ISLINGTON 11/18

I0571254

ʟ GIRL IN
HIS EYES

by
Jennie Ensor

www.bloodhoundbooks.com

Print ISBN: 978-1-912604-66-1

Praise for Jennie Ensor

"The Girl in his Eyes is an incredible novel that will really stay with me. It's such a prescient novel about the lasting damage of sexual abuse but it's so beautifully and sensitively written that you'll find yourself utterly absorbed in the story and won't want to stop turning the pages. I read it in one sitting because it had me gripped from the opening chapter. I highly recommend it!" – **Hayley, Rather Too Fond of Books blog**

"It's riveting reading, albeit uncomfortable at times, but it tackles the subject of abuse so brilliantly because it shows the ease with which a man can justify his actions and how those closest to him can accept them too. The concept of deception at all levels underpins this book and fascinates the reader. THE GIRL IN HIS EYES disturbs, shocks and disconcerts. It is also convincing, captivating and all too credible. It's a book I won't forget in a hurry." – **Linda Hill, Linda's Book Bag**

"The Girl in his Eyes is an edgy, compulsive read with a disturbing sense of unease that doesn't let up until the end. I devoured it in two sittings." – **Linda Huber, author of** *Death Wish, Baby Dear* **and** *Ward Zero*

"A well written domestic noir that is both unsettling and compulsive reading. An addictive story that will grab your attention from the very beginning!" – **J.A. Baker, author of** *The Other Mother* **and** *Undercurrent*

"A dark and compelling psychological thriller that bravely takes us inside the heads of both the abused and the abuser. The characters and their thoughts come alive on the page with a raw honesty, and the dilemmas they face feel frighteningly plausible." – **M.R. Mackenzie, author of** *In the Silence*

"This slow unfolding of chaos beneath the façade of middle-class respectability is a real page-turner; I read it over three days and couldn't wait to get back to my Kindle every time. What makes this novel about this most heinous of crimes stand out is that Jennie Ensor has been bold enough to write from the point of view of the perpetrator, as well as the abused." – **Terry Tyler, author of** *The Devil You Know,* *You Wish* **and other titles**

"A book with a moral dilemma at its heart, and yet one that so many young girls and women face, and what better way to explore it than in the hands of Jennie Ensor who has already proved herself to be a fearless author." – **Cleo Bannister, Cleopatra Loves Books blog**

"A brave and important book that unflinchingly tackles subject matter lesser authors struggle with. Ensor ensnares her readers in a cold, clammy grip of dread and helplessness. Simply riveting." – **Kerensa Jennings, author of bestselling literary thriller** *Seas Of Snow*

"An all-too-real tale of domestic abuse and the lies that people tell themselves and each other. Disturbing, moving and compelling." – **Ian Skewis, author of bestselling crime thriller** *A Murder Of Crows*

"Jennie Ensor will set on fire every emotion in you because you will feel it through her characters, including the shame. The shame that the victims shoulder that it must be their fault and the shame of the abuser for being found out, not for what they have done." – **Susan Hampson, Books From Dusk Till Dawn blog**

"The Girl in his Eyes is a challenging and compelling read that draws you in from the very first page - and will stay with you long after you have read the last." – **Alex Day, author of** *The Missing Twin*

"Ensor's novels are brave and bold; she is never afraid to broach challenging topics. In *The Girl In His Eyes* she tackles a controversial subject, exploring the far reaching consequences of one man's actions and the devastating impact on everyone involved." – **Katherine Sunderland, Bibliomaniac blog**

"*The Girl in His Eyes* is a book that will keep you awake well into the early hours. Grizzly, compelling, and absolutely necessary, this is a perfect thriller to cut right to the heart of some of the most prevalent issues in society today. Ensor shows real skill throughout!" – **C.S. Barnes, Bloodhound Books author**

In Memory of my Mother

1

Laura

29 December 2010

The face in the window stared back at her. Hers, yet not hers, it blurred into a jelly of reflected faces and the shifting darkness beyond.

She would be there, soon. With her mother – with *him*. She would have to say the right things, laugh in the right places. Pretend everything was alright.

Laura picked up her overnight bag, left the station and began the slog up Wimbledon Hill. Lorries shuddered past, splashing her jeans. She forced her umbrella into the wind. Her body felt flimsy, like one of those skeleton leaves clinging to the trees along the road.

At the top of the hill she turned into a side road then left into Elgin Drive. Slower now, past the line of stern 1930s houses. Number 31 loomed behind its ten-foot, ruler-flat hedge. The Porsche wasn't in the driveway.

She opened the gate, hesitating. She didn't want to go into this house again – not now, not ever. What if she turned around and went home, said she wasn't feeling well? It wasn't far from the truth. The warning signs were back: a thudding heart, a prickling beneath the skin. But she drew in her breath and made herself walk up the path and press the doorbell.

The hall light came on behind the frosted glass panels. She waited. Then her mother appeared, a little out of breath. Her hair, now highlighted blonde, bore the signs of her favourite Toni & Guy stylist.

'Hello, Mum. I thought you weren't in.'

'The radio was on, I didn't hear you.' She was enveloped by arms, bosom and a cloud of floral perfume. 'You're soaked! You should have called, darling, I would have picked you up at the station.'

'It's only ten minutes. I don't mind the walk.'

Laura followed her mother into the kitchen. The cactus on the windowsill had sprouted a third lobe, a spooky shade of orange. On the worktop, plastic containers competed for space with her mother's collection of herbal and homeopathic remedies for everything from insomnia to swollen ankles.

'Dad isn't back from work yet?'

'He shouldn't be long. How was your trip?'

'It was just what I needed, I didn't want to come back. How was Christmas?'

'Oh, you know. Your father wasn't in the best of moods.'

A thick paperback lay beside the toaster – one of those self-help books with instructions for how to transform one's life. She opened it and read the underlined sentence:

Picture affirmations as seeds that you are planting in the garden of your mind.

Laura put down the book. Her mother was a sucker for all that New Age stuff.

'Did Stephen miss you while you were away?'

'I doubt it. We're not seeing each other anymore.'

'Oh, Laura.' Her mother's brightness vanished. 'What happened?'

'He was seeing other girls,' she explained. 'He said he didn't think our relationship had a future. He said I didn't trust him. Stuff like that.'

His words were stuck inside her head. *I don't know who you are, Laura. You never let me see the real you.*

Their parting had been brief, though not painless. Evidence of his betrayal had been left for her to find: an unfamiliar hair slide on his dressing table, a blonde hair on a pillow. She'd yelled, hurled things. He'd told her she was being hysterical.

'I'm so sorry, darling.' Her mother approached, arms opening. 'Why didn't you tell me?'

Laura bit her lip. The tears were banked up behind her lids, ready to flow. But she stiffened and pulled away. She didn't want to cry here, with her father liable to walk in any moment. In any case, she had cried quite enough lately.

'I just needed time to sort things out in my head.' It wasn't only that. She couldn't talk to her mother about lots of things. Explaining herself to her mother was just too difficult. Keeping things inside was easier, was what she was used to doing.

'How about a cup of tea?' Her mother was already removing a bottle of milk from the fridge, which was crammed with cling-filmed bowls. A damp ginger cat squeezed with difficulty through the flap and padded towards her. Laura glanced into the hall. She had to be on her own for a few minutes.

The downstairs toilet was fragrant with air freshener. On the shelf, dried flowers sprayed prettily from a vase. The basin, spotless, boasted a pristine block of Royal Jelly soap. Her reflection startled her: ghost-white face framed by a damp tangle of nearly black hair, eyes smudged with kohl. They stared back at her, as sad and shiny as a spaniel's.

3

She turned the tap on full, wondering if the sound of pouring water would hide the howl that might erupt from her. No, almost certainly not. She neatened her hair and splashed cold water on her face.

'Don't take this too much to heart, love,' her mother said as they sat at the kitchen table. 'You never know who might be round the corner.'

No one, hopefully. She'd had enough of love, enough of men who wanted too much or too little. Enough of men full stop. Her mother meant well but she just didn't get it. They were too different, they would never understand each other. They were never going to be the best buddies that she wanted them to be. How could that happen when her mother still loved Dad, thought he was as white as snow? In all this time she'd never guessed the truth.

'Daniel's bringing Karen with him tomorrow, did he tell you?'

Laura shook her head. Her brother, two years older than her, was a project manager at a high-tech company in Bristol. She envied his focus, the way his life appeared to go wherever he willed it. Her own life was waiting in vain for some direction. Engrossed by her history course at Durham University, she had graduated with an upper second, better than she'd expected given her erratic performance in exams. But now, eighteen months later, she was starting to wilt. Try as she might to latch on to some sort of career, something vital to success always eluded her.

'He said it was about time we met her,' her mother said with a knowing look.

It was serious then – Daniel never brought girlfriends to the house. Although she was glad Daniel would be around tomorrow for their father's birthday, she wished she'd been able to think of a good enough excuse to not be a part of it.

Her father arrived shortly after 7.30pm. When her mother went to greet him, Laura didn't get up. His footsteps smacked the wooden floor as he strode along the hall. She saw, as he entered the kitchen, that his face and neck were still tanned from the summer. No sign yet of a beer belly. He was a tall, athletic man, quite decent looking. A man she ought to be proud to have as her father.

'Hey, sweetie, how're you doing? Good to see you again.'

He put down his briefcase and momentarily stood before her, arms at his sides as if hoping she might hug him, before leaning over and offering her his cheek. She barely touched the stubble with her lips. Faint, woody notes of his scent, peppermint mouthwash on his breath. He lifted his briefcase onto the worktop, pulled off his tie and took a beer from the fridge, as any other man might do.

Over dinner, her father's mood worsened. He grumbled about a scratch he'd discovered on the passenger door of his car, which he suspected wasn't accidental.

'It's that kid down the road, I bet. The one who rings on people's doors for the hell of it – his parents let him roam the streets at all hours. I've a good mind to call the police.'

Her mother nodded, looking worried. 'How was work today?'

'Not so good.' He scowled, picking at a patch of candle wax on the dining table. 'Orders are down, profits are down, and bonuses will be too, most likely. It's the worst it's been in nine years. This recession is …' As he went into detail about the problems the company was facing, Laura drifted away from the conversation. Instead, she found herself contemplating the large bruise-like mark on the wall beside the display cabinet, and the gaudy flowers spreading over the heavy curtains. The smell of geraniums hovered behind everything, and that web of small familiar sounds – the murmur of a radiator, the plaintive mews of the cat, the occasional rhythmic clack-clack of a distant train. The house seemed to be drawing her in, as if she'd never left.

'You're very quiet, Laura,' her father remarked suddenly in a loud voice, startling her. 'How's the job going?'

'I spent all day typing out captions again,' she replied. 'If I stay there any longer, my brain will turn to mush.'

It had sounded like an interesting, possibly exciting job – trainee production assistant in a TV production company. But they didn't make documentaries anymore, only film trailers with booming voiceovers, and adverts for DIY stores and dog food. Worse, a large part of every day was taken up with whatever tedious tasks no one else wanted to do, which, by 5.30pm, made her want to scream.

'You'll keep on with it, won't you?' Her father's tone fell somewhere between sharp and resigned. 'All you've done since leaving college is float from one job to the next. If you don't get stuck into this one, you're going to be unemployable.'

She said nothing. Her father was probably right. Three months into this job, her third since leaving university, she had no idea what she wanted to do with the rest of her life. Her first job, in the V&A museum shop, had gone well until they'd made her redundant after four months. After temping in various offices she'd finally found another 'permanent' job, in the customer service section of a telecoms company. But she'd walked out after a month, sick of the constant supply of disgruntled callers.

The problem was, she didn't know what she wanted to do. She wasn't interested in politics, journalism, or the civil service. She couldn't imagine being a teacher – in any case, there was no need for history teachers at the moment.

Research, maybe. But there were no jobs for researchers without experience. It wasn't the right attitude, she knew, but lately she'd had less and less expectation for her future.

After dinner, Laura sat with her parents in the living room. When the *BBC Ten O'Clock News* was over she told them she was tired and she'd see them in the morning.

Across the landing from her parents' room, her old bedroom waited, its door ajar. These days she hardly ever slept in it, apart from a night or so over Christmas. The room smelled of the lavender pouches her mother used to ward off moths. Its walls were still covered in the lilac shade of paint she'd chosen, aged eleven. On the shelf, her battered straw hat lay atop a row of the hunky volumes on archaeology and ancient history collected over her teenage years. Her overnight bag had been placed on the single bed and her battered childhood slippers lay side by side beneath the dressing table, which had been carefully arranged with her left-behind jewellery and hair accessories.

Everything looked homely and welcoming. She pushed away a sudden sense of confinement and loneliness, of boundaries slipping, of time slipping. She was her twelve-year-old self again, waiting for something awful to happen.

Laura undressed, pulled on a long, stretchy top, and lay in bed with the bedside lamp on. A hundred sounds percolated into her brain, each demanding attention. The drone of a plane heading towards Heathrow. A soft scraping from downstairs that she couldn't identify, followed by a hollow clatter – her mother cleaning the cat's bowl, maybe. Footsteps on the stairs. A series of creaks from the landing. Subdued voices from her parents' bedroom then the click of their door closing. Finally, she switched off the lamp.

There's nothing to be afraid of, she told herself.

***

The garden seemed smaller and neater than she remembered. Its grass verges were trimmed, the rose bushes pruned. The earwig-infested tree stumps had been taken away. No fallen leaves cluttered the lawn. It was hard to recognise the sprawling garden she'd known as a child, with its endless places to play and hide.

Laura looked up at the featureless layer of thick cloud obscuring the sky. It was nearly midday. She had woken late after another bad night's sleep and taken a cup of tea up to her room before getting up. Then she'd done her best to help her mother, who'd been trying to peel carrots, look for fluted glasses, and season the guinea fowl. Her father was in good spirits, popping in and out of the kitchen to make sauces and help himself to nuts and wine when he wasn't occupied with his latest stereo, a birthday present to himself. She was thinking she ought to go back inside and offer to lay the table when her mother appeared in the doorway of the conservatory.

'Laura! Daniel and Karen are here!'

After the greetings were over they were corralled into the living room, where her father opened his presents. Flurries of conversation were helped along by a bottle of Prosecco and her father's well-honed charm. Despite this, the occasion felt awkward. Her mother kept rushing out to tend to something in the kitchen, and said little. Her brother seemed less relaxed than usual, and Karen smiled nervously, from time to time glancing at Daniel for reassurance. He had no doubt warned Karen about Dad's uncertain moods. And maybe she sensed something else besides a bad temper lurking beneath his jovial surface.

They all sat around the dining table eyeing the pot of stew her mother was ladling onto plates. *Pintard* something or other.

Daniel raised his glass. 'Happy birthday, Dad. Roll on sixty!'

Laura wished her father a happy birthday with the others.

'Start, everyone,' her mother urged, before turning to Karen with a smile of encouragement. 'So, what made you want to be a vet?'

Laura shifted in her chair. She was uneasy again. She watched her father as he discussed the latest Test match with her brother. As usual he was nicely turned out, in a dark-green silk shirt, open at the neck, black trousers and polished leather shoes. He sounded more than ever like an Englishman, only occasional traces of his Canadian accent coming through. He was on his best behaviour, she could tell. Her brother, with his shirt pressed and hair combed, looked oddly well-groomed for a weekend. Karen had made an effort too, with a smart velvet dress and carefully applied make-up. Her own make-up was minimal and her outfit simple – a blouse and short cardigan over narrow black jeans.

Karen and her mother were on to facials and their favoured remedies for open pores. Her mother laughed suddenly, and reached across to touch Karen's arm. Already there was a warmth and ease between the two women. Laura looked away. She felt the echo of some long-ago emotion, one she'd almost forgotten. That ache of being left out, of wanting to join in but not knowing how.

Daniel caught her eye and winked at her. 'Alright, sis?'

'I'm fine.' She turned her attention back to her plate, her serving mostly uneaten.

As their plates emptied, there was a hiatus in the conversation.

'Does anyone want to hear a joke?' Daniel looked around expectantly.

'Go on then,' said her mother.

Daniel waited until he had everyone's attention. 'What do you say to a black man in a suit?'

'Who's your tailor?' offered her father.

'Will the defendant please rise.'

'That's really bad,' her father said.

'Daniel,' her mother began in a weary tone. 'Don't you know any jokes that aren't racist?'

Her brother scratched his head, mischief on his face. 'Okay, how about this one. What are Belgium's most famous inventions?'

Around the table, vacant looks.

'Tell us, for God's sake,' she urged her brother.

'Chocolate and paedophilia – and they only invented chocolate for the paedophiles.'

Her mother frowned. Karen plucked up her glass, her cheeks flushed.

'Daniel,' her father snapped, 'I think we've had enough jokes for now.' He looked straight at her. 'Has anyone been watching that awful show on TV? What's it called …?'

Laura pushed aside the remains of her food. She wanted to get away from this room, away from this house. It was a reminder of everything she wished she could forget. Around her, familiar objects – hanging on the wall, her childhood sketch of a vase of tulips, now confined by a conspicuous frame. In the display cabinet, above her father's coin collection and gleaming swimming trophies, a row of school photographs of herself and her brother. The house was pulling her back, stripping away the years. She'd sat at this table ten years ago, on her twelfth birthday.

Mum is bringing in a huge cake studded with pink and yellow candles. Around the table, friends are cheering and clapping.

'Blow them out!'

'Go on, all in one go!'
One, two, three puffs. The last flame wavers and goes out.
Mum is smiling at her. 'Make a wish, darling.'
Straight away, it comes – please, make him leave me alone.

After lunch, Laura helped her mother to clear up in the kitchen while the others sat in the living room. Every so often she could hear her father's robust laugh from down the hall.

'Jane heard from Neil yesterday,' her mother said, feeding a plate to the dishwasher.

Jane? Oh yes, Jane was a friend of her mother's. Neil, Jane's husband, had left her for a woman of twenty-eight he'd met in an Argentine tango class.

'Is he still with that girl? What was her name?'

'Yes, they're living in a flat in Luxembourg. Neil rang Jane to wish them all a happy Christmas and she told him to get stuffed.' Her mother's voice got louder. 'She's not going to forgive him for running off like that. It's been a huge struggle for her, working full-time and coping with the kids – and now Emma's playing up.'

'Playing up?'

'Answering back, refusing to do anything round the house. Jane's really worried about her.' Her mother slammed the dishwasher door. 'Did your father tell you he's going to take Emma swimming?'

'No – how come?'

'Jane asked him if he'd mind taking Emma to the pool with him on Saturdays. To give her a break, partly – the kids are such a handful. But it'll be good for Emma too. Jane says she's always stuck in her room playing computer games and messing about on her iPhone.'

'Dad doesn't mind?'

'No, he's happy to help out. He likes the idea of teaching again, he misses working with kids. I think it'll be good for him, a chance for him to feel valued outside the office.'

'I suppose.'

It sounded sensible, on the surface. Her father had been a hotshot swimmer. He'd coached children at his swimming club in Canada, she remembered him saying – they all looked up to him because he'd won a big swimming competition, the state 100m freestyle title, or something. But a fuzzy sense of unease filled her.

'Suzanne, are you two still in there?' Her father's head appeared around the door. 'I thought we were going to have coffee?'

'We're just finishing, Paul. Give me a minute, will you?'

Her mother reached up into a cupboard then shrieked as a cup hurtled out and broke into small pieces that scattered across the floor.

'Jesus.' The veins bulged in her father's forehead. 'I've never in my life known anyone as clumsy as you!'

'For God's sake, Paul, I didn't do it on purpose.' Despite its attempted firmness, a tremor caught her mother's voice. 'Leave us alone, won't you?'

His footsteps thumped away down the hall.

'Are you okay, Mum?'

The colour had gone from her mother's cheeks. As she stared down at the floor in dismay, she looked as if she might break too.

'Sit down, let me clean up.' She went to the cupboard and took out a dustpan and brush. I'll make us more coffee.'

It had happened again, as it had so many times in her childhood. She had always been in a constant state of waiting for her father to let rip over some inconsequential thing. She or her brother hadn't tidied their bedrooms properly, or her mother had burnt the toast – anything would set him off. His rages would end with her mother dosing herself with pills and retreating to a darkened bedroom.

Daniel and Karen appeared in the kitchen and announced they were leaving – they were worried about driving on dark roads.

'Bye, sis.' Daniel gave her a quick squeeze. 'Look after Mum.'

'See you, Dan. Give me a call if you're ever in London.' Even as she said this, she knew he wouldn't. He was always busy with something. They got on well enough but their lives were mostly separate now.

Her mother put her hand on her arm.

'You'll stay on for a bit, won't you, dear? I'm going upstairs to lie down for half an hour.'

Laura made the coffee as slowly as she could then took the two cups into the living room. The thought of being alone with her father made her skin prickle, as though she were a child again. But she told herself she ought to make an effort. She was an adult now – trying to avoid him the whole time was ridiculous. Anyway, she wasn't going to let him get the better of her. Not anymore.

Her father was slumped in his armchair, his eyes shut and his legs, crossed at the ankles, stretched out in front of him. She put his cup quietly on the coffee table, which was temporarily unburdened of her mother's *Healthy Living* magazines.

'It's all right, I'm not asleep.' His tone was friendly. He pushed himself upright. 'It's good to see you again, Laura.'

She backed away. 'I know I haven't been over much lately. I'm sorry.'

He nodded, picking up his cup. 'I expect you're busy, these days.'

Reluctantly, she lowered herself onto the sofa. It would be rude to leave the room now. But what to say to him? A minefield lay between them, un-crossable. How could he talk like this, as if everything was perfectly alright? As if the past had never happened?

'Mum says you're going to take Emma to the pool with you.'

'That's the plan.' Carefully, he replaced the cup in the saucer. 'I'll help her with her swimming.'

'What about your own swimming? Won't Emma get in the way?'

He smiled, a generous smile that showed off his perfectly crowned teeth. 'I won't mind. It'll be fun.'

His tone was light, anodyne. But something was out of alignment. The door would not quite fit the jamb.

They talked some more – safe, impersonal topics. The recent severe weather, plans to give prisoners the vote, the farmer fatally gored by his own bull. Laura watched the coloured lights on the Christmas tree blink on and off. The standard lamp cast fuzzy shadows on the milk white carpet, which matched the antique white sofa and the hospital-white walls. The carpet had been chosen by her father, despite her mother's protests. As predicted, it was now bearing signs of spillage, which the recently placed rug didn't quite hide.

Outside, street lights came on. The contents of a lit room in the house opposite were clearly visible. A figure moved inside it – the old man who used to leave notes on her father's windscreen, complaining about him taking up too much space when parking.

Laura listened to the carriage clock ticking on the mantelpiece. Each tick was louder than the last and seemed slower coming. A kind of helpless resignation came over her. Neither she nor her father had spoken for a while.

Somehow, she was incapable of speaking. Even now, all these years later, he was controlling her.

Suddenly, her father leaned forward and placed his hands onto the arms of his chair, palms facing down. Her heart raced. He was going to get up and come over. Any second now, he'd be sitting beside her. There'd be that distant look on his face, as if his usual self had shut down.

Don't be so stupid. Of course he's not going to do anything.

No, she was twenty-two years old, not a child. What was the matter with her? She should just say something to break the silence.

With a small groan, her father pushed himself up off the chair. Her breath stopped. He walked over to the window and reached up. He was going to close the curtains. The curtains … Deep inside her brain, a switch flicked on. He was going to close the curtains, just as he used to, before coming over to sit beside her. Even when it was still light outside, he'd draw the curtains. After that first time.

She shivered. It had happened in the garden. She'd not thought of it for years. She'd pushed it deep inside her brain where it would be safe, where she'd never be able to find it again. But the memory sneaked up on her, without warning.

She's in her swimsuit, lying on her side on a towel on the lawn. Her back is warm from the sun. A book is open in front of her. It's a Saturday or Sunday, just after the start of the school holidays. Her mother has gone out to see a friend. Her brother is away somewhere too.

Her father comes over and sits down beside her on the grass. She glances up, thinking he's going to talk to her. But his face is closed down, a mask hiding his normal face.

15

He begins to stroke the back of her thigh. Gently, not like when he used to tickle her. She looks up from her book, confused.

'What are you doing?'

He doesn't reply. Instead, he slips the strap of her swimming costume off her shoulder and clamps his hand over the small mound of her breast. She is cold. She can't move her tongue. It's stuck inside her mouth, useless. Her heart hardens in her chest like a big stone. He explores her breast with his fingers, as if it belongs to him.

'Dad, stop it.'

It is as if she hasn't spoken.

Silently, she prays for him to stop. If only she could get up and run away. But she is unable to move. Her entire body has turned to stone.

Then she remembers the sex education class, what they are supposed to say if they ever get unwanted sexual attention.

'Please, leave me alone. I don't want you to do that.'

He doesn't seem to hear, he is so absorbed in his task. He lowers his head and his tongue is rough and hot on the sensitive tip of her breast.

At last, he puts the strap of her costume back on her shoulder.

'Did you like that?'

His voice is shaky and higher than usual. She shakes her head.

'You will, sweetie, I promise.'

She stares at him.

'You mustn't talk about this to anyone,' he says. 'And you must never tell your mother. If she finds out, it will kill her.'

When she has sworn not to tell, he leaves her alone. Alone except for the strange tingling sensation, and a certainty that everything will be different from now on. Something has been taken from her that she'll never get back.

When her mother gets home, he goes back to being the father she used to have. He tells her in a cross voice to go and tidy her room, as if nothing has happened.

In the long hours before she succumbs to sleep that night, shame and confusion take over. Why did she let him touch her like that? Why didn't she stop him? What had made him do such a thing?

After that first time, he does it again. Always when he is alone with her. Usually in the living room. Touching her body with his fingers, his lips. He talks to her like she is his girlfriend, his lover. Sometimes he holds her hand, squeezes it hard. Sometimes he kisses her on the mouth. She hates it, tries to turn away her head. He tells her he adores her, he needs to be with her like this. She's becoming a woman now. She turns him on so much, he can't help himself.

No one ever sees him do these things. Occasionally, her mother comes in when he isn't expecting it – she gets back early from visiting a friend, or a yoga class. But he's too quick. He just moves away and pretends to be watching TV or reading the newspaper.

She never says anything to her mother. She behaves as if her father is the same man he's always been, because she has no choice. Because she knows perfectly well, without him telling her, what would happen if she told: it would break up her family and ruin all of their lives. And maybe what her father told her is true, maybe it really would kill her mother if she ever found out. How could she be responsible for such a thing?

She knows she can't stop her father from doing what he does. He is the man who makes everyone do whatever he wants them to. He is the head of the family, the one who sets the rules. She is his daughter, not yet twelve, who must follow the rules. Most of all, she knows she should have said something the first time, and now it is too late.

The three of them clustered in the hall. Her father held out her coat.

'You'll come over again soon, won't you, sweetie? Are you sure you don't want me to run you home?'

'No, really, I'm happy to get the train. I'd like to get some fresh air – thanks, anyway.'

If she stayed here any longer, she'd suffocate.

Her father went into the kitchen and returned with a foil package. 'Here, put this in your bag. I wrapped some birthday cake for you, in case you're hungry when you get home.'

'Thanks, Dad.'

A sudden rush of affection overcame her, some remnant of her childish love for her father. She swallowed to clear the tightness in her throat.

'Cheerio, sweetie. Safe journey.' He put his arms around her, awkwardly. She froze as he made contact. 'See you again soon, I hope.'

Her mother hugged her tightly, holding on for a long time.

'Promise you'll phone soon – to let me know how you are.'

Laura sat on the District Line train, opposite a short-skirted, ponytailed girl, and a middle-aged man. He was the girl's father, clearly.

The girl chattered non-stop, her shining eyes darting around the compartment and beyond the window, but always returning to the face of the man beside her. What was it about her? She seemed so innocent, so vulnerable. She must be eleven or twelve – the age she herself had been when her father began to see her differently. Emma's age.

Laura stared out of the window, not seeing the houses hurrying past.

He wouldn't think of doing anything to Emma – would he?

The thought wedged in her brain, blocking out everything else. Small hairs stirred on the back of her neck.

It had never occurred to her before, that her father might do the same things to another girl. He had done those things to her because … What? She was special, he'd told her. There'd been something about her, something he couldn't resist.

But what if she hadn't been so special? What if he'd said the same thing to other girls?

West Kensington, she realised, several seconds after the train had stopped. She jumped out, escaping just before the doors clamped her between them.

The platform was empty. She walked up the steps, scarcely seeing them.

She should say something to her mother, or to Jane, or one of Emma's teachers. She must protect Emma from any possible harm.

Only that would mean telling on her father. She'd never told anyone – she'd kept it a secret, just as she'd promised.

If she finds out, it will kill her.

As a child it had been easy to believe him. She'd imagine her mother crying, sinking onto her bed, shutting the bedroom door and never coming out. And what might he do, if she broke her promise? When her father got angry, he could be frightening. Her mother, her brother, herself – they had all cowered before him, dreading what he might do. He'd chased her out of the house once, when she was fifteen, for daring to answer him back, his face red, yelling that she needed to be taught a lesson; after that she'd spent even less time at home.

Now though, she was a grown woman. Surely, she would be able to deal with her father now, however angry he might get.

What about her mother, though? Her mother loved him, depended on him. How would she cope if she knew the truth?

Laura turned in the direction of her flat.

It was impossible. Telling was as bad as not telling.

But her father should face the consequences of what he'd done, shouldn't he? Her mother would get through it somehow. Wouldn't it be the best thing, to tell the truth?

It's dark, except for a glimmer of light just above the horizon. The place is nowhere she knows. There's no shelter. The ground is strewn with small rocks that rip into the soles of her shoes. She is running as fast as she can, every so often stumbling then righting herself. She keeps on running.

Someone is coming after her. There's a thud-thud-thud like distant explosions. Bullets, or machine-gun fire? She runs faster, desperate now. But the thuds get louder and the interval between them gets shorter, and she knows that to try to escape is useless. Whoever is chasing her will not give up. Soon they will catch her and her life will be over.

For hours after the dream, Laura lay in bed with the light on, alert to the slightest sound. Her skin was still clammy, her heartbeat hard in her chest. She had never dreamed such a thing before, or felt such fear.

It's not real, she told herself once again. You're safe at home. No one is coming after you.

Yet she knew, in a way, she was wrong. It was her father who was chasing her – there was no doubt in her mind. She couldn't get away from him, not even in her sleep.

2

Suzanne

New Year's Eve, 2010

S uzanne removed the green silk dress from the hanger and let its cool smoothness linger on her skin. She put the dress down on the bed. It made her cleavage deeper and her waist narrower – she knew perfectly well – and her eyes startlingly green, as if all the grey flecks had been washed away. It was just the thing for Katherine's party.

Her skin looked brighter and firmer than usual, she thought with a spike of pleasure as she removed a blob of mascara from beneath her lower lashes. She could pass for forty-five, or younger. She brushed powder onto her cheeks. Paul's birthday came into her mind again, and his outburst in the kitchen. What had made him so bad tempered, on his birthday of all days? He'd made the children leave early, and she'd been hoping to talk more to Laura about how she was getting on. Oh, well. Laura hadn't been in the mood to talk anyway. She'd been withdrawn for most of her visit. Not just withdrawn. Strained, on edge, almost as if she thought something terrible would happen.

Suzanne put down the make-up brush and let out a long breath.

She'd noticed it many times, Laura's reluctance to engage during family get-togethers. Family get-togethers wasn't quite the right term – her family didn't joyously come together as they did in adverts and American films. The kids came to visit more from a sense of obligation, because they didn't want to let down their mother. This time though, Laura's uneasiness had been palpable. Her silence during the meal. The way she'd darted away after talking to Paul, and then insisted on leaving virtually immediately ... Laura was uncomfortable around her own father.

She had an instinct to deny the thought. But a deeper part of herself knew it to be true.

From outside, the lazy growl of a powerful engine. At the squeak of the front gate, she sprayed Chanel No. 5 into her cleavage and reached for the dress.

Paul stepped towards her, two bunches of red roses outstretched.

'Darling,' he said, 'you look stunning. I'm not sure I should let you out in that dress.'

He went to the fridge and helped himself to a beer, talking non-stop of his day at work. He and his sales team had thrashed out the details of the new incentive scheme to everyone's satisfaction. Not only that, the managing director had promised Paul and the other directors a five per cent pay rise, unexpectedly generous after the year's disappointing results.

They left shortly afterwards. Suzanne climbed into the Porsche that was parked next to her reliable Toyota hatchback. Paul drove too fast as usual, continuing through the first flash of red at the traffic lights and slowing just in time at the roundabout. She looked at him sternly, but did not speak, bracing her left leg against the door, a position she half hoped might afford greater protection in the event of a crash.

He had taken extra care getting ready, she noticed. He wore his cashmere jacket and black linen shirt; his hair, damp from the shower, was combed back from his forehead. He had the same forties film star look about him that he'd had the night they met – at a dreadful party where she'd known no one except the host. For an interminable time, she'd floundered among a gaggle of self-important people, who all seemed to be either excessively successful entrepreneurs or TV producers, all the time trying to ignore the fact that it was impossible to walk properly because her heels were ridiculously high. The very moment she decided to leave, Paul appeared and said, 'I've come to rescue you. You shouldn't be miserable, you're the prettiest girl here.'

Clouds of white billowed from their mouths as they walked along the icy pavement to Katherine and Jeremy's house. Jeremy greeted them and asked Paul to show him the new car; Suzanne went inside, alone.

The hall walls were a deep shade of burgundy. Nothing in Katherine's house ever looked out of fashion or out of place, as it did at home. She was a good hostess too, introducing the people who needed introducing, remembering what they had in common, and never getting flustered when something burnt or the bottle opener disappeared.

Suzanne hesitated in the doorway of the spacious living area. It appeared to be stuffed with a significant proportion of Wimbledon's population. At one end of the room, couples were swaying to a Latin rhythm; Katherine's daughter was dancing with a young man who didn't look like her boyfriend. There were familiar faces from previous parties. James, from Jeremy's bridge club, and Sheila or Shauna, from Katherine's wine tasting group. And who was that woman with the long nose, a purple boa draped around her neck, chomping down things on cocktail sticks?

She ventured inside. Katherine emerged from a group of glamorously-dressed women, all talking loudly and at once; newly-cut hair framed her jaw.

'Hello, m'dear.' Katherine plonked a kiss on Suzanne's cheek. 'Love the dress! Let me take that bottle.' She tugged at her arm. 'Come with me, there's someone I want you to meet.'

Beside the buffet table, Jeremy's barrister friend was talking to a tall man in a casual shirt and jeans. 'Excuse me for butting in. Suzanne, meet David. We worked in Melbourne together, yonks ago. David's an architect. He's come back to live in England after fifteen years in Chicago.'

He had silver streaks in his hair and a worn face that dimpled when he smiled.

'Pleased to meet you, Suzanne.'

There was more than politeness in his voice. She felt keenly aware of her breasts, more exposed than usual. Katherine turned away to the barrister, leaving her alone with David.

'So,' Suzanne said quickly, 'how are you finding life over here?'

'It's a refreshing change, to be honest.' He paused, his grimace just visible before it became a smile. 'After my marriage ended I needed a change of scene.'

She nodded.

'I bought this cottage a couple of months ago,' he went on. 'It keeps me busy, which is just as well. I spent most of yesterday in the garden trying to decide which plants were weeds.'

'That can be tricky, can't it? I'm not much of a gardener either. But I love to sit out on the patio when it's sunny.'

Glancing towards the mantelpiece, she saw Paul with Jeremy and an older couple she remembered from a previous party. She caught a quick movement of his head away from her.

'Your husband?'

Suzanne nodded. Paul wouldn't like her chatting to another man. But she quickly forgot about him as the conversation continued, somehow veering off to ancient Egypt. As David enthused about the Valley of the Kings and how she ought to see it, she warmed to him. She didn't feel, as she often did at parties, that she ought to justify herself for being a rather ordinary, unaccomplished woman whose children had left home, and who earned an unpredictable income from correcting dull articles in magazines that most people had never heard of. True, she had a degree in English, a passion for classical music, and could play the piano quite well considering her sporadic childhood lessons. But she wasn't witty or knowledgeable about things in the way some people were – in the way her husband was.

'Would you like to dance?' David gestured to some couples dancing to 'Blue Suede Shoes'.

She glanced over to the mantelpiece again. But Paul wasn't there.

Before she could protest, David put her into a firm dance hold and propelled her backwards. She tried to keep up with him but her feet couldn't move as fast as his. He spun her unexpectedly under his arm and she lost her balance. Just in time, he caught her. They tried again, their legs tangling together. She laughed with him, relaxing into the rhythm of the music.

The song ended. They danced the next one, and the next. While she recovered her breath, David stood apart from her, watching her face.

'It's about time I was getting home, I'm afraid,' he said quietly. 'It's a long drive back.'

'Goodbye then, David.' She was disappointed that he was going, and wondered if he could tell. 'I enjoyed our conversation – and the dancing.'

'Bye, Suzanne. I hope things go well for you.'

He touched her hand lightly and left the room. For a few moments she felt wistful, then remembered herself with a twinge of guilt. Had Paul noticed them together? And where was he? Usually at the first sign of another man's interest he'd be over like a shot.

After checking he wasn't anywhere in the room, she went to the kitchen. Inside, two middle-aged men, with protruding bellies and receding hairlines, swigged from Heineken bottles and argued about politics. Paul was standing at the far end with a young woman – no, not even that, just a girl. She stood very close to him. Long, glossy hair, reaching towards the curve of her back. Her skirt was ultra-short, exposing very long, lightly muscled legs. Sheer tights, little make-up. A trace of concealed acne on her chin. She could be no older than fourteen or fifteen.

Suzanne took a few steps towards them. Neither had noticed her. The girl carried on talking, eagerly, in a low voice. Paul was listening intently. Then the girl rolled up her sleeve and moved a white arm towards him. He inspected something there and touched the flesh, entranced.

The girl saw Suzanne first, and stared back, boldly.

'Hello, darling, have you met Lindy?'

Paul's eyes were too bright, his voice too loud. He said something else but she couldn't hear it. The girl waved a hand at Paul and loped away.

'What were you doing with that girl?'

'She was only showing me her tattoo.' He drank the rest of his wine. 'What's the harm in that?'

At that moment, the barrister came in and began to rummage in the fridge.

'Let's go back and join the party,' Paul said.

Suzanne followed him, unsure what to say. She felt unsettled. His expression had been so … intense. But he hadn't done anything wrong, had he?

They rejoined the crowd and were propelled into one conversation after another. As usual at parties, Paul was gregarious, energised by the crowd. After the New Year toasts, he asked her to dance. They danced very well together, she knew. Whatever the dance – rock 'n' roll, salsa – he was always nimble, sensing her next movement.

They left the party soon after 1am. Paul accepted her offer to drive home. She turned the key in the ignition. Instead of reversing, the Porsche shot forward. She swore, braking hard to stop the car from slamming into the one in front. The thing was impossible to drive at the best of times.

'Look out! You nearly hit that car.' Paul's face was scrunched tight with anger. 'Do you have to be so damn careless?'

'If you didn't have to drink so much, you'd be able to drive the bloody thing yourself!'

'I drink too much, do I?'

'You know you do. It always makes you bad tempered and miserable.' The small amount of alcohol she'd drunk had loosened her tongue too. 'And, by the way, who was that schoolgirl you were talking to? You were lapping up her every word.'

'I think you've got it the wrong way round.' His voice was scornful. 'I was wondering when you'd finally extricate yourself from your new friend.'

'His name's David,' she hissed, finally putting the gear into reverse. 'Katherine introduced us.'

'When I saw you two, he practically had his dick out – and you were enjoying it.'

Relief flowed through her. Paul had been jealous, that's all.

'There's nothing to worry about, Suzanne,' he went on in a conciliatory tone. 'She's just a kid, for Christ's sake – she's studying for her GCSEs. Do you seriously think I could be interested in a fifteen-year-old?'

They drove the rest of the way in silence. She wondered why she had reacted so strongly to that girl.

***

Suzanne gave the fruit bowl a final flick with the feather duster and turned to the framed photographs on the sideboard.

The first one was her as a child, aged three or four, on her father's knee. Bright sunlight making her hair blonde, her face split by the hugest smile. Her father's hand on her shoulder, his face bearded and weathered by the many afternoons he'd spent sailing, the tip of his nose red. His expression was serious yet happy – and proud, too. In the next, her brother, Richard, was surrounded by friends, holding up a pint glass and laughing. Untidy curls skimmed the collar of his shirt – one of those gaudy, fashionless shirts he loved. It was in the Lamb & Flag on his fortieth birthday, four years before he died.

At the third photograph, she lowered the duster.

Herself and Paul on their wedding day. His unwavering gaze into the camera contrasted with the teary brightness of her eyes and her generous smile, a trace of shyness lingering. She was so young then, much younger than her twenty-five years. You could see it in her face – the face of a girl so hopeful for her future and so inexperienced in the ways of men.

Everyone had been surprised at the news they were to be married. Especially Irene.

'You've only known him for five months,' her sister had said, gravely, as if she thought Paul might be a spy or a bank robber. 'Why don't you wait until you know him better?'

She hadn't waited though, had jumped straight in. Had their marriage been a mistake? Paul hadn't wanted to have children nearly as much as she had. Being a father often seemed more of a burden than a delight. And his moods hadn't got any better over the years.

He'd come home from work, scowling, and scurry to his armchair to watch TV, or into his office to sit at his computer. She'd be taken to task for leaving creases in his shirt, or one of any number of things he might find fault with. Every now and then he'd say horrible things to her; afterwards he'd tell her he was sorry, he hadn't meant it. His words would burrow under her skin though. She imagined them slowly dissolving her, like acid eating into metal. She was too soft, that was the trouble. Yet, after a big sale, or some good news at work, he'd be bursting with boyish enthusiasm, and he'd become the affectionate, undaunted man she used to know. The man who gently teased her, who would come up to her in the kitchen and give her a hug. 'You're my woman, Suze,' he'd say. 'I love you.'

An ache lodged in her throat. Why was he like this? Whenever she tried to comfort him, or offer support, he would pull away, shutting her out. Something seemed to be gnawing away at him, something he couldn't share with her.

An image of the girl at the party came into her mind – she could see again the whiteness of her arms, and her animated, unlined face. And Paul, clinging to her arm, unable to take his eyes off her.

She dabbed the duster clumsily at the photograph. It fell over with a clatter. She set it right, gritted her teeth, and fiercely buffed the sideboard until a grainy reflection of her face appeared in the oak. From the corner of her eye, she saw something dark move away from the sofa. A spider, bulbous and hairy, the size of a plum, heading straight for her. She flung the duster at it but missed by a foot. She grabbed the thick Collins dictionary on the coffee table, waited for the thing to reach her, and walloped down the book. Pressing her foot down on the book, she imagined the mangled body beneath. The horror of it prickled in her scalp.

Suzanne made a cup of strong tea and took it onto the patio. She loved this garden. A path cut through the lawn, leading to a cluster of fruit trees and a vegetable plot. Rhododendrons blazed purple in spring and later there were blood-red roses. The trees and shrubs were bare now though, except for a single yellow leaf clinging from a twig, flapping furiously in every movement of air.

She closed her eyes and tried to concentrate on each breath. Mindfulness, they called it at the meditation group. It was a good way to let go of stress, everyone said, only she hadn't quite got the hang of it yet. Thinking about her breathing tended to make her feel *less* relaxed. Besides, household tasks she had forgotten to do and all manner of things always intervened – and cats.

'Eeeeaaaow.'

Marmaduke pushed his body against her leg. She stroked him then got up and walked to the other side of the garden. At the rockery, patches of weeds filled the gaps where stones had fallen. The pond was covered with dead leaves. There had been goldfish, once. She stared into the murky depths. What was the matter with her today? Perhaps it was just this time of year.

No, it wasn't that. It was Paul.

He'd changed. When they first met he'd been affectionate, attentive, adoring. But now ... It was hard to pinpoint exactly when it had started. There were countless little things, each with its own rhythm. Some seemed to ebb and flow like the phases of the moon, others seemed to change imperceptibly, like yellowing paper.

His kisses, for one. Instead of a kiss on the lips when he came in, he'd go past her to get a beer from the fridge. He'd come home tired and withdrawn, not wanting to talk to or touch her. They only kissed when they were making up, or during sex. That too had changed. These days it was more like an over-familiar ritual than an expression of love, let alone desire.

Could he be seeing another woman? He had always denied it. He said he was tired out from work, and he had no interest in anyone else. He would only ever love her.

A brown leaf jiggled in the pond. Suzanne stepped closer. She could make out dark shapes among the reeds that didn't look like fish. She rubbed her arms.

No, she'd know if there was another woman. She was in a gloomy mood, that was all. Maybe things were getting better. This new interest in swimming coaching – perhaps it was a good sign. Paul needed something to take his mind off work. She'd said enough times that it was taking over his life.

Suzanne turned away from the pond and walked towards the house.

No one had a perfect relationship, did they? No marriage stayed the same for twenty-five years. They'd both changed. Before they were married, Paul said he loved her for being feminine – unlike other women who needed to prove how tough and clever they were. And hadn't she been drawn to his ambition, his confidence, his unrelenting alpha-maleness?

Only she wasn't a young woman any longer. Now, instead of giving in, she would stand up to him when they argued. She had joined a meditation group, in addition to her yoga class, despite him telling her she was taking on too much, and she'd stopped cleaning the house twice a week just because he liked it spotless.

Did he prefer her as she used to be? He'd never said it. But so many things were locked away inside him, unknowable.

Shortly after 7pm, Suzanne took out the rack of clean cutlery from the dishwasher. Paul shouldn't be much longer, she thought for the third or fourth time. He hadn't said he would be late. She put the final fork away, closed the drawer and went into the living room, giving a wide berth to the dictionary still on the floor. She switched on the television and flicked through the channels. Soaps, a documentary about welfare cheats, another on the mating habits of foxes. She switched it off, moving quickly away from the mirror above the mantelpiece. She didn't need to be reminded of the crows' feet gathering at her eyes, or her eyelids that were beginning to droop.

It came to her, then. Something had been trying to come into her mind since Katherine's party. That day, years ago. She'd yelled 'dinner's ready!' several times, but neither Paul nor Laura had answered. Flustered, she'd opened the living room door to find Paul sitting on the sofa, reading an Edward Lear poem to Laura, sitting beside him. Both completely absorbed – neither looking up as she entered the room – just as Paul and that girl had been at the party. Afterwards she'd scolded herself for her sudden jealousy, told herself this was wrong, she shouldn't be jealous of her own daughter.

There'd been other times too, when she'd felt excluded and even a little envious. Paul would be so eager to leave the house to pick up his daughter from her ballet class or swimming lesson, or he'd be so focussed on helping her with her homework he'd scarcely notice anything else. And that sailing holiday, the summer after Laura had turned thirteen. How many times had she noticed Paul watching her with that mournful expression? He regretted, she'd imagined, that his daughter was no longer the little girl who wanted him to read poems to her, but was on her way to becoming an adult. He hadn't confided in her, his wife, though. She'd been an intruder into his private grief.

The minute hand of the mantelpiece clock jerked forward, another step on its long journey towards the hour.

Suzanne made a gap in the curtains and looked out. A white van passed, then a woman on a bicycle. She came away from the window.

'How did it go at work today?' She made an effort to sound cheerful.

'Not great. Too many meetings, too much hassle. Usual story.'

She smelled beer on his breath. 'I didn't know you were going to be late. Did you go to the pub?'

He dropped his coat on the banister and walked towards the kitchen. 'A few of us stopped for a drink in the Red Lion. It was Tim's last day.'

'Oh Paul, hang on a sec. There's something I need to ask you.'

Is there someone else? Another woman?

But she couldn't say it. Not here, not now.

Paul frowned. 'What is it?'

'There's a dead spider in the lounge, under the dictionary. You couldn't …'

He smiled. 'Don't worry, darling, I'll take care of it.'

As so often happened after a day at work, Paul was half asleep soon after they had finished eating. They went to bed early.

'Suze, darling,' he began, coming up behind her as she took off her make-up. 'I want to apologise for being so grizzly. Things are frantic at work right now.' He unbuttoned his shirt. 'I've had to call a meeting for tomorrow morning to sort out what we're going to put in this new release. The customer is putting the screws on us, big time. They want us to put a stack of changes in the software or they're going to take us to court. Our guys say it's too much work. I've been running around like a maniac trying to deal with all this shit.'

'I know it's been hard for you at work,' she said. 'But you've been so distant lately. And when I saw you and that girl at the party—'

'Suzy, Suzy.' He kissed the back of her neck. 'I know I'm not the husband I should be. I know I behave like a fucking idiot sometimes. You're a wonderful woman, I don't deserve you. But, darling.' She turned to face him. 'There's no room for anyone else. I love you, Suze. Don't you know? I couldn't bear to be without you.'

They lay in bed, in the dark. Despite the rational, sceptical part of herself, she was reassured by Paul's words. She closed her eyes, enjoying his warmth and the gentle pressure of his arms wrapped around her.

3

Paul

8 January 2011

'Hello, long time no see.' Jane greeted him with a pallid smile. 'Come on in.'

Her hair was tied back severely. Her once attractive face was pale, almost haggard. Dark shadows hung around her eyes. She wore an unflattering sweatshirt and baggy tracksuit pants. She was still slim, though.

Paul stepped into the hall. Music bleated in his ears from behind a closed door, the banal repetitive beat thankfully muffled.

'It's so good of you to do this, Paul. I felt bad about asking, but I thought ... Honestly, I didn't know who else to turn to. My friends are fed up with me asking for favours.'

'It's absolutely no problem at all, my dear.' He gave her his most dazzling smile. 'I'm at the pool most Saturdays, it's the least I can do. It's a pleasure to help.'

'I just hope Emma will be better behaved with you.' A slow heave of the shoulders. Jane's sigh conveyed all the miseries of single motherhood. 'She's had a fight with Toby already this morning and she's refused to tidy her room or do anything I ask. I'm at my wits' end with her.'

He followed her into the living room. There was barely any space left on the carpet for the agglomeration of toy dumper trucks, *Glamour* magazines, Blu-ray cases and sheets of crayon-streaked paper.

Emma was strewn across the sofa, watching TV. Beside her, a cheap beaded necklace and an empty bottle of Fanta lemonade. She wore faded jeans, white Nikes, and a sweatshirt with GAP emblazoned across the front.

'Paul's here, Emma. For God's sake, turn that thing down.'

He hadn't seen her for at least a year, so he'd expected a few changes. But this girl he hardly recognised. He knew she was only twelve, yet she could have been fourteen. Her skin was flawless. Her hair shimmied down her back, thick and glossy brown like a model's in a L'Oréal advert. Gone was the awkward, gangly girl he remembered from Jane's dinner parties, back when Neil was around. Something else had emerged, poised and self-aware.

'Hi, Emma.'

'Hi.' She turned her head to him, smiled reluctantly and turned back to the TV.

Jane checked her watch. 'Have you got your swimming things ready, Emma?'

'They're upstairs. Can I just watch the end of this programme? There's only a few minutes to go.'

'No, Emma! Please turn the TV off now and get your things.' Jane's voice sounded infinitely weary.

Emma glared at her mother, dragged herself off the sofa and flounced out of the room.

Jane bent to pick up a glass from the floor. 'I hope she won't be any trouble, Paul. If she is, let me know.'

'Don't worry, I don't think Emma will act up with me. Anyway, I've had my own stroppy teenage daughter to deal with, remember.'

A paper-thin smile didn't erase the weariness from Jane's face.

'I can't thank you enough for your help,' she said. 'She'd be stuck in her room all day if you weren't taking her out.'

'It's no trouble,' he repeated. 'Believe me.'

Two minutes later Emma reappeared with a faux-fur trimmed jacket over her jeans, and a pink and silver striped bag hanging from her shoulder. The three of them clustered at the front door.

'Bye, Em. Have a good swim, won't you?'

Emma ignored her mother. She leaned against the wall, examining her nails with a bored expression. Her bottom lip stuck out sulkily.

'See you later, Jane.' He opened the front door. 'Come on, you. Let's go swim.'

Emma climbed into the Porsche, put on her seat belt and yawned.

'How long are we going to swim for?'

'It depends.' He started the engine. 'Usually I swim for three quarters of an hour. How long do you want to swim for?'

She shrugged.

He smiled. She could be as difficult as she wanted. He could handle anything this girl could throw at him.

'Do you want to choose a CD?'

'Mmm.' She scanned the titles without interest.

'How about the Rolling Stones? Or Fleetwood Mac, Pink Floyd, Stevie Winwood?'

She wrinkled her nose.

He turned on the radio. Billy Joel was singing 'Uptown Girl'. She probably wouldn't like that either, but it was too bad.

They inched their way through congested Putney, past thicker than usual crowds of Saturday shoppers. A week into January, the sales were pulling nicely.

'How far can you swim?' he asked after he'd parked at the health club.

Emma shrugged again. 'Not far. I'm not very good at swimming. I hate water in my ears.'

'That'll change when you get more confident in the water. I'll have you swimming up and down the pool in no time, I bet.'

She looked at him, stony faced, and reached for her bag.

He signed her in at reception without trouble – fortunately they relaxed their 'no under 16s' rule at weekends. Emma said nothing as they walked to the changing rooms. He could understand her lack of enthusiasm, it didn't bother him. The girl knew him only as a friend of her mother's, another adult on the fringes of her world. She probably wished it could be her father taking her swimming instead.

Paul waited for Emma at the tiled entrance to the pool, just past the shower and the foot bath. He glanced down at his belly, dented the skin with his fingers.

Good enough, he thought. Not quite as flat and firm as it used to be, but overall, he was in good shape. He had no excess fat and his muscles were strong from his weekly workouts. Emma would see he looked after himself – he wasn't one of that crowd of lard-arses, at the wrong end of middle-age, who came here to splash around and hang out in the steam room, kidding themselves they were still twenty-five.

After ten minutes, Emma still hadn't come out. He was about to go in and check she hadn't run off, when she appeared before him, hair hidden under a rubber cap, a red Lycra costume clinging to her slim white body. Her nascent breasts were encased by the fabric, which allowed a discreet rise at her chest, nothing more. Her face showed a tinge of shyness.

'Nice costume. Is it new?'

She shrugged – a twitch of shoulder with the slightest curl of her lower lip. 'Not really.'

He led Emma to the shallow end, where a collection of mothers and small children dotted the casual swimming area. Goggled swimmers zipped up and down the cordoned-off section. A lifeguard sat motionless in a chair.

'Coming in?'

Emma stood at the edge of the pool, hands on hips, studying the water with a look of disdain.

He walked slowly over to one of the faster lanes and dived in, striking the surface cleanly and gliding as far as he could. He emerged, arms slicing effortlessly through the water, legs propelling him, an efficient and powerful machine. This was his chance to impress her. He was in his element in the pool, no longer a man of fifty-three, with greying hair and a large number of titanium teeth, but a swimming champion. It might be nearly forty years since he won the title, yet he could still out-swim most people.

At the other end, he looked for Emma. She was sitting disconsolately on the edge of the pool, head down, feet dangling in the water, ignoring his performance. He swam back, stopping a short distance from her.

'Aren't you coming in?'

She looked at him as if he were an idiot, then back at the water. 'It's cold.'

'No it's not!' He scooped up some water with his hands and sent it in her direction. She made a face as a hail of drops struck her. 'Come in, scaredy cat! It's only water.'

She slid down, grimacing, and attempted a few strokes of front crawl. Her arms generated more splash than motion.

'Can I make a suggestion?' He demonstrated how her arms should strike the water. 'You try now.'

It was better this time. She turned back to him with a hesitant smile.

'You're getting it,' he said. 'Kick a bit more.' She got the knack after a while, though she still insisted on sticking up her head as she swam. 'Okay,' he coaxed. 'Can you swim all the way to the other end? Take it easy, don't rush.'

He swam alongside her until she lunged for the side of the pool.

'Made it!'

'That's a girl! You're a quick learner. At this rate, you'll be able to swim a whole length next time.'

Surprise and delight flashed across her face. She responded to his praise like a plant to the sun. There was a long way to go before she became a half-decent swimmer, though.

He watched her swim some more, calling out suggestions from time to time. An elderly woman swimming on her own gave him a friendly nod.

She thinks I'm Emma's father.

None of the other swimmers seemed to suspect anything either. Why would they? There was no sticker on his forehead announcing: THIS MAN CAN'T BE TRUSTED. In any case, he told himself, he had no intentions towards this girl other than to help her swim better, and for her to enjoy their outings. Anything else wasn't worth the risk.

'I'm tired,' Emma announced after less than fifteen minutes. 'I want to get out now.'

'Okay.' Paul pointed to the café tucked behind a glass wall. 'Get changed and wait over there for me, okay? I'm going to swim a few laps.'

He watched her swim over to the steps, climb out and remove her cap. Damp hair tumbled down her back. Before she turned away, he saw the outline of her breasts under her costume. For a split second he could see her naked.

He pushed himself off the wall and swam lengths as hard as he could, until his arms ached.

When he saw Emma again, her hair was blow-dried straight and her lips were glossed. She sat with her elbows on the table, studying the menu.

'Can I have something to eat?'

She pleaded with her big brown eyes. Something about her reminded him of Laura at that age. He forced his mind back to Emma's question.

'What would you like?'

Instantly, her face brightened. 'Coke and chocolate fudge cake, please.'

He sipped his coffee as Emma consumed her cake in large, almost continuous, mouthfuls, ignoring the fork he'd got for her. She ate as if the cake was the only thing that mattered in the world. Her fingers became flecked with brown. A brown smear appeared below her mouth. Crumbs fell into her lap.

Their outing had gone okay, hadn't it? He considered. She hadn't been badly behaved, only a little offhand. That would change, next time. Maybe. The girl seemed to like him, but she wasn't sure of him yet. She would let him see a glimmer of her real self, and then retreat, afraid of letting him get too close. But she would start enjoying herself soon enough. They were only on the first square of the board.

'What did you do for Christmas?'

'Granny and Granddad came over.' Emma frowned, swallowing cake. 'Then we went to stay with my uncle.'

'What about the rest of the holidays? Got any plans?'

A roll of the lower lip. 'Don't know. Watch some DVDs. Maybe go ice skating.'

It didn't matter if they didn't talk. Silence was fine.

He watched the last piece of cake disappear into her mouth. Emma slurped Coke through her straw, meeting his eyes. He couldn't help smiling. What was it about her? She was just as Laura had been – floating inside her own secret world, a mysterious, ever-changing creature.

Emma licked each finger in turn then wiped her mouth with the paper napkin. Without warning, a smile transformed her sullen face – a come-and-get-me smile, he thought. As if she was daring him to react, to do something. Was she playing with him? Or was it just his imagination?

'Do you like school?'

'No.'

'Why not?'

'I don't like the teachers, and the subjects are so boring. I hate having to learn things I don't like.'

'There's no subject you like?'

She took a while to answer. 'I like art. And sport.'

'What's your favourite?'

'Netball.'

'Do you have lots of friends at school?'

'Hannah's my best friend.' She coiled an elastic hair band around her finger. Her voice was low and musical, a rain of silky notes. 'My other friends are Zara and Kylie. And Mandy, sometimes. But my mum doesn't like her, she's always getting into trouble at school.'

'Do you see your friends during the holidays?'

She hesitated. 'Sometimes we go to each other's houses and stuff. I go to them if Mum can take me – she doesn't let me go on the train on my own. Anyway, I usually have to look after my little brother when she's out at work.'

'That's not so easy, I guess. Little brothers can be tough. I didn't have a brother but my two sisters were bad enough.' He waited for her to respond, not wanting to turn the conversation into an interrogation. But she'd turned her attention to her Coke.

He wondered how it would end, their first outing together. Would it be their only outing? That would be up to Emma, partly. Jane wouldn't force Emma to come to the pool with him if she told her she'd hated it.

Suddenly, the thought of Emma not wanting to swim with him again was unbearable. He knew it was gaining strength, this urge inside him. He knew he should tell Jane he wouldn't be able to take Emma to the pool again. He was too busy, or she was too difficult, any excuse would be fine. It would be the right thing to do. Then there would be nothing to tempt him.

'I enjoyed our swim, Emma,' he said as they got up from the table. 'I'd like to do it again soon, if you would?'

It was the other man who had spoken. The man who had no concern about the consequences of his actions. The man whose needs could not be denied indefinitely, who was waiting impatiently for his next fix. The man prepared to sacrifice everything for the impossible joy of a girl in her first bloom.

Emma looked at him gravely. He prepared himself for disappointment. She didn't like him, or she sensed somehow what was on his mind. Or maybe she would refuse to go with him again just to spite her mother, who thought swimming with this boring older guy would be good for her.

'Yeah, okay.' Quietly, yet without hesitation.

They walked back to the car. The sun was golden above the horizon and a row of trees cast long shadows over them.

She came to him as he fell asleep that night, in that enchanting place between alertness and oblivion. Laura, in her swimming costume, spread out on the grass, drops of water sparkling on her bare shoulders. No matter how many times he replayed it, the image was as clear as it had always been.

She had been standing under the garden hose, trying to cool herself down. Now, propped up on an elbow, she was engrossed in a book. *Riddles in Philosophy* it said on the cover, the sort of book she'd taken to reading of late.

He sat down beside the discarded sun hat. Though not yet a woman, his daughter was beautiful. In only a few months, the bones in her face had become visible. He watched the side of her face, its sharpness of concentration, the little furrow in her brow. She was ignoring him. She wanted him to leave her alone so she could get on with her book.

The tan of her thighs glistened against the white of her costume. The cheeks of her bottom stretched the skimpy material. He could see the curves of her breasts too. Last year they had only been tiny buds.

He glanced up at the houses on either side. The back windows of one were curtained, and those of the others were obscured by a nearby tree – now strung with small apples – and a mass of roses poking up from the fence. No one could see them here, at the far end of the garden.

He knew that what he was about to do was wrong. Only that wasn't enough, not anymore. He closed his eyes, the electric fizz of anticipation building inside him.

4

Laura

25 January 2011

'Alison wants to see you in her office,' Jan said cheerily as she strutted past, a stack of DVDs in her arms. 'I'd go straight away, if I were you.'

Laura looked up from her computer. She was in trouble, she guessed. Alison was finding fault with everyone today. One of the editors had been rebuked for allowing his honeymoon to coincide with the week of the annual company get-together. Then Alison's PA had been reprimanded for making a spelling mistake in a presentation to potential clients – pubic instead of public – loud enough to send the whole office into a fit of sniggers and giggles.

Yes, she must have done something wrong, despite her renewed efforts to do everything as if her life depended on it, to make up for her recent lack of concentration. Nightmares had disrupted her sleep more than ever lately. By about mid-afternoon, she'd have to go outside for a quick walk around the block to stop herself from dropping off at her desk. Today had been worse than usual. All morning she'd found it hard to focus on the simplest task.

Her boss's door was open. Laura knocked and went in.

'That was Charlie on the phone,' Alison announced in her thick New Zealand accent, not issuing an invitation to sit. She was standing behind her desk, bouncing a paperweight between her hands, her eyes hard and bright. Her bulk seemed more mountainous than usual. 'He said he left a message with you this morning.'

Laura waited for Alison to continue. Her gaze wandered from the paperweight, to Alison's clunky watch, to the large ruby on her finger. The message stayed obstinately out of reach.

Alison's frown embedded itself deeper. 'I'll give you a clue. It involves Mr Beale.'

Then she remembered, with sickening clarity. 'It was for Charlie to call Tim at Flamingo.'

'That's the one.'

Someone had distracted her with Jeff's leaving collection as she was about to write it down, and then she'd had a call to go and help in the edit suite.

'I forgot about it. I'm sorry.'

The volume of Alison's voice shot up by several decibels. 'You forgot about it? You *forgot* about it?'

Laura opened her mouth to speak, but Alison got there first.

'Charlie is off his fucking tree. Flamingo have decided to go with the fuckwits down the road instead of us – thanks to you.'

'I'm sorry, Alison. It won't happen again, I promise.'

A cursory flick of the hand. 'I have to go back to work. I'll see you later on.'

At 5pm Laura started on her last task – booking next week's facilities. The summons still hadn't come. Anxiety lodged inside her gut, the vague unease slowly building into a churning, icky sensation, until she couldn't think of anything except what would happen next. Alison was well known for her temper – even some of the men were reluctant to say anything that might set her off.

At 5.30pm, people started to leave the office. While most ignored her, some gave her curious or pitying stares. Laura sorted the papers on her desk into neat piles and sharpened her pencil. She was sorely tempted to slip away with the others. God only knew what Alison would say to her. Perhaps she'd have calmed down. Or was she waiting for everyone to leave so she could let rip?

At 6pm, Jan beckoned to Laura.

'Alison will see you now.'

Alison was sitting down at her desk, examining a sheet of paper. She lowered it and motioned for Laura to sit.

'Laura, I'm not going to beat around the bush. You've been here for nearly three months now. How do you think you're doing?'

Alison's tone was scathing. This interview wasn't going to go well. Laura wet the inside of her mouth with her tongue and fought the urge to swallow. She tried to speak confidently without any trace of a wobble.

'I could be doing better, I suppose.'

'Yes, I'd agree with that. Let me give you a few reasons why.' Alison leaned forward, emphasising her heavy jowls and extensive cleavage. 'One, you obviously dislike what you're doing, or think it's beneath you – since you arrived here you've shown no interest in your work, and rush home as soon as you possibly can. Two, you keep making mistakes when you should know better. Three,' Alison thumped the desk with the heel of her hand as her voice increased in pitch and volume, 'you go around in a daze not knowing what the hell you're doing. Someone asks you to do something and you forget to do it, and we lose an important contract.' A speck of saliva landed just below Laura's eye. 'Is there anything I've missed?'

Laura shrank into her chair, staring at her hands huddled in her lap. What could she say? That she'd been doing her best, only it was difficult to concentrate on anything after so many nights of broken sleep? That a dull ache clouded her head most of the time, like someone pushing their knuckles behind her eyeballs? That she wanted just one last chance to prove herself? That she needed this job?

There was no point.

'You can go now, Laura, and don't bother coming back. You'll be paid for the rest of the month. I suggest you find yourself a job you're better suited to.'

***

Rachel gave Laura an interrogatory glance. 'So, you've been looking for something else?'

Rachel's pale, red-tinged hair was piled behind her head as usual. Today she was wearing her new camel coat, its collar turned up in the late January chill.

'Of course. I spend all day looking.' Laura sighed. The frustration of it all made her want to tear up her CV on top of the head of the next person to ask her where she wanted to be in five years' time. 'There's not a lot out there, though, unless you're an IT genius or you want to spend the day asking passers-by to make donations to Greenpeace. Everyone's looking for the same jobs as me, I think.'

'Better sign on for the dole, in case you don't find anything soon. Damn, we'd better go back.'

Water stretched across the towpath in front of them, barring the way. Laura reluctantly turned and followed Rachel's slight figure. The stillness of the scene soothed her. It seemed to deepen after being broken once in a while by the hoot of geese, or the hypnotic lap of water against muddy stones. Beside them the river, fat and brown, crept up into the meadows like a giant slug.

'Oh, I forgot to tell you, you'll never guess what happened at rehearsals the other day.' Excitement bubbled up through Rachel's voice, sending its pitch even higher. 'Roger tripped over my cello case and nearly went flying. I couldn't help laughing. He gave me this really dirty look and I grovelled. Anyway, we got talking ...'

Laura smiled. Such meetings were typical of Rachel, who was never shy of capitalising on social opportunities. Though she tried to follow the story, her friend's voice began to blend with the squawks of ducks chasing bread, and the chug of a receding boat. She watched a heron trawl the mud. Above, the clouds began to darken.

'Sorry, Laura. I'm going on and on and you can't get a word in.'

Sometimes, Rachel's vivacious chatter could be irritating. Today, she didn't mind, for it stopped her from having to think about what she was going to say – if she had the guts to go through with it.

They reached Richmond Bridge. Rachel suggested they sit on a bench with a view of the river.

'So, what was that thing you wanted to talk about?'

Laura thrust her hands deep into her jacket pockets. 'I'm not sure if this is the right time.'

Her decision to reveal her secret – her father's secret – had been definite. Only, as the moment approached, her certainty was receding. To tell Rachel would be to betray her father, she couldn't help thinking.

'Come on, Laura,' Rachel pressed. 'When is it going to be the right time?'

It was as good a time as any, wasn't it, to finally let go of this thing? She'd been holding on to it for long enough; it was starting to fester inside her. If she didn't tell someone, the truth would burst out. And why should she have to hide it anymore? She was a big girl now. Nothing would happen to her.

'You know these bad dreams I was telling you about?'

'Where someone's chasing you? You're still having them?'

'They're worse, lately. Sometimes I can't sleep for hours afterwards. The man chasing me – he's dangerous, he's going to hurt me, or kill me. But I'm trapped, I can't get away.'

Rachel frowned. 'Do you know who it is?'

'Not really. I never see his face.'

'What, it's just some random guy?'

'I think it's my father.'

'Your father? Why would he be chasing you?' Her friend sounded interested, as she'd expected. Rachel was always interested in anything psychological – the darker, the better.

'It's a bit ... heavy. I've never told this to anyone.'

Laura looked at Rachel's pretty, almost angelic face. Though Rachel was her closest friend, sometimes she had the disconcerting feeling that Rachel looked on her as an object of curiosity, much as a biologist might examine the contents of a petri dish.

Rachel smiled enticingly. 'Tell me.'

She checked no one was within earshot. This was like the moment before diving into a pool of icy water on a sweltering day. Wanting to, and not wanting to, in equal measures.

'When I was growing up he ... he used to do things. When no one was around.'

The afternoon light was dying. Clouds towered into the sky, giving the river a steely hue.

'Go on, I'm listening. What did he do?'

'He used to touch me. He said I—' She stopped. Rachel's smile had gone. Why go on? She could stop this now, if she wanted. But something was starting up inside her, unstoppable, like a huge wave curving the sea, way out from the shore.

'He used to put his hand on my thigh, and I'd push it away. It was like a game we played.' The games had started years earlier. Games of hide and seek that would end in giggling and shrieking when her father grabbed her and swung her high in the air. Games of how long she could keep quiet while he tickled her feet with blades of grass. Games that they only played when they were alone together. 'Then it went on to other things.'

Rachel's eyes widened. 'What things?'

Laura took a deep breath. The wave was closing on the shore now, carrying her with it.

'The first time he actually did anything … I was sunbathing in the garden and my mother was upstairs. He pulled down my costume and started touching my breasts.'

'My God, Laura.'

'I was eleven. My mother had bought me my first bra a few months before. I wanted to push him away, but I didn't. I couldn't.'

It sounds pathetic, she thought, startled by the look of disgust on Rachel's face. *As if I had no free will whatsoever.* But she had been unable to stop him. He had taken temporary ownership of her body, rendering her approval obsolete.

'He did it quite often, after that. He kissed me too, sometimes. I hated it.'

For so long, she had tried to forget what her father had done – now, most of the separate incidents had blurred together in her mind. Could she actually have enjoyed any of it? That was the worst thing, imagining that.

Rachel scratched her head, frowning. 'Did no one see him while he was doing this?'

'No, I was always alone with him.' She was riding the wave now. 'My mother would be out, shopping or whatever, and my brother would be out with his friends. Usually he did it when I was downstairs watching TV or doing my homework.'

'No one ever saw him?'

'No, never.'

'What if someone had? Didn't he worry he'd be caught?'

'I've no idea.'

Rachel bit her lip. 'Did he ever … do anything else?'

'Sex, you mean? No, nothing like that, thank God. Except one time.'

'What?' Rachel leaned forward.

'Mum was away for a few days, staying with a friend. I think my brother was on a camping trip. I found some pictures on my bed, of a man having sex with a girl. She was about ten or eleven. They were disgusting. I screwed them up and chucked them in the dustbin. I thought it must have been my father who put them in my room, but I didn't say anything. Then, the next night, he came into my room when I was asleep. He lay down beside me and opened his dressing gown. I honestly thought he was going to make me have sex with him. But he didn't, he just made me do things.'

'What things, Laura?'

Though it was too awful to say, she would have to say it now.

'Hold his … you know. Then he asked me to put it in my mouth. He said he needed me to know how much he wanted me.'

It was the worst thing she'd ever done. A flash of memory snuck out before she could push it back. That musty, festering smell. Wiping her face on the towel he'd handed her. Her gut clenched. Something fluttered inside her like a small, dying animal.

'Then he went away again. He went downstairs and played his music.' He'd played Beethoven's fifth symphony, the volume high.

'My God, Laura.' Rachel stared, her face drained of colour.

'He never did anything like that again. I always thought he might, though. After that night, I kept thinking he would make me do it again, or he'd make me have sex with him this time. He never did, thank God.'

'How long did all this go on for?'

'A year or so. I'm not sure why he stopped. Maybe he thought I'd had enough by then. Or maybe he was scared someone would find out.'

'You didn't tell anyone? Not even your mother?'

'No, I didn't tell anyone. He made me promise.'

Looking back now, it seemed so obvious. Why hadn't she just told her mother what he'd done that first time? She must have asked herself a hundred times, now it was too late to change a thing.

'I know it sounds crazy, I didn't tell my mother. Or my brother, a teacher, someone.' She heard her voice weak and scratchy in her throat. 'But he said it would kill my mother if she ever found out. He meant it would actually kill her, not just "Oh, it'll kill her". I couldn't tell anyone.'

Her heart drummed in her chest. Finally, it was out.

Rachel tucked an escaped strand of hair behind her ear. She seemed deep in thought.

'What do you think would have happened if you *had* told her?'

'Maybe she would have asked for a divorce, and we'd have all carried on happily without Dad, and he wouldn't have come near me again. I don't know.' She heard her shrug reflected in her voice. 'But maybe not. He was the boss in our family, we all had to do what he said. Mum didn't stand up to him, Rachel. She tried to, but he always had to be in control, everything had to be done his way. If I'd told her, she probably wouldn't have been able to do anything at all, she'd have just crumbled, fallen apart. And I'd have been left alone with him, apart from my brother.'

'Your mother might have left him.'

'No, she wouldn't have. She was tied to him, she still is. She says she loves him even though he makes her so unhappy sometimes.'

Neither of them spoke. Invisible specks of rain hung in the air. The wind broke up the reflection of the street lamps on the bridge.

It was done, for better or for worse. The awkwardness, anxiety and exhilaration were gone. The anger she knew she ought to feel was still lost somewhere inside her. All she felt was relief, and the ache that never went away – a longing for things to have been different.

'I'll never understand why he did it, Rachel. A father is supposed to love and protect you. What's the point of having children otherwise?'

Rachel's arms surrounded her. 'You poor thing. I can't imagine what it must have been like. Your father was the pits. I'm surprised you can bear to see him now.'

'I got used to pretending, I suppose. I wish he wasn't my father. I wish I had a normal father, one like everyone else.'

'It's hard, isn't it? My mother used to do crazy things to me and my brother, and I couldn't tell anyone.'

Laura looked at her friend in surprise. She knew Rachel hadn't had a happy childhood, though she hadn't talked about it much – at least, only those bits she could manage to laugh at.

Three women in office clothes and heels ran past, yelling. The first raindrops were falling, splattering loudly on the ground.

Rachel reached for her bag. 'Let's go up to that bar,' she said, nodding to the terrace. 'It's going to pour.'

They found a table by the window. While Rachel went to get the drinks, Laura watched people scurrying for shelter. She was getting scared now. What if her father found out? Had she done the right thing, telling someone? Gusts of wind ruffled the surface of the river, creating vast silvery lakes. A pelican landed on the cabin of a moored boat, bobbing crazily.

'I got us mojitos, it's two for one. I could do with a drink after what you told me.'

She thanked Rachel and took a gulp of the drink.

'I find it hard to believe your father could do those things and your mother didn't know,' Rachel said all of a sudden, as if she'd been dwelling on it for some time. 'Surely she had an inkling what was going on? What planet was she on, for fuck's sake?'

'Well, if she did know, she's never said anything. Dad's clever. I think he made sure she never had any reason to be suspicious. But I suppose it's a bit odd she never twigged what was going on.'

'Aren't you angry with her for not protecting you?'

Laura slammed her glass on the table. 'It wasn't my mother who did those things! He did.'

But wasn't Rachel right? That was part of the reason she avoided seeing her mother, wasn't it? She was angry with her mother for not seeing the truth, for not being a stronger person. Because her mother couldn't stand up to him, he'd thought he could get away with anything. Her mother hadn't seen what was wrong with Dad. Why hadn't her mother protected her – why had she been the one to protect her mother? *Even now, I'm going around on tippy toes to save her from the harsh reality.*

Laura lowered her voice. 'I'm sorry, Rachel. It's so hard to explain. Things aren't right between me and my mother. I guess part of me *does* resent her. I've always hidden things from her. Maybe it's because I've had to keep this big secret. I just can't imagine telling her about all this.'

An uneasy silence.

'I'm glad you told me,' Rachel said at last. 'It must have been really difficult for you.'

'I had to tell someone. It seemed like the right time.' She waited, summoning the long-stored question to her lips. 'I've been thinking. Do you think my dad could do the same thing to someone else?'

'What do you mean?'

'He's started taking this girl swimming. Emma, her name is. She's twelve. Her mother's on her own, her husband left her. My mother's been friends with her for ages.'

'This woman must be very trusting.'

'Dad's friends with her too, she trusts him. Do you think I should tell someone about what he did to me? Emma's mother, maybe?'

Rachel stabbed her straw into the ice at the bottom of her glass. 'I think you should tell *your* mother about everything your father did to you. Tell her you think he might do it to Emma too.'

'What if she can't deal with it? What if something happens to her? She loves him, Rachel. She'd be devastated.'

'And what if he does do something to this girl? After what he did to you …'

'I know. But he probably won't get the chance to do anything. He's only going swimming with her. There'll be other people around—'

'All the time? What if he *does* do something? How would you feel then?'

She shook her head, unable to put her feelings into words. An icky swirl of foreboding, brooding and strengthening.

From above, a long, deep rumble.

'That can't be thunder, can it? In January?' Rachel's voice was charged with excitement. They both turned to the window. Another flash of lightning forked in the sky, causing a stir around them. 'Let's get out of here before it buckets. I'll come with you to the station.'

They went out, onto the street. Rachel stopped and struggled to open her tiny umbrella, jabbing at buttons and shaking it. The wind tossed an empty crisp packet high into the air.

'It's stuck. Hold on, let me fix it.'

'We're going to be soaked, hurry up!'

Finally, the umbrella opened. They huddled beneath its inadequate canopy.

'Hold it straight, will you?' Laura clung on to Rachel's arm. 'I'm getting a river of water down my neck.'

'It's hard to hold it straight in this wind.' Rachel started laughing. 'You try.'

They narrowly missed crashing into someone running umbrella-less towards them.

'Slow down, we'll crucify someone! There's a vicious spike on the end of this thing.'

A fierce white light bathed the street. Almost immediately, a crack of thunder. Rachel looked up.

'Shit, it's right on top of us, we'll be struck! Let's wait here till it's over.'

'No, let's run to the station. We'll be alright.'

'We'd better be,' Rachel said. 'It'll be your fault if we're struck by lightning.'

It would be his revenge. The thought had slipped out before she could stop it.

They ran past the shops, reached the station and stood dripping inside the entrance hall, laughing and panting. Her jeans were soaked. Rachel's fringe clung to her forehead and she had a dark smudge under one eye.

'Look at us.'

'Your mascara's running!'

When the rain eased, Rachel readied her umbrella.

'Good luck with the job hunting. And I'm glad you told me about your dad and everything. Let me know what happens, won't you?'

The train was waiting at the platform. Laura sat down in the first empty seat, smiling to herself. Her head felt light. She was cold and damp but she didn't care. Finally, she'd revealed the truth about her father. Why had she got so anxious about telling Rachel? She'd even wondered whether Rachel would still want to be her friend.

Of course, if she had other close friends, Rachel wouldn't be so important. She'd never made friends easily, not since the end of primary school. Back then, she'd gone around with her three closest friends. The four of them would always be over at each other's houses, having parties and sleepovers, playing with Lizzie's karaoke set and Allie's roller skates, or acting in Alex's plays. Then, the year she turned twelve, everything changed. Her closest friends went to a different school and drifted away, and new ones didn't come. She went around by herself in the breaks, longing to be included. But something stopped her from getting close to the others, an invisible cloak separated her from the world, containing within it all the bad things her father had done to her, and all the bad things inside her that she couldn't let anyone see.

Even as an adult, looking at the world with adult eyes, she sometimes felt like that withdrawn and lonely schoolgirl.

On some days she felt utterly alone. But those days were fewer, thankfully, since Rachel had come into her life.

Laura smiled. They would never have met if Rachel hadn't started chatting to her on a bench at Wimbledon station, while they waited for a delayed train to Waterloo. She'd been prickly, not in the mood to talk. Rachel had persisted, asking questions about her life with a peculiar ease and openness she had, which made meeting people seem natural and inevitable rather than a chore you did your best to avoid.

It had been like discovering an unsuspected sister. They'd talked on the phone for hours about the books they'd read and films they'd watched, the things they disliked the most, what they would most like to do but had never dared, what they would do if they won a million pounds. They'd confided in each other about their bodies, their jobs, their relationships. She'd shared more with her friend than she had with anyone else – including her mother and her brother, and every one of her past boyfriends. And now she'd shared the secret about her father, too.

She's in her room, back at the house. The sky is dark and branches flail in the wind, scratching and tapping against the window. Her mother has gone away, won't be back for a long time. Outside, a light flickers. Her father is calling, she realises.

'Laura! Where are you?'

He thuds down the hall and starts climbing the stairs. She runs out of her room and into the bathroom, bangs the door shut and slides the bolt across, leaving the light off so he won't know she's there.

Thud, thud, thud. He's on the landing now.

A tap on the door. 'Laura! I know you're in there! Open the door, sweetie.'

She turns on the bath taps so the gushing water will block him out. But she can still hear the tapping at the door.

Tap, tap, tap.

A flash lights up the room, brighter than any lightning she's ever seen.

Tap, tap, tap.

'No! Don't come in!'

A scream pierced her head. Her own scream.

Laura jolted upright. Sweat drenched her skin. Her heart was beating wildly and irregularly, as it must do when one is in the throes of a heart attack.

Then, slowly, her body returned to normal. She was safe now. She was an adult again, back in her flat. She'd dozed off against the beanbag. Outside, rain was beating against the roof and the wind was gusting. But inside was warm and cosy, just as it should be.

5

Paul

5 February 2011

'Bet you can't catch me!' With a splash, Emma vanished.

'OK, missy, I'm coming to get you!'

Her head bobbed to the surface, way down the pool. Another shriek and she was off again, churning up a wake with her frenzied kicking. Paul launched himself towards the flash of red costume, dodging shoals of bodies. He was catching her up. Any second now he'd have her.

He reached out and grabbed her foot but she wriggled free. He stood up, pretending to give up the chase, then flung himself at her with all his strength, managing to grab a flailing arm. 'Gotcha!'

He reeled her in, held her tight around the waist. Suddenly she was helpless in his arms.

'Okay, you win,' Emma said, pulling away. 'Let me go.'

He drank in the slippery, fluttery feel of her body against his and let her escape.

'Time to go home, little mermaid.'

She floated away from him, a smile curling her lips. Of course, she wouldn't want to leave just yet.

'Your mum will be wondering where we've got to. I said we'd be back by four.'

No answer.

'Come on, Emma, let's go.'

She stayed floating, ignoring him.

'I'm going in to get changed.' He turned away as if he didn't care what she did. 'See you at the entrance.'

'Wait, I'm coming!'

Paul closed the door of his cubicle and pulled a towel from his bag. It was their fourth swim together, and she was finally starting to let down her defences. He was getting glimpses of a laughing, mischievous Emma. The sullen stares and long silences were on their way out and Little Miss Wilful was getting an airing instead. He was up for whatever games she wanted to play. He could play games too.

He imagined Emma's glistening body as she stepped out of her wet costume, her tresses clinging to her back. The small breasts and the tender slope of her stomach leading to a dark patch above her legs. He was getting a hard-on. How could he help it? She was a wispy, sulky, feisty little thing, her flesh secretly moist, ripening with each passing week. And just out of reach.

He finished dressing and went outside to wait. Emma would be a while yet, messing around with her hair and her lip gloss, trying to look like the models in her *Glamour* magazines. In her head, she was a woman already.

Suzanne would go nuts, he thought, if she knew how much time he spent picturing Emma undressing. She was getting a tiny bit suspicious now, since that girl with the tattoo at the party. But in all these years, she had never picked up on anything untoward.

He had been careful, cunning even; Suzanne wasn't stupid. He had one big advantage over her, though.

At heart, his wife was a good woman, kind, affectionate and loyal, the sort who could see only good in others.

He'd fallen in love with a sweetly shy, girlish, tender-hearted twenty-four-year-old. He'd been something solid for her to cling to. In her gratitude and love, she'd dedicated herself to him – in those early years, at least. Her naivety had appealed to him, her foolish fears and fancies had amused him, her giggles had loosened the crust around his heart. He'd known from the start that she wouldn't see there was another part of him, which needed more than she could offer. Hadn't he even hoped, for a while, that she could crush this demon inside him, that marriage and a family would be enough – or at least would prevent him from placating the hunger for something more?

For a few years it seemed to work – or perhaps he just kidded himself it was. As Suzanne's lure diminished, the resentment and hostility built up inside him. She came to embody the reason he could not satisfy his deepest desires. And these days ...

He sighed, thinking back to last night's sight of Suzanne's bare backside before she draped her pyjamas over it. She was no longer young and curvy. Her breasts hung towards her thickened belly. Sometimes it was like going to bed with his mother, not his wife.

He rubbed his hands together and put them inside his jacket pockets. It was fucking freezing out here. But the ache of cold in his hands and feet wasn't nearly as bad as the ache in his groin when he looked at Emma. The grinding, useless ache of wanting something you couldn't have. He kicked the concrete bollard in front of him, scuffing the leather of his shoe. The craving was as strong as ever. He could no longer ignore it and pray it would go away.

He'd been drawn to young girls since he was a fresh-faced trader on the money markets, back in Canada.

The ones just beginning to ripen, delighting in their newly-found femininity, sunning themselves in the park on hot days in the latest show-all fashions. Just looking. Casually, but carefully, so no one would notice. He'd had girlfriends his own age, but none had done much for him. Then Maxine swaggered into his life, that spoiled, rich kid desperate to get back at her parents. She'd told him she would be fifteen in two months and she needed to find out about sex because her parents were absurdly strict and didn't like her even looking at boys. It was only when her parents found out about the late-afternoon sessions in his apartment, and threatened to call the cops, derail his career and generally make his life hell, that he found out she was actually thirteen.

He'd escaped to London and found Suzanne. He'd wanted a normal life, to have a wife and kids like other guys. He told himself he wasn't going to turn into some saddo, sneaking off to do things in secret, perpetually looking over his shoulder for cops and deranged parents.

And then came Laura.

Laura was his adored little girl. He read her stories, and built her a doll's house and a tree house. He took her to ballet and swimming lessons and he comforted her when she fell over or came home crying. He loved her as a father should love his daughter. Only, when he carried her on his shoulders and she would scream with excitement, or she looked at him with serious eyes as he read to her, he would imagine her freshness, her softness, her willingness to please.

He'd done everything he could to resist her.

After his wife had gone to bed, or while she was out for the evening, he feasted on clips of girls he'd downloaded from the internet, putting his sessions down to eBay or Amazon, or networking with ex-colleagues on LinkedIn.

Occasionally, usually during business trips, he'd sought out girls in the flesh, girls who looked younger than they dressed and never gave their real age. He went to terraced houses in the back streets of cities, places far enough from home that he wouldn't be recognised, where you could get girls of indeterminate age – runaways or illegals – with broken English, half of them on drugs, judging from their robotic responses. He never saw the same girl twice and he never told them his real name or anything about himself.

Only, it began to feel like *he* had a drug habit. The relief was always short-lived and spoiled by his desire, which came back stronger than before.

Then one day, he hadn't been able to resist Laura. It had been easy, that slide down. It had felt quite natural, like stepping into a hot bath at the end of a long journey that had left you mentally and physically exhausted.

At first, he'd limited himself to kisses and caresses. The thought of going further had crossed his mind, of course. He'd resisted that temptation, mostly. Laura had been hard to resist, though. It was only when she began to show the first signs that she would soon reject him, maybe even out him to Suzanne, that he'd been able to stop. Otherwise, he might have gone all the way with her.

The thought of it had freaked him out. He'd vowed never again to let himself get hooked like that. He'd told himself that Laura would be the end of it. From now on, he would steer clear of girls: girls on the game, girls walking in parks, girls coming home from school, friends' daughters, neighbours' daughters, girls on the internet. He could never again take the risk of being found out, of being hounded by the police, or, heaven forbid, dragged before a court and locked up.

He'd not wavered, until now. Day by day, hour by hour, his will was eroding. Emma was awakening the same yearning inside him that Laura had. She was indefinable, contrary, quiet yet mischievous, fragile yet tough. Something in her called out to him, yet at the same time pushed him away.

He had to find a way out of this, before it was too late. He could go to prostitutes again, couldn't he? He could get it up for some girl who'd already done it with so many guys, doing it with one more wouldn't matter. A girl who would do whatever he wanted. He could save Emma from the demon inside him. That would be useless, however, he knew in his heart. There was one inescapable fact: the girls he could pay for were nothing compared to Emma.

Emma was the real thing. Not an image on his computer screen, or one of those dirty, desperate girls doped to the eyeballs, thinking only of her next fix as she passed herself from man to man. This girl was untouched by other men. And it wasn't just that – he would get to know Emma gradually. He would find out how she ticked, get past her defences. With the right encouragement, she would come to him willingly, bit by bit.

He kicked the bollard again, harder. The jolt of the impact travelled up his leg. Suzanne would be out of her tree, he thought, if she knew one quarter of what he'd done, and Jane would probably piss herself. But fuck it, he wasn't the only guy alive to have these feelings, so did thousands of other men, all of them hanging out for what society wouldn't allow. How many guys gawped at internet porn behind their wife's back? It was young flesh they wanted to see, not aunties with facelifts. Half the men in the country were turned on by a pretty, young thing in a school tie and a short skirt. The red-blooded ones, at least. Only most of them didn't have the balls to do anything about it.

'Hiya.'

Paul turned around. Emma was standing there in her denim jacket and jeans, shiny-lipped, hair in two cute bunches, sucking on another sweet. She loped ahead to the Porsche, which was glinting like new after yesterday's visit to the car wash. She was impressed by it, he guessed, but didn't think it cool to say so. Jane drove around in a zit of a car that no one would give a second glance. A pity it was still chilly February, or he could have taken the roof down and impressed her even more.

He climbed into the driver's seat, checking his reflection in the rear-view mirror. He'd left a layer of stubble on his face this morning, especially for her. It gave him a touch of the rogue and would appeal to her. He'd also dug out his best sheepskin jacket and black Ralph Lauren sweater. Well, he could afford to take pride in his appearance. Emma was into fashion. She wouldn't want some cheap scruff taking her out.

He revved the engine until its powerful rumble turned heads in the car park, and drove fast towards Putney, squeezing into gaps between cars and accelerating through the lights before they turned red. Emma liked going fast too. A half smile came to her lips as he stepped on the gas.

As he slowed for a red light, he glanced at her. She seemed perfectly relaxed. Her legs stretched out in front of her, so sexy in that tight denim. If only he could put his hand on one for one second. Just a fleeting touch, she'd hardly notice.

'Nice jeans, Em,' he said.

Emma was staring out of her window, lost in her own world. His hand on the gearstick loosened. He held his breath and imagined what would happen next. His hand would land on her thigh, like a stupid moth that had lost its way. He would feel the warmth of her flesh below her jeans. He would move his hand to her zipper, then touch the soft fabric of her panties ...

No, not yet. He pressed his hand into the gearstick.

The traffic became heavy. They crawled past litter-strewn pavements, mums with pushchairs and shopping bags, sour-faced youths in wool balaclavas. He looked at Emma again. The ache was stronger than ever. He wanted to stop the car, hold her in his arms, and kiss every inch of her.

'Can we go to that shop, Paul?' Emma's voice was bright, expectant.

'What shop?'

'On the right. We're passing it now.'

He looked to where she was pointing: Claire's. It had a gaudy, uninviting exterior.

'Okay, but we mustn't be too long.'

Emma trotted ahead, clutching her tiny handbag, then turned. 'Do you have any money? Mum gave me five pounds but it might not be enough.'

Oh, those angelic, imploring eyes. This girl really knew how to turn it on.

'Don't worry, sweetie,' he said. 'Wait till we get inside, I'll see what I've got.'

The shop was too hot and too bright and heaving with teenage girls. Pop music blasted through the speakers. He couldn't put up with this for long.

Emma positioned herself in front of a stand of garish earrings and began trying one pair after the other.

'I want these ones – they're six ninety nine.'

He handed over some coins.

'Okay,' he said as they left the shop. 'Let's head back. Jane will be wondering where we are.'

She looked so glum, he put his arm around her shoulder and gave her a squeeze. 'How about an ice cream?'

'Can we go to McDonald's?'

'Alright, if we're quick.'

It was hard to say no to her. And why should he?

The place was packed. He left her to find a table while he waited in the queue, trying to ignore the medley of odours reaching his nostrils.

'Here you go.'

Emma seized the huge paper cup and slurped the chocolate milkshake through two straws.

'I went for a trial last week,' she announced cheerfully, pushing away her empty cup. 'For the school netball team. The under-thirteens.'

'How did it go?'

She gave him a toothy grin. 'I got in. Mr Kingly said I'm one of the best players in my year.'

'That's fantastic, Em. I hope I'll be invited to see you play sometime.'

Her cheeks flushed. She was so eager to please, so craving approval. It wasn't surprising, after her cretin of a father had walked out.

'So, you're enjoying school more now?'

'Yeah, it's alright.' She giggled. 'I quite like art, now – I'm getting really good marks.'

'Maybe you'll go to art school when you're older. You could be another Picasso, or someone like that Damien Hirst guy who made the diamond skull.'

'I'd like to be a fashion designer when I grow up,' she said coyly. 'Or a model.'

'You could do some modelling first, then go to college and study fashion.'

'I've already tried out for an agency.' A shy smile. 'My mum doesn't know. I sent in some pictures a friend took. They said I showed promise but I was too young for them.'

'There's nothing to stop you trying other places. You'd make a great model, I bet.'

Emma began preening her hair, a dreamy expression on her face. 'I love watching *America's Next Top Model*. I'd do anything to be on a show like that.'

As they got up to leave, an idea came to him. 'I could help you, maybe,' he said. 'I know a woman who works at a model agency. She's pretty high up. I could mention you to her.'

Emma's eyes widened. 'Really?'

She'd nibbled at the bait. One day, he might pull her in.

The journey back to Jane's was hassle-free. As they were pulling up outside the house, a red-brick terrace in one of the less desirable streets of Putney, Jane's face appeared in the gap between the curtains. Moments later, the front door sprang open and Jane was greeting Emma with hugs, as if she'd been kidnapped by armed guerrillas. Guilt at leaving her offspring, most likely. No sign of any suspicion, not a whiff.

'Hi, Paul.' Jane smiled at him quickly then turned her attention to Emma. 'Did you have a good swim, darling?'

Emma mumbled something.

'Emma swam really well,' he said. 'Even better than last time.'

'That doesn't surprise me. She's quite capable at lots of things when she puts her mind to it.' A sideways glance at her daughter, who frowned in reply and scuttled upstairs. 'Paul, you'll stay for a coffee, will you?'

He followed Jane into the kitchen. She'd put on a little make-up but her hair was still all over the place, grey peeking through the brown dye. She had great bones in her face and a decent figure, but she'd stopped bothering to look after herself, which was handy. If Jane had been a well-maintained blonde, Suzanne might have viewed his visits differently.

'She was OK today?'

'Yes, she was fine – much chattier this time. And she was swimming up and down like a fish, I almost had to drag her out of the pool. So, did you find what you wanted at Brent Cross?'

'I've ordered a lounge suite. I just hope the kids don't wreck it inside a month.' Jane put two mugs on the table and rifled in her handbag. 'Sorry, Paul, I'm dying for a fag. You don't mind, do you? I need to wind down. Toby was a little terror today.'

He did mind, but he could hardly stop Jane smoking in her own house.

'When did you start smoking again?'

'A couple of weeks ago – it was stress at work that did it. Sometimes I think I might jack it all in and go on the dole instead. The kids don't have a father anymore, and they scarcely have a mother.' She began to laugh, a deep belly laugh, and took another puff of her cigarette. 'I feel guilty about asking Emma to mind Toby when I'm away. She's good with him, she helps him with his homework and all sorts. I know she resents it sometimes though. She's been starting fights with him, which is a worry. And she gets lonely too, and she misses her dad.' She turned away to exhale smoke. 'I should have let him visit at Christmas, I suppose. But we'd made plans already, and Yasmin was with him.'

'That would have been awkward.'

'You're not joking. I would've given the little slut a piece of my mind if she'd come anywhere near the kids.'

There was something endearing about Jane, although she dressed like a bloke and was a real slob around the house. The fruit in the bowl was often mouldy, and the same magazines and scraps of paper were left lying around for weeks. But she always spoke from the heart, even if it got her into trouble. She'd never sit there thinking of what to say so as not to hurt your feelings – as Suzanne did – or how best to get someone where you wanted them – as he did. With Jane, it was all out there: take it or leave it.

'Emma told me she's been picked for the school netball team,' he said.

'Yes, she's over the moon. She'll have to practise every week and play matches on the weekend – I just hope she can keep it up. There's been quite a change in her lately, she seems to be coming out of herself, thank goodness. The other day she told me she wants to go to sessions at the local drama school.'

That could be inconvenient. With netball and drama school, he'd never get to see her.

Jane tapped the ash off her cigarette and looked directly at him.

'Paul, I do appreciate you making the time to help Emma like this … keep out of there, Toby! We'll be eating dinner in an hour.' He turned to see Toby rummaging in the fridge.

'It's no trouble, Jane, I told you. I enjoy taking her out.' He took a last gulp of coffee and got to his feet. 'Well, I'd better be going. We're off to the theatre this evening.'

'Oh, anything interesting?'

'It's a satire about married couples. Suzanne wanted to see it. Not my thing, really.'

'Well, have fun. I wish someone was taking me to the theatre.'

'Jane, darling, I'd love to take you to the theatre. Only Suzanne wouldn't be too pleased.'

'Cheeky devil!' Jane gave him a playful thump on the arm then went to the hall and called out at the top of her voice. 'Emma, where are you? Paul's going! Aren't you going to say goodbye?'

Feet thumped on the landing. A head peeped over the banister.

'Bye Emma!'

'Bye-eee!' She waved back and he melted, like chocolate in warm fingers.

Jane opened the front door. 'See you next Saturday, then.'

Paul flicked the key in the ignition and revved the engine hard. He was a devious bastard, lusting after the daughter of one of his wife's best friends, and the poor girl barely past teddy bears.

Well, so what? Soon she'd be whisked away from him into a whirl of activities. He wouldn't actually do anything, he'd just look. Emma enjoyed being with him, so why shouldn't he appreciate her in return, while he still had the chance?

Laura, that's why, piped up the spoilsport inside him. You did more than just look at Laura, didn't you?

He pressed his foot firmly on the accelerator and closed the gap to the car in front.

He'd been lucky to get away with it. But Laura had tucked their secret safely away and hadn't told anyone, as far as he knew. With any luck, she never would – not anyone who mattered, at any rate. He'd made sure she would never spill the beans to Suzanne. Anyway, why would she want to dredge up the past now, after all these years? Unless she guessed the temptation that Emma posed.

He shouldn't press his luck, he knew. He should let Emma go. If he had any sense, that was what he'd do.

Paul switched on the stereo. He turned up the volume of his *Best of Eric Clapton* CD, loud enough to rattle the speakers, and cruised the final stretch home. Sure, he could make up some excuse as to why he couldn't see Emma anymore. Yet how could he not see her? He couldn't just walk away. His life would be too thin without her smiles, scowls and flounces, without the thrill of her body next to his in nothing but a thin, nearly see-through costume. Without her, he'd shrivel into a sexless old man.

6

Suzanne

9 February 2011

Suzanne took out a tissue and mopped her face and neck, both uncomfortably hot and damp after her dash along noisy, fume-filled Wimbledon High Street. She opened the door and went inside. The room was refreshingly quiet and cool. People – mainly women – clustered around a trestle table bearing an urn and a collection of plastic cups, drinking tea and talking. The session hadn't started yet.

A thin, unsmiling man peered at her through thick glasses. 'Hello, PK.'

His name was either PK or KP, she couldn't remember which. Then Zac waved at her cheerily from his solitary cross-legged position on the large, bare wooden floor. He looked as eccentric as ever with his long black ponytail and almost-as-long beard. He would often come up and hug her unexpectedly, and tell her all manner of things she would otherwise never give a moment's thought. Last time, he'd asked her the reason why water only went one way down the plughole, the answer to which she'd forgotten. Another time, he'd told her with glee what chaos would ensue if the earth's magnetic poles were to flip.

Suzanne hung up her coat and hurried over to the refreshment table. She returned Adele's smile. Adele, who was taking the session that evening, had a torrent of corkscrew curls, and large, liquid eyes that always seemed to radiate kindness and generosity towards everyone. Then she noticed her friends, Carol and Jilly, chatting to each other in the corner, and went over to join them.

'Hello, guys!' She hugged each in turn.

'You look puffed out, dear,' Carol said.

'It was fraught getting here,' she replied. 'The District Line was up the spout again.'

'Will everyone please form a circle.'

It was Adele's voice. The chatter stopped. Suzanne went into the middle of the room with the others.

'Join hands and close your eyes. Let go of any distracting thoughts. Feel the irritations and disappointments of the day drift away. Take a deep breath … and slowly let it out.'

The background bells and chants started up. Adele's voice continued, coolly hypnotic.

'Feel your weight pulling your body into the ground. Feel the person on either side of you connecting you into the circle. Feel yourself unite with each person in the circle. Now, open your eyes and turn to the person on each side of you. Look into their eyes. Show that you accept them in their totality. Send them your deepest love.'

Suzanne opened her eyes with a sigh. She always disliked this part of the evening. She didn't like the look of PK, who was now looking into her eyes with indifference verging on hostility. He had only just started coming to the meetings. Who knew what he might get up to outside of here, what bad things he might have done? Maybe everyone *was* worthy of love – even murderers and rapists, people she'd never be able to understand in a million years. How could she accept such a person, though, let alone love them? Trying not to look at the slack skin under his jaw, or the greasy lens of his glasses, she attempted a smile. It came out as more of a grimace, no doubt. He stared back, unsmiling.

The evening went on as usual. After the breathing exercises, the yoga, chanting and meditation, her body began to relax, lighten. Her mind lightened too, untroubled by the usual nagging worries. If only she could feel like this all the time.

Adele made some announcements about the group's next meeting, and events coming up, then everyone was putting on coats and saying their goodbyes. 10pm already.

'Are you going to the retreat?' Jilly asked, as they made their way downstairs. 'It's going to be a cracker this year, from what I've heard. Adele's found a Tibetan monk to take the meditation sessions, and there's a healing workshop ...'

Several in the group were healers or therapists of one sort or another, or hoped to be, including Jilly. She wasn't anywhere near that stage herself, and doubted she ever would be, but she felt a tug of interest.

'I don't know. When is it?'

'The second weekend of March. I'm going, so's Carol. You ought to go, Suzy.'

It was the weekend after her silver wedding anniversary. Nothing was planned.

'I'd love to,' she heard herself say. 'Paul won't be keen on me going though.'

'Why's that?'

'Oh, he doesn't approve of all this. He thinks we're a bunch of overgrown hippies who just want an excuse to grope each other.'

'If only!' Jilly looked aghast. 'No one's groped me lately, unfortunately. You should bring him along and let him see for himself. He might be surprised.'

'He wouldn't come in a million years. Whenever I mention anything in the least alternative he laughs and says I'm losing my marbles.'

Jilly was sympathetic. Her husband didn't share her interest in meditation either.

Suzanne walked slowly to her car. It would be wonderful, she thought, to be able to share this part of her life with Paul.

By the time she'd driven home it was nearly 10.30pm.

The street was quiet. Driveways were filled, curtains closed. Infrequent street lamps did little to relieve the darkness. Pushing open the gate, she glanced up at the house. It was imposing, rather than welcoming: its tall, elegant windows and deep eaves suggesting a house in deepest France rather than Wimbledon. Paul had fallen for its charming period features; she'd pointed out it would be dark and chilly in winter. Still, it was their home now.

She turned her key in the lock. The TV was blaring from the living room. She opened the door, saw Paul slumped in his armchair, a bottle of beer on the table beside him. He hadn't changed out of his suit.

She went closer. 'Hello, darling.'

He seemed not to notice her. She would have bent down and kissed him, but sensed that was not a good idea.

'So, you decided to come home after all,' he said, in a caustic tone, not looking away from the TV. Gun-toting cops were chasing the bad guys again.

'You didn't forget, did you? I always have the group on Tuesday evenings.' He flicked channels, to a bird's-eye view of a glossy car being driven around a hairpin bend.

'Have you eaten?' She knew she ought to go upstairs and leave him to it. He flicked to the next channel. 'There's some risotto in the fridge, I can heat it up if you like?'

'Don't trouble yourself. I can do without yesterday's leftovers, thanks.'

A flash of anger. 'Do you have to be so goddamn rude? What's the matter with you?'

He swigged from the bottle then looked at her.

'If you really want to know, I've had a shit day at work. Chris dropped me right in it again, making me look like a prize idiot in front of the directors.'

'Why, what happened?'

'He pulled me up for giving the customer an earful about fucking us around with their requirements – he said I was harassing the customer and the whole project was in danger. Carlton was sitting there, lapping it up.'

'I'm sorry. You've been working so hard on this project. I know how stressful it is at the moment.'

Paul laughed, a mirthless eruption from deep in his throat.

'That's a joke. You go rushing around like a twenty-five-year-old, forgetting you've got a husband at home.'

'I'm not your slave, you know. I have a right to my own life.'

'Well, why don't you fuck off then?' He got out of the armchair, pointing the remote control at the TV. 'Go back to that pack of weirdos you hang out with.'

Her composure vanished, along with any trace of compassion and willingness to understand.

'For God's sake, Paul, you should hear yourself! What the hell gets into you?'

'I'd like to be able to come home once in a while and know that you're going to be here and not getting up to God knows what.' He stood over her, glaring. 'The house is a fucking disgrace, if you hadn't noticed. When did you last get round to cleaning the bathroom?'

Her mouth fell open. For a moment, she was unable to speak.

'Well,' she said at last, anger overtaking her, 'if you weren't so bloody paranoid, accusing the cleaning woman of snooping around your things, I wouldn't have to fucking well do it all myself!'

'Oh, give me a break, will you?' He lowered his voice. 'You've really let yourself go, haven't you? Is it my fault you don't turn me on anymore?'

She had a fleeting urge to pummel her fists into his body.

'You can talk, you …' She couldn't think of any words strong enough. 'You arrogant bastard. Who do you think you are, Robert bloody Redford? You've got all the charm of a … fucking gorilla!'

She stomped upstairs, slamming the bedroom door. Then she undressed and climbed into bed, teeth unbrushed, face unwashed. His words swirled around in the darkness, making her seethe. How dare he sneer at her and everything she believed in? But, what stuck in her mind, what really hurt, deep down, was his final thrust:

'Is it my fault you don't turn me on anymore?' As if she were a sack of potatoes. If that was true, then what was left?

***

Suzanne opened her eyes. Chill morning light leaked through the drawn curtains. The images in her dream lingered, and with them a sense of profound sadness. Snow hurling in through gaps in the ceiling, swirling into her face, covering the furniture. Piling up into deep mounds, trying to obliterate her. She must get out, before she was buried forever.

I've hung on too long. This wasn't the life I was meant to have.

Paul was kissing her brow, she suddenly realised. She turned her head away, pushing herself up in bed. The night before came back.

'Darling,' he said in a soft voice. 'I want to apologise for the things I said last night. I shouldn't have got so angry. It was just that I so much wanted you here with me last night, after what happened at work.'

He was trying to find his way back into her heart. It was uncanny how easily he could do that. The hurt welled up again, strong as ever.

'Is it true, what you said to me?' She held her breath. 'I don't turn you on anymore?'

'I didn't mean it, Suzanne. I just wanted to hurt you.'

She caught sight of her reflection in the dressing table mirror. Her face, crumpled with sleep, the texture of an old apple. She turned his words over in her mind, examining their inflection. He might be telling the truth, or half the truth, or none at all.

'Darling.' His voice suddenly anxious. 'Please, I didn't mean it. You know I didn't.'

'Just go away and leave me alone. I'm going back to sleep.'

He rustled around the room getting ready for work.

'How about dinner this evening? That French place you like in the village?' She opened her eyes. Paul's hand rested on the door handle. He wore his pinstriped suit, the one she liked best. 'I can call and book from work. You can get all glammed up.'

'No, thanks, I'd rather not.'

'Come on, Suze. Don't be so hard on me.'

He waited, but she stayed silent.

She heard the front door close, the Porsche's low, powerful rumble and, for a long time after he'd driven away, the resigned, melancholy tone of his last words.

I've been too hard on him. I should have let him make peace with me.

No, he's gone too far. He has to understand that.

Her thoughts came and went. A sort of deadness seemed to have taken root inside her. Through the window, the sky was flecked with cloud, promising a fine day ahead.

She could go downstairs and make a cup of tea. Or she could just lie here and do nothing. She looked at the pair of thin, wavy cracks that travelled along the ceiling then diagonally down the wall. They had been there for months; Paul said it was from the speed bumps, there was nothing to worry about. Even so, sometimes she couldn't help thinking that if it were to rain very hard one day, the ceiling might cave in.

It came back suddenly, another strange dream she'd had, a few hours before. With it came the sense of desolation. She'd been alone, clinging to the side of a hulking ship. There'd been no lifeboats or survivors, only endless iron-grey water all around. Again and again, the ship lurched down, taking her with it, towards the water.

She shivered. It meant nothing. It didn't mean she was going to drown one day, as her father had. Though she didn't want to, she found herself imagining his last seconds, floundering in that cold, merciless sea while the yacht sped ahead without him. What had gone through his mind? Had he prayed? Had he begged God to save him?

It would have been a quick death, her mother had said. He hadn't been wearing a life jacket – none of the crew had. The weather had changed a few hours into the race and surprised them. By the time they'd turned the boat around and headed back to where he'd fallen overboard, her father had disappeared.

Suzanne heaved herself out of bed. Perhaps she was drowning already, only very slowly.

No, she must stop thinking like this. She must get up and do something.

Downstairs, Marmaduke greeted her. She fed him and went back to bed with a cup of tea and her laptop. It contained all four features from the upcoming issue of the dry, jargon-filled magazine. She was supposed to finish subbing them by the end of the week. She opened the first piece, about advances in call centre technology, and began to make changes. Soon, red blotches of crossed-out words and altered punctuation were breaking out all over the screen, like an attack of chickenpox.

After ten minutes, she'd had enough. Why was she doing this? One didn't need a degree in English to change it's to its, or delete a herd of unnecessary apostrophes.

What about her affirmations? She hadn't done them lately.

Suzanne took the list from her bedside drawer and read the first one aloud.

'I trust the universe to bring joy and harmony into my life.'

She frowned. Living with Paul was one guarantee of not having joy and harmony. What was the universe going to do about that?

She went on to the next.

'I am a beautiful, desirable woman.'

She put down the list. She wasn't in the mood for affirmations either. Perhaps Katherine would be able to meet her for lunch. She went into the kitchen and put two thick slices of bread into the toaster.

Paul used to like her curves, she thought as she sat down and crunched into her toast. He used to say they were womanly. That was before the children came though, and she'd put on a few kilos. Now, however much she dieted and went to the gym, her weight stubbornly stayed the same.

It was no use hoping that one day she might shrink back from a size 14 to a size 12… However, Paul was ageing too. His hair had started to thin and he had to take pills to control his blood pressure. His teeth had seen rather a lot of the dentist lately. Apart from death, of course, there was no way either of them could avoid getting old.

'Hello, m'dear.' Katherine wore a T-shirt, jeans and a leather jacket. Debbie's jacket, probably – Katherine was always swiping Debbie's clothes.

They ordered salads and a bottle of wine. The café was Katherine's choice, fashionable and expensive, the latest eating place to spring up in the village. Voices echoed in the airy, light-filled space, competing with shouting and clanking from the open-plan kitchen.

'You'll never guess,' Katherine announced. 'Debbie's got the job with BT. In their marketing department.'

'That's great, Kat.' Suzanne hoped she sounded sufficiently pleased. Lately, good news about other people's children only served to remind her of her own daughter's troubled career, or, more precisely, her string of unsatisfactory jobs punctuated by unemployment.

'I hope Laura finds something too, soon,' Katherine said quickly. 'So, how are you? Things are bad with Paul again?'

She related what had happened the night before, aware of the progressively grimmer expression on Katherine's face.

'Suzanne. You can't keep on letting him do this to you.' Katherine's response was as it had been at least five times before. 'Tell him you'll leave him if he carries on treating you like a doormat. Tell him if he talks to you like that again, you'll walk out – to a solicitor.'

'Katherine, I love him. I couldn't leave him. If I didn't love him, it would be different—'

'Well, he doesn't show his appreciation for you much, does he?' Katherine cleaved her beetroot in two without mercy. 'Maybe you need to make him realise that you're a human being too, you haven't been put on this planet just to tend to his needs—'

'He told me I don't turn him on, I'm too fat.'

Her friend made a face. 'Well, he's hardly a sex god himself, is he? I know he works out and swims 'n' all, but really.'

'I've been worried about Paul, lately – something's going on, I'm sure. Do you think he could be seeing someone else? He says it's the stress of his work, but I don't think that's it. He's been so withdrawn lately. His moods seem to be getting worse and he's wound up so tight. I don't know how to describe it. He just seems so ... *strange*, lately.'

'Suzy, listen.' Katherine squeezed her hand. 'I really don't think he's having an affair, or he's becoming unhinged. I'm sure it *is* all down to the stress of work – and realising he's getting old. His work is challenging and he feels pressure from the young ones coming up below him. He knows he isn't a spring chicken anymore. I've had it from Jeremy, I know what it's like.' Her voice hardened. 'You need to make him understand how his behaviour affects you, and you're not going to put up with all the shit he throws at you. You're not chained to him for life, are you? Alright, my love?'

Suzanne nodded, summoning a smile. It was good advice, no doubt.

The waiter cleared their plates. Katherine whipped out a compact and retouched her lipstick.

'So, how are the swimming sessions going?'

'Very well, by the sound of it. Paul says Emma's really coming on. She can manage several lengths non-stop now.'

'It's good of him to help her like that, I must say. How long is this going to go on for?'

'He's happy to take her for as long as Emma is happy going to the pool with him. Jane told me she's pleased about how it's going, she thinks it's having a good effect on her. Emma's behaving much better now.'

'I must give Jane a ring, we haven't chatted for ages. Maybe the three of us could meet up in Covent Garden and treat ourselves to an evening at The Sanctuary, like we used to. Oh, by the way.' Katherine leaned towards her. 'David phoned the other day. He asked me to say hello to you and to pass on his best wishes. I think he fancies you.'

There was something undeniably pleasing about the thought.

'Why don't you give him a ring?'

'I might be pissed off with Paul, but I'm not looking for an affair.'

'Maybe you ought to be.'

She pictured David on his knees, slowly unrolling a sheer stocking from her leg, and laughed. 'I'm too old to have an affair, Kat.'

'Don't be daft! Since when did age matter? It's not as if women have to worry about getting it up, is it?'

'Shush, not so loud,' she said, and then found herself laughing as loudly as her friend, provoking curious stares.

'Seriously though,' Katherine said, after their mirth had subsided, 'if you made Paul a little jealous, would it be such a bad thing?'

Paul arrived home early that evening. Before she could say hello, he'd thrust two bouquets of red roses into her hands and kissed her on the lips. An unusually long and tender kiss, as if they were new lovers who'd been parted for too long.

'Suze, I don't deserve you,' he said. They sat on the sofa in the living room. On the coffee table, two of their most expensive crystal glasses, filled with a Bordeaux from the cellar. 'You have every right to be upset. All I can say is, I'm sorry. I love you, I didn't mean those things I said last night.' He leaned over and looked into her eyes. 'You believe me, don't you?'

She swallowed the lump in her throat. He wasn't going to sweet-talk her out of what she had to say, not this time.

'I don't know anything for certain, Paul. When you talk to me like you did last night, I don't know who you are. You say you love me. How can you love me when you're thinking those horrible things?'

'Darling, don't talk like that.'

'Please, listen to me.' She gulped her wine. 'There's only so much more of this I can take. If you keep on treating me like this, I … I'm going to leave you.'

There, she had said it, those words she had never said before. The look on his face almost made her wish she hadn't – as if he were a child who'd had his favourite toy taken away.

'Please, stop. I'll change, I promise. I don't want to hurt you anymore, please, my darling. Let me make it up to you.'

Later, he insisted on cooking dinner.

'Why don't we go away somewhere different for our holiday this year?' he said as they sat down at the table. 'For two weeks this time.'

She thought of the ten days they'd spent in Barbados last year. Paul had spent most of it thinking about work and checking his emails, then, just as he'd started to unwind and enjoy the holiday, it had been time to go home.

'How about Mauritius, or Madagascar? You've always wanted to go there. And why don't we go somewhere special for our anniversary? What about that hotel Andy and Fiona liked?'

Her throat tightened. Apart from her father and her brother, she loved Paul more than any man she had ever known. How could she not forgive him?

They went to bed early.

Paul kissed her mouth and brought her towards him, pressing his hand into the small of her back. He began caressing her. Her skin became super sensitive under his touch, every stroke of his fingers sending a shiver through her. Then she was floating, falling from the tops of great clouds, then rising up again, weightless. She had no choice except to go with him, wherever he took her.

'I love you,' he said as she lay beside him. She knew it was probably foolish of her to be reassured by his words, but she needed his love now, more than ever. For a few moments she felt elated, as if she'd unexpectedly come across a dear possession given up as lost.

Then she remembered. What was it Paul had said last weekend after he had come back from the pool? Jane had wished he could be taking *her* to the theatre; that was it. Jane hadn't been serious, surely. Paul was stirring, that was all. He'd said it in the joking way he often said things, so you weren't sure if he meant what he was saying or not.

Was Paul having an affair with Jane? Was that why he was so keen to help her out with Emma's swimming lessons? She was slim, even now, without effort. A little younger than her, Jane had attracted plenty of male glances in her prime. She still had an I-don't-care-what-you-think glamour, that careless, sassy swagger that men loved. Even without make-up, her face had acquired a steely beauty.

Paul could hardly be shagging Jane at her house, though, with Emma and Toby around. Anyway, he wasn't interested in Jane, not sexually. He'd said once after a dinner party that she was slovenly and wore frumpy clothes, and she really ought to pluck her eyebrows, people would think she was a lesbian. They got on well, that was all. He wasn't having an affair with her, or with anyone else. He wasn't that type of man.

Then she wasn't so sure. What if he *was* that type of man, but she'd never realised?

7

Laura

16 February 2011

Water dripped from the bath tap. The splash against ceramic echoed around the flat like gun shots. Down the hall, her neighbour's door slammed.

Laura lay on the beanbag, listening. It was well past midnight, past the time she usually went to bed. However there was no point going to bed, she knew she wouldn't sleep. She pulled the rug over her in an attempt to get warm. The flat was cold most of the time. It was on the top floor of the block and there were only two storage heaters, which she didn't turn on often enough to try and cut down her electricity bill. Though it was described as a one-bed flat, the bedroom was more like a large cupboard, and the bathroom had no bath, only an erratic shower that squirted insufficient streams of tepid water.

This room made up for those deficiencies, however. It needed maintenance and hadn't been decorated in a long while, but it had a large sash window that let in the afternoon sun, and an ever-changing view of rooftops, trees and streets interspersed with church spires and big stretches of green towards the horizon. Sometimes, when she was really down, she'd stand at the window for ages, just watching the changing colours and shades and shapes as the day went on. It made her feel light and free again, like a bird in its nest, ready to soar.

Her attention wandered among her sparse possessions, rendered sparser by the spacious, high-ceilinged room. Her laptop, earphones, *The Sunday Times Magazine* from last month, a half-eaten slab of Tesco finest chocolate, and other bits and pieces lay on the coffee table. On the other, not much bigger, table she ate at, an art deco lamp she bought from an antique shop in Durham, the first homey thing she'd bought while at university. A screen print, in the vague shape of an owl, from a charity shop. The vase Daniel gave her as a housewarming gift when she moved in. Three cherry-red, silk-covered cushions to brighten up the disintegrating sofa. That was about it. All the furniture had come with the flat, except for the bookcase her father had delivered, stuffed with paperbacks and textbooks from uni.

Her life was emptying out, and it wasn't exactly full to begin with. But now it was definitely thinning, a little less substantial every day. She thought of the day ahead, alone, indoors, scouring internet ads for jobs, the occasional, brief phone call her only contact with anyone. Work had been pretty crap, but at least it had provided some social interaction, some sense of belonging to the everyday world that other people belonged to. Rachel had vanished too. The relief after her revelation to Rachel had turned into an anticlimax, then a niggling sense that perhaps she'd done the wrong thing to confide in her friend. Rachel hadn't called for a week and hadn't returned her last message, though that didn't necessarily mean anything. Her friend was always busy with something or other.

Voices in the street outside interrupted her thoughts. Slurred words. Loud, happy sounding.

It arrived then, that feeling of terrible isolation. As if she must have done something so very bad, her punishment was to be excluded from the world forever. Not comforting or deadening. It surrounded her like a flock of angry birds. Sharp, jabbing. She couldn't take refuge in it and she had no faith that she could find a way out.

Laura closed her eyes and began to hum.

She's at school, in the playground. A slender, serious girl with sad eyes. She's sitting against the wall, separate from the others. Pretending to read, to be absorbed in her book. Anything to look busy, like she doesn't care that she has no one to talk to, that she isn't part of any group with their excited chatter, their games, their pranks and dares.

She longs for someone to ask her to join them. But no one ever does. She doesn't know how to ask, or maybe she knows they wouldn't let her. Some of the girls jeer at her, some make snide remarks. 'Why are you such a numpty? You're a les, aren't you?'

Most of the girls just ignore her. They know she's not like them. Something marks her out as different, something they don't understand, that she herself doesn't understand. It's just there. As if her skin is green.

Sometimes, one or two of them follow her around, calling out horrible things, and she has to walk over to the park to hide among the trees, or wander around the shopping centre. Other times, when it's raining or she can't get out of school, she locks herself in a toilet cubicle. Not for long, usually. Once, though, she stayed there for the whole of lunch break.

When it all gets too much, she squeezes her eyes shut and hums softly to herself. Sometimes she sings the words too, very quietly.

When you walk through a storm, hold your head up high ...

She knows the song by heart. It makes her more hopeful, less alone. Though not always. Sometimes she just wants her body to disappear. She longs to let go of everything she knows and for her body to evaporate, so she can be carried far away from this place.

Laura hummed louder. Her heart beat loud and fast and the birds still swarmed about her, a dark, diving, fluttering cloud. She started to sing. The words came without striving, taking away the emptiness inside her.

In an instant, she knew what she must do. She couldn't keep it from him any longer. She would have to go to the source of her pain.

On the way to her parents' house, she realised it would be more difficult than she'd thought. She'd never confronted her father with what he'd done to her. He'd never alluded to it, or acknowledged it. Each year, this unspoken thing that lay between them had grown bigger and more intractable. Now it was so dense and heavy it seemed impossible to address with mere words.

Around her, the signs of a normal weekday morning in Wimbledon Village. Joggers plugged into earphones. Shoppers hurrying along the street. Office workers slumped at walls, chatting over a cigarette. Mothers towing dogs and small children. Stylish women getting out of four-wheel drives, talking on their mobile phones.

The day was cloudy, less cold than it had been. No wind, not the faintest flicker of a breeze. No green yet, even on the smallest trees.

Laura stopped on the pavement at the turn into Elgin Drive.

'It's going to be alright,' she said aloud.

She put her hand over her heart – it was pumping furiously. She took a few sips from her water bottle before carrying on.

This was a stupid idea. What good could it possibly do to confront him now? The past was the past and nothing he could say would change it. He would try to downplay what he'd done. He might blame her for everything, ask why hadn't she spoken out at the time, even say she'd wanted it. He might say all sorts of things. And if he was up to something now, he wouldn't simply admit it, would he? Whatever she said to him he was bound to have an answer, a story that would justify everything.

She wasn't a coward, though. She couldn't just turn around and go home. This was something she had to do, she knew in her heart, even if it ended up a dismal failure. This time, she had to stand up to him. For how could she blame her mother for never standing up to him, if she couldn't do so herself?

The house was opposite her now. It looked taller and seemed to frown at her. Her father was in there somewhere, alone.

She walked to the front door and drew in her breath. She'd called his mobile earlier to check her mother would be out, told him she had something to ask him, in person. Her mother would be having lunch with a friend in Sussex, and wouldn't be home till around 4pm. It was only 11.30am – there was plenty of time.

After a few seconds, she pressed the bell.

'Hello, Laura.' Her father looked taken aback for a moment, then he beamed at her. He wore one of his unending supply of grey suits, the tie removed and the top button of his shirt undone. In this suit, he was a successful businessman, a man whom everyone respected. 'This is a pleasant surprise. I didn't expect to see you again so soon. How are you?'

'I'm okay.'

Laura stepped past him into the hall. A tang of floor cleaner overlaid with garlic. She took in the familiar mahogany chair and drop-leaf table, the brass ship's clock on the wall and the framed sketches by her grandmother – the arty one on her mother's side, not the stern one on her father's side who she'd never met. Further along, a row of her father's morose Lowry prints alongside her mother's Georgia O'Keeffe White Rose. More stuff in this one space, she thought, than in the whole of her flat.

Her father touched her arm. 'Come and sit down,' he said warmly. 'Can I get you anything?'

Laura gripped the banister, draped with her mother's yellow mohair cardigan. Her heart was thumping like crazy.

'Why are you seeing so much of Emma?'

The question came out of her mouth awkwardly, without warning. This wasn't what she'd planned. She hadn't even taken off her jacket.

He shuffled his feet before replying.

'You know why. I'm helping her with her swimming. I take her with me to the pool on Saturdays. Come and sit down, we can talk in the kitchen.'

With a jerk of his head, her father turned and strode into the kitchen. She followed him, waiting as he poured a tumbler of Bell's, which he put on the table.

'Anything for you?'

'Water's fine.'

He handed her a glass. The kitchen was neater than the last time she'd visited, all its objects back in their rightful places. Herb bottles, pill bottles, recipe books, empty envelopes, a pack of parking permits. The worktops had been cleared, except for a garlic clove and a sprawl of dark red tomatoes beside the cooker. The cactus on the windowsill had faded to a yellowish hue. One of the orchids was strewn with purple bumps close to flowering. Her gaze snagged on her mother's Pagan Love Goddess fridge magnet, decorated with a reclining, scantily clad woman.

Her father lowered himself into his usual place at the table. Reluctantly, Laura pulled out a chair opposite him.

'What do you get out of it exactly, Dad?'

'Excuse me?' His face was a picture of perplexity.

'You know what I mean. Are you doing this just so you can have time alone with Emma?'

A scowl crossed her father's face, erased moments later by a smile – the sort of tolerant smile one might give to an old woman who'd farted at a vicarage tea party.

'I want to help her, that's all. I've taught her how to swim properly. She enjoys herself, she's getting a lot out of it. Things are tough for her at home – her mother's worn out from work and her little brother gets all the attention. All she needed was for someone to show some interest in her.' Casually, he added, 'I would never do anything that might harm her. You know that.'

As if she were dotty for having thought of such a thing. As if she'd imagined everything that had gone before.

'So, you're not planning to do the same to Emma as you did to me? Or have you done something to her already?' Her heart was thudding loudly enough for him to hear.

'Don't be ridiculous, Laura.'

She wanted to hear him admit what he had done to her – and why – and find out whether he was a danger to Emma. Now the moment had come, though, her confidence was leaking away. She picked up her glass of water, trembling as she brought it towards her mouth. She put it down quickly and took a deep gulp of air, clasping her hands firmly together.

'Why did you have to do those things to me? I don't understand. I'm your daughter. I loved you. I trusted you to look after me.'

His fingers fluttered around his glass. On his face was confusion, and then something else, but she wasn't sure what. Not fear. A disturbance to his composure, tinged with hostility. In the silence that followed she concentrated on letting each breath come and go, trying to overcome her body's manic reaction, trying to push down her fear as far as it would go.

'It wasn't that I didn't love you, Laura,' he said, very softly. 'You must understand. I loved you too much.'

'You loved me so you thought you could do anything you wanted to me?'

'No, it was just …' His gaze flitted about the kitchen. 'There was something about you. I longed to be close to you. When you were small, I loved how you listened to me, you didn't judge me, you forgave me for things. You were what I needed, it was like … like I'd fallen in love with you.'

A shudder went through her. What sort of explanation was that? She couldn't bear to be in the room with him any longer.

Her father was staring at the floor. He cleared his throat then took a gulp of Scotch before speaking again.

'Maybe I went a little too far—'

'A little too far? What you did to me was abuse. You know that, don't you?'

'I think you've exaggerated things in your head, it was a long time ago—'

'Don't you remember? You put your hands all over me. You forced me to …' She couldn't say the words.

'Whatever I did, or didn't do, Laura, you must know this. You were special. I will never feel those things for anyone else, ever again. Not anyone.'

He was earnest, as earnest as she'd ever heard him. Could he be telling the truth?

'Why should I believe you? You couldn't control yourself with me, and I'm your daughter. You didn't care what you did to me, how much you hurt me. I meant nothing to you.'

'You're wrong, you're so wrong. You meant the world to me.'

'Then why couldn't you love me like any normal father? That's all I wanted, Dad. Was it so much to ask?'

He stayed silent.

'You forgot I had feelings,' she carried on. 'You made me keep quiet so I had no one to turn to. You didn't care what happened to me.'

The rest was waiting to burst out of her mouth.

I'm not like other girls, do you know that? I don't trust men, I can't let them love me. I try not to feel anything, because I know deep down I'm only a girl for guys to fuck. That's what you did to me.

Nothing came, though. He was waiting for her to run out of steam. He knew she would.

'Why shouldn't I tell Mum, right now, about everything you did to me?' She heard the edge of anger in her voice, her words losing their firmness. 'How you stalked me around the house, waiting for a chance to get your hands on me. How you showed me those disgusting pictures, and what you made me do that time.' Her heart began to race at the onset of the memory, even now, all these years later. The rest came out in a whisper. 'Don't you think she has a right to know the truth?'

'It wasn't like that, Laura. You're confused, you're getting things mixed up. I was affectionate towards you, yes. I loved you so much, it was hard for me. I'd never experienced that intensity before. I may have crossed the line sometimes, I admit. But I never meant to hurt you.'

'No, that's not how it was.' It was what she should have expected, surely, that he would downplay or deny everything she said.

He carried on as if she'd said nothing. 'I wish I'd been a better father to you, I've wished it a thousand times, but you shouldn't feel you have to tell your mother all these things you're convinced happened, just to get back at me.'

'That's not the reason I have to tell her.' Her voice sounded weak, irrelevant. 'She should know who she's really married to—'

'Laura, there's something you should know.' He exhaled heavily. 'Do you remember that time your mother went to stay with her friend in the New Forest? After Richard died. It wasn't just a trip away. She had a breakdown. She didn't want you and Daniel to see her in the state she was in. She was crying all the time, knocking back tranquillisers and sleeping pills, you name it. When she got back she started to see a therapist.'

'A breakdown?' She blinked at him. Of course, her mother had been upset when her brother died of a heart attack after a routine game of squash – Richard had been in his mid-forties with apparently no serious health problems. She'd heard nothing of any breakdown.

'She didn't want to admit it was so serious,' her father went on. 'But that's what the therapist told her. He said she had difficulty coping with sudden change – the loss of loved ones especially – probably because of the trauma she suffered as a small child when her father drowned.' He paused for a few seconds, jiggling his glass. 'The point is, Laura, mentally she's very fragile. Another severe shock to her system could trigger another breakdown. It could be much worse next time.'

He drank the rest of his Scotch.

How convenient, she wanted to say. *This is all ridiculous. My mother's not like that.* But shock was seeping into her brain, jumbling her thoughts. A breakdown. Her father wouldn't lie about something like that, would he?

'Laura, I understand why you feel the need to say something to her. She's your mother, after all. But think of the consequences.' His tone was calm, rational. He had seized on her doubt, turning it to his advantage. 'What's the point of dragging up the past now, after all these years? What good could it possibly do? I'm not going to do anything to harm Emma or anyone else.'

She sat, fixed to her chair, a rigid block, unable to move or speak. The last of her self-possession was leaving her body. He'd turned her into a child. Once again, he was exerting his paternal authority over her and she could do nothing.

'Your mother and I have been together for twenty-five years. We've built a life together. Do you want to take all that away from her? Everything would be tainted; her happiest memories would count for nothing. Imagine what effect it could have on her. It would always be on your conscience.'

Before he could say anything else, she got up from the table and hurried towards the door, nearly stumbling in her effort to get away from him. He still had his power over her, even now she was a grown woman. Yet again he had taken control and turned everything around.

On her way home, she remembered her words to her father.
I was your daughter, I loved you.
She sat on the Tube to West Kensington, not noticing the jerking and swaying of the train, or the people seated around her. Her throat clogged up and tears filled her eyes. She wiped them away, too proud to let herself fall

apart in public. But she wanted to howl, to cry until she had run out of tears, on and on.

It was true, she *had* loved him. A long time ago, back when her family had seemed not so different to any other family. Back when she'd thought her father was special, in a good way.

She'd been someone else, then. A little girl who trusted those she loved as a matter of course. And why shouldn't she have trusted him? He'd seemed like a good father. He'd encouraged her to learn things, to do things.

He explained how planes stay in the air and why the sky is blue. He showed her pictures of Vancouver Island, Montreal, and the Rocky Mountains, and all the places he'd loved as a child. He played her his favourite music. He said she was clever and praised her when she did well at school. He bought her a book about the ancient Egyptians for her ninth birthday, and took her to the British Museum and encouraged her when she told him she wanted to be an archaeologist when she grew up. He taught her to play chess and tennis, to swim, and to dive from the high board. He read to her on winter afternoons – *Alice in Wonderland, The Lord of the Rings, Tales of the Unexpected*. They took turns to read poems aloud – *The Rime of the Ancient Mariner* and *The Dong with a Luminous Nose* had been her favourites.

They'd done so many things together, just the two of them. She'd done things with her mother, too – pruning the roses or making pastry – usually things that weren't so much fun. Anyway, her mother always seemed to be too tired, or busy with something or other.

That morning by Lough Derg in Ireland, where they had all gone for a two-week holiday, it had been just her and her father.

'We must swim in the lake before we go home,' he says. 'It's only fifteen minutes' walk.' Her mother says she'll have to spend the morning packing if they're to be ready for their afternoon flight back to London. Her brother takes one look out of the window and says he'd rather stay watching TV. So, she goes with her father to keep him company, despite the swollen clouds resting on the hills, as they have done for most of their stay, and the storm they watched last night, hissing its fury upon the lake.

They change on a small strip of beach beside a huge, shivering sea. A vicious breeze makes it feel more like winter than the height of summer. There are a handful of people, all dressed for cold weather, sitting on rugs and drinking from flasks, or strolling, hands in pockets.

Before this morning, the idea of swimming in sunlit open water seemed quite reasonable, tempting even. If only because Lough Derg isn't the school pool, where for most of the spring term she's had to swim up and down, up and down, for an hour, twice a week, with all those super-fast, super-keen nine- and ten-year-old girls, because her father thought it would be a good idea for her to 'train properly', until she'd told him she hated swimming endlessly up and down, confined to lanes, nearly always at the back of her group, and she was never going to become the champion swimmer that he'd been.

She grits her teeth and pulls off her snug fleece and track pants, revealing her black swimming costume. She runs after her father towards the small lapping waves.

'Dad! It's FREEZING!'

This isn't an exaggeration – the water around her feet must have been ice recently enough. Resolutely, knowing her father won't let her get away with not swimming, she wades out to her hips. Then she stops. The coldness knocks the breath out of her, feels like blocks of ice jammed up against every inch of her skin.

Her father stands.

'Just get yourself under, Laura. It's not so cold once you get in.'

No, she definitely can't do this.

'Come on,' he coaxes, 'be a brave girl. You'll get used to it in no time.'

She braces herself and plunges into the water, screaming. She's never swum in anything so cold.

But he's right – the cold water is soon cool water, warmer than the air above. She kicks out, and rolls over and over like a seal pup, then floats on her back. It's wonderful to be swimming in the open like this, with no roof, no lanes, no chlorine, no one trying to overtake her or yelling for her to swim faster.

'Let's swim over there, shall we?' Dad points to a small wooden platform protruding from the land, quite a long way off. 'Can you manage to swim that far?'

She squints at it. 'I think so.'

It's no further than all the lengths she's endured in a typical session at the pool, she tells herself. If they go at a steady pace, she'll manage it.

They swim out towards the intense green hills rising beyond the shore. She gets into a rhythm, alternating between breaststroke and front crawl. Soon, the platform is closer than the beach they've come from, and the thrill of being so far from the shore makes her momentarily forget her worries about getting tangled up with the underwater weeds and being so far out of her depth. Nothing bad is going to happen. Her father will make sure she is all right.

'Well done, you made it!' They clamber up onto the platform. Her father hugs her. 'Are you okay, sweetie? That was quite a distance, not many girls your age could swim so far. I'm proud of you.'

She glows. She has shown Dad that she's a good swimmer, after all – herself, too. She's a bit puffed out, that's all, and it's cold out of the water. The wind is stronger out here.

He stands on the edge of the platform looking out into the distant corners of the lake. When he says they should go back, she dives in, as he's taught her, without splashing, her body a straight line from head to toe. On the way back he swims beside her, or slightly behind, calling out encouragement whenever she begins to flag. Her arms are tiring, yet she's still certain she can make it back. The cold gets worse, seeping through her muscles and bones. She has to stop and float on her back to rest for a while. She watches the sun's rays slant through a gap in the clouds, turning the indeterminate colour of the water to a brilliant turquoise, and the nondescript shades of bird plumage to snowy white. Only when they're almost on the beach, and the tiny figures on the sand are once more real people, does she start to panic.

'Dad, help me!'

Invisible fronds drape around her legs. She feels her arms fail and all the strength drain out of them. The lake is sucking her down. Her nose and mouth are filling with water. Frantically, she tries to surface.

He's there in no time at all.

'It's OK, sweetie. I've got you.' He puts his arms beneath her legs and, without effort, pulls her out of the water and carries her onto the beach. 'Let's get you warm and dry, now. I'm so proud of you, swimming all that way.'

He rubs her dry and helps put on her warm things. She sits on the rug with his big jacket wrapped around her, gulping warm tea from the flask. Slowly, the feeling returns in her hands and feet and she stops shivering. The shock and fright are leaving. What do they matter, compared with her achievement? She smiles at her father.

'Thanks for saving me, Dad.'

'Don't be silly, honey.' He kisses her cheek. 'You're the most precious thing in the world to me. I'd never let anything happen to you, ever.'

Her happiness swells inside her as if it would burst through her skin — for managing to swim so far, and for her father having rescued her. And for simply being here, beside him, knowing he loves her.

8

Suzanne

5 March 2011

They reached the end of the gravel path that bisected the smooth lawn, and turned to look back at the hotel. On impulse, Suzanne reached up and kissed Paul's cheek.

The memory of their lovemaking lingered in the tender places of her body with a pleasurable ache. She recalled his slow, purposeful touch under the bedclothes, awakening her in the early morning chill, then, in the dazzle of the early spring sunshine, eating croissants and marmalade in bed, feeding him her crispy corners. As it had been in the early days, before the demands of a career and children had taken their toll.

They walked on, towards the distant fir tree where Heinz, one of the hotel staff, had pointed. He had insisted that they do the walk he recommended, presenting them with a package of food to take for lunch and afternoon tea. First, they had to find the lake, then they'd see a path up to the lookout.

Suzanne took off her jacket. It was past midday and quite warm. The sun played hide and seek behind islands of cloud. Daffodils rippled in the breeze and birds chirped from fat-budded trees. The path swept past towering tree trunks and weather-beaten statues of ancient gods, crossed a stream, and led them to a white-painted gazebo overlooking a lake.

'Let's stay for a few minutes, shall we?' she said, sitting down on the bench. They watched a pair of moorhens negotiate the water lilies. A line of little ones trailed behind, stepping over the leaves. 'I wonder what it's like being a duck. You wouldn't have to go to work or anything. You'd just paddle around all day, looking out for tasty morsels, making sure your ducklings didn't swim off or get eaten.'

He squeezed her hand, laughing. 'You'd have to enjoy swimming in cold, slimy water all day, and screwing in public. You wouldn't be a good duck, Suzanne.'

They lapsed into silence. The lake's surface became still. Paul was sitting very close to her, his hand resting loosely over hers. The gremlins in his head had gone somewhere, thank goodness. He seemed relaxed and happy, more so than he'd been for ages. If only he could stay like this forever.

They followed the path further into the woods. Suzanne scanned the grounds for the promised pheasants, but saw nothing – except for what looked like a hen scratching in the dirt. Then, as open grass replaced the woods, she made out something large and dark behind a nearby bush. A head thrust towards them, crowned with a mass of antlers.

'What's that?' she cried out.

'Only a deer.'

'What's a deer doing here? He looks fierce.'

Paul took her hand. 'He won't hurt us, don't worry. Walk on slowly.'

When she turned back a few seconds later, the deer had gone.

The path inclined gradually at first, then more steeply. Below, far away, fields merged into a blur of bluish hills. Paul wrapped her hand inside his. She breathed in the pine-scented air, glancing up every so often to his unshaven face, with its bold contours coated with stubble, and his always-alert eyes. A feeling of almost overwhelming happiness grew inside her, tinged with wonder. How could she help loving this man? How could she stop loving him?

It took a while to reach the vantage point. They sat against a fallen log, where they could take in the expanse of Somerset below. Paul pulled Heinz's box from his backpack and brought out two bottles of pear juice, two filled baguettes, two apples, and two slabs of fruit cake.

'We should head back.' Suzanne opened her eyes. She'd dozed off – they both had. Paul was pulling on his leather jacket. 'If we stay any longer, we'll be going back in the dark.'

She checked her watch, surprised at how much time had passed. Quickly, she gathered the remains of their picnic.

The sun glared, too low in the sky for her liking. The breeze was getting chilly. Though they were going downhill, it seemed a long time before they reached the woods.

Suzanne stopped at a fork in the path. 'Are you sure it's left?'

'Come on.' He spoke impatiently. 'I know the way.'

A twinge of doubt. Paul had a good sense of direction but the light was slipping away. If they took a wrong turn they could end up lost.

They hurried on, past the one-armed statue and the vine-clad tree trunk. Fir trees stood darkly against an orange-pink glow. The hotel was among them, somewhere.

They crunched acorns underfoot, heard the last flurry of birdsong. A dot glowed high above the line of trees – Jupiter, perhaps.

'Do you recognise any of this? I don't.' She stopped at a dead, hollowed-out tree. Its bark had warped into a crust of blackened ridges.

When there was no answer, she turned, and looked all around. Paul wasn't there.

It didn't make sense. He'd been right behind her a few seconds ago. The path was empty now. She bit her lip.

'Paul, where are you?'

Something crackled in the undergrowth. Suzanne peered into the gloom. A squirrel ran towards a tree and disappeared up its trunk.

'Paul, are you there? Stop playing games.'

She strained her ears for a sound. He couldn't have just disappeared. But all she could hear was the creak of branches.

Then everything went black. Something clamped itself over her eyes – a hand. A gasp bubbled up in her throat.

'Gotcha!'

The hand fell away. She turned and stared at Paul, her relief turning to anger as a damp patch spread in her underwear. He'd sprung out from behind the dead tree.

'Sorry, Suze, I couldn't resist it.' He was laughing.

'Jesus, Paul! You gave me one hell of a fright. What the bloody hell did you have to do that for?'

'I'm sorry, darling. I didn't mean to scare you that much. I was only fooling around.' He pulled her against him and tried to kiss her. 'Don't be upset.'

'Paul, you're unbelievable.' Suzanne pulled away. 'You haven't grown up at all, have you?'

They walked on, not talking. She was too angry with him to care if they never got back to the hotel. Then he pointed ahead. 'I recognise that tree over there,' he said. 'We'll be back in a minute or two.' He squeezed her hand. 'Come on, Suze.'

She was wondering if he was right, even as she saw the hotel through the trees right in front of them, its windows bright and a coil of smoke unfurling from the cluster of tall chimneys. As they approached, she studied the plinths on either side of the heavy wooden door. On top of each one, perched an alarming winged creature, each with a grotesquely shaped, wide-open mouth. A shiver slipped down her spine.

Safely upstairs, Suzanne shut the bathroom door behind her. She ran the water as hot as she could bear then lay outstretched, her body invisible under the foam. Her sigh billowed into the steamy air. Why had Paul wanted to frighten her like that? Sometimes it seemed he was still a boy at heart, the one she'd glimpsed during his occasional childhood stories, who got a kick out of throwing the family cat out of his bedroom window, and laughed when his drunken friend tripped on the kerb and knocked out his front teeth.

However, he had another side – a wonderfully warm and generous one. He was always thinking of her, in different ways. Without warning he would bring home her favourite chocolate truffles, or an M&S orange cake, or a stunning bouquet of roses. He made an effort to plan and to arrange things so as to surprise her – in a good way. The hot air balloon ride he'd arranged for her fiftieth birthday, the handbag he'd bought after her operation, the trip to Paris on Eurostar last year. Katherine complained that Jeremy never did anything romantic. If Paul were always as calm and predictable like Jeremy, she would probably die of boredom.

Suzanne stepped carefully onto the rather grand staircase, gripping the handrail. Her heels were higher than usual, designed for glamour rather than steadiness.

Downstairs, a suited young woman greeted them and showed them into the lounge. Paintings of dark rural scenes lined the walls, their frames heavy and old-fashioned. She scanned the menu while Paul immersed himself in the wine list.

Heinz came in and walked towards the fireplace, a taper in his hand. A lick of flame grew from behind the grate.

'Did you find the lake?' he asked.

'Yes, thank you,' Suzanne replied. 'It was lovely in the sunshine, watching the ducks.'

'There's not so many now. We've had a few fox attacks – they've taken most of the ducks, unfortunately.'

Paul grinned. 'Sitting ducks, were they?'

Heinz nodded, blank-faced, and left the room.

They ordered drinks and settled into the leather armchairs. She looked around the conservatively decorated room. On the mantelpiece, a pair of marble frogs squatted, their heads tilted upwards on thick necks like bulldog's heads. Further along, a black wolf-dog reared, its paws grasping a tray with a white candle on top.

'The decor's a bit morbid, don't you think? I wouldn't want to come here on my own. This place would give me nightmares.'

Paul grunted. He was peering into his glass, lost in thought. Not pleasant thoughts, by the look on his face. But she knew if she asked he would probably say 'it's nothing' in an irritated voice.

The dining room was full of sedately seated couples. It contained more large, gloomy, ornately-framed paintings. A black-suited waiter brought over a bottle of wine and poured some into Paul's glass. Suzanne watched Paul bring the glass to his nose and swirl the liquid, before taking a sip and nodding to the waiter. Whereas she always felt slightly uncomfortable with the formality of this sort of restaurant – where heavy silver cutlery rested on crisp white linen, your napkin was instantly placed on your lap, and your glass was refilled every few minutes – Paul was in his element. He always knew which wine to order, how to pronounce everything on the menu, and what was in every dish.

'Happy anniversary, darling,' Paul said when the waiter left them, holding his glass over the candle. 'Here's to our first twenty-five years.' Glasses clinked. Across the room, a young man began to play the grand piano. 'You look fabulous in that dress.'

It was her sexiest dress, the hemline a couple of inches above the knee, made of loosely woven black jersey. She didn't wear it much these days.

The waiter arrived with their starters. Suzanne took a mouthful of lobster bisque, taking care to sip from the side of the spoon and not to drip any liquid on the spotless white tablecloth, or her dress for that matter. The napkin was large and spread across as much of her lap as possible.

'Fiona, don't do that!'

The outburst came from a table across the room. A woman in her forties was scolding a slender, thick-lipped girl, with very long, intensely red hair, who looked to be in her early teens. The man beside her busied himself with the menu, while a sullen, younger boy dropped his fork repeatedly on the table. Unable to suppress a smile, Suzanne glanced at Paul. The scene took her back to some of their own fraught family meals. He too was watching them, his head cocked.

She took another mouthful of bisque. 'I hope Laura will be alright.'

Paul didn't answer. He'd put down his soup spoon and was still gazing intently across the room.

'Paul?'

'Sorry, what did you say?' He frowned and made an impatient clucking noise. 'Why shouldn't she be alright?'

'I told you, I had a feeling when she phoned that something was bothering her.'

'She's unemployed still. She'd be bothered about that, I should think. How on earth is she going to manage without a job?'

'It wasn't that. Not just that. There was something else.' She couldn't quite nail what it was. It had struck her that Laura was holding something back, something was definitely not right. The phone, though, made it even harder to communicate with Laura than face to face.

'Did she say anything?'

'No, nothing.' She finished her soup and patted her mouth with her napkin, relieved that none of the liquid had found its way to her dress. 'I'll find out when I go over next week, I suppose. She's asked me over for lunch.' *At long last*, she silently added. She'd forgotten when she'd last visited Laura.

'You invent things to worry about, Suzanne.' He tore a piece of bread from the freshly baked sourdough roll on his plate, not looking at her. His mind was somewhere else, again.

'Did you reply to your sister's email?' she asked, remembering his news of the previous week. His mother had no more than two months left, the doctors thought; the cancer had reached her brain.

Paul drummed his fingers on the table. 'I told her I'm not going.'

The familiar frustration grew inside her. Why was he always so rigid about things?

'Canada isn't so far away,' she said. 'You haven't been back once in all the time we've been together. You might not get another chance to talk to her.'

He gave her a warning look. Her instinct was usually to keep quiet so as not to upset him. This time, curiosity, or something else overcame it. He'd left home as soon as he could to get away from his parents. His father had been strict and distant, had cared only about him being top of the class, Paul told her soon after they'd met. And he'd hated his mother.

'Was she really that bad?'

He tilted his head upwards, eyes shut, and let it rest there for a few moments. A rush of breath escaped his mouth as his eyes met hers.

'She was fucking terrible. What she did to me ...' His gaze retreated from her and he went to some place she couldn't reach. 'I came seven years after Vicky. She never wanted me from the start. Vicky and Tania were everything to her, her perfect family.' He paused. 'I told you this before, didn't I? There was some problem with her coil. I read about it in her diary. She didn't want another child, and definitely not a boy.' His mouth twisted into a smirk, making his face ugly. 'But she was from a good Catholic family, so she couldn't get an abortion.'

Although she had heard this before, it still shocked her to hear about his mother. She had met her briefly, during their three-day visit to London to see their son get married. Lucinda. A tall, thin Canadian woman, who carried herself like a dancer, his mother had been reserved, aloof at times, though hardly the ogre she'd expected. In contrast, his father, a heavy, boxy man, abrasively forthright in manner, had reminded her of a prowling bear. Paul had treated them both with cool politeness, as if they were an aunt and uncle he was obliged to tolerate.

'Isn't there a chance,' she began cautiously, 'that you two could heal the rift somehow? Or to at least come to some resolution. Once she's gone, you won't get another chance.'

'Don't you think I know that already?'

'I'm just saying. It's up to you, of course it is. It just seems such a waste, to shut them out of your life like this—'

'Those are your issues. You can't get over losing your parents, let alone Richard, so you try to turn everyone else's into what you never had.' His voice softened. 'Sorry, sweetheart, I know you're only trying to help.'

Her own parents had meant so much to her; her father's death in a sailing accident when she was eight years old was the worst thing she'd ever known, by far. Twelve years on, her mother was struck down by a lorry as she cycled to the shops. And then it was Richard's turn. The unfairness of it all still rankled, especially when she was with people who'd never had to face such loss. In her worst moments, she wondered if she had been cursed.

'So,' Paul began, breaking off another mouthful of bread. 'You'll be off to that thing of yours next weekend?'

'The retreat, you mean? Yes, I've booked a room.' She braced herself for his reaction. He would no doubt tell her what a waste of time these mumbo-jumbo activities were, and try to persuade her not to go.

'When are you leaving?'

'Friday afternoon. I'm taking Jilly. She'll share the cost of the fuel.'

'You're not back till Sunday?'

'Around six in the evening, depending on the traffic. You'll have to fend for yourself, darling.'

'Oh, I'll manage.' He smiled. 'I hope it goes well, Suze. And you get what you want out of it.'

Goodness, that was unusually positive. A band of tension left her neck and shoulders. They should go away more often.

As she was scraping up the last of her dessert, Paul's head moved. His eyes were tracking something behind her.

She turned around. The family of four were making their way out of the dining room. The parents were followed by the boy and, some way behind, the redhead. Her hips swayed as she walked. Her hair came down almost to her waist, shimmering sunset tones under the chandeliers.

Paul turned his head to follow her until she left the room. His expression as he turned back was odd, almost shocked. He picked up his large, tulip-shaped wine glass. When he put down the glass, there was only a purplish residue above the stem.

An uneasy sensation pooled in her gut. First it had been that girl at Katherine's party. Then she'd caught him waving to the leggy girl at number 39, who went past with her family's dog – a huge Boxer that always snarled at Marmaduke. The other Sunday, Paul had stopped cleaning the car and stood chatting to her on the pavement. She'd seen them from the bedroom window. It looked as if they had been conversing for quite a while, with frequent smiles on both sides. She hadn't made out any words. After a minute or so she'd become uneasy, standing there behind the curtain like a paranoid wife, and had hurried back downstairs before anyone saw her. And now, this girl. All of them would still be at school, not even halfway through their teens. That was odd, wasn't it?

She tossed the thought away, wondering at herself. Surely, she couldn't be jealous of girls who were young enough to be her own daughters – or granddaughters? She was putting two and two together and making five. When he chose to be, Paul could be charming and friendly with all sorts of people – men and women, young and old – it was just his way.

They took their cognacs into the lounge. The embers in the grate glowed red. As they sat down on the sofa there was a sharp crack, then a thud as a large log fell, sending up a shower of orange sparks. Suzanne relaxed. She was glad to be away from the formality of the restaurant. They talked of the places they wanted to visit, and friends they would like to see in the years ahead, while they were still healthy and active.

She put her hand on Paul's.

'Do you think we'll still be together in another twenty-five years?'

'I'm sure we will, Suze, if we're still around by then – if you haven't worried yourself to death.' He swallowed the last of his cognac then squeezed her hand. 'Come on, let's go upstairs.'

She followed Paul along the hall, her heels tapping on the polished wood floor. They passed the enormous antlered head that lunged out of the wall and began climbing the stairs.

A sudden blast of sound from below startled her, like someone banging on a giant gong with all their strength. She stopped, jerkily, nearly losing her footing on the stairs.

'Oh my God! What's that?'

'Careful, you'll knock that cat over. It's only the grandfather clock.'

Heart thudding, she stepped away from the window ledge, which bore a heavy-looking statue of a creature bearing some resemblance to a cat – a sinister, wolfish cat. It was wobbling, but wasn't going to fall, thank goodness.

The lamps on either side of their bed cast a yellowish glow over the room. A vase of mauve heather stood on the antique dressing table, which had been polished to a high shine. Suzanne opened a small window and leaned out, taking a deep breath of soft, clean air. The sky was huge and so magnificently black, not the patches of washed-out, yellowish brown they had at home. Stretching across it, the lacy swathes of the Milky Way. There were too many stars to take in, as if a child had thrown handfuls of glitter at a black canvas. A rush of awe inside her. How could anyone not look at this and marvel? The universe was vast, unknowable, and greater than anything anyone could imagine. It made her worries seem insignificant.

Paul unfastened her shoes then removed her dress. They kissed on the bed with an unusual intensity, then he undressed and they started to make love. Her responses seemed muffled, weaker than usual. Suddenly, he stood and moved her to stand against the window frame. He thrust harder from behind. She shivered in the cool air, hoping it wouldn't take too much longer. Then, without warning, she began to moan. Her body had come to life. He moved more urgently, pushing her into the wall. A shudder went through her, a gasp escaped her mouth. The orgasm thrilled her, its unexpected intensity drenching her.

Lying in the darkness, wrapped in his arms, thoughts of their marriage came and went. Were things really as bad as she'd imagined? Their sex life might be less varied and, in general, less passionate than it once had been. It certainly wasn't over, though. Emotionally too, she'd felt closer to Paul this weekend than she had for a long time. Had he just needed a break from the demands of work? Or could this all just be an act he'd put on to please her, mindful of their anniversary? Was he secretly fed up with her, waiting for an opportunity to meet someone else?

No, that was ridiculous.

Although she willed them to stop, the thoughts carried on. Perhaps he had met someone already. He was always so keen to leave for Putney on Saturdays. If he wasn't interested in Jane, could he have his eye on Emma? After all, she was young, slim, attractive.

Emma? No, that was totally crazy. Emma wasn't even a teenager. Her husband wouldn't be attracted to a child of twelve. He was helping Jane, that's all, doing her a favour.

God, she really was getting paranoid. This had to stop. She wasn't going to let herself become one of those sad women who lived in permanent fear of their partner straying. She had to trust Paul – at least, until she had a good reason not to.

9

Laura

10 March 2011

Laura sat up and rubbed her eyes. She felt sluggish, unrefreshed from her night's sleep. The sun glared through a gap in the curtains. At least there was one good thing about being unemployed: no one gave a hoot if you spent half the morning in bed. Then the dart of memory, a shadow falling and darkening everything. This was the day. Her mother would be here in just two hours.

In the bathroom, Laura splashed her face with cold water. The basin and mirror weren't particularly clean and patches of mould were sprouting from cracks between the tiles. She inspected the rest of the flat. In the living area, the carpet looked wearier than ever, alongside the meagre furniture and a clutter of newspapers, the discarded cups and CDs. In the kitchen, unwashed crockery queued next to the kitchen sink. Above it, bottle-green cupboards flaked paint.

Why had she suggested her mother come here – and what were they going to have for lunch? She removed a cookery book from the shelf, leafed quickly through its glossy photographs, and returned it. The recipes were far

119

too complicated and time-consuming. It would have to be pasta.

After a quick shower, she set to work with as much vigour as she could muster. The physical effort of cleaning helped her to stop thinking about what would happen later that afternoon. Every time she paused for a few moments, the knowledge of it returned, along with a sloshing and roiling inside her gut, like something nasty was stuck there.

At 1.30pm Laura sat down and waited for the buzzer. Everything was ready. The dirt and mess had gone and every surface gleamed expectantly. Fresh fruit salad in glass bowls. A bottle of wine chilled in the fridge. A vase of assorted bright flowers from the local supermarket overlooked the table, which was now covered in the unused tablecloth her mother had given her. A clean, folded towel on the bathroom rail.

Ten minutes later her mother arrived, wafting a crisp floral scent, a daffodil-yellow silk scarf tied at her neck.

'Hello, darling.' Her mother stepped inside, arms opening for a hug. 'You've got the flat looking spick and span. I love the new cushions.'

'Thanks, Mum. How was your weekend away?'

'The hotel was fabulous – we had champagne in our room when we arrived, breakfast in bed.' Her hands began to dance, as they always did when she became enthusiastic.

'What about Dad? Did he enjoy it too?'

'He was happier than he's been for ages – that was such a relief. I wasn't treading on eggshells the whole time.'

After her mother had visited the bathroom, they sat down at the table. Out of the window they could see a squirrel leaping about on the corrugated roofs of the row of garages below.

'Mmm, this is very good.' Her mother waved a fettuccine-laden fork. 'How's the job hunt going?'

'Not so well. Everyone wants someone with loads of experience. Having a degree makes no difference.' A first-class degree probably put people off, she thought. They'd assume she was the clever but impractical type, who wouldn't know how to liaise with printers or send out mailshots. And they were right, weren't they?

'What about that job you went for the other week? The editorial assistant at that magazine?'

'I haven't heard anything. I don't think I have much chance of getting on the shortlist, to be honest.' Over a hundred people had applied, they'd told her; they'd been interviewing all week. They'd asked her to list her three biggest career achievements, and why she'd had so many jobs since leaving university.

'Will you be OK to pay the rent, darling? What if you don't find a job for a while?'

'I should be OK. I've got some money saved, and I'm getting Jobseekers Allowance now.'

That was being optimistic, she knew. Her student loan was nowhere near paid off. The small amount she'd managed to save was dwindling rapidly. The JSA wasn't nearly enough to cover the rent, and her housing benefit, so they told her last week, could take another month to arrive because of a claims backlog.

'We can always lend you some money to tide you over, if you need it.'

'Thanks, Mum, but I'll be alright. I'll find something soon, don't worry.'

Taking a handout from her parents would be admitting that she was still a child who couldn't look after herself. Worse, it would be her father's money – her mother earned peanuts compared to him.

'You know you're always welcome to come and stay with us for a while,' her mother went on. 'I know you don't like the idea much, now you're so independent, but it might be more sensible than renting.'

'Thanks, but no. I'm sure something will come up soon, Mum.' The words came out a bit too sharp. But she couldn't live in the same house as him again, not even for a week.

Silence grew in the room like an invisible fog. Her mother looked out of the window, sending off a cloud of hurt and disappointment. Laura concentrated on eating more of the pasta on her plate. Somehow or other, she had to tell her mother the truth. But how? She and her mother didn't do heart-to-hearts. How would she go about destroying this false conception of her father? Should she dismantle it in one blow, or slowly, piece by piece? And what if what her father said about the breakdown was true, and telling the truth about Dad triggered another one?

'I'm glad you asked me over. It's been a long time since we've had a chance for a good talk, just the two of us.' Her mother paused, a trace of a smile on her face. The sun was turning her hair into a halo of golden threads. 'It would be good to meet up now and then for a chat, do you think? You've been so preoccupied lately. We don't even talk on the phone nowadays.'

Laura didn't reply immediately. She had an instinct to defend herself. But what her mother said was true. She'd kept Mum just out of reach, not letting her get too close. It was as if the silence she'd kept about her father for all these years had come between them, and squeezed out all the normal things they might have talked about, all the closeness they might have had.

'I know, Mum. I'm sorry about that.'

It sounded lame. She wanted to say something better, but could think of nothing else to say. Laura picked up the plates and took them into the kitchen; she placed a spoonful of ice cream in each glass bowl, on top of the fruit salad, and brought them to the table.

They were quiet again. Outside, the roof glared silver, making the room bright.

'Do you think there's something strange about Dad?'

The words came out of her mouth before she knew it. Her mother froze, a piece of kiwifruit impaled on her fork. Then she put down the fork and laughed.

'So many of the things Paul does are strange. He seems to get stranger as time goes on, are you thinking of anything in particular?'

Laura dug her spoon into the fruit and let it stay there. It would be so easy to tell her now, the easiest thing in the world.

'Laura?'

'Oh, lots of things … the way he used to get so angry, then suddenly be all smiles. The way he …'

Her mother's frown deepened. 'He's been like that more often, lately. I think there's something wrong, something he's keeping from me. I've been wondering if he might have some condition that's gone undiagnosed. A few years ago, I asked if he could get a referral to a psychiatrist. He said I'm the one who needs treatment, not him. He'd never go in a thousand years.'

There is something wrong, Mum. There's something I have to tell you.

The words waited inside her head. A magpie landed on the roof, pecked out a piece of moss and flew away.

'Is something the matter, Laura? Aren't you going to eat any dessert?'

'There's something I have to …' she began. The moment passed. She swallowed, suddenly voiceless, aware only of her mother's face, concerned and confused. 'There's something I have to ask you about.'

'Go on.'

'Remember when Uncle Rich died? I asked you why you were taking pills, and you said they stopped you feeling unhappy. Was that true?'

Her mother put down her spoon and looked at her in surprise, then she rubbed the bridge of her nose and sighed heavily.

'It was an awful time, really awful. I'm surprised you can remember so much, that far back. July 1999. You'd only have been ten.'

'Were you having a breakdown?'

'That's what they said. It wasn't the worst kind, I didn't hear voices or anything. I just found it hard to keep going.'

A shiver hovered about Laura's shoulders. 'What happened, Mum?'

'It was so sudden.' Her mother tugged at her scarf. 'No one had any idea there might be something wrong with his heart.' Her voice wobbled slightly. 'I didn't know how to cope without Richard. He was such a wonderful brother, always going out of his way to help. I was much closer to him than to Irene. It was as if my father had died all over again. The same feelings came back that I had then. One part of me was determined to carry on, to look after you and your brother. But part of me just wanted to go to sleep and not wake up.'

'And the drugs helped you get through it? That was when you started taking them?'

'I'd taken antidepressants before, on and off. After Richard died, I started taking them regularly – anti-anxiety drugs too. I went to see a therapist – he said I had an anxiety disorder. He helped me deal with the shock and the grief, he helped such a lot.' Her mother gave a small, sad smile. 'I'm so sorry to shock you, darling. I didn't want you to know, I wasn't proud of myself for caving in like that. I didn't tell you and your brother because I didn't want you to think I wasn't coping, that I wasn't there for you. But maybe it's time you knew.'

'How long did you see him for? The therapist?'

'Six months. I got a referral from Doctor Edwards.'

She couldn't speak. A thousand questions whirled in her brain. Had she always known about the breakdown, or half known? The pills, the crying, the long rests in bed – they all made sense now. That was why, for much of her childhood, her mother had been only half there. Why her mother hadn't noticed things that other mothers would have.

'Laura, are you alright?'

'He used to impersonate people, didn't he? Uncle Richard. I remember him talking like Patrick Moore, wiggling his eyebrows.'

'Oh, his Patrick Moore was unbelievable. He'd have me and Irene in stitches.' Tears shone in her mother's eyes. 'How I wish he were still around.' She dabbed at them with a tissue. 'I'm glad I've told you all this – I don't like having things we can't talk about. I've wanted to, but I was worried how you might react. I didn't want you to think your mother was some sort of fruit-loop.'

'Come on, Mum, you've had such a lot to deal with, that's all. Your dad dying suddenly when you were so young.' She thought of her own father, and her innermost wish when she was growing up – that he would disappear.

'I suppose certain things can affect you more than you'd ever imagine,' her mother replied.

Laura looked at her mother's hand, resting on the table. Her skin was thinner than it used to be, strung with blue veins. It was odd, she thought, how they had both been keeping secrets, waiting for the right time to reveal them. Only her mother had got there first. She put her hand over her mother's.

'Do you think you could have another breakdown, Mum? If something like that happened again?'

'Someone dying, you mean? No, I don't think so.' A frown. 'You mustn't worry about that, darling. I've talked things through ad infinitum with the therapist. I'm much stronger than I used to be.'

Her mother sounded a little too certain. Was it true, or was it only meant to reassure? Mum was a lot chirpier these days than back then, when she and Daniel had lived at home. Laura felt a growing impatience with herself. Now was the time. She had something to share too. Why not just spit it out and be done with it? Her mother would have to find out sooner or later, wouldn't she?

She got up and took their bowls into the kitchen, then put her head around the door to ask if her mother wanted coffee. She was fiddling with something in her bag. Her stash of pills. She popped a pale blue one into her mouth.

No, she couldn't do this. Not yet. How much could her mother have changed from the woman she'd been twelve years ago? How would her mother handle the truth about Dad? It would be such a terrible shock. Worse, even, than a death. How would she cope with losing her husband, on top of losing her brother?

Laura put down her cup of coffee. 'How's Dad? Is he taking Emma swimming on Saturday?'

'He was supposed to be, but Jane cancelled. Emma wants to see a friend instead that day, and from the following week on she's got netball practice every Saturday.'

'So, he's not taking Emma to the pool anymore?'

'That's right.' Her mother's voice sharpened a fraction. 'Why do you ask?'

'Oh, no reason. I just wondered.'

Her mother said she'd better be going, there was a man coming to the house to fix the gutter.

Laura kissed her goodbye. She promised to phone soon.

She slumped on the sofa. The room slowly became quiet, except for occasional doors slamming on the landing and the faint whoosh of passing cars. Images came to her, fragments of early memories.

Sitting in Uncle Rich's garden, listening to him put on the voices of celebrities and politicians, her mother teary from laughing. Standing in the kitchen waiting for her mother to let her lick the cake mixture spoon, or press the cutter into the pastry. Watching Mum expertly toss an omelette, shake the stir-fry pan, or blend the perfect strawberry smoothie. Back then the kitchen was the centre of the universe, her mother a warm, reassuring presence, always around on weekends and after school, the bright star beside her father's uneven light.

Until Uncle Rich died.

It's her first funeral. They're standing by his grave, stiff and silent, she and her brother, Mum and Dad. A man is speaking to the clump of people around them. Everyone's in black despite the bright flowers and the hot sunshine. Everyone looks sad, dabbing at shiny eyes. Except Mum, who seems beyond sad. Her eyes are dry and empty.

'Can I take this off now?' she asks, when the man stops speaking and everyone starts to move away.

But her mother ignores her, not noticing, even when she tugs on her sleeve and asks a second time. Her brother rushes off to the toilet. Her father takes her hand and walks with her, leaving Mum behind, staring at nothing.

Eventually they got back to normal, more or less. But her mother faded. She spent less time in the kitchen or the garden and more time upstairs. And she stopped noticing things. Mum would let her go to school without her hair tied back, or with a stain on her tie, and would forget when she needed a clean PE kit.

Not long after that, her father started to notice her in ways he hadn't before.

Laura got up from the sofa and went to the window. Her spirits lifted as she watched the distant green spaces under the open sky, the last minutes of sunshine colouring in low ribbons of cloud.

Her thoughts turned back to her father. She tried to decide what to do about him. Now she knew what he'd said about her mother's breakdown was true, didn't it change things? And there was even less reason to say anything to Mum, now she knew her father wasn't going to take Emma swimming anymore. But maybe she should warn Jane, just in case he had another chance to get to Emma.

It was hard to imagine that her father would ever be desperate enough to pursue Emma, or any other girl. Why would he take such a risk? He had everything to lose. And how would he get close enough to do anything to Emma, even if he wanted to? As his daughter, trusting him and loving him, living in the same house day after day, she'd been an easy target. Other girls, even the ones he knew already, would be far more difficult. They were constantly warned by their parents and teachers about the dangers of paedophiles. She'd met Emma a few times, years back. The girl had been a feisty thing, seemingly quite able to stand up for herself. Surely, even if her father did see Emma again, she'd never let him do anything.

But what if he *did* do something to harm her? How would she be able to live with that?

10

Laura

11 March 2011

Laura reached out to ring the doorbell then lowered her arm. From inside, raised voices. A boy and a girl, arguing. The boy's voice wobbled with suppressed tears. The girl's was sarcasm-inflected, bored. Clearly, Jane wasn't in – or was she in another part of the house?

She scanned the front of the modest semi. It was the same as she remembered. Its modernish, bland exterior matched all the others in the street, though the paintwork looked fresh and the windows boasted wooden blinds, not net curtains. She pressed the bell, which set off a loud electronic chime. The voices carried on. She pressed the bell again, for twice as long this time.

Silence, then the hurried thump of feet. Emma opened the door.

'Hello?' She wore her school blouse and skirt. She had grown half a foot, into a skinny teen. A sullen line of lips had replaced the eager-to-please smile.

'Hi, Emma, I'm Laura. My mum is friends with yours—'

'I remember.' Emma's expression didn't alter. 'Hi there.' Her voice was flat.

'I'm really sorry to disturb you, but I wanted to speak to your mum.' Laura paused, hoping for Jane's voice to intervene. 'Is she in?'

'She's at work. She won't be in till seven thirty, maybe eight.'

She hesitated, checking her watch. It was only 6.45pm now. For some reason, she hadn't considered that Jane might be out. 'Can I come in and wait for her?'

'Yeah, sure. If you like.' Emma pulled the door open a fraction further and made way for her to pass. Blue painted fingernails. Skin bitten at the edges.

Laura stepped over a plastic dumper truck in the hall and followed Emma into a long room, a living area at one end and a dining table at the other. Toby leaned over the table, his legs dangling off the floor, mopping up the mound of peanut butter on his plate with a slice of toast.

'Hello, Toby. How are you doing?'

Toby stared at her in silence. His fair hair, slightly too long, tickled long-lashed, intensely blue eyes. He had the angelic features of a boy destined to become a heartbreaker – a boy who was probably used to being admired by grown women. Laura did her best to smile. She was always awkward around small children, never knowing what to say – they seemed such alien creatures. Emma sat down beside Toby and helped herself to a taco chip from a large bag in the middle of the table.

'I'll wait over here, shall I?' Laura gestured to an armchair.

Emma made a wordless mumble in reply.

Laura took off her jacket and sat in an armchair, with the dining table to one side of her. From here, she could see the children without having to face them. She took her phone from her bag and checked her emails. Two replies to her latest job enquiries. She opened the first.

Thanks for your interest, but we've been overwhelmed with the response to our ad and are no longer taking applications.

The other was from an agency. She would be welcome to come in to register, but she'd need recent experience and the ability to type 60 words per minute. With a sigh, she put her phone back in her bag.

'You're making a mess all over the table!' Emma hissed at Toby, and their squabbling resumed.

Laura checked her watch, nearly 7.30pm. She felt uncomfortable. This was not what she'd imagined; she'd wanted a short chat with Jane, alone. It seemed wrong to sit here listening to the children's increasingly loud verbal thrusts, without intervening. She fidgeted in her chair, taking in the room. It was all quite tasteful, middle class. Expensive looking furniture. Framed paintings – all originals, abstracts – everywhere. But there were signs of stagnation. She counted a dozen marks on the walls. A wooden side table bore a deep scratch. What looked like the base of an iron was imprinted on the carpet near the TV.

'I am not!' Toby yelled. 'Stop kicking me!'

'Shut up, dick-brain.'

She thought about what she'd planned to say to Jane, who would be coming home tired from a long day at work. This probably wasn't the best time to mention that Dad might pose a serious danger to Jane's daughter, given he'd taken Emma swimming every weekend for the past six weeks.

A loud bleat made her start. Surely, they didn't keep sheep in the garden? No, it was Emma's mobile.

Emma stopped glaring at Toby and studied her phone. 'It's Mum.'

Laura got to her feet. 'Will she be long?'

'She's going to be another forty minutes probably. The District Line is stuffed.'

'Oh.' Disappointment ballooned in her chest. She considered staying for forty minutes more. No, that wasn't possible.

Toby sprang up and pointed a remote control at the TV. A smiling, smooth-skinned, lightly-tanned, late-teen girl ran through a sunny room in skimpy shorts. An advert for deodorant.

'What I wanted to say to your mum, it's to do with you.' Her words petered out. Emma was frowning at her. She glanced at the glass panelled door that led into the kitchen. She couldn't talk about this in front of Toby. 'Could we go in the kitchen for a moment?'

The kitchen was modern, designer. No one ever tidied here, it looked like. The surfaces were cluttered with papers and toys and books, and the cooker was scabbed and stained.

Emma waited for her to speak, jiggling from one foot to the other.

'I heard you're going to the pool with my dad.'

The girl stopped jiggling and looked down at her fingernails. 'I'm not going there anymore, I've got other stuff to do. I'm in the netball team now. Our matches are starting soon.'

'Did everything go OK, then? With the swimming lessons, I mean. Did you enjoy going to the pool with him?'

'Yes, I suppose.' A quick smile. 'I'm a much better swimmer now.'

'And he's not done anything ... unusual?'

Emma righted a toy car that lay on its side on the worktop. She seemed uncomfortable, as if she wanted to say something but couldn't find the words.

'You shouldn't let my dad take you swimming again, Emma. He's not ...' *Not right in the head*, she nearly said.

In the other room, the TV volume increased. Men shouted angrily against a volley of gunfire. 'He's not the sort of person you should be with – alone.'

Emma shrugged and studied her nails again. 'Sure, OK.'

'There's something you don't know about him. I don't know for sure, but …' In her head, a succession of words came and went. They all sounded too dramatic, or plain scaremongering. 'You should be careful,' she said at last. 'He could try to take advantage of you. I don't think you should spend any more time with him.'

Another shrug. 'Sure. I'm not figuring on that anyway.' From next door, a rattling blast of bass. A scowl rucked Emma's features. She yanked open the door. 'Toby! Shut up in there, will you? What did I tell you?'

Laura followed Emma into the living room. Toby was now sitting on the sofa, knees up, feet on the coffee table, watching cars screech across the TV screen. She reached for her jacket.

'I'd better go now.'

There was no point in staying any longer. She needed to be away from this house now, alone, in the quiet. How did Jane put up with this commotion? It was a mystery to her how mothers looking after children on their own managed to carry on without walking out or strangling them.

At the front door, Laura stopped. Should she leave a note for Jane?

An image thrust its way into her mind. Her mother, sobbing hysterically in the back of a car, on the way to some terrible place where the flowers were changed daily and listless people sat about with medicated smiles, a cross between a psychiatric ward and a care home for the elderly. Then she imagined a policeman, taking her father's arm, tugging him into a police car.

No, she'd already talked to Emma, and Emma would be bound to tell Jane. Leaving a note would make this too formal, somehow.

Laura opened the door. Male voices boomed from the TV.

'Thanks, Emma.'

Emma shrugged, her lower lip jutting out sulkily. 'No worries.'

She tried to read Emma's face. Should she kiss the girl goodbye? But Emma didn't look like the kissy type. She touched her arm.

'You'll remember what I said, won't you?'

'Yeah, of course.' Emma's lips puckered into a smile. Her next words were the friendliest sounding so far. 'See you, then.'

11

Paul

12 March 2011

Paul tapped his fingers against the coffee table, willing Toby to dislodge himself from the Sony tablet that he hadn't looked up from for about ten minutes. Why couldn't Jane just take her son away, and leave him and Emma in peace? Time was ticking by. He didn't want his last afternoon with Emma to be frittered away watching her mother flap about like an old woman. But he must try not to appear impatient. He was grateful for these last precious hours, hours that had almost been snatched away from him by a shopping trip. Instead of going swimming with him, Emma had wanted to go shopping instead, with her friend Mandy.

Jane's text last Sunday morning, saying he wasn't needed anymore, had plunged him into gloom verging on despair. He'd lost his appetite, stopped listening to music, had taken no pleasure in anything. Then, salvation. Mandy had been suspended from school that afternoon for scrawling graffiti over the walls of the gymnasium, he learned yesterday evening, when Jane had called. He'd been on his way home from work. Jane didn't want Emma to spend any more of her spare time being influenced by Mandy – a smoker and troublemaker, as well as a graffiti artist – could he possibly take Emma swimming tomorrow after all, one last time? She had to take Toby to a soccer match in Watford and didn't want to leave Emma alone in the house, tempted to slip out with the likes of Mandy.

'No problem at all,' he'd replied, with an exaggerated tone of goodwill.

For added certainty, he'd texted Emma immediately after speaking to Jane. True, he felt like a lowdown git for doing so. He had resisted messaging Emma after Jane cancelled Emma's Saturday outing, trying to convince himself that it was probably best this way. But, after the relief of the last-minute change of plan, he hadn't been able to stop himself.

Great news, Em! My friend at the agency wants to help you out. Will tell you all about it when I see you tomorrow. Maybe best if you don't say anything to your mum just yet, till it's sorted. Lots of women don't like their daughters going into modelling at your age. Paul.

'For God's sake, Toby!'

Once again Jane burst into the living room, this time wrapped in yards of red scarf, as if about to set off on an Arctic expedition instead of driving a few miles to watch her son play soccer. 'Get your coat on this second and stop messing around with that damned game. You'll miss the match if you don't get a move on. I'm not going to ask you again.'

Toby made a gargoyle face and dawdled out of the room. Emma, sprawled on the floor in front of the TV, flicking through music channels, looked up with an expression he couldn't decipher. Bored, mainly. Cautious too, maybe. And wasn't there a hint of anticipation, just below the surface?

'Thanks again for helping out, Paul, you're a lifesaver. Let me know if she's any trouble at all. I've had just about enough of the both of them, after last night's performance.'

'They've been fighting again?'

Jane's expression said all he need to know.

'We'll be back by six,' she said to Paul in a tone of pained resignation and turned towards the hall. She hesitated, brushing the arms of her coat. Suddenly, she seemed reluctant to leave. 'Bye, Em, see you soon. Behave yourself, won't you?'

Finally, the front door clicked shut. Paul glanced at Emma. The girl was seemingly oblivious to Jane and Toby's departure. His body tensed, his senses became alert, like a gladiator preparing for combat.

'This is gross.'

Paul looked at the television screen. A female, around eighteen, showing off her jewelled belly button, gyrating her slim hips as she bleated out a pop song. An idol to girls of Emma's age, no doubt. She couldn't sing, but she sure knew how to dance.

Emma aimed the remote control at the TV. A *Sky News* presenter appeared, and in serious tones gave the latest on yesterday's earthquake in Japan, and the stricken Fukushima nuclear power plant: thousands dead, evacuations around the plant, fear of radioactive contamination ... He shuddered. At least in the UK they were safe from that sort of thing.

Before he had a chance to say: 'don't rush, we could hang round here for a while', Emma sprang to her feet and galloped upstairs. A minute later she reappeared, Nikes on, a candy-striped bag slung over her shoulder. He paused at the bannister, lost in the Cheshire cat grin enveloping her face as she padded up to him.

'So, what did your friend say about me?' Her eyelashes flickered beguilingly. 'She really wants to help me get into modelling?'

Don't blow it now, he thought. One step at a time.

'Yes, I talked to Mona at the weekend.'

'Mona?'

No, not Mona. What the heck was his model agency friend's name supposed to be?

'That's Monica's nickname. She was very helpful. She suggested something we could do to get the ball rolling.' He gave Emma what he hoped was an enigmatic smile. 'I'll tell you the rest later. Let's get a move on, or the pool will be crawling. Got your keys?'

'Of course,' she replied, a sharp edge in her voice. 'I'm not a complete floss head.'

He walked behind as Emma loped towards the car. Her legs looked longer than ever in her jeans. The material was stretched tight over her backside, peeping out pertly below her fake fur jacket. She had blue varnish on her nails, he saw as she got into the car. Had she worn it just for him?

'So, this will be our last visit to the pool,' he said, as they inched along car-filled Putney High Street. 'I know you wanted to go shopping with your friend, but I'm pleased we can go for another swim. I'll miss our swims together.'

She looked at him and didn't reply. He knew she probably wouldn't miss him at all. But their outings were special to him. *She* was special to him. Without her, his life would be robbed of something vital. He would no longer wake up early on a Saturday morning, impatient for the hours to pass until he could be with her.

'We've gotten used to each other, don't you think?' he asked, tentatively.

'Yeah. At first, I thought you were going to be like my Dad and tell me what to do all the time. But you're alright.'

She liked him, no kidding. Joy surged through him like the first taste of beer on a hot day. Or was the little minx just trying to get him hooked?

'You're not allowed to see Mandy anymore?'

Emma made a loud sweet-sucking noise. 'I don't mind not seeing her. She's been acting so crazy lately.' They carried on, past the dismal strip of grocers, betting shops and identikit houses while Emma chattered away about her friend. 'She wrote the graffiti to piss off her P.E. teacher, because he wouldn't let her off gym when she had her period. And the smoking ... She thinks puffing on a fag makes her look grown-up, but she's so stupid. Boys in year eleven don't go for girls our age. Anyway, smoking's mad. I tried it once and it made me sick.' She stuck out her tongue and pretended to gag. 'I can't believe people actually want to do that to themselves.'

He listened to the words bubble out of her, overtaking themselves in their hurry to get out. She had an endearingly girlish habit of raising her voice at the end of every sentence. This was a different Emma from the brooding girl he'd taken out that first time. Yet, in a few hours she would be only a memory.

She was half gone already. Her interest had moved to more important things: netball, drama classes, boys at school. Perhaps he could conjure up other opportunities to see her – he could take her to netball matches, or they could go swimming again in the summer holidays. But it would be difficult.

Jane's sixth sense had begun to operate. He'd almost tasted her unease this time, as she relinquished her darling to him. Suzanne's antenna had kicked in too, he was certain. She'd seemed inordinately pleased to hear he wouldn't be taking Emma to the pool again. Suzanne was on the wrong track though, with all her questions about Jane. Fortunately, she'd hotfooted it to her retreat yesterday evening before he'd had a chance to mention today's outing with Emma. His phone was switched off too, in case Suzanne called. She would find out about it later, when it was safely in the past.

His thoughts turned to Laura. If she had any inkling of how much he yearned for Emma, she would tell her mother everything, with no fear of the consequences. No, this would be his last time with Emma. This would be his last chance to show her what she really meant to him.

He was ready before Emma. He waited for her in their usual spot at the entrance to the pool, past the showers. The smell of chlorine was harsher than usual. There were a handful of women swimming today. He recognised them as Saturday regulars: gym freaks finishing off their workouts.

After five minutes, Emma emerged. She gave him a reproving look, ran towards the water and jumped in. It was the first time she'd done that. Usually, she immersed herself inch by inch, yelping because the water was too cold. When she was nearly two-thirds of the way, he dived in and powered after her, passing her before she reached the end. He turned expertly at the wall and swam past her again, cleaving through the water, a lean, mean swimming machine.

Twenty, he counted, touching the shallow end. He glanced around the pool. For a few anxious moments, he couldn't see Emma. Then he caught sight of her floating on her back in the shallow end. He swam over.

'I'm dying,' she said melodramatically. 'I did six lengths. My arms are like lead.' She stayed floating, looking up dreamily through the roof.

He laughed.

'You've become a regular little mermaid, Em. Remember how you were when we first started? You couldn't manage one width without stopping. I can hardly believe it's the same girl.'

She righted herself, her eyes on his face. No smile. Pensive. Thinking about the boys at school, perhaps. Or Mandy, or netball. Or her father shagging some hot babe he met at a tango class.

'Watch out!' He grabbed Emma's ankles and set off, pulling her along. She screamed and thrashed. When he let her go she retaliated, sending a shower of spray over him.

'Can we go now?' she said a few minutes later, a sad look clinging to her face. 'I'm frozen.'

It was after 2.30pm by the time they got back to the car. He waited for Emma to fasten her seat belt. He had no intention of wasting time in McDonald's and cheap boutiques, not this time. He had a better idea.

'How about we go back to my place?' He raised an eyebrow encouragingly. It was too good an opportunity to miss. Suzanne was away, immersing herself in her New Age rituals – there would be no one to disturb them. They'd have some time alone together, at last, away from prying eyes.

'I don't know. Can you drop me at home? I've got homework to do.'

Her reply stung him. He hadn't expected that. And he hadn't told her the news from the model agency yet. If he didn't do something quickly, he was going to lose her. All his plans would be dashed.

'Isn't there a film you'd like to see? How about a movie? There's a Blockbuster near my place. It has every film you could possibly want.'

Emma had mentioned how much she liked horror films. Jane had banned her from watching anything that might give her bad dreams, or interfere with her impressionable young mind, since she'd found her and Mandy together on the sofa watching *Scream*. But she didn't seem tempted by his offer. She stared into her lap, her hands gripping her knees. The nail polish had chipped on a couple of nails.

'You trust me, don't you, Emma? You know I'm not going to turn into a bogeyman or anything?'

He said it jokingly, and waited for her to smile back. But she didn't. Time for the trump card.

'I haven't yet told you what Monica said.'

She looked up at him, interest rekindling in her eyes.

'She said, if I send in some shots of you, she'll take a look at them. She promised to do what she can for you.'

'I wouldn't be too young for them?'

'That's no problem at all. This agency is looking for younger girls especially, they want to get new talent on board. You're their ideal age.'

Emma's focus on him was instant and unwavering. Her eyes widened, ready to swallow it all. She wanted so much to believe. He explained more about the agency. As he talked, Monica and the agency were becoming almost real. Monica was his friend back in Montreal and they had stayed in touch – she was a senior director at the Bright Young Things agency, and one of its key people. She looked at the most promising applicants and had final say over whether to sign new girls.

'I've got a new Nikon at home,' he added quickly, 'it takes great photos. I'll take some shots of you, if you like. I know what sort of thing they're after.'

Emma dipped her head again, eyes on her hands. His heart went out to her. She seemed stricken, unable to make a decision.

'What do you say?'

'OK, then.' She looked up, her face earnest. 'Do you really think she can help me?'

He breathed again. *Thank you, God.*

'Absolutely, sweetie. Monica is the best there is. If anyone can get you started in the modelling game, she can.'

He drove as fast as he could without looking like he was in a desperate hurry – not slowing enough over speed bumps and racing to get through traffic lights. Time was slipping away. Emma chewed on a Mars bar, humming the pop song from the TV.

'Can we still get a film?'

They were waiting at yet another set of traffic lights. He met her eyes, surprised.

'Of course. I thought you didn't want to, though.' It would take up valuable time, he thought. Then again, it might help to put her in the mood.

'Can we see *Ginger Snaps*? It's meant to be really scary. Mandy's seen it.'

Fortunately, the store had a copy of the film. Emma insisted on him buying a huge bucket of popcorn too.

'It'll rot your teeth,' he said. He'd never seen anyone get through as much junk food as this girl. But, right now, he would be happy to buy whatever she asked for.

Paul swung the car into the driveway, narrowly missing Marmaduke who scarpered under the side gate as if his life was in danger. The creature had been sitting nonchalantly in the middle of the driveway, cleaning itself. It beat him why Suzanne was so dotty about the stupid animal. One day she would find it squashed flat, a marmalade-coloured rug.

He inserted his key into the lock and hesitated.

What was he doing, bringing Emma here? Suzanne would flip out if she knew what was on his mind – so would Laura, and Jane, too. He was risking losing all he had – a wife and kids, his house and car, sixty grand a year plus commission. Not just that. He was risking prison and all its horrors.

Then he pictured Emma, lying beside him, naked. How could he simply let her out of his life with nothing special ever having taken place between them? He wasn't an ordinary man. He needed more than Suzanne and the sanitised version of sex she provided.

He pushed open the door. Emma followed behind him.

'You've got a nice place.'

'Thanks.'

The girl hovered at the sideboard, picking up framed photos and replacing them. He took a can of Fosters and a bottle of Coke out of the fridge and put them on the coffee table. Then he switched off his phone and set up the Blu-ray player.

'Stop nosing about, come and sit down over here.' He patted a cushion on the sofa. 'It's the best place to watch, or you'll get a sore neck.'

She gave him a look but did what he said. He went over to the window. No sign of anyone.

'I'll draw the curtains. The film will be scarier in the dark.' And he wouldn't have to worry about the neighbours peering in either. He sat down beside her, leaving a reasonable gap. 'OK, are you comfortable? Take off your trainers, if you want. And turn off your phone, will you? We want the full cinema experience.'

The room reverberated with bass from the rear speakers. The extra-wide flat screened TV and integrated sound system was top-of-the-range home cinema, no comparison to the cruddy old thing Emma had to watch at home.

'Too loud?'

Emma shook her head. She'd kicked off her trainers and was slumped back on the sofa, one yellow-socked foot resting on the edge of the coffee table. She dug into the popcorn with one hand and gripped her glass of Coke with the other, taking an occasional slurp through the straw.

He tried to keep looking at the screen, but his gaze was being drawn back to Emma. She had a fresh, sweet smell after her usual long, post-swim shower. Her eyelashes curled upwards, incredibly dark and thick. Her lips, soft and plump, enticed him. Her long, glossy hair was tucked behind her delicate ear. Inside it he could see dark, spiral caverns like a seashell's. He wanted to put his lips to her ear and softly breathe into it.

'Shit!'

Paul turned back to the screen. It was dark. Something nasty was coming towards the two teenage girls. Emma gave a breathy little scream.

He touched Emma's arm, gently, as if to comfort her. She didn't move. He wondered if she'd object if he rested his hand companionably on the thick denim covering her thigh. She was cocooned in layers – a sloppy, cheap woollen sweater, and below that, a cotton garment. He wished he could take off all her clothes right now, so he could look at her, feel her skin and her warmth. But he dared not do a thing.

A gasp escaped from Emma's mouth. She hid her face behind a cushion.

Slowly, carefully, he leaned over and put his hand on her thigh. Surprise flashed over her face. Her eyes narrowed as she studied his. Then, she turned back to the screen.

She wasn't going to stop him. She didn't mind. Perhaps she wanted something to happen as much as he did.

After a few minutes, he moved his hand away. Emma resumed chomping her way through the popcorn. He watched the green digits advance on the Blu-ray player's display: 3.13pm. Time was running out. There was the drive home still to come; he had to get her back home well before six or Jane might suspect something. If he didn't do something soon, it would be too late.

'I'll go and get the camera,' he said.

Emma shrieked as he opened the door. One of the sisters had turned into a werewolf.

'I can't watch!' She raised the cushion to cover her face.

He returned and put the camera on the coffee table.

'Shit, this is so scary.' She flopped back on the sofa, dispatching the cushion to one side.

Finally, the credits started to roll. He took the remote and pressed eject.

'OK, Em, are you ready?' He took off the camera's protective case and switched on the lights. 'We need five or six really good shots of you.'

'Wait one minute.' She fussed around with a compact, dabbing candyfloss-coloured goo on her lips. Her cheeks were already flushed.

He pointed to the wall behind, a perfect backdrop, white enough for good light reflection. 'Stand over there, sweetie, and look into the camera.'

She got up immediately and posed quite naturally, one leg bent against the wall, arms loose at her sides, smiling nicely. Click.

'Can I look?' She skipped over to peer into the camera. The result was fine. Better than he'd expected.

'Now,' he said, 'let's have a few more. More attitude, this time. Think of Rosie whatever-her-name-is.' What was her name, Emma's current favourite model? 'Rosie Huntington-Whiteley, that's it.'

He knelt on the sofa, digging his elbows into the top of it to steady the camera, and zoomed in on her face. The modelling contests she watched on TV must have rubbed off, he thought, as she slipped with ease through a range of poses and expressions. She probably would make a good model – she had no shyness whatsoever in front of the camera.

'Em, that's great. Monica will love these, I'm sure. But we need a few bikini shots. You have to show them you're nearly grown up, not some dopey twelve-year-old.'

She shook her head. 'I don't have a bikini. Only my costume from the pool.'

'No, that won't do. It's fine for swimming, but it's not exactly fetching, is it?' Mock despondently, he scratched his head. 'I know. Why don't you take off your things and I'll take a photo of you in your underwear? That's the same thing, pretty much. Better, in fact. It'll add a touch of spice. That's important, these days.'

She giggled, as if he'd told her a risqué joke. 'OK, then.'

His heart was going like the clappers, it would burst out of him any second. Christ, she was going to do it. Pursing her lips, she pulled off the wool sweater and cotton top together, revealing a simple blue cotton bra. Padded, by the look of it. A moment's hesitation then she quickly pulled down the zipper of her jeans and stepped out of them. She looked at him with a coquettish smile. Her panties matched the bra. They only just covered her pubic hair.

'Will this do?'

'You have a fabulous body,' he said.

Her eyes fixed to his, as a shy horse inspects a stranger at the fence. It wanted the sugar in your hand, only it didn't trust you enough to let you come near. He came around the side of the sofa, settled himself on the arm, and raised the camera. She was going to do whatever he asked. His groin strained against the tight denim.

'Come on, give me some raunch. Pretend you're a naughty girl. Yes, like that.'

Click, click. Click, click, click.

'Pull the strap down a bit. Let's see a little more – that's it. Don't be shy. Give me that teasing look again … perfect.'

Paul looked at his watch. 'OK, that's enough.'

Emma strode to the pile of clothes on the floor.

'Hey, no need to be in such a hurry to get dressed.' He gestured to the sofa. 'Come and sit down for a sec and look at these. We might need to repeat one or two shots.' She perched awkwardly on the edge of the seat beside him, clutching her cotton top in one hand. He held the camera close as the photos skipped by in the viewfinder, aware of the fascination and pleasure passing over her face. He reached the last photo. It was extra special – he would treasure that one. Her eyes shone with the knowledge of her beauty and its impact on him. Her parted lips and slightly raised eyebrows seemed to dare him to do something.

'You're a natural model, Em. Like the ones in *Glamour* magazine, but better.'

She looked pleased, but a little uncertain, one hand still holding on to the cotton top. He put the camera down on the coffee table. He had to act quickly.

'Take your bra off, sweetie.'

'Why? We've done the photos.'

'Please. Just for me. Let me see how beautiful you are. I'd like to see what you look like underneath, that's all.'

Stubbornness crept into her voice. 'No, I don't want to.'

'Please, Em. I just want to look. You have a beautiful body.'

She stared, about to bolt.

'Go on,' he cajoled. 'I won't do anything, I promise.'

She sighed in protest but let go of the top. Then she pulled down her bra straps, dragged the fasteners to the front, and unhooked it, placing it on the seat beside her. And there, before him, were two perfect, creamy peaks, their tips darkening to a dusky mauve.

His breath drew in. Her breasts weren't quite as small as he'd expected, just big enough for a first bra. But he hadn't realised how lovely they were. She always kept them hidden under her baggy tops.

'You're beautiful,' he said.

Hardly daring to breathe, he leaned across and brushed his lips against her velvet earlobe, then the downy rim of her ear. When he touched her mouth with his lips she jerked her head away, looking at him wide-eyed, as if she'd just been kicked. Her eyes were bigger and darker than he'd ever seen them.

'It's alright, sweetie,' he whispered. 'I'm not going to hurt you.'

He reached out and felt the softness of her breast. She didn't move. Her eyes seemed so big in her pale little face.

'Don't be scared, Em. I'm going to give you the most wonderful feeling you've ever had.' He could almost hear her murmur of delight.

'No, I want to go home.'

She removed his hand and tried to stand up. He pushed her back down, firmly enough that she'd know he meant it. She tensed, protested. He wondered if she would yell and if he should put his hand over her mouth. He had the fleeting thought that he ought to give this up now and let her go – this could only end in disaster.

But he couldn't stop. His need filled him, a desperate, insane need that went beyond any boundary. This time, he would do what he craved. Slowly, gently, without hurting her too much. Soon, he was certain, she would enjoy it. This dark angel would surrender to him.

'I'll never forget this,' he said. 'Not for as long as I live.'

It was over. He wanted to hold her close for a little while longer. But they had to leave now.

'Put your clothes back on, sweetie. Don't you want to have a wash in the bathroom before we go?' She didn't seem to hear him. A cloudy dribble was making its way down her thigh. 'Sit up, that's a girl.'

Emma looked bewildered. He left her sitting on the sofa, naked, hugging her knees.

In the bathroom, he quickly examined the mess of red scratches on his lower back. Luckily, most weren't deep. They would heal before Suzanne had a chance to notice – if he was careful. He would leave his T-shirt on in bed for a while.

He washed himself quickly. The joy and exhilaration were fading. In their place, a heaviness, pressing down on him, trying to suck the air out of him. He heard a voice from somewhere.

Scumbag. You shouldn't have done that.

He stood for a few moments, holding on to the basin. A voice in his head? This wasn't like him. He wasn't one of those nutters who heard voices. He was sweating royally now, his heart all over the place.

Come on, he silently replied. *This isn't fair. She wanted it too. The blush on her cheeks, the hot little breaths. They were evidence, weren't they?* He'd intended to loiter on the edges, stay a gentleman to the last, but it had been easier than he'd imagined to break through that little barrier – perhaps she'd tried it before, with one of the boys at school. She hadn't pushed him away, had she? Not after that first bout of resistance, that sudden attack with her nails. She'd let him slide in to taste those sweet depths.

They wouldn't see it that way, would they? The people she told. They would make out he'd done something wrong.

Shit.

Paul turned on the tap and lowered his hands beneath the gush of water. He tried to think straight, to get control of himself. What had he done? He shouldn't have let himself go like that. Christ, he was a fucking idiot. He was pushing his luck to think he could get away with it a second time. After all these years, Laura had never said anything to Suzanne as far as he knew – yet it was always there, lurking in his mind, the thought that one day she might break her promise and expose him. Lately, since her visit, the thought had pressed down on him more than ever, waking him in the stillness of the night. And now, he'd gone and strung a second weight around his neck. They could get him for this. They could well and truly hang him up by the balls. What would happen now, for Christ's sake?

Emma will go blabbing to her mother, that's what. She'll tell her mother, and all her friends at school, that she was raped by the man who was meant to be looking after her.

When he came back into the living room, Emma was dressed. She sat on the sofa, head lowered, both arms wrapped around the bag on her lap. The lace of her trainer trailed across the carpet.

'Don't look so miserable, Em.'

She didn't respond. A smudge of pinkish gloss hung below her bottom lip. He reached into his pocket for his handkerchief and wiped it off.

'I want to go now,' she said in a small voice, not looking at him.

He checked his watch: 5.11pm, Jane would be back at home soon. He switched on his phone in case she called.

'Before I take you home, Emma, I want you to promise me something.' He waited for her to look up at him. 'You must promise not to tell anyone about this.'

Her eyes flickered slightly, as if assessing the seriousness of his request.

'You promised you wouldn't do anything,' she said. 'You lied.'

'I didn't mean to do that. I'm sorry.'

Why did you then? her eyes demanded. But she stayed silent.

He moved so his face was level with hers.

'Emma, you mustn't tell anyone about what we did just now – not even your mum. If you tell her, or anyone else, do you know what I'll do?'

She moved her head slightly.

He thought quickly. What the fuck could he do? It had better work, whatever it was.

'I'll show your mum the photos. And I'll put them on social media. They give it away, Emma. They show how much you wanted me, how you were trying to tempt me. Your face was full of it. No one will buy that it was all just meant for some model agency. You know what your mum will think about you then, don't you? What all your friends will think? That you're just a little slut, gagging for it. You wouldn't want that, would you?'

Her mouth opened. She blinked rapidly.

'I swear, I'll never tell anyone.'

'Remember, Emma. I meant what I said. Keep quiet, or you'll regret it.'

She nodded, her face white.

Thank God he'd got through to her. It was bad to talk to her like that, but now she wouldn't tell on him. If his luck held out, no one would ever suspect a thing.

On the way back, Emma stared out of the window. Despite his efforts to lighten the mood, her silence was unbroken, a cloud of poison filling the car.

He knew that it was his fault she was like this. It wasn't how he'd planned their last moments together. He wanted his cheeky, high-spirited girl back again. Not this sourpuss, off its milk. But he hadn't done anything so very bad, had he? He'd only given her a foretaste of what she would experience later. She would be back to her old self soon enough. One day, years from now, she'd probably brag to her boyfriends about this older guy who had taken her swimming, and taught her a thing or two outside the pool as well.

He turned in to Jane's road. Kids were playing with their bikes on the pavement. Suddenly, Emma looked at him.

'You lied about the photos too, didn't you? You don't know anyone in a model agency, do you? You just said that to get what you wanted.'

A knife twisted in his heart. *What could he say to that?*

'I'm sure you'll find an agency soon. Really. You have talent, looks—'

'I don't care about modelling anymore,' she said, quietly, looking ahead through the windscreen. 'You can keep the photos, I never want to see them.'

He pulled up in front of Jane's. Behind the curtains, the windows were unlit.

'Goodbye, Em. I'll miss you.' He squeezed her hand. It was cold, lifeless.

She pulled her hand free and stepped out of the car. The door clunked shut. The finality of the sound struck him, made his throat clench tight.

This was it then, the moment he'd been dreading. He watched Emma open the gate and walk down the path to the house. He waited for her to turn her key in the lock and go inside, then he drove home.

12

Laura

28 March 2011

Baked beans, 99p a can. Laura put three tins in her basket and hurried on to the breakfast cereals, ignoring the stacked freezer of ready meals. She chose Sainsbury's own brand porridge oats, the cheapest per kilogram, and made a quick calculation.

Three tins of baked beans, a packet of oats, four bananas, four apples, a wholemeal loaf, a packet of potatoes, a carton of apple juice. It wasn't quite ten pounds. She had just enough money for some eggs, and maybe a bottle of shampoo.

At the supermarket checkout, she handed over three five-pound notes and took the change.

The day was cool and drizzly. She glanced at the betting shop as she passed. A man in a cheap suit hurried out and strode off, humming under his breath. Perhaps she could bet thirty pounds on a horse or a football game, and win hundreds. Except for office raffles and wagers with her brother, she'd never bet on anything in her life. Then a woman of around sixty, with wispy dark-rooted blonde hair and a depressed expression, came out and trudged along the pavement, head down.

Laura hurried on along North End Road, wondering how long she would be without a job. Hopefully she wouldn't end up filling in the empty hours with visits to the betting shop. Rachel had phoned last night and had tried to be encouraging, told her it wouldn't be much longer before she found a job, but they were only words. Rachel's advice was to apply for a wider range of jobs, to lie about her employment experience, and to change the dates on her CV so there weren't any gaps in her work history. Well, anything was worth a shot, though she hated having to lie. It was eight weeks since she'd last worked, and each week that went by was more dispiriting than the last.

She slowed at a café and glanced at the daily specials board outside – shepherd's pie for £3.99. It was the sort of dirt cheap place she'd never normally go into, where everything was fried and the air stank of stale chip fat. But it was warm and bright inside, and there was a vacant table in the corner.

Studying the menu, she took out the last note from her purse – a fiver.

'I'll have scrambled eggs on toast, please.'

'Anything to drink?'

'A cup of tea, please.'

The waitress, a girl of eighteen or so, smelling of cigarettes, departed without enthusiasm. Laura looked around at the plastic tablecloths and picture-less walls. A calendar showed a topless blonde leaning over a sports car. Two rough-looking men in casual jackets argued at a nearby table. Behind them, a white-haired man in a hair-strewn coat hunched over a crossword.

She ate her meal quickly, feeling guilty for succumbing to temptation. The eggs were hot and fluffy but lacked flavour. As she sipped her tea, her thoughts turned to her worsening financial situation. It was on her mind constantly these days. She'd managed to pay the rent for February out of her last wage. But March's rent, due in advance on the first of the month, was still unpaid, and soon April's rent would be due. She'd applied to increase her overdraft at the bank but had been refused. She had no credit card and no way of getting credit without a job.

A rack on the wall held *The Sun*, a month-old copy of *Hello*, and two local newspapers. She picked up the less tatty newspaper and took it back to her table.

The employment section was less than a page long. Experienced receptionist wanted for a busy doctor's surgery. Gardener wanted for a large estate. Mini-cab drivers, lorry drivers, construction workers – nothing she had the remotest chance of getting, apart from the part-time jobs for cleaners, shop assistants or pizza delivery staff, all of which stated variations of 'experience and references essential'.

An advertisement in a small box at the bottom of a column caught her eye:

Girls wanted for stylish gentlemen's club. Previous experience not essential. Good money available.

She pictured herself in a black dress, carrying a silver tray of Singapore Slings into a high-ceilinged, dark, wood-panelled room, delivering drinks to aristocratic types and retired company directors lounging on high-backed armchairs, smoking cigars, and talking in muted tones about the best investments, accompanied by some chap in a black jacket playing Cole Porter on a grand piano.

But no, of course it wasn't that sort of place. It was the other kind of gentlemen's club, where near-naked girls strutted about to stir the lust of city chaps.

The 'good money' was tempting, certainly. But she didn't want to go down that road. She'd never worked in such a place and had never known anyone who had.

Gentlemen's clubs, as far as she knew, were sleazy places full of cocaine-snorting louts and desperate girls who would do anything for money.

She put the newspaper back.

'Oh, by the way,' she said, after paying the woman behind the counter, 'you don't need any staff do you, by any chance?'

The woman regarded her with a gaze that was both curious and pitying, her plastic gloved hands temporarily coming to rest on the sandwich she was preparing.

''Fraid not, love. Try at the Italian café up the road, if you haven't already.'

She *had* tried them – three or four days ago. Like all the other places, they trotted out a well-practised line: 'no thanks, maybe come back in a month and check again'.

Oh, well. It was the expected outcome, not even disappointing. She smiled, thanked the woman and left the café. She would go home now and apply for some of the jobs from this morning. There had been a few advertisements on Totaljobs website that she might have a punt on, more out of habit, and for something to occupy the afternoon, than from any real hope of landing a job.

***

Laura sat down at the table and read the letter from her landlord once more. It was printed on officious, headed notepaper, the crisp expensive kind. All afternoon the letter had nagged at her, like a toothache you tried to wish away so you wouldn't have to go to the dentist:

Dear Miss Cunningham,
I am afraid I am no longer prepared to tolerate your non-payment of rent for the flat you currently occupy. If you do not pay the rent owed for the months of March and April

in full by April 16th (a total of £890), I will consider the terms of the lease broken.

In this event, I shall unfortunately have no alternative but to ask you to vacate the flat immediately. Please note that in this circumstance I shall not hesitate to take immediate legal action (and any other that may be appropriate), to obtain your removal from my property.

Regards,
Mr Francis Taylor

She put down the letter. April 16th was less than three weeks away.

Picking up a piece of scrap paper, she scribbled some figures. Her bank account was £280 overdrawn, close to her limit of £300. On top of that, there was the cost of food, travel, electricity … How would she be able to produce £900 by the middle of next month? It was next to impossible.

Stupid though it probably was, she hadn't seriously considered the possibility of losing her flat. *You'll find a job sooner or later*, she'd told herself for weeks, despite the recession. Yet one thing after another seemed to have conspired together, making losing her home a distinct possibility.

A job was as far away as ever. In the two months since her last day at the film production company, she'd had a grand total of three interviews and zero job offers. She was considering almost anything now. For weeks she'd sat at home, checking recruitment websites and filling in application forms. With each application the result was the same: no, thank you. Not even that most of the time, just a monotonous silence in response to her stream of emails. There was nothing for her anywhere, it seemed, not even temping work in an office – they required references and recent relevant experience, thank you very much.

The housing benefit money she applied for weeks ago still hadn't turned up. There'd been a delay in processing her claim due to an error in her application form, a letter informed her. It could take several weeks more to decide whether or not she was eligible for support; there would be no payment until then.

She took out a packet of digestive biscuits from the dwindling food cupboard, and stood by the window nibbling one. Outside, black wings flapped across the darkening sky. Low cloud threatened to gobble up the church spire. She tried to think without panicking, while the question in her head became ever more insistent.

So, Laura. What are you going to do?

She could find somewhere cheaper to live, perhaps. But there weren't many places as cheap as this, even sharing with others – she'd found this flat after weeks of searching for the cheapest place going. It had a bedroom just big enough for a double bed, mould growing on the walls that had to be wiped off daily, a cooker – which looked unchanged since the seventies – with a broken grill and only two rings that worked, and a fridge that growled and shuddered most of the time and was scarcely cold enough to keep anything fresh. The landlord never took any interest in the flat, and never repaired anything if he could possibly avoid it – what did she expect for such a low rent? seemed to be the unspoken rebuke. And, even if she did find somewhere cheaper, what would be the point? Even for utter dumps you had to have several hundred pounds up front.

Maybe she could call Mr Taylor's bluff, and stay without paying rent until she found an income. She was only three weeks overdue, not three months. Wasn't he being a little harsh with her, threatening to kick her out so soon? Or, she could stay with someone for a while and stop paying rent on this place. Only no one she knew had a spare room, except her father's reclusive aunt in Wales, who suffered from a long list of phobias, only washed once a week, and constantly complained about 'young people these days'.

Or maybe she could borrow some money from her brother. Except he was always short of cash, and complained that it would take forever to save enough for a mortgage. He was paying an exorbitant amount of interest on a car loan, he'd told her recently. What about Rachel? Her friend had some money stashed away towards a deposit on her dream flat. She might lend her some, possibly. Not £900 though. That was too much to ask a friend – too much to ask anyone. How would she ever pay it back?

Had the time come to go to her parents for help? They would lend her the money, they would give it to her gladly, with no requirement to pay it back until she was ready. Yet the thought of asking made her cringe. It wasn't just that she would be taking her father's money, though that was bad enough, it would be yet another reason for her parents to sigh when they compared her with her brother. And it would be admitting to them that her life to date had been a failure.

No, borrowing money wasn't the answer. She could maybe pawn the antique necklace of sapphires and diamonds that used to be her grandmother's, which must be worth a few hundred pounds. But it was the only thing she had from her grandmother and it was the most beautiful piece of jewellery she owned. Anyway, she didn't need a pile of cash that sooner or later would be gone, she needed a job.

She went back to the table, picked up the handwritten sheet with details of the jobs she was considering applying for, and studied each of them in turn.

The cleaning job in Shepherd's Bush paid £7 an hour for a twenty-hour week. She could get there by Tube or bus. Only, the thought of getting up at 5.30am to clean dirty floors and toilets … anything, pretty much, would be better than that.

Tesco wanted someone to pack shelves three days a week. The bakery – mornings only – paid much the same, not much more than the minimum wage. Yes, she could swallow her pride, not mention she was a graduate, and apply for a job like that. But what was the point? A month ago, it might have been an option, but not now. It would take too long to earn the money she needed. She put down the sheet of paper. Suddenly, everything seemed hopeless. She imagined the summons to go to court for non-payment of rent, the burly man at her front door demanding that she leave immediately, the black plastic bags holding her possessions.

She went to the table and picked up the free local newspaper, which lay on the pile of papers beside her laptop. It was folded at the jobs page. She turned it over and searched for the small boxed advertisement, with a question mark beside it in ballpoint pen.

Laura reached for the phone.

'Hello, Rascals. Can I help you?' A woman's voice, syrupy smooth.

'Hello? I saw an ad, it said you were looking for girls.'

'We're always interested in taking on new girls,' the woman replied in a gruff tone. 'If they're suitable. Have you got experience?'

'No, but I'm a quick learner. I'm good at dancing.'

'How old are you?'

'Twenty-two.'

A sniff at the other end. 'You'd have to come in first and try out. We're selective about who we take on.'

'When can I come in?'

A long pause filled with rustling paper. 'Friday afternoon, does that suit?'

'You couldn't make it any sooner, could you?'

Another long pause. 'Four thirty tomorrow, then.'

Laura wrote down the details and hung up. Suddenly, the world didn't seem so grim. They'd take her on, wouldn't they? She could dance, she was good looking. She had a flat stomach and curvy breasts – not big, but big enough. Whatever she had to do, she would learn.

She opened her underwear drawer and rifled through the contents. Wear nice underwear, the woman had instructed. She took out the black lace bra and pants and held them up. Yes, they'd do. A surge of nervous anticipation went through her as she put them on the back of the chair, ready for tomorrow.

***

'Pleased to meet you, Laura. I'm Zoe, the supervisor here. I look after the girls and make sure everything goes to plan. You'll meet the manager another time, if you come back.'

Laura smiled back and shook the offered hand. She was starting to sweat. She felt fake in this outfit, not herself at all. The shoes she was wearing, the newest and smartest pair she owned, were beginning to rub at the toes. Her skirt was too tight around the thighs to be comfortable and made walking awkward. Her bra was visible under her white shirt, which she'd discovered too late to be the only washed, ironed and vaguely suitable garment in her wardrobe.

Zoe was jotting down something on the large sheet of paper in front of her. She had a heavy chin and opaque, humourless eyes. Her hair was expensively cut, scooped behind one ear, and her nails were professionally done.

She looked about forty. There was a faded glamour and a certain hardness about her.

'So, you haven't had any experience of this sort of work?'

'Not really.'

'You have, or you haven't?'

'No, I haven't.'

'Well, before we go any further,' Zoe put her pen down on the desk of the cramped, untidy office, 'this isn't a big chain, like Spearmint Rhino.' She said the name disdainfully. 'We've got our own way of doing things here, we pride ourselves on offering a good service, on giving our customers what they want. We're looking for girls who will be responsive to those needs. We'll treat you well in return, so long as you don't step out of line.' A brisk smile. 'Anyway, Laura, let's get down to basics. You seem like a nice, well brought-up girl. Do you think you'll be OK to go up on stage wearing only a G-string?' Zoe's eyes probed her face. 'And some of the time you may have to be completely naked. To put it bluntly, Laura, men are going to get a good look at you. Some girls find that difficult.'

Laura held Zoe's gaze. 'I could do it. I'm not embarrassed about letting people see my body.'

Zoe nodded briskly and checked her watch.

'OK then, follow me. I'll introduce you to Noelle. You can show us what you can do up on stage.'

They went down a corridor, into a room with small glass tables and fake leopard-skin sofas. It looked like a nightclub, with a stage at one end and a huge mirrored ball hanging from the ceiling. All the walls were mirrored too, making the place look huge. Her heart beat faster. Zoe stopped at a sofa in front of the stage.

'Take off your clothes, Laura,' Zoe commanded, easing herself into the sofa and languidly crossing one leg over the other. 'You can keep your underwear on.'

There was nowhere to change. Was she meant to undress right here, in front of Zoe? Fingers fumbling, she stepped out of her shoes then removed her shirt, skirt and tights and placed them on the arm of the sofa, trying not to fidget while Zoe looked her slowly up and down, expressionless.

Was her body good enough? Her breasts would have stuck out more if she'd worn the other bra.

Zoe nodded and motioned for Laura to stand aside. Her attention had shifted to something else. Laura turned to follow Zoe's gaze. A leggy black girl loped towards them, wearing a skimpy Lycra top and equally skimpy shorts. A mass of dyed-blonde braids fell behind her back.

'Noelle, Laura's here to try out.'

Noelle glanced at her without interest.

'Noelle checks out all our new girls,' Zoe explained. 'She'll show you some moves up on stage. Watch her then copy as closely as you can.'

Laura followed Noelle up the steps beside the stage.

'OK, I'll do an easy one first.' Noelle sat down with her legs straight out in front of her, spread them, and lowered her stomach onto the floor, as if she'd got into that position every night for the past ten years.

This was an easy one? She tried to coax her body into something vaguely similar, but her legs wouldn't open as far as Noelle's and her stomach was still miles from the floor. As she strained her body further, she saw, out of the corner of her eye, a man looking up at her. He slouched against the door at the far end of the room. His face was pitted with small craters and his lips were set in a narrow line. He was examining her as you might check apples for bruises.

That was the whole point of it though, wasn't it? Men came here to be entertained. They didn't care how undignified you felt.

The man went up to Zoe, said something, and walked away.

'That's Ken,' Noelle murmured to her. 'He owns the club. OK, Laura, watch this.' She sprang to her feet, fastened one leg to the pole and spun herself around.

Laura took a deep breath. She managed to copy the move, sort of, and awaited the next instruction. But Noelle was nodding to Zoe.

'Thanks, Laura, that's all.'

She pulled on her shirt and buttoned it up quickly. Sweat stuck the fabric to her back. She glanced over to where Zoe and Noelle were talking, without acknowledging her presence. After a good two minutes, Zoe beckoned. She didn't look pleased. Noelle left them to it.

'You were a bit stiff, Laura, you need to loosen up a bit. But I think you'll be OK with practice.'

Laura let out a long breath. 'Thank you. Thank you so much.'

'I'll ask Jade to put you down for this Thursday. If you can come in for a couple of hours tomorrow, Noelle will show you some routines on the pole. You'll have to commit to at least two nights a week.'

She nodded. 'That's fine. When will I get paid?'

Zoe raised her eyebrows.

'I'm a bit short of cash, you see. And how much will I get?'

Her cheeks warmed. Zoe would think she was desperate.

'I'll explain how it works, Laura. You pay us an entry fee for the night – that's forty pounds – and at the end of the night you take away whatever you've earned from your dances. There's no wages as such.' Zoe smiled frostily. 'You should do OK. You're young, good-looking. Most girls are taking home a reasonable amount by the end of their third week.'

165

'How much?'

'At first you'll probably take home around a hundred pounds a night. In a few weeks, after you've got the hang of things, it could be two hundred. Three hundred if you're really good.'

Two hundred pounds a night, twice a week. It would be worth putting up with this sleazy place for that. At this rate, she had a chance to make the money she needed in time.

'Some make more than others, of course. That depends on how much the customers like you, and how far you're prepared to go.' Zoe paused. 'But you'll find out for yourself, soon enough.'

13

Suzanne

31 March 2011

'Where the hell did I put the damn thing?'

Suzanne slammed shut the last drawer in the kitchen. This was the second time in a month she'd managed to lose her gym membership card. Her brain seemed to be more of a Swiss cheese than ever. She had better find it soon, she needed to leave the house in fifteen minutes for her weekly 4pm yoga class.

After searching once again in her raincoat, her purse, her gym bag, the bedroom and everywhere else it could possibly be, she found herself entering the small room facing the garden that Paul used as an office. It had been her office too once; she liked to work there in the late afternoon, when the sun flooded that side of the house. Paul had started complaining that the desk was his, and wasn't practical to share, so these days she worked at the desk in Daniel's old room instead. But it was possible that Paul had picked up the card by mistake, without paying it much attention, and put it away with his stuff.

Everything in the room was neat as usual and carefully ordered. Paul's *National Geographic* and sailing magazines, as well as a host of business, marketing and management books, were stacked in bookcases beside the filing cabinets. The desk was clear apart from an extra-wide computer screen, paperweights of varying sizes, a paper knife, a jar with a collection of pens, and a box of his business cards.

She opened the top drawer. It contained a calculator, a ruler, two staplers, a leather-bound desk diary, and a pile of assorted papers. She shifted through them: vehicle registration papers, a half-completed passport application form, a bundle of credit card receipts tied with an elastic band, an old newspaper clipping about a yacht for sale, and a brochure listing special offers on wine.

She started on the second drawer. Her membership card wouldn't be inside it, she was almost certain. But, now she had started looking, it was hard to stop. If she didn't find the card, she might find something else that had gone astray. There was a guilty pleasure, too, in looking at what you weren't supposed to see. She checked the top compartment, full of small items of stationery – more pens, paperclips and so on, then pushed it back, exposing the section below. There was a tear-off notepad, its top page full of Paul's handwriting, and below that, various letters and documents relating to his job.

The bottom drawer was fuller than the others, and less ordered. She lifted up some of its contents: old theatre programmes, maps from overseas cities that Paul had visited on business, a guide to hotels in Bangkok, business cards from cab firms and building contractors, leaflets that had come through the letterbox, and a humorous birthday card showing a drawing of a man with a fishing rod straining to haul out a giant fish. She opened it, and read, in large, childish letters: To Daddy, With Love From Laura. After replacing the items, she groped at the back of the drawer. Snuggled into a corner was Paul's Nikon inside its case. She fished it out. It was an odd place for him to put it, she thought. Hadn't he always kept it on the shelf behind the desk? Without hesitating, she unfastened the case and switched on the camera, curious to see what photos he'd taken. Clicking the button, she reviewed the photographs. There were several of herself and Paul with their friends, Andy and Fiona, on board Andy's yacht. A couple of close-ups of a small scratch on the rear of the Porsche, scarcely visible, and another of its wheel, and a photograph of Emma.

The girl was putting on an exaggerated pout for the camera, her bottom lip stuck out, hands on hips. Suzanne drew the camera closer. The picture had an intimate quality, as if Emma and the photographer had entered their own private world. Emma had on a sweatshirt and pink lip gloss with a streak of eyeliner. There something rather flirtatious about the way she was looking at the camera, wasn't there? Where had Paul taken it? Indoors, somewhere. The background was white, and didn't look like anywhere associated with a swimming pool. Could it have been taken here, inside this house? The date – March 12, nearly three weeks ago – was shown in white at the bottom of the picture. She did a mental calculation. The twelfth had been a Saturday. That must have been the day he'd taken Emma swimming for the last time; the day she was away at the retreat.

Was something going on between Paul and Emma?

A series of mental images came to her. Her husband with Emma. Paul trying to amuse the girl, making a fuss of her, taking an interest in her – too much of an interest – while Emma laughed, flaunting her taut, young body at him.

No, she scolded herself, that was ridiculous. She was jumping to conclusions based on nothing. The photograph didn't show anything like that. All it showed was the normal exuberance of a young girl, posing for the camera, aware of her own sexuality. Jane had said Emma was getting interested in boys. Perhaps Emma had been testing out her attractiveness on Paul. That would be natural, wouldn't it?

Suzanne put the camera back in its case and into the drawer. She'd ask Paul about it later. It was 4.50pm now, too late to go to her class. She would go for a walk instead.

Specks of drizzle wetted her face as she walked along the edge of the golf course. She burrowed her hands into her jacket pockets and brought out her gym membership card.

Paul was leaning against the fridge, drinking from a bottle of beer as she chopped vegetables for a stir-fry, telling her about his day. The directors of the parent company had flown back to Chicago, after unsettling everyone by talking about falling profits.

'They're going to bring in consultants to look at restructuring options,' he said. 'We all know that means redundancies. We've heard rumours, but there's been nothing definite till now.'

She put down the knife and looked at him. 'Your job's safe, isn't it?'

'They could combine my position with Dave's, I guess. But it's too early to predict. Coleman wants to make his mark, he's keen to chop out the dead wood. I reckon he wants to offload us from the group.'

Restructuring had happened before at his company and Paul had survived, but this time … What would they do if he lost his job? He was too old to get another job quickly, or at all. Suddenly the photograph seemed trivial. Still, it would be good to be reassured she was worrying over nothing.

'Oh, by the way, Paul. The picture of Emma on your camera, when did you take it? I saw it this afternoon while I was looking for something.'

He swigged on his beer again then walked to the pedal bin and dropped the empty bottle inside. Then he turned to her, a furrow on his brow.

'I took it that last time I saw her. After we'd been to the pool.'

'What, here? At home?'

A beat. 'That's right. What were you doing anyway, looking through my desk?' His voice louder, the tell-tale reddening of his face. 'I've told you before to keep out of there.'

'For goodness sake, I was trying to find my gym card. Why was she here, in our house?'

'I told you, I brought her back here after swimming and we watched a film – don't you remember?'

She shook her head. 'No, I don't remember you saying that.'

'You must have been thinking of something else, as usual.' A dash of contempt in his voice, not quite hidden. 'We came out of the pool early, so I suggested we came back here to watch a film. I thought she might enjoy watching it better here – and it would make a change for her to be away from the mess over at Jane's.'

She tried to fit the information together in her head. 'But why did you take a photo of her?'

'When she saw my camera on the table, she asked if I'd mind taking a few photos of her, she wanted to send some off to a model agency. I didn't see any harm in it.'

'Where are the others? There was only one of her on the camera.'

He shrugged. 'They didn't turn out too well – I deleted them. That one, I thought I'd send to Emma.' He carried the salad bowl to the table, sat down, and started helping himself to salad. 'Is anything wrong?'

She didn't reply immediately, examining her mental image of the photograph.

'It's just that she looked so … I don't know. Coquettish.'

'Oh, Emma loves posing, she was just acting up for the camera. She was trying to look like the models in *Glamour* magazine.' He put the tongs back in the bowl with a dull clatter.

'She looks like she was trying to come on to you, almost.'

'Yes, I know what you mean. But models look like that these days, don't they?' He sprinkled salt over his salad. 'Come and eat, Suze, stop worrying.'

She sat down at the table, opposite him, in her usual place. Paul had mentioned Emma being keen on the idea of modelling as a future career. She remembered that, at any rate.

There was nothing to worry about, she told herself. What he had said made sense. But she was still a little uneasy. Why hadn't he said anything before, about Emma coming to the house? Her memory couldn't be that bad. Surely, she wouldn't have forgotten something like that. Perhaps he'd said it while she was thinking about something else.

I'll ring Jane, she decided. Yes, she'd mention the photo of Emma and the modelling thing. They hadn't had a decent conversation for ages; Jane was so busy nowadays. Tomorrow, or over the weekend. Weekday evenings were never the best time to talk. Jane would be preparing dinner, in the middle of eating it, or collapsed in front of the TV.

After dinner, Paul went into the office to work on his computer. Suzanne watched Marmaduke squeeze in through the cat flap. He brushed against her legs and purred as she scraped the last of the chicken pieces into his bowl.

14

Laura

31 March 2011

A mass of people swirled into Hammersmith underground station, like water going down a plughole. Laura pulled her canvas bag closer to her side, forcing her way against the flow, up the steps and out into the damp evening. All her gear for tonight was inside the bag – the black silk wrap that she'd borrowed from Noelle, which just covered her bottom, as well as the three-inch-high silver platforms, shameless wisp of a G-string, black lace garter and fishnet stockings – everything except the elbow-length black gloves, which none of the department stores she tried had in stock. It was probably just as well – in total she'd had to fork out nearly eighty quid, paid out of money she had set aside for Tube fares and the electric meter.

She checked her watch again: 6.58pm, she was going to be late for her first shift. Why hadn't she left fifteen minutes earlier? It was just her luck, having to wait twenty minutes for a Tube, tonight of all nights. Her trainers slapped against the pavement. She walked as fast as she could, dodging shoppers and office workers. Her mouth was dry but there was no time to stop and take a drink.

She felt fear and excitement in turn. Soon, she'd be wearing next to nothing in front of a roomful of strangers, doing things that before this week she'd never imagined herself doing. And how would she ever remember all the things Noelle had shown her?

She shivered. What on earth would Rachel say if she knew? She'd be surprised, certainly, and probably none too pleased. And what if her mother found out? She'd be horrified. As for her father, God knows what he'd think. He'd probably fly off his perch, making out she was the lowest of the low.

Laura turned in to a side street, past spiky railings guarding smart terraces. At the fourth street on the right, she stopped. Was this the turning, the street without a sign? Everything looked different in the dark. She walked a little way down it.

This was the building. It looked similar to the offices on either side, except the door was painted in a deep plum shade, and a gold plaque on the wall proclaimed the name of the club in Gothic script: Rascals. She crossed the road and went up the steps to the front door.

I could go home now. It's not too late to change my mind.

No, she couldn't chicken out now. What would she do if she was kicked out of her flat? She pressed the buzzer.

A voice blared through the intercom. 'Rascals, good evening.'

She wet her lips. 'I'm Laura, Sarina, I mean. I'm starting work tonight.' Sarina was her working name. Noelle had suggested it, saying most of the girls had one, and Sarina sounded more exotic than Laura.

There was a loud buzz. She pushed the door and went in. A heavily made up girl in a strappy black dress eyed her from behind the reception desk.

'Zoe, there's someone new starting, can you come?'

Laura pulled the water bottle from her bag and recovered her breath. She drank some water and wiped her mouth with the back of her hand. For the first time, she noticed the shiny potted plants and the black leather sofas in the entrance area. The receptionist stared at her for a few seconds then switched her attention back to her magazine.

'Laura?' Zoe wore black leather trousers and a low-cut top. Her neck and arms were strewn with gold.

'Sorry I'm late, my train was delayed.'

Zoe's face stayed stony. 'Come in, I'll show you where to change.'

They went down a dimly lit passage, past framed drawings of nudes. Zoe opened a door and motioned for her to go inside. The air was overloaded with perfume, its sweetness offset with a sprinkling of stale sweat. There was scarcely room for anyone else to fit in the room. Benches and pegs disappeared under heaps of discarded clothes. Shoes, bags, towels and toiletries almost hid the floor. The place didn't look particularly hygienic. A patch of pale flakes garnished the floor where someone had been eating a croissant, and the waste bin was overflowing with blood-stained tissues. Girls in various stages of undress clustered around a mirror above a row of washbasins, applying make-up and false lashes and spraying hair. In one corner, a girl with vampish nails, a shiny black corset, a jet choker, and the shortest of shorts, sat cross-legged on the floor, peering into a thick volume that was open in front of her, as if she were quite alone. A cross-section of a heart stared out from the page.

The door closed. Laura hesitated. She felt like the new girl at school. She tried in vain to find an empty spot to put her things.

'Hello, darling. Squeeze in beside me, if you like.'

A girl with big brown eyes in an elfin face grinned at her. She had pink-streaked, jaw-length hair, and was wearing false lashes, a sparkly red bra with matching briefs, and dangerously high red platforms. A black and yellow striped snake with outstretched fangs coiled around her belly button.

'Hi, I'm Sam.' The girl plucked a dried apricot from the packet she was holding and put it into her mouth. 'This is your first time?'

Laura nodded. 'Yes, I'm Laura, I mean, Sarina.'

'Hi, Sarina. Sam's my real name, by the way. I couldn't be bothered to think of another one.'

Sam made space on the bench so she could put her bag down then bent to examine a shoe. A small blue butterfly flapped over the left cheek of her bottom.

Laura removed a smelly towel from the peg nearest her, the only one not burdened with clothes, and hung up her jacket. She sensed a multitude of eyes flicking in her direction, like curious animals watching a human who'd strayed into their territory. Someone bumped her from behind as she took off her T-shirt.

It was far too hot in this place. She sat down and wiped her palms on her jeans before taking them off. Everyone seemed to be ready, except for her, adding finishing touches to their faces or adjusting straps on their heels and lingerie. She took another swig from her bottle and removed her pants, snatched her G-string from her bag and wriggled into it. It was even more uncomfortable than when she'd tried it on. She put on her lace lingerie set, dragged the fishnets up as high as they'd go and attached them to her garter, and tied the black silk gown around her waist. Then she fastened her platforms and tottered over to the mirror, swaying from one foot to the other.

Yes, she looked different. Sleekly, decadently glamorous, as captivating as the others. The high heels made her legs look incredibly long. They were difficult to walk in, though, let alone dance.

'Hey, Laura,' Sam called. 'Put some blusher on, darling. And you need some redder lipstick. Here, have some of mine. You'll earn more if you look sexy.'

Laura took the lipstick. Reluctantly, she pressed it over her lips, brushed Sam's blusher onto her cheeks and stared the girl in the mirror. Her face looked gaudy, a tart's face. She took out the little zippered, elasticated pouch from her bag, and positioned it above her elbow, as Sam had done with hers.

'Girls, are you ready, is everyone sorted? Josie, have you put on weight again?' Zoe strode towards a big-breasted girl, who was wearing a see-through top over tight hot pants that accentuated the flesh beneath. 'I know the men like big boobs, but I don't think they're so keen on big bums.'

A few girls laughed loudly, turning to examine the culprit.

'I'm going on a diet, Zoe,' mumbled the girl under scrutiny. 'I'm going to lose five kilos by next week.'

Zoe moved on. 'Anabelle, that bra makes you look frumpy. It looks like something my granny would wear. Can anyone lend her something else?'

There was a flurry of activity while another set of lingerie was found, then silence as Zoe examined the rest of them. Laura felt Zoe's gaze on her own body, before the woman turned away without making any further comments. She breathed a sigh. She'd passed the night's first test. Everyone moved towards the door, except for herself and Sam.

'Don't look so worried, darling, you'll be fine.' Sam stuffed the last of the dried fruit into her mouth and tossed the empty bag to the floor. 'Stick with me, if you like, till you get the hang of it.'

The club was almost empty. Clumps of men in suits sat around tables in twos and threes, talking and drinking. Most were in their twenties and thirties. Zoe flitted about, businesslike, chatting to her customers. A burly guy in jeans and a dark shirt stood near the entrance to the room, looking bored. Girls strategically positioned themselves near the men, whom they greatly outnumbered, either alone or in pairs. Every so often, a girl went over to a table, sat down and started up a conversation. A minute or two later they'd move off to another table. No one wanted a dance yet.

Laura clasped her hands behind her back. The monotonously heavy beat of the dance music reverberated through her body. She was conspicuous here, standing under these bright lights so close to the stage. Though she didn't want to leave Sam, she'd prefer to stand in the darker area at the back. Here, she was on display. Every few minutes a man would look her up and down as if she were a car in a dealer's yard. Were her wheels scuffed? Was her steering off? She pulled down her garter a little, so it was less tight.

'Come with me,' Sam suddenly hissed, nodding at the nearest sofa where two guys lounged in business shirts, ties off and collars undone, their glasses empty. 'They've refused everyone so far. But we might get lucky.'

As they approached, one of the guys gave her a lingering look with no hint of a smile. He had small, deep-set eyes and an oddly pronounced forehead.

The other one was better looking. 'Hi, girls,' he said, introducing himself as Dave and the other as Roger.

Sam sat in the armchair near Dave. 'Hiya, guys. How're you this evening?'

Laura hesitated and sat down on the sofa beside Roger, the only spare seat. She let Sam do the talking.

They hadn't been here before, someone at work had suggested they give it a try. They were traders for an American bank in the City.

Roger scratched his thigh and cleared his throat.

'Have you been working here long?' He meant her, not Sam, but Sam answered for her.

'I've been here for two years. Sarina hasn't been here for long.'

'Is that right?' Roger cocked his head to one side and examined her with renewed interest.

'That's right,' she replied, not knowing what else to say.

They talked on, or rather Sam and Dave did, about the excesses of their day. Roger joined in from time to time with less enthusiasm. Laura fidgeted. They should leave these two alone, she thought, trying to catch Sam's eye.

Roger leaned over and spoke in his friend's ear then smiled at Sam.

'How 'bout a dance then, girls?'

Sam smiled back and uncrossed her legs. Laura forced a smile. It was what they were here for, but she wasn't ready yet. She looked around. The rest of the tables were filling up. A petite blonde with oversized breasts was swaying her hips at a nearby table.

Roger was holding out a twenty-pound note. She unzipped her money belt and put the folded note inside. When she looked up, Sam had arranged herself between Dave's legs.

Laura got to her feet. Roger opened his legs to make a space for her. She lowered herself into it, her back to him as Noelle had showed her. Her heart crashed against her chest. She was trapped. He was too close, she didn't want him to be so close, she didn't want to be anywhere near him. She took a slow breath and concentrated on remembering what she had to do next.

Her movements felt forced and awkward, not at all sexy. She drew herself slowly to her full height, leaving a hair's breadth between her back and his shirt, then stepped away from him. Her hands were shaking slightly as she fumbled at the hook of her bra. She turned to face her first customer, expecting interest or pleasure or amusement, something. But Roger's eyes were blank. She stepped forward, crouching, so her nipples brushed the middle of his shirt – as Noelle had done to her when they'd been practising – then inched upright until her breasts were level with his face. He jerked forward as if to catch one in his mouth. She moved away just in time. No touching, Noelle had said.

She knelt on the floor, her eyes locked on his, and slid her panties down to expose the shiny black G-string. All she had to do was concentrate on being sexy. She moved from one position to the next. The routine she'd learned was still in her brain, thankfully. She gyrated her hips, lay on her back, opened her legs wide and snapped them shut like scissors. She did all the moves she could remember. Finally, she stood in front of him and bent over double, until the tips of her hair touched the floor and Roger's face appeared through the V of her legs. Thank God she wasn't naked. Then she stood up and gave him a smile.

It's over. She wiped her palms on her thighs. *The first one's over.*

Sam, finished already, stood waiting a few feet away.

'You weren't bad, darl', considering it was your first time.'

'It was so weird.'

Sam laughed, making the snake on her belly wriggle. 'You'll get used to it. C'mon, let's keep moving.'

They walked slowly around the tables, searching. Sam pulled her bra strap off her shoulder.

An amplified male voice filled the room. 'First up, the lovely Noelle!'

Laura glanced back at the stage. Noelle was stripping to a G-string. A glistening brown streak with a flash of white over her crotch, she strutted towards the pole and began to twirl around it, her thighs bulging as her legs contorted into one unlikely position after the next, her breasts inscribing dizzy circles, her nipples erect, a cross between a ballerina and an acrobat on steroids.

Sam, not interested in what was happening on stage, nudged Laura's arm.

'Gotta pee, back in a sec ... see that one over there?' She pointed to a young guy, sitting alone in an alcove. 'He looks lonely. Why not go and say hi?'

Anxious and annoyed, she did as instructed; Sam was meant to be looking after her, not leaving her to fend for herself.

'Hi there. Can I join you?'

'Sure.'

The guy took a gulp of beer. He was barely twenty, she guessed, casually dressed with steel-framed glasses. Ordinary looking. More nervous than she was even.

His name was Ben. He supported Tottenham Hotspur and he was studying civil engineering, he told her readily, without elaborating. There was an awkward pause while she tried to think of suitable topics of conversation. Football and hobbies to start with, Noelle had recommended. The weather, TV programmes, and the news, if you're really stuck. Never work, wives or girlfriends.

'So, what do you do when you're not studying?'

He gave her an awkward smile and looked into the table. Oh, shit. It sounded like she was chatting him up. She sipped her Diet Coke. All this was so artificial. She didn't want to know about his hobbies. She knew what he was here for and so did he. Why not just get on with it? All this waiting made it worse than ever. She gathered up her courage.

'Would you like a dance?'

'Great.' He reached for his wallet and handed her a few notes. She glanced around. Two other girls were dancing, she wouldn't be the only one. And they were tucked away in a corner here, away from the others.

She nestled between his legs. It was strange, switching to this sudden intimacy after the stumbling conversation. But dancing was easier than talking, in a way – she knew how to be sexy, there was nothing complicated about it. She closed her eyes, sent her mind back.

It was all there, somewhere inside her.

She hadn't needed to do anything except stay, and go along with whatever her father had wanted. Her body, for those minutes it was required, was his to watch or to touch as he pleased. It had been their private ritual, a repeated performance that never failed to satisfy. She had seen his desire close up, and known that she was the reason for it. All she had to do now was dig down to find that place, become that girl again.

Laura opened her eyes. With her back to her customer, she moved herself slowly up and down in front of him. She removed her bra, this time without fumbling, turned to face him and came up close. His eyes followed the movement of her nipples as they moved up the buttons of his shirt. She could sense the excitement in his breath, in the shine of his eyes. She stood, her legs astride him, and cupped her breasts in her hands – just as the small blonde had done – slowly circling her hips. He blinked, his eyes fixed on her. She was getting the hang of this. It wasn't so scary anymore.

'Thanks, that was great.'

He sounded sincere. Perhaps this was his first time in a place like this too. She plucked her lingerie from the floor.

A shard of light pierced her eyes from a mirrored ball above. She turned away, drawing stale air into her lungs.

'Next up – Anabelle!' A stir went through the room. Laura turned toward the stage. Lacklustre applause as the next girl ran up.

'Come on, fellas, give her some encouragement!'

A spasm of anxiety went through her, settling low and icky inside her stomach. She'd be up there soon. It was one thing dancing for a single guy, down here. But up there, under the spotlights, for everyone to see?

Sam reappeared at her side. 'Fancy a drink?' She stuck out her tongue. 'I'm parched. Come on, it'll help you dance.'

On stools at the bar, three girls were seated. They were allowed to drink two glasses of alcohol during their shifts, as long as they didn't get drunk or misbehave.

'Zoe's in a strop tonight,' a tall girl said in a South African accent. 'I'm glad she didn't have a go at me for looking like an old crone. I'll be thirty next week.'

Moments later, Zoe appeared and tapped the blonde's forearm.

'Lucy, aren't you on next? You should be over there ready to go by now. And, Sarina, you go on after Heather.' Zoe appraised her with cold eyes then turned to the South African girl. 'Heather, make sure you're ready in plenty of time.'

Laura took her drink and followed Sam to look for another dance.

'All the guys like Lucy,' Sam said, rotating her neck while she massaged it. Lucy was up on stage, an impish smile on her face as she approached the pole. 'She looks so innocent, but she'll do anything with a bit of encouragement. She's only eighteen, you know.'

'Are those real? Her boobs, I mean.'

'She had them done just after she started here. Lots of us have, you earn more money with big tits.'

'You too?'

Sam was nicely curvy on top – a C cup at most, she guessed.

'Not yet. I might one day, if I need to. I've had Botox though, I get it every month. And I'm always at the beauty salon. You've got to look after yourself if you want to earn good money.'

'How long have you been here?'

'Three years in June, and two years before that in another place. I know, it's a long time.' Her gaze slipped away. 'I wanted to be doing something else by now, uni, or something, but this is better than a lot of jobs, believe me.'

'Go, girl!' shouted a leather-jacketed man from a table at the front, waving a bottle of beer. The men around him looked up at the stage and winked at one another.

'I Want Your Sex' by George Michael ended. Lucy waved and pulled teasingly at the G-string, flashed her shaved pussy then skipped offstage. She seemed to have no inhibitions whatsoever.

One by one, the others went up on stage – black, white, Asian, mixed race. Most were in their twenties or early thirties, she guessed, and slim. Some were fluid and graceful, spinning and stretching their bodies like haughty peacocks. Others seemed to just put their bodies through the motions, their faces lifeless, as if they'd done their routine too many times.

'Better get ready now,' Sam said, after they'd done the rounds of the floor and found no takers for dances. 'Heather's about to come off.'

Another song started.

Laura put down her glass. The tables in front of the stage were all full now. Everyone would be watching her every move – literally – they'd be sure to know this was her first time. She took a deep breath. What if they didn't like her?

Her song, 'Sex Machine', boomed out of the speakers. She waited for her cue to go on then ran up onto the stage, late. She was Sarina now, not Laura. The light was dazzling. She could see nothing below the stage, only darkness.

She dropped her gown and walked uncertainly towards the pole. No one clapped or cheered. Her feet seemed glued to the floor.

'Get on with it, darling!'

She tried to concentrate. If she could block out everyone around her, she'd be fine. She gripped the pole with one hand, positioned her foot on it, and launched herself. Once, twice, three times she swung around, her other arm limp at her side. Her hands were so damp it was hard to get a grip. She did some other moves that Noelle had shown her, and stepped away from the pole.

'Show us your pussy, sweetheart!'

She stared down into the glare of the lights but couldn't see who had shouted. Suddenly, it was all wrong. Titillating men who cared nothing about the person she really was – what was she doing up here, for God's sake? She had an urge to run off the stage and keep going, out of the club.

But it had to be done.

She forced a smile, as if she did this all the time, as if she was loving every moment, and undid her bra. She went through her positions on the floor. Lastly, she bent over at the hips, bum to the audience, and wriggled her pants down to her ankles so her body was bare, save for the G-string and platforms.

The song ended. She hurried down the steps.

'Passable,' Sam told her afterwards. 'Try to enjoy it more, next time. Or look like you are.'

Things got better after that. She got a third lap dance, then a fourth and a fifth. Her confidence increased a little each time. One man, who said he'd been drinking all evening before coming to the club, left her a twenty-pound tip. The more they drank, the more generous they seemed to get.

Around 1am, she guessed, the club began to thin out. They weren't allowed to wear watches, Noelle had told her, as it didn't look good to be constantly checking the time. Laura sat on a stool at the bar. Her feet were aching from the high heels. She didn't want to do another dance before the end of her shift.

Zoe walked by with a frown cast in her direction. Laura got to her feet. She knew she should be hustling for business; even if you were turned down, you were meant to keep asking. She went up to a nearby table where Sam had danced a few minutes earlier. Three businessmen sat around a bottle of Krug in an ice bucket.

'Darling, come over, will you?'

He had cropped hair and an expensively-styled suit, as did the other two.

Laura looked at the money he was waving at her. At first it had looked like a couple of tenners, but no, it was two twenties. He rolled up the notes and put them into the top of her stocking.

'Take everything off, will you.'

He spoke tersely. She didn't want to dance naked, as Lucy and the others had done. Not yet anyway, even if it meant getting forty pounds rather than twenty. It felt too uncomfortable, too much like a violation. What if he reached out and touched her? It was against the rules, but that might not stop them.

She saw the flash of irritation on his face. No, she couldn't get out of it, not now. She took off her wrap and started.

The stale smoke and garlic on his breath turned her stomach. He had three deep lines on his forehead and a deep line curving around each side of his mouth.

The first part was easy enough. When that was done, her hands slid down to her stomach, fingers playing with the top of her G-string. He picked up his glass, his eyes on her moving hips. She arched her back and bent over, whisked the flimsy piece of material past her knees and stepped out, naked. This was the part they liked best, Noelle had said, 'you have to take your time at the end, wave your arse at them, let them see all your assets. Then they'll be happy and give you a good tip.'

Laura brushed her hair from her eyes, heart pounding, and picked up her things. She had finished the dance too quickly, and he didn't look pleased. There wouldn't be a tip.

In the remaining time, nothing much happened. The men had almost all gone or were in the process of leaving. She tried not to show it, but her spirits had sunk to the floor. How would she ever get used to this? But the first naked dance was always the hardest, according to Sam.

The club had almost emptied of customers, when an invisible signal sent every girl fleeing towards the changing room, like birds changing direction mid-flight. Laura followed. At last, her first shift was over.

Everyone was jostling for space, peeling off clothes and stuffing things into bags. She sat on the bench and pulled out the banknotes from her money belt. She unfolded each one as she counted. Forty, sixty, eighty ... one hundred and forty pounds. It wasn't as much as she'd hoped, and she'd already paid forty pounds to Zoe just to get in, but she'd make more next time.

She unfastened her platforms and placed her aching feet on the floor. The cold was soothing. She wiped off her lipstick, stuffed her gear into her bag, and dressed as quickly as she could. A squawk of voices filled the room – the birds were about to escape their cage. The first ones were on their way already.

'Sarina, before you go, will you go and see Ken in the office?' It was Zoe.

Had she done something wrong? Or was there something else she had to do, before Ken would let her come back? Half of her hoped he wouldn't want her to come back.

She hurried down the passage to the small room where Zoe had interviewed her. The door was open. Ken leaned back in a swivel chair, puffing on a cigarette, his legs stretched out on the desk. An angle-poise lamp cast a harsh circle of light on papers strewn over the desk, leaving Ken's face shadowed, without pockmarks. But his forehead was too narrow and his cheeks too sunken for his face to be anything other than ugly.

'So, how did it go, your first night?' His accent sounded like he was from a rough part of town and he was trying to pretend otherwise. Despite his smooth manner, neatly cut hair and expensive suit, his voice had a harshness to it and a slightly mocking tone. *He's a bully*, she thought.

'Alright, I think.'

'You seem to have got the hang of things. If you stick with it, you'll be making good money soon.'

Ken took a long pull on his cigarette, his eyes raking her body as he exhaled. It would have been an insolent look, were he not the club's manager. She waited for him to speak again.

'Zoe's put your name down for this Saturday.' He flicked through the pages of a large diary on the desk. His voice became brisk and businesslike. 'And for next Tuesday and Thursday. If there's any problem, please let Zoe know as soon as possible. Otherwise I'll expect you here Saturday, at seven sharp.'

He was shooing her away. She nodded, grabbed her bag and flew down the hall, out onto the street. The cold air stung her cheeks and ears. She thrust her hands inside her pockets. Sam was climbing into a cab with Heather and another girl.

Sam thrust her head out of the window. 'Are you coming back?'

'Yes, Saturday.'

'See you then!'

Another cab pulled up soon afterwards. There was no one else waiting, fortunately. Laura climbed into the back seat.

'Where to, love?'

She met the driver's eyes in the rear-view mirror. He was studying her expectantly, like a blackbird observing a tasty worm. He knew she had been working at a lap dancing club, of course. He could see what sort of girl she was. She looked down at her hands resting on her bag, suddenly ashamed. Yes, she was Sarina the lap dancer now, a girl who flaunted herself in front of a roomful of men in return for a few quid. She had become a thing for men to drool over.

15

Suzanne

11 April 2011

Suzanne put down the article with a yawn, went into the kitchen and switched on the coffee machine. Sunshine glinted from the cooker and the neat row of stainless steel containers lined up on the worktop. Through the open window she could see the trees in the garden, their branches puffed up with blossom. It was a glorious day, not a day to be sitting indoors.

She took her coffee outside to the patio. At last, spring had arrived. This winter had been surprisingly mild, yet lately, the bare branches and dreary, sodden days had weighed on her more than usual. As the sun warmed her skin, the aroma of coffee and damp earth mixed deliciously, removing all nagging thoughts about Paul and Emma. If only one could rein in the days as they galloped towards autumn. On days like this, the sun and the earth seemed to work their magic, turning lifeless twigs into supple shoots and flower-filled buds. She leaned her head back and basked, feeling a rush of contentment. It wasn't just the sunshine, or the quiet greenness of the garden. Once in a while, it was as if something new and vital was unfurling inside her, too. Something beyond words, something she couldn't explain to herself, let alone anyone else. As if the real Suzanne Cunningham was waiting to come out of hiding – not Paul's wife, not a mother of two, not the woman who edited articles in obscure magazines, but another woman altogether.

She sipped her coffee slowly, examining the garden. The fence was invisible under a deluge of yellow forsythia. Further down, the apple trees were a mass of white frills. Wedding dress frills. Suzanne smiled. Weddings, that was all she'd thought about these past few days, after Sunday's conversation with her son – along with much of the country, given the upcoming Royal splurge.

'Mum, brace yourself,' Daniel had greeted her when she answered the phone. 'I've got something to tell you. Can you guess?'

'I don't know. Tell me.' *He's going to work overseas, or he's in trouble with the police.* Which scenario would be worse, she wasn't sure. 'Have you got another promotion?'

'Karen and I have got engaged. We're going to get married.'

'Married?' It was the last thing she'd expected.

'You know – a wedding, in a church.'

'Daniel! I'm surprised, that's all. I didn't realise. I'm so happy for you, darling.'

'I know I'm young, we both are. But I love Karen. I want us to have kids together.'

'She's not pregnant, is she?'

To her relief he had laughed for about a minute, and the conversation turned to his wedding plans – it would have to be the end of summer, probably, or there wouldn't be enough time to organise the event. She avoided saying what was in her head – that the end of summer was only a few months away and he was quite young to be getting married, that it would be better to wait and get some experience of life first. There was plenty of time for that conversation.

But afterwards, she tried to reconcile her son's planned marriage with the mischievous, irresponsible Daniel she'd always known. He had never talked of love. He'd always seemed disinterested in marriage, joking about older work colleagues who had succumbed to children and resented losing their former carefree lives. She'd always pictured him marrying in his thirties, after he'd had time to accumulate property, status and experience. Not at twenty-four, in his first job, to his first serious girlfriend. Then again, if he were willing to give up his freedom to marry the woman he loved, how could she argue with that? He'd known Karen longer than she'd known Paul when they got married.

She sighed. If she'd known Paul for several years, long enough to see all aspects of him, would she still have married him? A wistfulness drifted over her. She got up and walked across the lawn, her shoes sinking into the dew-soaked grass. Every blade had been daubed in a glossy overcoat, except where a trail of dark paw prints led across the lawn. She scanned the rockery and the patio wall, half expecting to see a familiar flash of fur. But Marmaduke wasn't in any of his usual places. No doubt he was hanging out with Toby, next-door's noisy Siamese.

At the beech tree, she stopped and looked up to the tree house. The rope ladder hung down limply, its lower end frayed. Paul had built it for the children, years ago. Back then, it was the perfect hideaway, for Laura especially. She loved going up there and having tea parties with her dolls, and when she was older, she spent long summer days up there with a book or sketchpad, deaf to all pleas to come down.

Suzanne walked past the apple trees to the end of the lawn. The grass was long and straggly underfoot. She took

a large step to avoid the half-consumed remains of a bird –
Marmaduke's doing, no doubt – and reached the semi-circular
platform backing on to the fence, below an overhanging horse
chestnut. Worn steps led up to a statue of a mermaid. Her tail
was flecked with moss. The structure was draped in shadow,
apart from a shaft of sunlight that tickled the mermaid's
back. There was something mysterious about this part of the
garden, the way it was shielded by trees on all sides as if it
had been purposefully hidden. A breeze stirred in the leaves
above, putting goose pimples on her arms. She turned and
walked towards the house, past the banks of rhododendron.
Time was getting on.

It was lying in wait for her – a hideous spider web
stretched across the path, glinting in the sunshine. A
collection of insects squirmed on silky threads. She stopped
mid-step, a bleat of distress emerging from her mouth. One
more inch and the thing would have wrapped itself around
her face. She tore off a woody stem from the bush beside
her and thrashed at the web until it was a white tangle at
the end of her stick.

The phone was ringing, she realised, and had been for
some time. She tossed down the stick and ran inside.

'Hello?'

'Hello, Suzanne. It's me, Jane.'

She panted into the phone. 'Hi, Jane, I was in the
garden. Did you get my message? I left it yesterday.'

No answer. A surge of irritation.

'Are you phoning from work?'

'No, I've taken the day off.' Jane's tone was oddly flat.
'There's something I have to talk to you about, Suzanne.'

She went over to the kitchen table and sat down. 'What
is it?'

'It's about Paul. I've got something to tell you.' Jane
cleared her throat.

Her body went cold. Normally Jane would just come straight out with it. Were Paul and Jane having an affair after all? No, it wasn't that. Somehow, she knew this would be about Emma.

'Emma slept through her alarm again. I tried to get her up this morning and she said she wanted to stay in bed, she wasn't up to going to school. Her breath smelt bad – she admitted she's been taking my sleeping pills. I'd noticed a packet was missing but I thought I must have made a mistake.'

Her mind raced. How was this about Paul?

'Why is she taking your pills? Why are you telling me this? I don't understand.'

'She didn't want to tell me at first. But I said I wasn't going to leave the room until she did.'

'So, what was it? What was the matter?'

Silence at the other end.

'She told me what happened. The day Paul took her swimming for the last time.'

Her breaths were coming faster and shallower; she couldn't suck up enough air. This was turning into a childish guessing game. Only she knew it wasn't a game.

'*What* happened, Jane?'

'Did he tell you he brought her back to your house afterwards?'

Somewhere inside her head, a dull roar began.

'Yes, I knew about that. Paul said they came out of the pool early, so he asked if she'd like to come back here to watch a film.'

'Emma told me that after they'd watched the film, Paul took some photos of her.'

'I know.' Why couldn't her friend get to the point? 'She asked him to take some photographs of her, to help her get into modelling. I saw one a few days ago, that's why I called—'

'It was his idea.' Anger transformed Jane's voice. Quieter than normal, the words precisely enunciated, leaving pointed gaps between each word. Jane had never spoken to her like this before. 'It was just his ploy to get her to take her clothes off. He said he knew someone in an agency, and he could take some photos to help her get in. She's an impressionable girl and he knew it. He worked out exactly what he had to do to get her where he wanted her.' Jane's voice began to tremble. 'He told her he had to get pictures of her in her underwear, or the agency wouldn't be interested.' A pause. 'And did he tell you what else he did?'

'What are you talking about?' Suzanne gripped the handset, her breath sucked out of her. What did Jane mean, 'what else he did'?

Jane carried on.

'I really don't know what induced her do it. She sat beside him, wearing next to nothing. He promised he would only look. But he ...' Jane's voice cut off then resumed with grim determination, the tremble more obvious now. 'He stuck his fingers into her. He wouldn't let her go. And then he put his fucking prick inside her. My beautiful, innocent daughter, who's never been with anyone. He was too strong, too heavy, she tried to stop him but she couldn't get him off her. She had to lie there while he did his vile business.'

Jane's voice collapsed. Only a stretched-out, sibilant sound. A hiss, not quite a wail. Then only breathing, the ragged, clutching breaths of pure grief.

The strange roar filled her head again. She opened her mouth to speak but no sound came out.

Jane's voice reappeared, its strength back.

'You do understand what I'm saying, don't you? He violated my little girl and she'll never be the same again.'

Suzanne listened to a sound from outside in the garden – the thin, repetitive note of a bird. She was unable to think, let alone speak.

'He made her promise not to tell anyone. He threatened her. Emma said she wanted to tell me that day but she thought I'd blame her for what happened. She blamed herself for letting him take the photographs – she thought she'd encouraged him, that somehow, what he did was her fault. She believed all the nonsense he told her.' A snort of contempt. 'She was even scared I'd be angry with her.'

Jane's words bobbed up and down inside her head like drunks who couldn't find their way home. *He put his fucking prick inside her* …

'I can't believe it,' she said at last. 'Paul couldn't have done that. He couldn't have.'

'I'm sorry, Suzanne, it's not a nice thing to have to tell someone.' Jane's voice was breaking up. 'But it's not a nice thing to have your daughter tell you she's been molested and raped by your friend's husband. How could he have done that? She's only twelve, for Christ's sake.'

'It can't be true.'

'It *is* true – don't you think I'd know when my own daughter is telling the truth?' Jane's voice blasted in her ear. 'Do you think she would make up something like that?'

'I just can't believe Paul could have done a thing like that.'

She felt sick, as if she'd just been forced to eat a large carton of chocolate ice cream in one go. This couldn't be right. Someone was playing a terrible trick on her.

'Why don't you ask him?' Jane said, in a mocking tone. 'He knows what he did to my daughter. Ask him to tell you all about it.'

'Can't we talk about this face to face? I'll drive over now.'

A sneering little chuckle. 'I'd rather you didn't, actually. Our friendship is over, don't you get it? And I swear, if your husband comes near me or my daughter ever again, I'll kill him with my own hands. He's a disgusting pervert—'

'Jane, don't—'

'He should be locked up so he can't molest anyone else. I'm going to report him to the police so he gets the punishment he deserves.'

'No, you're wrong.'

The phone buzzed in her ear.

Suzanne poured out half a tumbler of Gordon's. She drank it neat, holding on to the worktop to steady herself. The liquid numbed her tongue and burned her throat. She drank the rest then sat at the kitchen table. A shudder went through her. It seemed to pass through her skin and carry on, into her blood and bone, going deeper and deeper, until it became a repugnant, evil thing, slithering inside her. She shut her eyes.

Oh God. How could such a thing be true? Surely, such a frightful thing could not have happened.

A yellow wedge of sunlight slanted in through the window. Outside, a bird piped cheerfully as if everything was normal, and Marmaduke was meowing at the back door.

Paul's key turned in the lock. With the words she had selected earlier, Suzanne went toward the door. Fear had been working on her body all afternoon, turning her insides to a pulp. She stopped in the hall, a few feet away from him. He put down his laptop case and took off his jacket.

'Jane phoned this morning,' she said. 'She's accused you of something, something very serious. It's to do with Emma.'

He froze, his hand outstretched, about to drop his jacket over the banister. He turned to her, his eyes black and shiny as a crow's. 'What are you talking about?'

'Emma says you assaulted her. That day she came over here, after you took her swimming.' Without replying, he put down his jacket and walked into the kitchen. She followed him. He was rinsing his hands under the tap as if he hadn't heard her. She forced herself to say the rest. 'She said you touched her, inside. Her vagina. And then you … you forced yourself on her.'

He snapped his head towards her, leaving water pouring from the tap.

'Is it true, Paul? Tell me, is it true? Did you have sex with that girl? Did you rape her?'

She held on to the kitchen table. Bile erupted into her throat. He looked at her, his face unreadable, then he turned off the tap, walked casually to the other side of the table, and took off his tie.

'She's lying, Suzanne.' His tone was resigned. He undid the top button of his shirt. 'Emma was angry with me so she's gone and made up this story. It's her revenge. But it defies belief that she could come up with something as twisted as this.'

'What do you mean? I don't know what you're talking about.'

'Sit down. I'll tell you what really happened.'

She did so. Paul sat down in the chair opposite her. He seemed calm, not at all surprised. Then he sighed heavily.

'I was taking the photos, as I told you. I was kneeling on the sofa to get the best shots. She had all her clothes on, there was nothing untoward. Then she gave me a weird smile and said she was going to take her clothes off for the next one, she wanted me to take one of her in just her underwear. I said no, she shouldn't do that, but she took them off anyway. I put the camera down and said "Photo session's over, please put your top back on". That seemed to greatly upset her. All of a sudden, she came over and kissed me.'

Suzanne stared at him.

'It was some kiss, she put her tongue right into my mouth. I was shocked, I pushed her away and asked what the hell she was doing. She laughed. I guess I lost it – I slapped her face, hard, and called her a little brat. She started crying hysterically, it took her ages to stop. Afterwards, she said she was sorry. She begged me not to tell anyone, not even you. She said she'd die if her mother found out.'

She tried to make sense of it. Emma had kissed Paul? How could that be? Finally, she found her voice.

'I don't understand, Paul. If that's what happened, why didn't you tell me before? Even if you couldn't have told Jane, you could have told me. I'm your wife. I don't understand how something like that could happen and you didn't tell me. You told me you'd taken photographs of Emma, but you said nothing about any of this.'

Paul leaned towards her. His knuckles stood out white against the tan of his hand.

'I didn't know what to do, Suzanne. I didn't have the heart to tell on her. That's why I didn't say anything about it to you – I thought you'd feel you should pass it on to Jane. I didn't want to upset Emma any more than she was already.' He sighed. 'It was a mistake, I guess.'

So, Emma really had tried to come on to her husband, just as she'd imagined? Or was everything he'd told her simply a story he'd made up?

'You do believe me, don't you?' His eyes fixed on hers. 'I know I should have told you before, now it's blown up into this goddamn mess. The only reason I didn't was to protect Emma.'

'Why would she kiss you? Did she fancy you?'

'I think she had some sort of girlish crush on me, yes. But I didn't realise, not till later. Once, when we were driving to the pool, I said something about her hair looking good and I thought it was strange how pleased she was. And there were a few other things.' He sighed again. 'I think you were right, Suze. It wasn't just Emma posing in that photo, trying to look like a model. She wanted me to respond to her as a man. I knew her head was muddled, that she always wanted me to notice her, but I truly had no idea of the extent of it. When I told her to put her clothes back on, she looked so terribly hurt. She kissed me, because she wanted to make me kiss her back.'

It was possible, wasn't it? Suzanne thought about what she knew of Emma. The girl hadn't been doing very well at school for some time, lacking in confidence and self-esteem, according to Jane. After her father had left, she started getting into trouble with the teachers, and playing up at home. Her own impression of Emma – formed years earlier – was a girl, hungry for attention, who yearned to be liked and admired.

'Did you send the photograph to Emma?'

'What?' He frowned.

'You told me you were going to send it to her.'

He stroked his jaw, looking thoughtful. 'I decided it would be better not to, in the circumstances. I thought it best if she wasn't reminded of that afternoon.' He put his hand on her arm. 'Suze. You do believe me, don't you?'

Did she believe him? Or did she believe that her husband was a child molester? What sort of choice was that?

He stood and pulled her head onto his chest, running his fingers through her hair. Her vision blurred; she closed her eyes.

'Darling,' he said. 'I couldn't bear it if you didn't believe me. I couldn't bear it.'

'Paul, I want to believe you. But I don't know if I can.' Her words sounded distant, as if they'd come from a woman in another house, another city, another world. How could she be saying these things?

'Suze, I love you. I couldn't possibly do what Emma's accused me of – not ever. You know I couldn't have.' He stepped away from her. 'I could never do anything like that. You have to believe me.'

She was silent. She was trapped between two opposing forces: doubt, and the urge to believe. It was intolerable. One had to give way.

'Please, my love. I'm Paul, your husband, the man who loves you. Do you really think I could do something like that?' His eyes implored her. Finally, weary of the struggle, she nodded.

'Alright. I believe you.' Her voice was low, scarcely there.

He looked at her, saying nothing. His Adam's apple moved as he gave the slightest nod.

'Jane says she doesn't want to see either of us again,' she said. 'She says if you come near Emma again, she'll kill you.'

'You're joking?'

'No, she was almost hysterical on the phone. She believes Emma. She might report you to the police.'

'That's crazy, absolutely crazy.' He turned away. 'I'll call her right now and tell her the truth.'

She went into the hall after a minute or so and listened through the door to Paul talking in the office. She couldn't make out most of his words. He wasn't getting angry, or raising his voice; he sounded eloquent yet insistent, as he had when he'd persuaded the phone company to refund the cost of the broadband service because it hadn't been working for three days. She sat in the living room and waited for him.

After a few minutes he came in, shaking his head.

'She doesn't believe me. She still thinks Emma's telling the truth.'

Suzanne stared at him. *Jane doesn't believe him.* The thought meandered along and registered somewhere, far away. A numbness was settling over her. Nothing else could happen now that would make her feel anything.

'We just have to accept it,' he said. 'That's what Jane chooses to believe. Maybe when she's had a chance to think it over, she'll see things differently.'

'Would you get me a gin and tonic please, Paul?'

While he was away, she wondered if it was possible that Jane would ever see things differently. It seemed more likely that she would never speak to either of them again, continuing to believe that Paul had raped Emma. And what would happen if Jane reported him to the police? Would *they* believe him, or would they believe Emma?

Her face and back were soaked in sweat. She was chilled to the core, her heart galloping in irregular bursts. She gripped the arms of her chair. She wasn't strong enough to withstand this; it was going to overwhelm her. The landscape of her world was going to change forever. What had once been solid ground was now giving way beneath her feet. How would she face the devastation that would ensue? Once again in her life, she was utterly lost.

'You sit quietly for a while,' Paul said, handing her a glass. 'I'll fix dinner.'

They ate in silence. Then Paul said he'd had doubts from the start, about whether he should be helping Emma, and that events had proved him right. She'd struck him as a flaky kid with the potential to be destructive. He thought Jane had always spoiled her daughter, but neglected her real needs, and her instinct now was to defend her.

Suzanne said little in reply. She couldn't think clearly. Could all this be a trick to make her believe him? But, she too had seen another side of Emma. As a little girl, she had often been selfish and attention-seeking, and worse. At one birthday tea, the girl had been spiteful towards one of her friends, pulling away her plate and making her cry. And Jane had complained often about Emma stirring up trouble with her brother, breaking one or other of Toby's toys.

After they'd eaten, she went to sit in the living room. Paul cleared the plates then put on some Vivaldi. Later he turned on the *Ten O'Clock News*; Gatwick had been closed for several hours because of the threat of a terrorist attack.

She couldn't take any of it in, something vital inside her had shut down. All she could do was stare at the flickering screen.

16

Laura

20 April 2011

Laura hung her jacket on the corner peg as usual and put her bag on the bench. The changing room was empty. She sat down and opened her purse, took out the slip from the cash machine, and read the balance again: *£350.37 CR*. It was more than she'd had in her account for ages.

Not quite three weeks in this place, and she'd earned over a thousand pounds. Her rent was paid in full and the landlord wasn't going to kick her out. She'd done what she'd come for. She could look for another job now, one that didn't involve taking off her clothes and being inspected by leering men.

Then again, she could stay on a bit longer … just in case. To make sure she'd have enough money to live on in case it took a while to find another job.

She sat on the bench. A thought was tugging at her.

This place had become a habit. Two, sometimes three nights a week. She was getting used to men ogling her as she shimmied about in next to nothing in front of them. She was learning to put her feelings aside and focus on the money she would take home at the end of the night – two hundred pounds most nights, sometimes more.

But the money wasn't the only thing, was it? Wasn't it a tiny bit exciting, dancing for these men, these strangers who came here to watch and weave their fantasies?

She unlaced her trainers. Sometimes she did get a buzz out of it, yes, when the men were young and nice to look at. She was being appreciated for what she did and there was a sense of power almost – now she was getting more adept at the job – from being the one in control.

At other times, showing herself off to whichever guy happened to ask made her feel uneasy, cheapened. Deep down, she knew this place was wrong for her. It was hurting her, bit by bit, taking something vital away. It was as if she'd given up on making things better, so they could only get worse. To make things better would require too much effort – too much hope, for a start. It was easier to just let things carry on as they were.

'Hi, Sarina, how's it going?'

Sam dumped her bag on the bench, fished out a red corset and held it up for her to admire. It had come from a lingerie shop in Covent Garden, where the day before she'd spent over three hundred pounds. Laura fastened the straps of her platforms and looked in the mirror. A dab of concealer to hide the dark circles forming under her eyes, then a slick of frosted eyeshadow.

The remaining girls arrived. Heather brought out a new pair of strappy work sandals, leading some of them to discuss where they had bought shoes lately and how much they'd spent. Lucy rushed in, out of breath. She'd got pissed on cocktails the night before and slept through her alarm, she said, frantically pulling off her street clothes.

Minute by minute, the chatter grew louder. It was a Wednesday evening. Tomorrow evening would be the start of a four-day weekend for many. Some of the girls had plans to go away for the Easter weekend with husbands, boyfriends or lovers. Not her, though. She'd be working Saturday night, earning whatever she could.

As soon as they were let out onto the floor, Laura headed to the bar. She caught Danny's eye and nodded as he pointed to the bottle of Jack Daniels. The place was getting busy but no one seemed to be getting any dances.

The first girl was called up on stage for her pole dance. Laura looked around as she downed her drink. It was her turn next.

'And now, the lovely Sarina!'

She adjusted her G-string and walked into the glare of the spotlights. She began to move in perfect time to the insistent beat. The pole first, then the floor. Each part of her routine flowed smoothly on to the next. Her body knew what to do. Her legs could stretch further than last time, her back arched higher. She would make every man in here want her to dance for him.

The music ended. She spread her legs, pinged her G-string and smiled as raunchily as she could. The punters liked you to look as though you couldn't wait to shag them, Sam said.

Once the club got going, she was busy for a long stretch with no time to even go to the toilet. A group of men in their twenties began to yell at each girl going up on stage, cheering and heckling as they guzzled bottles of beer and champagne. The security guy did nothing. As long as the customers didn't make an obvious nuisance of themselves – fighting or spilling their drinks, trying to leave without paying, openly kissing or touching a girl, or trying to get up on stage with them, as had happened the week before – he didn't seem to mind how they behaved. Lucy was grabbed in the crotch once, and had reported it to Zoe, according to Sam, but Zoe had said that Lucy must have provoked it. Sam said you had to look out for yourself, to always be prepared for the worst.

After her eighth dance, Laura sat on a stool and swigged from her bottle of water. She hadn't checked her money yet but it would have to be over two hundred pounds, tips included. She looked across the room to the booths along the wall. A lone, middle-aged man in designer casuals, overweight with thinning hair, was beckoning her over. She drained her glass and slipped down from the stool.

'Hi, honey. My name's Pete.' His voice was loud and had a nasal twang. The accent was American, from a part she couldn't determine.

'I'm Sarina.' She sat down on the sofa beside him. He had a pudgy face and his breath smelled of cigar smoke.

'How are you, Sarina? You seem to be enjoying yourself.'

'Not bad, thanks.' She wasn't in the mood for another inane conversation.

'Going away for Easter?'

'No, I'm working Saturday. How about you?'

'I'm in London on business. I fly home tomorrow. Back to the wife and kids.' She felt his hand on her shoulder. 'You're gorgeous, babe,' he said, close to her ear. 'I've been watching you all evening. I love the way you move. You give me a warm feeling in my dick.'

She looked at him, repulsed. He was looking her up and down with relish.

'Will you dance for me, Sarina?'

'Naked or G-string?'

His tongue darted, lizard-like between his lips. 'As naked as possible, honey.'

He slipped some rolled notes under her garter. Laura removed her wrap. She didn't want to dance for this jerk. The guy was a sleazeball. That didn't make any difference, though – you were supposed to accept every offer of a dance, or risk a fine from Zoe. She'd never seen a girl turn down a request for a dance since she'd started at the club. Everyone seemed to care only about making as much money as they could by the end of the shift.

She steeled herself and began. Her nipples skimmed his shirt. She stepped back and moved her hands lightly over her breasts.

Pete leaned back in his chair, his lips parted.

'Come on, baby,' he said. 'Let's see the rest of you.'

She removed her G-string and finished the dance as quickly as she could.

When it was over, she put her things back on. The sooner she was away from him, the better.

'Do you do any extras?'

She shook her head.

'Could we go somewhere private?' He leaned closer, so she could smell the booze on his breath, and whispered. 'I'd make it worth your while.'

'No, I'm sorry, we don't have a private room anymore.'

He shrugged, making a disappointed face.

It was what she'd been told to say if anyone asked. Some undercover police had been nosing around, making trouble, someone had said, so the private room had been closed. But she was pretty sure it was still in use. She'd seen Noelle leave the main area once, with an evening bag on her shoulder, and return forty minutes later.

Near the end of the evening, Zoe told her to go and speak to Ken in reception. She found him arguing with an unhappy customer and waited until the man had reluctantly backed down and left.

'Sarina. A word, please.'

Ken was wearing his usual well-cut suit and shiny black shoes. He gave her a cool smile.

'That punter you were with earlier – Pete – the American. He's asked if he can go to the private room with you.' Ken waited for her to speak then went on. 'It's a room we only use for special customers. Those we decide to offer an extra service, if you like.' His narrow lips stretched into a leery curve. 'Come with me, I'll show you where it is.'

She followed him along the corridor. She wanted to go home now. She was tired, she wasn't interested in the private room. But she couldn't tell him that. He stopped at the door next to the office, took out a key and unlocked it.

Two low, black leather sofas faced each other across a shiny parquet floor, which was lit by spotlights in the walls and ceiling. There was a hi-fi cabinet against one wall. A large mirror and framed café scenes hung on the others. The glass table beside the sofa was empty except for a box of Kleenex.

She looked at Ken.

'You won't be disturbed, darling. The security guards don't come over here. You can do a dance for him, as usual, then ask if he wants you to do anything else.' Ken had spoken casually, as if he was talking about offering a cup of tea.

'Sex, you mean?'

'You don't have to do anything you're not comfortable with.' He moved closer, so she could smell the scent on him. The pockmarks in his cheeks looked uglier than ever. 'What you do is up to you.'

She nodded, trying not to show her alarm.

'It's not prostitution, just consenting adults in private. You don't ask for any money up-front.' A hint of eagerness entered his voice. 'They'll pay you afterwards, before they leave the room. You'll earn good money from it.' He waited for her to speak and when she didn't, glanced at his watch.

'Pete is waiting out there, shall I bring him over? There's a bathroom through that door where you can freshen up.'

'No, please don't,' she said, a little too quickly.

Ken's eyes widened in surprise. He hunched a shoulder.

'It's up to you, darling. I thought you might appreciate the chance to top up your earnings. But no worries, there's plenty of others who'll do it.'

The changing room was empty except for Sam and Heather. Both seemed to work practically every night.

Laura stood in front of the mirror and began to wipe off her make-up. Ken had expected her to say yes. But she earned enough from dancing. She wasn't one of those girls who'd do anything.

'What's the matter?' Sam bit off a chunk of her fruit bar.

'Ken asked if I wanted to go in the private room with someone. The American guy I danced for.'

'Pete, you mean? He's a mate of Ken's – they have a business thing together. We've both done him a few times. He likes new girls better though.'

'You told Ken you didn't want to?' Heather spoke sharply. Her face looked thinner and older without make-up.

'I said I'd think about it.' Embarrassed, she looked from Heather to Sam. 'You both go there, then? To the private room?'

Sam rolled her eyes. 'We're the biggest tarts in this place, darling.' She sighed and inspected the side of her nose in the mirror. 'Damn, my skin is always full of blackheads! Ken knows we'll do extras – and he trusts us. Anyhow, I need the money.' Sam met Laura's eyes in the mirror. 'I have expenses, you know.'

'Drugs, you mean?'

'Only booze and fags. I wish I could get off them.'

Heather gave a caustic laugh. 'Come on, Sam, admit it. You like a good shag, don't you?'

Sam smiled. Her eyes were serious, though. 'Yeah, that's right, Heather. Insatiable, that's me.'

Laura kept looking at Sam, curious. The girl was about her age.

'How long have you been working here?'

'Three years, nearly four.'

'Do you enjoy it?'

A look of horror. 'God, no. I don't know why I'm still here, I should be doing something else with my life. But I can't just walk into a decent job, not with three GCSEs. I've got to get money somehow – I've got a mortgage to pay and a five-year-old kid to look after.'

She couldn't hide her shock at the idea of Sam being a mother. She looked so young. What did she tell her child? But, of course, these days, with the recession and everything ...

Sam shrugged. 'A lot of the girls here are supporting their kids or working their way through uni. Or they have money problems—'

'Not Lucy,' Heather interrupted.

'No, Lucy likes it here. She doesn't do it for the money, she gets off on guys lusting after her. She told me her mum's boyfriend started screwing her when she was fourteen, and her mum was too off her face to do anything about it.'

'You shouldn't repeat things like that, Sam.'

'Oh, Lucy wouldn't mind. She tells everybody everything, doesn't she?'

Laura finished dressing and picked up her bag. Suddenly, she was fed up with this place and everyone in it. The private room, the sordid stories – everything. On the surface, it was as glitzy and alluring as a Paris boulevard at night, decked with glittering cafés and scented women in their finery. But something nasty hung around underneath, occasionally rising like a foul smell from a drain.

'See ya Saturday,' Sam said.

On impulse, Laura leaned forward and called out to the cab driver. She couldn't go home yet, despite the fact she was wearing her grungy jeans and flat shoes, and tiredness dragged on her eyelids.

'Excuse me, would you mind pulling up along here?'

It was a nightclub. She had never been inside it, or even thought about going inside. It wasn't exactly inviting – a windowless brick wall with a heavy steel door barred by two surly bouncers. Inside was equally unappealing – a large room, with black painted walls, that was noisy, crowded and dark. But there was plenty to drink, and she wouldn't have to be on her own. The solitude and silence of her flat always made everything worse. Sometimes, without warning, she would experience the wrongness of what she was doing – the shame and the stupidity of it – magnified over and over. Then the only way to escape was to fall asleep, exhausted, or drink something strong, until the alcohol smoothed away all her troublesome thoughts.

She squeezed alongside the counter at the bar and ordered a double Jack Daniels and Coke. The guy standing beside her watched as she moved away from the bar and stood against a shaded pillar in a darker part of the room. He was thin and tall with black hair. When she looked back at him, he looked away. She turned her attention to her drink.

Time passing. Sounds coming, going. People coming, going. She drifted away, trying to forget what she had done that evening – all the things that had earned her a little more than last time, and the ease with which she'd done them. Tonight, at the club, she'd again had a strange sense that she was losing her grip on who she was, as if another girl was waking up inside her, one who'd lain dormant for years. A character in a play that had been written and put away in a dusty cupboard, biding her time until she had the chance to come alive in a theatre. And now she had her chance, this girl who didn't care what happened to her, who didn't mind that she earned a living by arousing desire in strangers.

Laura took another gulp of her drink. Suddenly, she was afraid. It was only three weeks since she'd started at the club, how would she be in another three weeks? But she ought to keep on going, just a little longer, to be sure she didn't end up in the same perilous situation all over again.

The sensations of the moment began to take over – the noise of her surroundings and the warm rush of alcohol through her body. Her thoughts stopped, her memories of the hours just gone began to blur, her fear subsided. It was all falling away now, sloughing off like sunburnt skin.

'Can I buy you another drink?'

It was the guy from the bar. He was handsome, in a gaunt sort of way. He wore a silver ear stud in the shape of a guitar. He had a warm smile.

She told him a double Jack Daniels and Coke. When he came back, he asked if she always came to bars on her own.

'Not usually. Do you?'

He smiled. 'Not usually. But my friends haven't showed – I think I've got the wrong place, or the wrong time. What's your name?'

'Laura.'

'I'm Dylan. You didn't look as if you were having much fun, that's why I came over.'

He smiled again, pulling hair from his eyes.

'No, I don't like it here much. I just came to … to wind down, I suppose. It's been a long evening.'

'What are you winding down from?'

She decided to tell him the truth. She was tired of pretending to be other than she was, and what did it matter, anyway?

'I work in a gentlemen's club.'

He looked puzzled.

'You know, lap dancing. Like Spearmint Rhino.'

His eyebrows raised. 'Do you enjoy it?'

'I wish I didn't have to do it.'

'Why do you?'

'I need the money to pay my rent. I was out of work for a while.'

'Everyone needs money, don't they?' He looked into her eyes. 'You're lucky you're so attractive.'

'I guess if I was fat and ugly, I'd have to do something else.' She smiled, flirtatiously. He was a bit older than she'd first thought – probably twenty-six or twenty-seven.

'I'm sure you do very well. What were you doing before?'

'Not much. A job here, a job there. I was fired from my last one. I've got a degree in history but I haven't found a good use for it yet. What do you do?'

'I'm a biochemist. I've started doing research into the causes of dementia. My dad had it. I'd like to help find a cure, some day.'

'It must be wonderful, to do something you believe in. I've never had that. I've no idea what I want to do with my life.'

His face stayed serious. 'Don't leave it until it's too late.'

She finished the drink. It had done the trick. The bad thoughts had left. Her mind was slowing, getting fuzzier. She wanted to lie down in a quiet place and close her eyes …

'Are you OK?'

'It's been a busy night. And I've had too much to drink, on an empty stomach.' She smiled brightly. The drink had loosened her tongue. She wanted to tell him everything. 'I'm not drunk though, not yet.'

'Do you want to be?'

She shrugged. 'Maybe.'

'Why?'

'It makes me feel better.'

'Being drunk isn't good – I know from experience. Don't you have someone to talk to?'

'Not really, no one I can talk to about everything. I don't have many close friends.'

'That's a pity. Everyone needs someone to talk to.'

'There's only Rachel, and I don't think she would understand. I've told her about the club, but not what it's really like. I don't think I should tell her too much.'

He came closer. Gently, he placed his arm around her. 'You're in a bad way, aren't you?'

'I suppose.' She looked straight at him. 'I came here because I didn't want to go home by myself. But I'll be OK now.'

'How are you getting home?'

'Taxi. I'll get one outside.'

She tried to remember his name. Yes, Dylan, like the poet.

'It was good talking to you, Dylan,' she said. 'I'd better go now.'

He moved away from her. She moved away from the pillar. The room swayed.

'Do you want me to come home with you? I won't mind if you say no.'

'Yes, OK. Come home with me.'

She hadn't done this for a long time – meeting a stranger in a bar and going with him. But tonight … She wanted it

215

suddenly, so badly. Skin touching skin, the heat of bodies moving together. She could kiss him, easily. There was something about this guy, the way he looked at her. He wasn't going to judge her – or use her.

He held her close as she walked, his arm around her waist. She nearly fell on a kerb, and laughed it off. Her key got stuck in the lock and he helped her. For a moment, she wondered if this was safe, and why she was inviting someone she hardly knew into her flat.

She made coffee then took him into her room. They sat on her bed with the heater on, a red silk scarf thrown over the lamp so its light wouldn't show up the damp marks on the walls and the dust on the table.

'Sorry it's such a dump.'

'Don't worry. My place isn't much better.'

He was only saying that to be polite – or to make her feel better. He really was a nice guy, far nicer than the ones she normally met.

'You're really out of it, aren't you?'

'Yes, I'm sorry.'

He looked into her eyes. 'It's none of my business, but do you … do you ever sleep with the guys in this place where you work?'

'No, I wouldn't do that. I just dance for them, that's enough.'

He nodded, sipped his coffee. She asked if he had a girlfriend.

'I was seeing someone. It ended last year.'

'Relationships always go wrong for me, sooner or later.' Laura laughed. 'It's my fault, I always choose guys that don't care about me or the other way around. It's pretty stupid.'

'I don't think so. Whatever we do, there has to be a reason.'

'What do you think the reason is, in my case, then?'

'You don't think you're worth much, so you treat yourself as if you're not.'

'I see.' A dart of pain went through her, as if he'd jabbed her with a needle.

'I didn't mean to hurt you.'

'No, it's OK. You're probably right.'

She leaned forward and kissed his lips, softly. He looked surprised. Surprised but pleased.

'Look, Laura, are you sure you want to do this? I could leave, if you like. Or just stay here and sleep.'

'I'm sure. Aren't you?'

She knew she was more than slightly drunk. But not too drunk to know what she wanted.

He kissed her, took off her blouse and jeans, and caressed her until she was aroused, then he undressed. He kissed her again and held the top of her arms tightly as he fucked her.

It was intense, too intense. She seemed to be passing into another world, and she wasn't sure if she could come back to this one. From somewhere far away, she heard his shower of curses as he came. A shudder grew at her core, and she let go. He stroked her head on his chest.

For a while she was elated. As that passed, something else floated in, some long-ago forgotten joy. Then everything got mixed up and she couldn't tell if she was happy or sad. A river of tears began to rise inside her, prickling her eyeballs and constricting her throat.

A small choking sound burst out of her like a misplaced hiccup. She pushed her head into the pillow to stifle the sobs.

Next morning, he was still in bed beside her, sleeping. She showered then ran down to the local shop and bought croissants and fruit for a late breakfast.

'Why are you called Dylan? Are you Welsh?'

He sat at the table, watching her, as she waited by the grill for the croissants to brown.

'My dad was.' A note of pride entered his voice. 'He liked Dylan Thomas. His poems.'

She thought of her own father, the man she couldn't talk about.

'Do you want marmalade?'

'No thanks – jam, if you've got it?'

She joined him at the table. They talked almost continually as they ate. She felt as if they'd been together for weeks, not one night.

'You've really cheered me up, Dylan,' she said, after their third cup of coffee.

'You don't look so pale now. I was worried you might collapse, after last night.'

'Work takes its toll, I guess.'

'How often do you have to work?'

'Three times a week. But it's good money, that's why I do it. I've already paid off the rent I owe, pretty much. I just need a bit more to tide me over till I find a real job.'

She went over to the sink with their dirty plates.

'I like you, Laura.' He came up to her. 'You've got a lot going for you.' She waited for the rest. She could guess what he was going to say: she was doing damage to herself, she needed to change pretty quickly or she'd end up on a cold slab. 'You should stop working there.'

'I know,' she said, turning to him. 'I will, soon.'

It wasn't what he'd wanted to hear, she knew that as soon as she'd said it. She wasn't sure why she hadn't just said yes, why she hadn't promised to stop there and then.

He said he would call the next day, but he didn't.

The disappointment went away after a few days. It wasn't that she'd expected him to call her – she was a lap dancer now, which didn't make her the sort of girl that a stable, intelligent, good-looking guy with a career would want to hang out with. But it would have been good to see him again.

17

Laura

22 April 2011

'He said if I didn't behave, he'd pull down my knickers and give me a good smack on the bottom,' Rachel said with a giggle, puckering her small mouth. 'I said "OK then, go ahead".'

Laura swallowed another hunk of bread and cheese. She hadn't expected this meeting with her friend, but it was a relief to have this meandering, light-hearted conversation on a warm April afternoon.

They were sitting on a rug in Richmond Park. Below, the hillside tumbled into fields and clusters of distant buildings. Further out, church spires punctuated a whitish haze. Food cluttered the rug, mostly from Rachel's local deli. Her friend had called at 10 o'clock that morning and suggested they have a picnic somewhere since it was Good Friday and the weather was fine. Despite feeling tired from the previous night, she'd agreed straight away – they hadn't met up in over a month.

'What are you doing next week? Do you want to go and see a film?'

'I don't know.' Rachel helped herself to another olive. Her hair, fastened behind her head with a slide, gleamed in the sun. 'Jake keeps texting that he's got to see me. And I've got dinner with a friend on Tuesday, and a rehearsal on Wednesday.' Rachel smiled, brushing a strand of hair behind her ear. 'I could do Thursday evening, if you're free?'

'I'm working at the club on Thursday. Can we make it Friday?'

A couple of weeks ago, she'd admitted to Rachel that she was working in a lap dancing club. Rachel was the only person she'd told, apart from Dylan. She'd told her brother and her mother that she was serving drinks in a nightclub.

'I thought you were going to give that up and look for another job?'

'I am, but I haven't found anything yet.'

'What happened with that job you applied for the other week?'

'I didn't even get an interview.'

'Have you got any interviews coming up?'

'There's one next week – an admin assistant job at an insurance company.'

'You can't get anything better than that?'

'There's not a lot of work out there, Rachel. I can't just waltz into my ideal job.'

'Which is what?'

'I don't know. I wish I did. I'm not like you. You're lucky, you always knew you wanted to work with kids.'

Her friend was in the middle of a work placement at a school for children with autism, part of her Masters in Educational Psychology. She had impressed them so much that they had virtually promised her a full-time position upon completion of her course.

Rachel chewed a stick of celery, her face thoughtful. A breeze stirred the grass, lifting a paper plate off the rug. A dog barked as it chased a small boy who was struggling to steer his kite.

'You're managing to pay the rent OK now?'

'Yes, thank goodness. I'm getting some good tips at the club.'

'What happens at this place? You've hardly said anything about it.'

Her friend stopped eating and looked at her intently. What could she say? She knew it would be better not to tell Rachel in too much detail what went on at Rascals, or her friend would be even more displeased than she was already. But she didn't want to lie about it either.

'We dance – up on stage and one-on-one.' She hesitated. She'd better not mention striptease, or the pole. That would definitely give the wrong impression.

'One-on-one?'

'They sit and you do a dance for them. You wiggle your hips, stick out your boobs and try to look sexy. They're not allowed to touch.'

'You have to take all your clothes off?'

'Mostly it's just down to a G-string.'

Rachel stared. 'My God, Laura. I didn't imagine you doing something like that.'

'Well, that's what you have to do in these places. That's what they expect.'

She looked down at her hands. It had been a mistake to tell the truth. Why hadn't she kept her big mouth shut?

'Don't you mind men looking at your body?'

'I don't like it, of course I don't. It was really hard, at first.'

'At first? So, you're used to it now, are you?'

'I had to get used to it.' Panic flurried inside her. This was going all wrong. 'It's not that bad, Rachel. You're imagining it to be worse than it is.'

'You don't have to keep on working there, do you?'

'I'm not going to be there forever. It's only until I get something better.'

Rachel sighed and stared into the distance. 'I know you can't see it, Laura,' she said slowly. 'But you seem to be doing your best to fuck up your entire life.'

Laura picked up a lump of cheese and put it into her mouth. It tasted like nothing at all.

They sat in silence. Eventually, Rachel looked up.

'Are you still having those bad dreams?'

'Yeah, the same one keeps coming back.'

'Which one?'

'Someone's chasing me. I know I have to get away from him, or he'll kill me.'

She stopped. Rachel was looking at her strangely.

'What's the matter?'

'Your father really messed with your head, didn't he? I think that's why you're still working at this place. You need these guys to salivate over you, just like he did. Don't you see? You're just repeating everything that happened before.'

'Rachel, will you stop trying to psychoanalyse me? I can do without it, thank you very much.'

She bit her lip. Her reply had escaped without warning. She shouldn't have retaliated like that.

'If that's what you want, fine. But I'm not going to stick around to watch you going downhill. You're worth more than that, Laura. If you keep on like this, I dread to think where you'll end up.'

Rachel started clearing away the uneaten food and putting containers into bags. It wasn't yet 4pm and they still had half a bottle of wine left.

'Where are you going?'

'I have some things to do at home.'

'Can't we talk about this?' Her gut felt distinctly odd, as if a hundred fingers were inside it, poking and pulling the

223

tubes, twisting them into knots. 'You're my friend, aren't you? Are you going to walk out on me just because I work in a lap dancing club? That's crazy.'

Rachel put more things into plastic bags and hurriedly stuffed them into her rucksack. She spoke without looking at her.

'I'm sorry if I'm hurting you, Laura. I know we've been good friends … But you've changed. I can't handle what you're doing. I can't cope with it happening again.'

'You're not making sense, Rachel. With what happening again?'

'I've had it before, with my sister.'

'The one in New York?'

'She's not in New York anymore, she lives in Nottingham. She used to work for Morgan Stanley. She was doing really well, then she lost her job. It was four years ago. She got depressed, started drinking too much. Then her boyfriend left and she got even more depressed. She stopped talking to me, to Mum, to everyone. We found out where she was staying, tried to help her, gave her the numbers of the local alcohol recovery service and so forth. It didn't make any difference.'

'What's she doing now?'

Rachel took a few seconds to reply.

'When I last saw her, she was staying in a hostel. A place where homeless women go. Most of them are alcoholics or drug addicts. It's hard to believe, my sister living somewhere like that.' Rachel's eyes glistened. 'If you want to end up in the gutter, Laura, go ahead. It can happen to anyone, even you. But don't expect me to hang around watching while you do it.'

A chill went through her. Her best friend, no, her only friend, was walking out on her.

'I know you're right, my father fucked me up. I need to change my life, I know I do. But please, don't go.' She took a deep breath, tried to stop the press of tears behind her eyes. 'I don't know if I can get through this alone.'

'What do you mean? You might top yourself?'

'No, I just meant—'

'You did try once, didn't you?' A sharp note entered Rachel's voice. 'You told me once you tried to jump off a roof or something. At school.'

'They thought I was, that was all.'

'So, what happened? Do you want to tell me about it?'

Laura cleared her throat. She might as well tell the story – there was nothing to lose.

'It was the lunch break. I was sitting on the grass, reading. The others were playing some game, I could hear them yelling, getting excited. Suddenly, I didn't know if I could stand it anymore. Feeling so apart from everyone, I mean. I went up to the science labs and climbed out of the window. It had a flat roof. I sat there ages, watching everyone below. I didn't hear any of the bells ring for lessons. Somehow it was better, sitting up there where no one could see me. Like I was properly alone.'

'You weren't going to jump or anything?'

'I did imagine stepping off the edge. I remember thinking it was only the second floor so the fall might not kill me, I'd probably end up crippled for life instead.' She heard the quiver in her voice. 'I knew I didn't want to be dead, I just wanted to be happy again. I wanted my mother to be happy and my father to go back to normal.'

She wanted to cry, to put her head in Rachel's lap and let the tears slip silently. But Rachel's face was closed. Her arms were folded across her body, as if to protect herself.

'Did they find you up there?'

'Two teachers came with a ladder to rescue me. I told them I was just going up there to think about stuff, but they didn't believe me. They thought I'd been about to jump. There was a huge commotion – they made me see an educational psychologist. He asked if everything was OK at home. I said my parents seemed very unhappy together and I wished my father was nicer to us.'

'That's all? You couldn't tell him what your dad was doing?'

'I thought of how heartbroken my mother would be, how shocked my brother would be. Even though I wanted Dad gone, I didn't want it to be because of me. I thought if he was taken away from us, my mother wouldn't be able to deal with it. And I was a bit scared of him. He could get so angry.'

Rachel let out a long breath then turned her head towards her rucksack.

'You should have told them about him back then. When you had the chance.' Her voice was different. Not hard, but without sympathy. As if she'd already left.

'I so wish I had.'

'You need help, Laura. I'm sorry, but I can't be the one to help you.'

Laura put her hand on Rachel's arm. Her tears welled up again.

'Please, Rachel. Don't go.'

She watched as Rachel got to her feet, pulled the rucksack onto her back and walked resolutely up the path, out of her life.

The flat greeted her with its familiar melancholy air. It needed laughter, visitors, cheerful conversation, a bright spray of flowers on the table. Instead there was the same jumble of tatty furniture and the same exhausted clatter of the fridge. Voices echoed along the stairwell. Harsh, unforgiving voices.

A chill went through her. She was alone. Rachel wouldn't come back. There was only her brother left, in Bristol, who might as well be light-years away, and her mother.

Laura took the bottle of Jack Daniels from the kitchen cupboard. She drank without bothering to pour it into a glass, and drank some more. A fiery sensation grew inside her. She thought about how Rachel had judged her then abandoned her. Shame mingled with horror and then anger. How dare Rachel do that to her?

She stripped and stood naked in front of the wardrobe mirror. Her body was firm and slim, rounded in the right places. She ran her fingers down between her breasts, smiling at her reflection. She was young and sexy. Men looked at her with longing in their eyes – on the Tube and when she walked past in the street – even when she wore a scruffy T-shirt and jeans with no make-up. If she were at the club right now, she'd let some guy fuck her. To hell with Rachel. She didn't need a friend like that.

I'm going downhill, she thought the next moment. Rachel's right. If I don't get away from the club soon, it'll be too late.

She awoke in the middle of the night, clutching the sheets, sweat drenching her skin. Her heart struck her chest in a volley of irregular thuds like it was being whirled around in a washing machine. Was this a heart attack?

She sat up and turned on the bedside light. Slowly, her body returned to normal. She drank some water and lay down, trying to rid the images from her mind.

It was him again. Her father. For the last time, he was coming to get her.

18

Suzanne

23 April 2011

'Suzanne, wake up.'

'What time is it?' Paul was sitting on the bed beside her, in his dressing gown. Suzanne opened her eyes.

'Seven thirty. It's time to get up. We have to leave in forty minutes.'

What was he talking about? Oh, today was Saturday. It was the Easter weekend. They were meant to be going sailing with Andy and Fiona.

In an instant, everything that had happened over the past few days came back. A wave of weariness washed over her. She shook her head.

'Paul, I'm really not up to it. I can't face going sailing now after all that's happened. I hardly slept last night.'

He clucked his tongue in annoyance. 'Andy's been getting the boat ready all week.'

She said nothing.

'Come on, Suze.' His voice was upbeat. 'We have to carry on as normal. Don't let all this get you down.'

She looked at him in astonishment. How could she carry on as normal? How could she pretend that nothing had happened?

'You go on your own then,' she said. 'I'll stay here.'

He sighed. 'I guess I could, if you really aren't up to it. You'll be alright on your own?'

She lay in bed, listening to him take a shower and brush his teeth. All sounds were muffled, as if a heavy cloth had been placed over her head. For half of the night, she'd replayed over and over in her mind what Jane had said on the phone, and Paul's explanation, trying to make sense of it all.

But there was no sense in any of it. Any relief she'd felt after Paul had told her that Emma was lying had vanished. In its place, a bottomless well of confusion. All the questions she'd asked herself last night began to reappear, ghosts that couldn't be laid to rest.

Had Emma really kissed Paul? What on earth had made her do it? He was forty years older than her. Could she really have some kind of girlish crush on him? Perhaps her father running off to Turkey with Yasmin had affected Emma more than Jane had realised. Had Emma been trying to get back at her father in some bizarre way? Or was she just a precocious brat who thought it was fun to run around creating havoc in other people's lives?

She rolled over. From the gap in the curtains, dust motes jiggled in a slant of sunlight. Everything that had been clear three days ago was now twisted into a desperate muddle. This situation was beyond understanding. Why on earth hadn't Paul said anything at the time? If only he'd told Jane there and then.

One thing bothered her more than anything else. Why was Jane so convinced that Emma was telling the truth? As Jane had pointed out, surely, she would know her daughter well enough to be able to tell whether or not she was lying. Then again, Jane wouldn't find it easy to accept that her twelve-year-old daughter had brazenly kissed a fifty-three-year-old man – her friend's husband to boot. Maybe she'd prefer to believe that Paul was a … She grasped for the right word. A child abuser? A paedophile, even?

Paedophile. The hateful word drilled into her brain. What was Emma thinking of, accusing Paul of such a thing? It was beyond belief. Emma must be to blame, not Paul. Surely.

She heard a clink on the table beside her. Paul was standing next to the bed.

'I made you some tea, darling,' he said.

Suzanne pushed herself upright, arranged the pillows behind her back. She sipped her tea, watching him get ready. He pulled on his white sports shirt and his knee-length shorts, and stepped into his sailing shoes. Then he folded his waterproofs and placed them inside the bag of sailing gear.

'I can't believe this is happening,' she said, to herself as much as to her husband. She pictured Jane in the pub, after one of those Tuesday evening choral society rehearsals, guzzling beer like a bloke, putting on a meaty growl as she impersonated Geoff, their outspoken, rather bombastic conductor, and wondered if she would ever see her friend again.

'Darling, I know this is difficult for you. But we've both got to be strong.'

He sat down on the bed and rubbed his nose playfully against hers until she couldn't help a feeble smile. He took her hand in his and kissed her goodbye, saying he'd be back around 8pm. She heard more noises in the kitchen and smelt burnt toast. Then the front door slammed.

She stayed where she was. She couldn't sleep now, but she couldn't make herself get up. Her tea would be getting cold, but she couldn't be bothered to drink the rest. She was on the edge of losing herself, as if she'd had too many hash brownies – though the ones she tried years ago in that Amsterdam café hadn't produced anything quite like this. Patterns of light swirled on the wall, too bright. Her skin was no longer an impermeable membrane; every sight, sound and smell in the outside world seemed to assault her. She felt jittery, unstable. There was nothing solid she could latch on to for reassurance. She was trapped inside a situation she couldn't comprehend, like a butterfly on a pin.

She breathed in slowly to a count of five, held her breath for five counts, then breathed out for five counts, as they did in the mediation group. For a while she kept on with this, hoping it would have some effect. It didn't. She put her finger in her mouth and pressed her teeth into the flesh, meeting the resistance of bone.

If only she could turn the clock back to that sunny morning, before Jane's phone call. Once more, something had cropped up out of the blue and pulled the bottom out of her life, just when she had least expected it. She thought of the rambling, rather shabby house she'd spent her youngest years in, two miles from the Dorset coast. Her father had filled it with his presence – his smoky beard, his cheery humming as he'd tended his orchids and written up chimney inspection reports. On Saturday mornings, while Irene had her weekly piano lesson, Rich trained with the cycling club, and her mother did the weekly house clean, she would set off with her father down the path to the beach, glad to have him all to herself.

They went there for the last time a month before he drowned. Midsummer's day. The beach all theirs, stretching out, empty ahead and behind. Wind buffeting their faces; waves wild, spitting foam. As usual, as they'd walked the firm, wet sand along the shoreline, her father was throwing pebbles into the sea as she looked out for shells. Then he'd shouted, 'Let's get an ice cream, race you to the top!' Soon after, he went out in a sailing boat for some stupid race and didn't come back. His death had marked the end of her childhood, the end of those carelessly happy years.

And now her world had been torn apart, again, by a few words spoken by a friend over the phone. She tried to fasten on to some tangible, comforting thoughts, but none came. Suzanne pushed off the duvet. This was useless. She would go downstairs and make a fresh cup of tea. Marmaduke would be wanting his breakfast and the house needed a thorough clean – she hadn't done it properly for ages. She would keep busy, that would be the best thing.

Halfway down the stairs, the doorbell rang. She stopped to adjust her dressing gown.

Who was it at this time in the morning? It wasn't yet nine o'clock. Not the postman – today was a public holiday. None of her friends would visit at this time, unannounced. She opened the door a fraction.

It was Katherine, out of breath, her hair tousled.

'Jane called yesterday and told me everything,' Katherine blurted out before either had said hello. 'Sorry, Suzy, I shouldn't have barged in on you like this, but I thought I'd pop over and check you're OK. I've been worried about you.'

'I'll be OK,' she said, automatically. 'Come in, I was just making some tea.'

Katherine's eyes travelled down the hall. 'Can you talk? Is Paul around?'

'He's off sailing – I said I'd stay home.'

'I'm not surprised, you must be shattered by all this.' Katherine's arms wrapped around her. 'I'm so sorry, m'dear. It must be hell, what you're going through.'

Suzanne extricated herself from Katherine's hug and poured boiling water into the cups. Something in her friend's tone jarred.

'Paul says Emma's lying,' she said. 'He didn't do anything to her.'

Katherine didn't reply. Her friend leaned against the kitchen worktop, softly tapping her mug as if contemplating what she should say next.

No, surely not, Katherine didn't believe Emma, did she? Suzanne ran her tongue around the inside of her parched mouth.

'You don't think Emma is telling the truth, do you?'

Silence.

'Please, Katherine. Tell me you don't believe her.'

'I don't know for sure,' Katherine said slowly, 'what Paul did or didn't do. But it seems to me ...'

No, it couldn't be true. She knew what her friend was going to say. Katherine had swallowed Emma's version, just as Jane had.

'Paul didn't do anything to Emma, Kat.' The words came out in a desperate rush. 'Emma had a crush on Paul. She was flirting with him, trying to come on to him. She kissed him and he slapped her. She was humiliated. She was trying to get back at him by making up this lie.'

Katherine looked at her, slowly shaking her head from side to side.

'Suzanne, listen. I know that's what Paul has told you, but I don't believe it. Why did he bring her back to your house in the first place? Don't you think that rather strange? He could have taken her back to Jane's afterwards.' Katherine's voice swelled dramatically, as if she were trying to convince an entire jury of Paul's guilt. 'But he knew you'd be away until the next day, didn't he? He knew he wouldn't be disturbed if he took her back to your place.'

'He came here to watch a film, that's all. Come on, Katherine. If he really had done anything to Emma, why didn't she tell Jane straight away, as soon as she got home? Why wait until now to tell her, all these weeks later?'

'He threatened her. He made her feel ashamed.'

'So, you're saying Paul is lying, are you?' She got to her feet. 'You really think he molested Emma?' Her voice was shaking, with fear as much as anger. A sliver of doubt was already uncoiling inside her.

'I hate to have to say this, but yes, I do.' Katherine took hold of her hand. 'I think Emma is telling the truth and Paul's lying to protect himself. Listen, I know how awful it is for you, I know you don't want to hear this, but it's not unheard of. There are men like that around—'

'And my husband's one of them?' She snatched back her hand. 'You're wrong, Katherine, you must be wrong.'

Paul was a good man, he had principles. He couldn't have done it. Could he?

But what if he had? What if he had done the unimaginable, and lied to hide his guilt?

'I'm sorry, Kat, I didn't mean to shout at you. I just need to be by myself for a while.'

Katherine said she understood, she'd better be going.

Suzanne went into the bedroom and pulled the duvet straight. Paul's slippers were side by side under the chair, as usual. Beside them, one black sock. She picked up the sock and hung it on the back of the chair. She went into the bathroom, took off her dressing gown and hung it on the hook. Paul had left the toothpaste cap off, which he never usually did. She rinsed the white slime away and put the cap back on. Then she tucked her hair into her shower cap and stepped into the shower. She turned it on full and stood there, letting the hot water pound her body.

Paul had brought Emma back here on purpose to molest her? He'd done the most heinous act imaginable and made her promise not to tell anyone? It was crazy. Her husband wasn't one of those perverts who went after children.

She dried herself and went downstairs. Paul would be on the boat by now, miles away. She washed Marmaduke's bowl, dolloped in some Whiskas and replaced the bowl under the chair in the kitchen corner. She wiped the sink and picked out the food that had collected in the sink tidy: white grains of rice, yellow teeth of corn, and scraps of red pepper. Then she turned on the radio very loud and began to clean the house to Beethoven's fifth.

Dust, vacuum, polish. Plump the cushions, empty the bins, get everything straight.

The sun came out for a while then went back in. She lost track of time. After the living room and the hall, she started on the conservatory.

Water the plants, sweep the floor, polish the windows.

Don't stop, don't think.

Just after 4pm Suzanne switched on the kettle, her arms aching. Through the kitchen window, branches were flailing and the clouds were racing. Andy's boat would be on its side, ripping through the water at breakneck speed. It was just as well she hadn't gone – she'd be freezing and clinging to the side, trying not to throw up. But Paul loved sailing in rough weather, even though she'd reminded him often enough how her father had died. He seemed to almost enjoy the risk of something going wrong. Men were strange like that. She dropped a teabag into her mug.

From nowhere, a memory came.

She had come into the garden after lying down upstairs. It had been another sweltering day. Paul was watering the flowerbeds and Laura was on the lawn, leaning back on her elbows, legs stretched out. A book lay open beside her. She wore her white swimming costume and the wide-brimmed straw hat that she always wore when sunbathing. Her skin had gone a deep, un-English shade of brown, and her legs had seemed longer and slimmer than ever. Quite the Hollywood starlet, she'd thought with a pang of pride. And then she had noticed how Paul was watching Laura as he moved the hose, intently, with an oddly furtive expression, as if he knew he shouldn't be watching her.

The kettle spewed steam and clicked off. She came back to the present. Why remember that, after all these years?

Suzanne picked up the kettle. She poured water on the teabag then opened the cutlery drawer and took out a teaspoon. The liquid in the cup was dark. It would be too strong soon. She removed the teabag and dropped it into the tall metal pedal-bin in the corner of the kitchen. The lid clanged shut. Now all she had to do was go to the table and sit down.

But she couldn't move. A question was forming in her head, one which could not yet be put into words. Without permission, her thoughts rushed ahead. Paul used to bring home comics and sweets for Laura, sometimes drawing paper and felt-tipped pens too, little offerings he knew she'd like. Never anything for Daniel. He had taken Laura on visits to the shops and the park, just the two of them. She had been anxious to think of Daniel being excluded, had been a tiny bit envious of Laura. But she had always excused Paul's behaviour, told herself that fathers did have special relationships with their daughters.

Something horrible was unwinding itself in her brain, unstoppable. That time she'd come home after her gall bladder operation. Daniel had been camping in Scotland, leaving Laura and Paul in the house by themselves for four days. She'd sensed a tense atmosphere, as if there'd been a fight between the two. Had something happened while she was away?

Laura had started to change around then. Sometime after starting her new school, she'd begun to withdraw. She stopped talking about what had happened at school and what she was doing with her friends; often, she would hardly speak at all.

Had Paul done something to Laura while the two of them were alone?

Everything made sense now. The change in Laura hadn't been about her new school or becoming a teenager, as Paul and others had suggested, and as she herself had come to believe. It had been because of what her father was doing to her. Paul had been abusing Laura. And now he had abused another girl. What Emma had told Jane was true. Not Paul's version.

A wave of panic went through her, a wall of black coming down. There wasn't enough air to breathe. The room around her began to fade and the muscles in her legs seemed to be dissolving. She sank onto the pedal bin, holding on to the counter to stop herself from sliding to the floor.

The truth was staring her in the face: her husband was a child molester. He really had committed a depraved act against her friend's daughter, one that she could not even begin to imagine, that she could not bear to think about.

But already her imagination was clearing a space to allow in something dreadful. She saw Paul removing his jeans. His hands rough, insistent, pulling at Emma's underwear. Emma's confusion turning to fear. The cries submerged in her throat, his hand over her mouth, perhaps. A look of appalled helplessness on the girl's face as she realised what he was going to do...

Her stomach rebelled. Suzanne hurried over to the sink and vomited.

Emma's face came back to her, and that flirty expression. Suzanne ran into the office, rifled through the desk drawers and pulled the camera from its case. She swiped past the more recent photographs until she found the one of Emma. It had changed, though it was exactly the same as before. No longer was it a girl flaunting herself, trying it on. It was simply a girl eager to please in whatever way she could because she didn't know any better. A girl who was losing her way, a girl who needed a more attention, more love.

A girl who had stolen her husband's heart.

The twelve-year-old her husband had fucked.

A wave of nausea came over her.

She pressed the bin icon.

Are you sure you want to delete this photograph?

She selected Yes then she threw the camera across the room. It hit the wall with a dull thud.

19

Laura

23 April 2011

Laura picked up the bottle of iridescent green nail varnish from the magazine beside her on the sofa and put it down again. She hadn't yet called Daniel. There was still time before she had to leave for work. She grabbed her mobile from the coffee table.

'Hey, big brother, congratulations! I heard you're about to become a respectable man – or whatever it is that blokes become when they tie the knot.'

A chuckle at the other end. 'In big trouble, I think.'

'I couldn't believe it when Mum told me. I thought you were going to wait till you were thirty, at least.'

'It's Karen's fault. She told me she wasn't planning on staying single for the rest of her life.' His voice became serious. 'No, we've been thinking about it for a while, but we decided not to say anything till we were sure.'

'You have been a dark horse.' She twisted a strand of damp hair around her finger. 'I'm really happy for you, Daniel.' It was true. But for some reason she also felt sad.

'What about you, sis? When are you going to get hitched?'

'Not for a while, I should think.'

'You never know, you might bump into Mr Right next week.'

'I doubt it.'

'Are you working tonight?'

'Yes, I have to leave soon.'

She paused. It was on the tip of her tongue to tell him the truth, that she wasn't actually working in a nightclub, but a lap dancing club. The words didn't come. What if he told her how stupid she was to do such a thing? What if he was tempted to tell their mother? It would worry Mum to death if she knew where she really worked.

They talked a little more, mainly about houses that he and Karen had looked at buying in Bristol, then Daniel said he had to go, dinner was on the table. He would be in touch.

Laura put down the phone. Why couldn't she let on how she was really feeling, rather than pretending everything was OK? She had wanted to talk to her brother properly, to let him know she needed his help, that she couldn't talk to Mum and there was no one else to talk to now Rachel had gone. But she'd said nothing. Why could she not let him see the other Laura, the little girl hidden underneath her blasé exterior, the Laura who was now dangerously close to chugging off the rails?

She and her brother had shared so much as children. Cycling in the park, hanging out in the lido, skateboarding in the street. Saturday afternoons had been a refuge from their parents' constant fighting. All the games they'd played together – conker contests, darts matches, arm-wrestling – and the laughter ... An ache took hold of her throat. Once, after his trumpet lesson, she'd teased him when he was practising an obviously challenging scale. 'Dan, maybe you should learn the piano instead?' He'd thrown a cushion at her and they ended up having a cushion fight. One split open and made a mess of the living room floor, and another hit the cat, who screeched and hurtled away. They'd both fallen on the sofa, laughing like idiots.

Then, around the age of twelve, their relationship changed. It was hard to recall any details now, and she wasn't sure why. Had he sensed something wrong between her and her father? Or was it just about them going to different schools and growing up?

Laura let out a long breath and poured another glass of Jack Daniels.

Whatever the reason, she'd got used to keeping things quiet and he'd stopped wanting to know about them. Right now, she couldn't share the most important things in her life with him – like what she was going to do next. Yes, she knew in her heart that to carry on at Rascals would be choosing the path to nowhere, the start of a long slope towards self-destruction, but what else was she going to do? The future didn't seem real anymore. Tomorrow was hazy, and next week wasn't even above the horizon. She would go to the club tonight and do what she had to – whatever was wanted of her. It made sense in a way she couldn't explain to anyone, and in a way that Rachel couldn't possibly understand. This was what she deserved, wasn't it? To be nothing but a plaything, a piece of meat.

Laura pulled the brush from the bottle of nail varnish. In three deft strokes, she'd painted her big toenail.

When she arrived at Rascals, Ken was on the front desk training the new receptionist on the phone system. She was a heavily made-up young woman, with breasts that were thrust forward by her bra, her low neckline revealing a startling amount of cleavage. Every few seconds she nodded her head eagerly.

Laura waited, trying to catch Ken's eye.

'Sarina. How can I help you?'

'What we talked about last time – the private room – I've changed my mind. I'd like to help you out, whenever you need someone.'

Ken's face lit up. For the first time since she'd started he looked genuinely pleased with her.

'Good girl. I was hoping you'd have second thoughts. I have a job for you later on tonight, as it happens. I was going to ask one of the others, but if you're up for it?' He scanned her face. 'An important punter is coming in later on. I like to make sure he gets taken care of properly, if you get my drift.'

Ken's upper lip twisted at the corner, an expression somewhere between smile and snarl. 'He'll be in around one. I'll bring him over and introduce him.'

She turned away. The ease of doing what she'd just done was disconcerting. Had she really agreed to go into a room alone with a customer? The thought was scary, almost preposterous.

About seven or eight girls were already in the changing room, smelling of perfume, sweat and hairspray. She took her gear out of her bag, along with a water bottle, an apple, and a muesli bar. There hadn't been time to cook anything. Anyway, she wasn't hungry, she hadn't been hungry all day.

Sam stood in front of the mirror in a silk camisole, brushing her hair vigorously, a sour expression on her face.

'My period's due, I've been like a grizzly bear all day. I'm bloated and fat and horrible.'

'You don't look it, dear,' Heather replied beside her, imprinting red lips on a tissue.

'I really didn't want to work tonight. Ken asked me to do a job later, but I said no.'

Laura squeezed in front of the mirror. Her face was pale and her eyes stared out from dark sockets. She frowned. No one would want her to dance for them, looking like this. She smeared foundation into the dark patches and dabbed blusher onto her cheeks.

Sam greeted her. 'Hi, hun, how're you?'

'Alright, I suppose.' She followed Sam to her spot at the end of the bench. 'I told Ken I'd go to the private room tonight.'

'I thought you didn't want to.'

'I've changed my mind.'

Sam shrugged. 'It's up to you. But you might regret it afterwards.'

'Maybe.' She rummaged in her bag for her dangly jet earrings and looked into the mirror. 'Do I look alright?'

'Ten minutes, girls! Stop yakking and get a move on!' Zoe placed a bowl beside a washbasin. 'And help yourselves to Easter eggs.'

'You look simply stunning, darling,' Sam said, in a mock upper-class accent. 'I so wish I had your looks. The guys'll be queuing up for you.'

Laura sat at the bar with the others and asked for a Diet Coke. Everyone was waiting for the place to fill.

Heather looked into her glass and sighed. 'I hate all this waiting around. I wish we didn't have to come in so early on Saturdays.'

'Easter weekend is always slow at first,' Lucy said, in a know-it-all tone. 'It'll pick up.'

Sam said nothing, fiddling with her bra so her breasts stuck out more. Her silver bracelet glinted in the mirror ball's dancing beams. Zoe strode past the bar in skin-tight black leather trousers, turning a wary eye on them.

After about half an hour, the music went up in volume. Right on cue, three youngish men in jeans and casual jackets appeared at the entrance door. They sauntered in, had a good look around then sat at a table in front of the stage.

Lucy nodded to Noelle and the pair of them went across to join the new arrivals.

They returned five minutes later, Lucy shaking her head. 'They just want to talk.'

The minutes crawled by. Another girl got up on stage, and another. Laura looked around the club. More customers were arriving, but there still weren't enough men to go around. No one was getting any dances anyway, she had talked to everyone at least once with no luck. As usual, Lucy and Noelle rushed over as soon as anyone new sat down, determined to get picked first. Some of the others, less confident, or more calculating, preferred to hang back then pounce at precisely the moment the guy would be ready to part with his cash.

Eventually, after lots of fruitless conversations, it was her turn to go up on stage.

She grabbed the pole and began to twirl and slide, trying to keep an alluring smile on her face. But inside she felt uncomfortable. Someone was trying to have a word with her, her old self perhaps; the Laura who would have died rather than show herself off like this.

What are you doing, Laura? Why are you doing this to yourself?

Three men sat at the table nearest the stage. They were big-framed, sporty types, guzzling a bottle of Dom Pérignon. One of them – the leader of the pack she guessed, the loudest and the best looking – gave her an exaggerated smile.

After her performance she went up to him. Before she could say anything, he grabbed her and sat her on his knee. They weren't supposed to do this, and she didn't like it, but she said nothing to stop him. The security guard was nowhere to be seen – they occasionally went to the toilets to snort cocaine, she'd overheard Noelle saying to Lucy – but this guy was harmless, just out of it. His eyes shone as he told her about himself, rocking slightly from side to side and slurring his words.

His mates looked on in wry amusement.

'He's celebrating his divorce,' one said loudly. 'He's not been to one of these places before.'

She danced for him when he asked and he tucked another clutch of tenners into her garter. The sense of discomfort deepened, turning into a physical ache in her chest. A thought kept on at her, like a buzzing fly.

This isn't the real me.

The club got busy for a while and then quietened again. Minutes dragged by. Girls stood around looking bored, moaning that they wanted to go home.

Laura went to the bar and asked for a Jack Daniels and Coke. It had to be after 1am; she was tired, and anxious about what would happen. When was the 'special customer' going to arrive? How much longer was she going to have to wait? She could change her mind, tell Ken she didn't want to do this after all.

'Don't forget to use a condom,' Sam hissed in her ear. 'Sometimes they offer you extra not to.'

She nodded with a stab of alarm. Of course, condoms. She'd not given them any thought.

'Heather keeps some under the cushion of the sofa in there, if you haven't got any.'

It was another half an hour at least before Ken arrived, followed by a tall, well-built man, aged forty or so, with a leather jacket slung over his shoulder. His neat brown hair was greying at the temples. He walked with a slight swagger, looking straight ahead. Not the friendly type.

She watched from a nearby table as the two men approached the bar, the out-of-the-way one that she would sit at when she didn't want to dance anymore. They ordered drinks, then Ken beckoned her over. He shouted over the music.

'Martin, this is Sarina.'

'Hello there.' Martin smiled briskly. A trace of an East End accent. His eyes, cool and unwavering, appraised her in a second. Something about him made her uneasy.

Ken turned to Laura. 'I'll leave you to entertain Martin. The room's ready, when you want it.'

She sat at the table with Martin. He took a swig from his shot glass. She wished she had some of her drink left.

'So,' she forced a smile, 'how are you?'

'Fine, thanks. It's been a busy day, as usual.' He spoke quietly, not meeting her eyes.

'Are you a regular here, Martin?'

'You could say. I've been here enough times, over the years.'

Neither spoke. Martin tapped his thigh. Then he drained his glass and got to his feet.

'Ken said you could dance for me in private.' He jerked his head towards the unmarked door leading away from the main club. 'Can we go over there now?'

She contemplated making an excuse, she could say she felt unwell – something about him unnerved her. But it was too late now. He was expecting her to be available for him. He wasn't the type who'd appreciate being let down. She led him down the dimly lit passage, past the nude drawings, the dance music fading to a dull throb of bass.

They stopped at the door of the private room.

So, Laura, you're a hooker now, are you?

Martin stepped inside and she closed the door behind them. She noticed that the key had been removed – might someone come in and check up on them? It was a horrible thought. She sniffed the musty air, a combination of faded perfume, a leathery, old car smell, and sex. She tried to open a window for a blast of fresh air, but it wouldn't budge.

Martin gestured to the internal door. 'I'll use the bathroom, if you don't mind.'

She dimmed the spotlights, and angled the blinds to exclude the yellow glare of the street light, then sat waiting on the sofa facing the window. Her chest filled with the same fluttery tightness as before. Shivering, she pulled her wrap tighter. It was cool in this room, and beneath the thin layer of silk she was wearing only her underwear. She lifted the cushion beside her. Underneath, two small plastic squares: Durex.

Laura put back the cushion. They could stay where they were, for now. She unclasped a small shoulder bag containing her cosmetics and examined her face in the compact mirror. Her lips were a cupid's bow of vibrant red. Her hair, newly washed and sprayed into position, draped her shoulders. Her nails glimmered like butterfly wings.

Outside, a car alarm burst into a shrill warble then abruptly stopped, plunging the room into an uneasy quiet. She listened for the sound of the toilet flushing, or the tap running, but could hear nothing, just the tap of high heels on paving stones outside and a thudding down the corridor. What the hell was he doing in there? Why could he not hurry up and put her out of her misery?

At the same time, she was glad he was still in there. She didn't want him to come out.

Laura looked around the room, dominated by its square of parquet floor. A plant languished in a ceramic pot by the wall. Its shiny, pointed leaves were interspersed with dull brown ones, shrivelled at the edges. On one wall there were framed, rather twee, sketches of girls pouting and preening in front of mirrors. She turned to the wall behind her. A large painting hung that she hadn't noticed on her first visit – a striking impression of a young woman lying naked in long grass amid galaxies of tiny blue flowers. Her limbs were pale and ghostly. A clump of dark stems grew thickly from the V of her legs, part of the landscape.

Laura shivered. The bathroom door clicked loudly, making her jump. Martin emerged, unsmiling. He set his jacket over the back of the sofa and eased himself down beside her. He wore a light, inoffensive scent. She waited for him to say something, unsure of what ought to happen next. Noelle hadn't given her any instructions about private dances, and Sam had been unhelpfully vague.

'Um … would you like me to dance for you now?'

Martin nodded. 'Good idea.'

'I'll put some music on.' She went to the tower of CDs beside the stereo and selected Madonna's greatest hits. Music filled the room. Laura took off her wrap. Her heart thudded. What was she doing here? She walked into the middle of the square of parquet and started to dance to 'Material Girl'.

'Come closer,' Martin said. 'I can't see you properly.'

She moved closer. He leaned towards her, forearms resting on his thighs. His face gave nothing away.

A minute or so into the track she took off her bra, and then her pants, leaving only the G-string, stockings and platform sandals. She lay on her back and held both legs up then opened them wide. She glanced at his face. It was alert, waiting. There was a flash of impatience in it, like hunger.

Back on her feet, sideways on to him, she rotated her hips, moving her hands down over her breasts as she did so, and peeled off the G-string. Now she was naked except for her stockings and sandals. In that moment, she was as exposed as she'd been on her first night at the club. She had been naked in front of customers many times now, but in here it was different. She was alone with him and anything could happen.

The music was still playing. Martin's hand was on his crotch.

'Come here,' he said.

She went towards him, swirling her tongue around her dry mouth.

'Are you OK?' he asked, without concern.

'I'm fine.'

Did Martin know this was the first time she'd been in private with a punter? Had Ken told him?

'Sit down,' he instructed, unzipping his flies.

She did as he said, repulsed by his coldness, his expectation, by everything about him. He reached out and squeezed her breast. She stayed still, didn't object. But this wasn't what she wanted at all. Something was compelling her to go along with him – just as it had all those years ago with her father.

Yes, her father had trained her well, hadn't he? All his little gifts, all his unspoken promises that he'd be nice to her, so long as she did what he wanted and didn't blab to anyone. Whenever he'd wanted to touch her or ogle her, she'd obliged. It had all come in so handy for this job.

'You're beautiful.' Martin traced his fingers around her nipple.

She wanted to pull away from his hand and run. But she couldn't. He was smiling now, the same cold smile. He was enjoying this.

'Come down here and suck me,' he said. 'I need to get warmed up first.'

He was waiting – he expected her to obey, to do this as she'd done everything else. She only had to bring her head down and open her mouth.

Horror and disgust filled her. What the hell was she doing? She couldn't go through with this. Everything about it was wrong.

'No, I can't.' She stared at him, shocked at her own words.

'What did you say?' His face was uncomprehending.

She got to her feet. Her heart thudded painfully in her chest.

He frowned. 'What are you doing?'

'I'm going, I can't do this. I'm sorry.'

'No, you can't go yet.' He grabbed her arm and yanked her back.

'Leave me alone!' She pulled away from him, about to run for the door, but Martin was ready. He shoved her hard in the chest, sending her reeling backwards. She hit the floor with a thud, landing awkwardly, and cried out in pain. He crouched beside her and pressed down hard on her arms. His face moved closer. It showed the extent of his anger. His mouth was open. He wanted to humiliate her, to pay her back for refusing him. And he was far stronger than she was. She would have no chance.

Instinctively, she scratched his face. The soft flesh did not resist her nails. A trickle of red ran down his cheek. A strange noise came from his throat, not quite a gurgle, not quite a gasp. He tried again.

'Bitch!'

Before he could retaliate, she'd covered herself with her wrap. Without looking back, without collecting her bag or her underwear, she yanked open the door and fled along the corridor.

The changing room was empty except for a scattering of food wrappers on the floor. Her bag was on the bench, below her outdoor clothes that were hanging on the peg. In seconds, she'd pulled on her jeans and jammed her arms into her cotton sweater. Her fingers stumbled on the laces of her trainers. She grabbed her jacket. She had to get out of here before Martin came after her, or Ken found out what she'd done.

Ken wasn't in the reception area, thank God. There was no sign of him or any customers. Laura pressed the button to open the front door and slipped out. The street was deserted – no waiting cabs, no passers-by, no girls from the club. She began to run.

Five, ten minutes later she stopped and checked the road behind her once again. No one was coming after her. She could slow down now. For a few moments, she was overcome with relief. Nothing on earth would make her set foot in that place again. Her body felt light, as if she'd been released from a death sentence.

20

Suzanne

Easter Sunday, 24 April 2011

Suzanne pressed the buzzer to flat five and waited. The large communal bin against the fence was overflowing again, she noticed. It was surrounded by bulging garbage bags, sodden pizza boxes and a stack of empty bottles. An unshaven man, wearing sunglasses and a khaki jacket, got into a dirty BMW parked on the street outside the block of flats.

She buzzed again. Finally, Laura's voice came through the intercom. She pushed open the front door and stepped into the dark hall. The dank smell greeted her as it had the last time, and what looked to be the same pile of unclaimed envelopes lay on the floor against the wall. Slowly, she started to climb the stairs. Her legs were like dead weights. A coldness was spreading into her hands and feet, down into her fingers and toes. She reached the landing and walked towards Laura's door. Dread circled her, drawing closer, a vulture about to land and feast on her defenceless body.

Laura was draped in a white towel. Her hair dripped water onto the carpet.

'Hi, Mum. I was just in the shower.'

'Hello, Laura.' She stepped into the dark, cramped space, too small to be called a hall. 'Sorry to turn up at such short notice, but I need to talk to you. Whenever I phone I get your voicemail.'

'I disconnected the landline so the phone didn't wake me up. I must have forgotten to switch it on again, sorry.' Laura waved at the armchair. 'Sit down, I won't be long.'

The room was untidy and needed a good vacuum. There was a red rug on the floor now, which jollied the place up. On the coffee table, a vase holding a spray of white chrysanthemums, a wine glass imprinted with red lipstick.

Her daughter reappeared wearing faded jeans and a black T-shirt. Her feet were bare, exposing polished toenails. Her hair was tied back in a ponytail and her face had no make-up. She could be seventeen again.

'Cup of tea – PG tips or peppermint?'

'I don't mind, either.'

Suzanne followed Laura into the kitchen. She had an urge to busy herself, to pick up the tea towel and dry the two mugs that were upside down on the draining board, or to wipe up the crumbs around the toaster.

The kettle boiled. She watched her daughter prepare the tea. Under the fluorescent light, Laura's face looked unhealthily pale.

'What's up, Mum? You didn't come over just for a chat, did you?'

'Let me sit down first.' She took her tea to the armchair. The cushion still had a ripped cover. 'I need to ask you something, Laura.' She bit the inside of her mouth hard, girding herself to continue. 'I don't know how to say this.'

Laura stopped winding the strand of hair around her finger, and perched on the sofa.

'What is it? Tell me.'

'When you were growing up, did your father ...' She forced out the words. 'Did he ever do anything ... Did he ever do anything he shouldn't have done, to you?'

The room darkened as the sun went behind a cloud. Laura sat perfectly still except for the movement of her chest as she breathed. Suzanne was about to repeat the question when Laura found her voice.

'Why?' Laura's jaw tensed. 'Has something happened?'

'He's been accused of something, something awful.' She readied herself. 'Jane's daughter Emma – you remember he was taking her swimming? Well, after the last time they went to the pool, about six weeks ago, he took her back to our house. I was away for the weekend. Emma says your father touched her – indecently touched her. And then he – I don't know how to say this ... He had sex with her.'

A warm, itchy sensation crept up the base of Suzanne's neck and into her face. She felt ashamed, as if she were the one who had been accused of this crime.

'At first, I couldn't believe it. Your father denied it all, said Emma was making it all up. Then I didn't know what to believe—'

'Oh, fuck.' It was little more than a whisper. Laura sat rock-still, eyes fixed ahead, unseeing. 'I didn't think he would, I really didn't.'

Suzanne recoiled.

'It's true, isn't it?' But she knew now, beyond doubt.

'Yes, Emma's telling the truth. I had an odd feeling about Dad taking Emma swimming. I wanted to tell you but I couldn't, I didn't think you'd be able to cope. I never thought he'd actually do anything—'

'He abused you too, didn't he?'

'You really want to know?'

She tried to speak but only a grunt came out. She cleared her throat and tried again.

'I need to know, darling. Please, tell me.'

Laura's face changed. She had an absent, faraway look. The look she'd sometimes had as a child, wandering around the house as if lost in a perpetual daydream.

'It started when I was about eleven, I guess. He started doing weird things. One morning, he came into my room when I was getting dressed – I only had my knickers on – he didn't go away, he stood there looking at me. I just looked back at him, I didn't know what else to do.' Laura ran her fingers through her hair. Her gaze skittered about the room. 'After that, he did other things.'

Suzanne's finger went to her mouth. Her teeth bit down hard, searching for bone.

'What things?'

The words swarmed from Laura's mouth like a plague of insects. She wanted to block them out but she listened to the end. So, her husband had lied to her all along. And she had believed him, she had always believed him. She tried to imagine how it had been for Laura, Paul's hands on her body like that. Bile entered her mouth. She needed to retch.

The next question formed in her mind, one she dared not voice.

Laura bit her lower lip. 'I didn't want to tell you, I knew how much it would upset you.'

She had to ask it though. 'Is there anything else? Did he do anything else? Did he ever touch you … inside?'

'No, I don't think so. He used to complain when I wore my black gym knickers. He said they weren't sexy. What is it?'

'So, he didn't … he didn't ever have sex with you?' The question erupted from her like a piece of indigestible food.

'No. The worst thing he ever did …' Laura's voice trailed off. She looked uncertain.

'Tell me. I must know everything.'

'It only happened once. I was alone in the house with him. He came into my room and took off his dressing gown. He made me do things.'

Her heart stopped. 'What things?'

'He asked me to touch him. His penis. Then he asked me to put it in my mouth. He'd been drinking whisky. I was so scared, I didn't think to say no.' Laura's voice was so quiet her words were barely audible. 'I tried to forget that night, Mum. For years I just tried to forget it ever happened.'

She saw the pain in her daughter's eyes, borne for so long, hidden for so long, and yet so obvious now. She tried to speak but the words stayed trapped inside her. How could this have happened? How could her own husband have done such an unspeakable thing?

Laura leaned into the base of the sofa, head dropped, eyes closed, her face so pale and beautiful. Neither of them spoke for a long time.

'It was weird,' Laura said, as if talking to herself. 'Like suddenly he'd become a total stranger. It freaked me out. I wish I'd told him to fuck off out of my room, to get the hell away from me. But I didn't – I couldn't.'

Suzanne gripped the armrest. The room was breaking up into a jumble of disconnected shapes, as it did whenever she had a bad migraine attack. The vase glittered savagely. Above it, an array of white, stalk-less heads. A rectangular wedge of table floated over a bright red square of rug.

'Mum, are you alright? Mum? Say something.'

She couldn't answer. She'd been taken to an alien planet. All that was safe and familiar had vanished. Or was she losing her mind? That would be welcome now. She shut her eyes. Yes, she would just drift off into a parallel world, one where bad things didn't happen. This one was too difficult, too painful. How was she supposed to keep on going, knowing what she knew?

From somewhere far away came Laura's voice, now laced with fear.

'Don't lose it, Mum. Please, keep it together. I'm here, you're not alone.'

As if from inside the room, she heard Adele's strong, resonant voice speaking, as she did at the meditation group: 'Imagine a light flooding into you, a pure white light, a healing light.'

Later, seconds or perhaps minutes, she realised that Laura's hand was pressing against hers. Her daughter was crouching on the floor beside the armchair, her long, delicate fingers wrapped over her own. Suzanne opened her eyes. She noticed the flesh of her ring finger, dented, deformed by the wedding band.

'I'll bring you some water, hang on.'

Laura stood and bent down to pick up the mugs, revealing a white swathe of back. Her jeans were tight, showing off her slim figure. Even as a little girl she was slim.

So, Paul had been turned on by his own daughter. He had used her to gratify some perverted need; he'd done a terrible thing to Laura, worse in a way than what he'd done to Emma. Laura was his own flesh and blood. She put her hand over her mouth, fighting the urge to throw up.

'Here, have some of this.'

Suzanne sipped the water offered by Laura. A hundred questions filled her mind. One was pressing to go first.

Why didn't you tell me?

'Have you told anyone else about what he did to you?'

'Only Rachel, a few months ago. After you told me about him taking Emma swimming. She thought I should tell you.'

'Why didn't you tell me? Years ago, I mean.'

'I should have, I fucking should have.' Laura lowered herself onto the coffee table. Her eyes glittered, wet now. 'Ages ago, soon after the first time he touched me, Dad made me promise not to tell you. He said it would kill you if you found out. I guess I was scared he might be right. I never imagined him going after someone else, not once. Not till he told me about Emma.' A bitter smile caught hold of Laura's mouth and she wiped the tears from her eyes with a swipe of her fingers. 'It was stupid of me, I know. But I always had this idea that he did those things because of something about me. He used to tell me I was so sexy, he couldn't help himself.'

She jolted, a small electric shock through her body. *Sexy*. The word penetrated to her core. He used to call her that, sometimes. 'Come here, sexy woman.' How could he have used that word to their own daughter? Her thoughts swirled, overtaking her. So many emotions: bitterness, anger, resentment, envy.

Then guilt and self-loathing. Laura was a child, she wasn't to blame for what had happened.

You're the one to blame. You're her mother, you let this happen. You didn't protect her.

This had all happened right under her nose and she hadn't noticed. Paul had callously abused her daughter and she'd done nothing to stop him. What mother could let her own daughter go through that, without seeing the truth?

'I should have protected you,' she said at last. 'I should have seen what was going on. You didn't deserve that.'

Laura looked at her steadily. 'Didn't you ever suspect anything?'

'No, I had no idea.' A well of unease deepened inside her as a memory flickered to life. That wasn't true, was it? Not entirely. 'I just had a feeling …' She took a deep breath.

'You and your dad were so close when you were small. He was always making a fuss of you – reading you stories, taking you to classes, buying you sweets and magazines, bits of jewellery – I wondered if that was normal. Sometimes, the way he looked at you ...'

She couldn't get her breath; her lungs were snatching at the air.

Just say it. Tell her the truth.

'I think I had an inkling something was wrong, way back. Only I brushed it aside and pretended it wasn't there. I didn't trust my own judgement. Paul used to say I was unstable, he made me doubt my own mind. I let him convince me that everything was about me, not him.'

Finally, she'd admitted it. She must have known all along that Laura was being abused. Only she'd never been able to believe it.

'Do you blame me, Laura? Is it my fault, what he did to you?'

A tear rolled down her daughter's cheek, unchecked. Laura swallowed, her head moving slowly from side to side.

'No, I don't blame you, of course I don't. Dad hid what he did from you, I know that. I just wish you'd noticed something was wrong. I wish you'd asked why Dad was always so nice to me and why I wasn't happy anymore. I wish you could have done something to stop him.'

'I'm so sorry, Laura. Please, forgive me.'

Suzanne reached across the gap between them and gave Laura's hand a squeeze. They sat, she in the armchair and Laura on the coffee table, the silence broken by occasional noises: doors slamming in the block, cars passing, the clatter of an object being tossed into a wheelie bin.

'Have you talked to Emma, Mum?' Laura's voice was urgent, suddenly. 'Did she tell you what happened?'

'No, Jane told me.'

'When did Emma tell Jane?'

She tried to work it out; days had seemed like years recently. 'A few days ago. Four or five days ago.'

'Emma waited all this time before saying anything?'

'She thought her mother would blame her for what Paul did.' Suzanne dug her fingertips into her brow. Anger ignited inside her, directed at her husband. 'He had it all worked out, he must have been planning it for ages. Emma was desperate to be a model and he knew it. He got her to come to the house to take some photographs of her, then he tricked her into taking her clothes off.' She skipped over the next bit, though images were already in her head. She mustn't think about that, not yet. 'Afterwards, he blackmailed her so she wouldn't tell anyone. He manipulated me, too. When I told him what Emma had accused him of, he denied it all. He made up a story about Emma kissing him and I believed it. I must have been mad.'

'I thought you said Dad wasn't going to see Emma anymore?' Laura's face was flushed. Her eyes had the hard shine in them that came into Paul's eyes when he was very angry. 'You said she had something else to do.'

'After I spoke to you, Jane asked your father if he would take Emma swimming again. She was worried about her seeing a school friend who'd been getting into trouble. She thought it would be better for her to be with Paul.' The irony of this hit her. If only Jane hadn't made that request. But it was too late now, of course.

'If I'd known,' Laura said, 'I could have done more to stop him.'

'What do you mean?'

'I went over to Jane's house, to warn Jane about Dad, but she wasn't in and I got fed up with waiting. So, I talked to Emma instead.'

'Emma?' She tugged at her blouse. A mesh of sweat clung to her skin.

'I told her she shouldn't see Dad anymore, that she shouldn't be alone with him. I said he might take advantage of her. But I didn't spell it out, I didn't say he was dangerous. I should have made it clearer.' Laura frowned and kicked a leg of the coffee table. 'I thought she'd tell her mother – I *asked* her to tell her mother. I was expecting Jane to call me sometime. Then, when she didn't, I guess I got caught up with other things. Trying to get a job then working late at the club.'

'She couldn't have told Jane,' Suzanne said. 'Jane would have stopped your dad coming over if she'd known.'

'Maybe Emma forgot to tell her. Or she didn't want to tell her.'

'Why wouldn't she want her own mother to know?'

'I have no idea. She really believed he could help her become a model?'

Neither of them spoke. Suzanne searched in her handbag for the small white tablet. Amitriptyline. She didn't like to take them anymore – they made her calmer and flat, drained of emotion – but she needed one now.

Laura went over to the window and stared out.

'Has Jane gone to the police?'

'The police?' Laura's question hung in the air for a while before the words began to make sense.

'For sex with a minor. It's a serious crime.'

'No, no, not yet. Not as far as I know.'

'I guess there's no evidence that he did anything to Emma. Not after all this time. If they charged him and he denied it, it would just be his word against hers. It might not even go to court.'

'You think Jane should go to the police?'

'Of course. What if he does this again, to someone else? He might have already, for all we know.'

Suzanne closed her eyes. Her brain felt like a full rubbish bin, trying to eject any extra items she crammed in.

'I thought I'd forgotten most of it, you know.' Laura spoke in a distant voice, as if to herself. 'But the things he said, the way he looked at me. It's still there in my head, somewhere. It's like he's haunting me.' Her voice hardened. 'I'll never forgive him, you know. For what he did to me, and for what he did to Emma. I hate him.'

Suzanne flinched, went cold. What could she say to her daughter? She couldn't defend Paul. Emma would be deeply affected by what he had done to her. For years, if not her entire life. And what about Laura? What would become of her? Would she ever recover from the damage he'd inflicted? Paul wasn't just a man she'd known for a while and had grown to trust, he was her father. He'd knowingly taken away Laura's innocence, just as he'd taken away her trust and her faith that the world would provide what she needed. He had been prepared to ruin his daughter's life — for what? She got to her feet.

'Laura, come here.' She was slight in her arms, all ribs and shoulder blades. 'I'm so sorry about what happened to you.'

'I know.' It was no more than a murmur.

Suzanne let herself sink into the armchair again.

Laura went away and came back with two small glasses of amber liquid. 'Get this down you. It'll do you good.'

She drank the alcohol gratefully.

Thick shadows crowded the room. It would be dark soon. Outside, a crow landed on the roof. Its beak dug into the moss. She thought of Paul, at home, waiting for her.

'I have to go now, darling,' she said, reaching for her handbag. 'It's getting late.'

'You can stay here tonight, if you like? If you don't want to go back home.'

Home. The word sounded wrong, somehow.

'I'll go for a walk, I think. I need to sort out some things in my head. Then I'll go home and speak to your dad.'

The sun was low as Suzanne drove away. She didn't really know where she was going. She passed a row of shops and several sets of traffic lights then turned onto a dual-carriageway.

He's betrayed me.

The thought ran on in a loop. Paul had spoilt everything. Their marriage was a lie and she'd never even noticed.

She opened the window to let in some air.

Later, she realised she was driving towards Wimbledon Common. There were spaces to park on the road alongside it, past the pub. She parked and set off on her usual path towards the wooded hill.

A breeze swirled her hair. She stepped across a large puddle; the path was muddy from recent rain. Her feet would get wet in these flimsy shoes and her jacket wasn't waterproof. But no matter. A large dog bounded past, trailed by a sullen-faced man. She scanned the common. No one else was in sight. Normally she'd never come out here by herself so close to dark. But that didn't matter now either.

Near the brow of the hill she sat against a tree and looked down at the distant buildings silhouetted against the sky. The sun hid behind wisps of rose-tinged cloud. Damp seeped through her jeans.

I'll stay here a while, she thought.

She recalled the look on Paul's face a few hours earlier, when she'd told him she was going to visit Laura. He must have worked out why she was going. He must have known she would discover the truth sooner or later, or had he imagined that he could do those things to Laura and

Emma and somehow get away with it? Perhaps he thought he was invincible.

It was quite clear, finally. The pieces of the jigsaw fitted perfectly. Paul had driven Laura away from both of them. He had sacrificed his family and his marriage. He had poisoned everything.

'Damn you, Paul! I hope you burn in hell!'

The rawness of her cry disappeared into the trees.

An hour later, perhaps two, she realised she was shivering; her bottom, hands and feet were numb from the cold. She looked at her watch but it was too dark to make out the hands. Through patches of scudding cloud, a faint glow that could have been the moon. An aircraft light bleeped through the murky sky.

She started to walk downhill. Though she tried to keep to the path, it kept changing direction and she could scarcely see what lay beneath her feet. Every so often she splashed into invisible puddles and stumbled over sudden spiky clumps.

Eventually, she stopped. The path had gone. There were only vague outlines of bushes and trees. She was lost. She would never find her way out.

'Come on, Suzanne,' she said aloud. 'Don't be so bloody silly.'

For a moment, the moon shone brightly through a gap in the cloud, turning the landscape a ghostly silver. A breeze tugged at her clothes. She waited, watching the sky until there was another gap in the clouds. The moon reappeared. Now she could see the path, further to the right.

She ran over the grassy mounds, her feet sinking into the sodden earth. When the ground levelled out she could see the row of houses along the road where she'd parked the car.

The living room curtains were closed; behind them, a light was on. He was still up then. Suzanne pressed the doorbell.

Paul came to the door blinking, his reading glasses perched over his head. His hair was dishevelled. He must have fallen asleep in the armchair.

'Where have you been?' He looked her over. 'You're covered in mud.'

She removed her jacket then sank onto the hall chair and pulled off her soaked shoes.

'Where the hell have you been?' His voice surged through the house.

Behind the anger, she heard his fear.

'I know what you've done to Laura. She's told me all about it. And you don't have to pretend anymore about Emma. I know what you did to her. You've been lying to me all along, you bastard.' She went into the kitchen and filled a glass with tap water. With trembling hands, she drank.

'Suze, it's not like you think.' In the dim glow of the fluorescent up-lights, Paul's eyebrows hung heavily over his eyes, which seemed to shrink into the recesses of his face.

'I didn't mean to do those things.' Paul's Adam's apple moved. 'They just happened, I couldn't help it. I've wanted to tell you for a long time, but I was afraid of what you'd do. I was afraid you'd stop loving me.'

She wondered if she'd heard right. Surely, he didn't mean to offer that as an excuse for what he'd done?

'You must think I'm an absolute idiot. For months, you abused my daughter behind my back. You kept it carefully hidden from me all this time, then you turned on my friend's daughter. You groomed her, then you groped her – molested her.' She gulped some air. 'How could those things have "just happened"?' Her words came straight out without hesitation, as if another woman was talking, a woman without fear. Not the tongue-tied woman, who was always trying to make things better, ever ready to forgive.

'I tried to stop but I couldn't. Suzanne, listen to me. I tried to stop, I didn't want to do anything bad. But I couldn't stop myself.'

'You're pathetic!'

He recoiled as if she'd struck him.

'You waited until I was safely out of the way, then you put your filthy hands on my daughter. Not just once, lots of times. What sort of man are you?' Words were spilling out of her in an unstoppable torrent. 'Laura was only a child, for God's sake! I can hardly believe what she told me. She said you made her put it in her mouth. Your fucking *prick*.' The word, new on her tongue, made a satisfying crunch of sound. She noted with relish the shock on his face, which seemed to freeze except for a tiny wobble in his lower lip. 'You bastard. How could you do that to your own daughter?'

'Suzanne, please—'

But he wasn't going to shut her up. He wasn't going to convince her to see things as he wanted her to see them, not this time.

'And you couldn't make do with just Laura, could you? You had to go and play your sick games with Emma too. Only you had to have more fun with her, didn't you? You had to stick your pathetic little willy into her.' She gasped for breath. Her anger was consuming her, like no anger she'd ever experienced. 'Are they the only ones you've preyed on? Or are there other girls that I don't know about?'

'No, there are no others.'

There was a chance, she thought, he was telling the truth. But that meant nothing. Why wouldn't there be others? How could she believe anything he said now?

'I swear, Suzanne, I've never done anything like that before. And it wasn't nearly as bad as you think—'

'Are you serious? Did you ever think for a moment how much harm you've done to that poor girl? She trusted you, she thought you were helping her, and all along … all along you …' She couldn't find any more words. She hated him then, more than she'd ever hated anyone. 'And did you ever imagine that Laura could be damaged by what you did to her? Or did you sit there with your stinking hard-on, thinking of nothing but yourself? Christ, I can't believe I didn't see who you really were for all these years. I've been an absolute fool.'

Paul didn't reply. He looked stunned, as if she'd just punched him.

'I'm going to sleep in the guest room.' She walked past him and up the stairs.

'Please, listen—'

'Leave me alone, Paul. Just leave me alone.'

She took out her pyjamas from under her pillow and opened the door of Daniel's old bedroom. His childhood dartboard stuck out from under the wardrobe, one of the many things she hadn't had the heart to throw away. She took off her damp clothes, sat on the bed, and started to cry. The man she'd loved for twenty-five years was gone. No, the man she thought she'd loved was gone, whoever he was.

21

Paul

26 April 2011

Paul drained the coffee from his cup. He looked again at the short message beside the toaster that had greeted him half an hour earlier, scrawled in red pen on the back of the gas bill envelope:

Gone to stay with Katherine.

Suzanne must have crept out when he was asleep – he'd not heard a sound from her. He crumpled the envelope into a tight ball and tossed it in the bin, then checked his watch: 8.10am. If he didn't leave soon he'd be late for his 9.30am meeting. He put his laptop inside his briefcase, picked up his raincoat, and closed the front door behind him. The sky was overcast, threatening rain. Moisture hung in the air.

He aimed his car key at the driver's door and froze. The words stretched across the windscreen of his Porsche in bright orange, two-inch-high capitals:

FUCK YOU TOO

The Porsche was parked in the street – Suzanne's car had until recently occupied the driveway – its windscreen visible to everyone passing by. Half the street might have seen it by now, this despoiling of his car by his demented wife.

Paul reached across and touched the F. The outline did not smudge; it was marker pen, he realised with a sinking heart. He spat on the F and rubbed in his spittle with a tissue then went back inside the house. He returned with a bottle of window cleaning fluid and a sponge. For ten minutes, he scrubbed until there was only a small hint of what had been there.

He turned the key in the ignition.

Pervert.

His heart kicked against his chest. The voice had come from inside his head. What was wrong with him? Mad people heard voices. They'd be putting him in a straitjacket next, locking him up in a padded cell.

He reached the end of Elgin Drive and accelerated into a gap in the traffic. Suzanne had been angry, she didn't know what she was saying. He wasn't a pervert. He'd only done what tens of thousands of men secretly longed to do. His yearning for Laura had tormented him, day and night. What man could have resisted her? A neutered half-wit maybe, not a man of flesh and blood, with a man's instincts. He'd fought against that yearning for so long.

And she'd never pushed him off, had she? She'd never fought back or run away.

OK, OK, he was making excuses. He should have left her alone. But he'd never intended to harm her. His desire had sprung from love.

He drove towards the station. Yet another squeak came from a rear wheel. He breathed a sigh of exasperation. What the hell was wrong with the car this time? First the driver seat motor had packed up, now this. You didn't expect a brand new Porsche to start falling apart after six months.

His train was delayed by ten minutes. He paced up and down the platform. A throb of pain was starting in his temple. At this rate, he'd only just make the meeting.

There were no empty seats on the train. He stood in the narrow aisle, holding on to the nearest seat, trying to ignore the other passengers who bumped against him, blared music through their headphones, and talked inanely on their phones. He tried to think about the meeting, to remember the points he needed to make.

But Laura came into his head. Laura aged ten or eleven, with that brace, and the fringe that kept flopping into her eyes. On her face that impish look she used to have, and the lightning smile that came from pure joy. It had stopped coming as she got older; she'd looked at him with sad eyes, eyes that spoke more than she'd ever said.

He thought of Emma, that night he'd driven her back to Jane's for the last time.

He hadn't meant to harm Emma either. He should never have agreed to take her swimming in the first place. He'd kidded himself that he could walk away if he wanted. But he'd been wrong. A kind of madness had taken him over. And now, he was paying the price. Everything was coming unstuck. The police would come to arrest him, sooner or later. His life would be blown apart. Soon, everyone would know what he'd done.

He got out at Vauxhall as usual. At 9.20am he arrived at the glass and steel tower near the Thames. The top four floors were Zenco Brand's UK headquarters.

'Morning, Paul,' James on reception called out in a gruff voice, accompanied by the reluctant smile he reserved for rainy Mondays and the first morning back after a bank holiday weekend. Paul nodded, and walked on to the lift. His headache was worse than before. The last thing he wanted was a goddamn meeting. And there was another one this afternoon, with the MD, to hash over what was causing falling sales revenues.

He got out at the tenth floor and turned left, swiped his card and entered the open-plan office.

'Hi, guys, hope you all had a good Easter.' Most of his team had been lounging at their desks, talking and laughing. Suddenly, they were all alert, straight-backed. 'Let's get this show on the road. We've got a meeting in the boardroom in five minutes.'

He sat at his desk – one of the more coveted ones because it was at the edge of the building and enjoyed a sweeping view across the Thames – and switched on the computer. The familiar messages scrolled down the screen: Login Name, Password; Welcome to Windows, Welcome to Zenco Brands.

It was time to leave all the other shit behind. He couldn't think about that in here. He had to be the tough businessman again, the decisive leader, someone who knew what the fuck he was doing.

The monthly sales figures, where were they? He found the document, printed it, then searched several folders for the file he'd saved Thursday afternoon, the one that contained the revised marketing strategy he was supposed to be going over in the meeting.

Jesus, it was hot in here. His shirt was clinging to the sweat on his back. He got up, poured a cup of water from the dispenser and drank it quickly. Linda, his PA, strolled towards him, her face dripping with goodwill.

'Hi, Paul. How was your weekend?'

Fucking awful, he almost said, to rid her face of its gormless smile. *My life is about to go down the plughole. My daughter has told my wife I'm the biggest slimeball that ever walked the planet, and my wife has left home and I've no idea when she'll be back.*

He assumed a neutral expression. 'So-so. I've had better.'

Linda was looking at him inquisitively, her nose twitching like a rabbit's, sniffing for clues.

He remembered that Linda had celebrated her 30th birthday over the weekend with a massive piss-up.

'How was the party?'

'Fantastic. We sang Abba songs until four in the morning.' Linda was peering at him through her speckled designer frames. 'Are you alright, Paul?'

'My head's killing me. Could you dig me out an aspirin from somewhere? And, Linda, will you find the latest marketing strategy document for this meeting?'

At 9.30am he took his folder of papers and walked over to the boardroom. Every seat was filled. He put his jacket over the vacant chair at the end of the table, closest to the flat screen on the wall. Opposite him hung a large, excessively colourful painting. It was meant to be an abstract, he supposed – someone must have thought it gave the company a suitably cutting-edge feel. But it looked more like the result of someone hastily retching on the canvas.

To one side of him, Sadie, the marketing assistant, doodled on her notepad. Linda's head was stuck inside the computer cabinet as she fiddled with the controls. He waited for her to pull out her head and smile at him before he cleared his throat, pushed back his chair and got to his feet.

All eyes were on him. A rush of adrenalin and another, scary, sensation, as if any moment he was going to lose it completely.

'First things first, we've had another good set of results this month.' He pointed to the top row of the spreadsheet that was displayed on the screen. 'Mark, congratulations for getting number one slot, yet again.'

Pervert.

He grasped for his next sentence. Sadie was looking at him with raised eyebrows. He frowned at her, trying to pull himself together.

'As you all know, we've had a few setbacks lately. We need to start making a significant improvement in sales volume.'

He gulped at his glass of water. It was too hot in here; the air conditioning didn't seem to be working. He had to keep going, stay focused.

'Kyle finally got the BAE contract signed last month,' he continued. 'Good work, Kyle.'

Another voice, different to the first.

Pervert.

Take no notice, he told himself. *The voices aren't real. Ignore them and they'll go away.*

The voices hissed in unison.

Pervert!

Sweat prickled on his forehead and the back of his neck. He loosened his tie. There was no air in this room. He swiped at his jacket.

'Sorry, guys, I have to go. Dan, take over, will you?'

He met a wall of stares. Everyone was eyeballing him as if he'd sprouted an extra head. Sonia touched his arm, her eyes wide with alarm. 'What's the matter?'

'I'm not feeling too well. I'm going outside to get some air.'

Thank God, he was out of there. He pressed the button for the lift, willing it to arrive before anyone came after him.

James at reception looked up with a blank face and carried on humming. Paul passed through the revolving doors, onto the street. He glanced at the sky. Dark clouds ganged up above the tops of nearby buildings.

'Spare some change, sir?' enquired the haggard old guy permanently installed beneath the cash machine on the corner. Paul shook his head and walked faster. The man muttered something unpleasant.

The lights were on in the café. Paul crossed over the road and went inside. No one would bother him in here, it wasn't yet time for the mid-morning cappuccino rush. Apart from a couple of tourists tucking into late breakfasts, the place was empty.

He ordered an espresso and sat on a stool at the counter alongside the window. A worn copy of the *Sunday Mirror* lay in front of him, the first headline read:

Family die in blaze

Then, further down, another, smaller headline:

Sex pervert jailed for five years

He started to read the article. A man had pleaded guilty to indecently assaulting his ten-year-old niece.

Paul put down the paper. His heart beat harder than ever, it was about to gallop out of his chest. He picked up a paper serviette from the counter and wiped his brow. He was an animal trapped in a cage. Some vicious sods were prodding him through the bars with a stick. They knew he couldn't escape. They were going to torment him until he couldn't take it any longer.

They'd got it wrong, though. He wasn't a pervert. No way was he one of those. He was nothing like that man who'd been sent to jail.

But what sort of man gets turned on by his own daughter? He'd told himself it was harmless, he hadn't hurt her. Had he been kidding himself? Once, she'd been bright-eyed and talkative. She'd turned into a girl who didn't laugh, a girl who kept things to herself. He'd told Suzanne it was nothing to do with him. *Wasn't* it all his doing, though? Had he taken away Laura's happiness, her spirit? And what about Emma? Would she stop laughing, too? He'd taken away her purity, hadn't he? He'd seen her fear and ignored it. She'd trusted him and he'd pissed in her face.

No, no, no. It wasn't like that. He wasn't a bad man. He loved Laura. He loved Emma too. He had taken it too far with her, yes, he admitted that, but it didn't make him the devil's spawn. They were all out to get him. They didn't understand how things really were.

A small white cup appeared in front of him. He stared at it, unable to pick it up. His mouth was dry, his heart was still hammering away like no one's business. He patted down his face again with the serviette.

When he looked up, the fat Italian at the coffee machine was eying him suspiciously.

Paul paid and left. He turned into a narrow street and followed it to the river.

No one was around. He stood and stared at the dull metallic strip of water. A gull landed on a piece of driftwood at the river's edge. Pages of an abandoned newspaper fluttered on a breeze.

A thought came, desolate like the wind: what would Laura think of him now she knew what had happened to Emma? His hope was that one day she'd stop treating him so coldly. Well, he could forget about that. She wouldn't want to go anywhere near him now. And what about Suzanne? He'd convinced himself she would always forgive him, she'd always love him no matter what he did. But she wasn't going to forgive him, not this time. He'd been an arrogant idiot. He'd finally managed to destroy her love, just when he'd found out he couldn't do without it.

He wiped his eyes with the back of his hand. If only he could let go and sob as he had as a small boy. There'd be some relief in that. It was more than half a lifetime ago, the last time he'd cried. As he remembered it, horror once again crept over his skin.

He's wearing only his T-shirt. His underpants are on the floor by his bed. His mother has come into the room. She has seen him. He pulls the covers over himself quickly. He can't stop what happens next. The hot wetness trickles down into the sheets.

He expects her to go away, to leave him to his embarrassment, but his mother doesn't leave the room. Her eye muscles twitch, as they do when she's concentrating. She walks towards him, stands over the bed.

'You should be ashamed of yourself. You're only ten years old and already you're doing that filthy thing.'

He does it in the middle of the night mostly, when there is no chance anyone will discover him, not in the bright, early afternoon with his mother and sisters around. But today he feels small and lost. Everyone has forgotten about him, no one seems to care about him anymore. He needs the good feelings to wash over him and wipe the bad ones away.

'Get out of bed.'

He hesitates. He can't. She will see.

'Get out of bed, Paul.'

Her voice won't let him disobey. He does as she says. She looks without speaking. He can't look at her but he can hear the disgust in her voice.

'I always knew you would turn out like this.'

She tells him not to move. He hears her go into the bathroom and she brings back a towel. White, spotless.

'Wipe it all off. Go on.'

He does what she says. She takes the towel from him.

He thinks he'll have to stay in his room for the rest of the day and go without dinner, as he has to whenever he accidentally breaks something or plays in the yard too loudly. Or she'll ask his father to give him the belt when he comes in from work, as she does for the most serious offences.

But this time it's different.

'Put those on,' she instructs, pointing. She watches him put on his underpants. 'Come with me.'

He follows her, afraid at the sudden coldness of her voice. They go downstairs. She opens the door to the cellar and gives him a push.

'Down you go. Right down inside.'

When he reaches the bottom of the steep stairs, the light goes off and the door shuts. He hears the key turning in the lock. All around is black. The light switch is on the outside wall. His foot hits a small hard object. He gropes for something solid, finds the fuse boxes. His hand brushes into something soft and wispy. He pulls it back.

He's always hated this place. Coming down here to fetch the stepladder, or to right a tripped fuse, he scuttles in and out, taking care to avoid peering into the grimy, shadowy corners. But he always puts on the light and keeps the door open. This time, he's trapped.

He calls out for his mother. She doesn't answer. He can see a bit more now, enough to make out a bucket on the ground and bicycles propped against the walls. He makes his way up the stairs and raps on the door. There is no handle, there's no way he can open the door from the inside.

'Don't leave me here! Please!'

His voice is frightened. He's five years old again and afraid of the dark.

He leans against the wall at the foot of the stairs. He wonders if there's a torch or a lamp somewhere, but he doesn't want to move from this spot to go into unknown places, where horrible things might lurk. He checks his watch, but the dial is too dark to read. His father won't be home for hours. He listens out for his sisters. He hears muffled voices approaching. One is the nasal whine of his older sister. She is back from somewhere. He calls out again. Footsteps running away; laughter.

It is their revenge too. They blame him for everything they do wrong and he is always the one punished. Juliet scratched Natalie's arm, leaving a red gouge, and both said that he'd cut his sister with his penknife. His mother is too stupid to see, or she just wants to take their side. He got beaten for it, with the buckle. His father thinks it's good to be tough with him, it will shake out the 'girly stuff'.

Soon, he needs the toilet. It's quiet outside the cellar, it has been quiet for ages. They must all be upstairs now, or outside in the pool. Where is his mother? He tries to distract himself by counting to a hundred slowly. If she doesn't let him out soon, he will have to pee right here.

He gets to forty then starts crying, and he can't stop. He pushes his fist into his mouth to muffle the noise, because crying during punishments isn't allowed and he doesn't want to be a cry-baby. His mother doesn't love him, he is sure of it now. If she loved him, she wouldn't make him stay down here, alone in the dark. She knows he is afraid of the dark. She taunts him about it sometimes, saying he is too old for such childish behaviour. And now there'll be another thing to taunt him with. The disgust was plain on her face.

Shame rises inside him, filling him. Then it turns to anger, and the anger turns to hate. His mother will mean nothing to him, he decides. He won't let her hurt him anymore.

Paul held himself very still. The pain of the memory was leaching out of the deep place he'd kept it all these years. His heart was tight, like someone with iron hands was squeezing it and trying to squash it into a pulp. For the first time since that day, he wanted to cry.

No, he couldn't let himself cry. He never cried. It was too late for that.

He walked on, along the path towards nowhere in particular, the first drops of rain wetting his face.

22

Laura

26 April 2011

Laura put down the casserole dish she was about to wash. The phone was ringing. The sound had hardly registered amid the chaos of her thoughts.

It was her mother, thank goodness. Mum hadn't answered any of her calls since their conversation at the flat two days ago.

'Mum, are you alright? I've been calling your mobile for hours.'

'I'm sorry, darling, I should have told you earlier. My mind's all over the place at the moment. I couldn't face being in the house any longer with your father, so I left this morning. I'm staying at Katherine's for a bit. I only got my phone up and running just now. I left the charger at home and the battery ran out.'

Her mother's voice was frail and distant. Laura pictured a thrush lying injured on the ground. There had been one yesterday, outside the entrance to the block of flats, just alive. She'd picked it up, covering it with her other hand, intending to take it to a safer place; so light, so tiny, from time to time gently fluttering against her hands. But when she uncovered it a minute later, it had stopped moving.

'Well, I'm glad you're still alive. Will you be OK?'

'I hope so. I'm doing my best to cope with everything.'

'Do you want me to come over?'

'You don't need to. Katherine's looking after me, plying me with tea, and gin and tonics. I couldn't ask for a better friend.'

'I did the right thing to tell you, didn't I?' Telling her mother what Dad had done to her years ago had been a relief, a burden finally lifted. But not for her mother.

'Yes, you were right to tell me. Only it's hard to take it in, what he's done.' Her mother's voice grew wobblier. 'I just can't get my head around it, how he could have done those things to you. I feel so bad that I wasn't there for you. That I didn't do anything to stop him.'

Laura said nothing. She too felt guilty. She'd guessed what her father might do but had done too little, too late. She'd hardly slept last night, thinking about what she should have done to stop her father from seeing Emma one more time. Then everything would have been different.

Her mother carried on. 'I've got to face it though, haven't I? Life doesn't always deal you the cards you're hoping for.'

'What Dad did to Emma, I think it's my fault.'

'How could it be your fault?'

'I guessed he might do something, that he might go after her. I should have done something to stop him. I should have waited for Jane and told her myself that Emma was in danger—'

'You couldn't read his mind, could you? You weren't there to see what he was up to. He manipulated us both, Laura. He made us see what we wanted to see.'

The words were meant well, but she knew she hadn't done the right thing. Why hadn't she tried harder to protect

Emma, rather than her mother? Why hadn't she waited a little longer for Jane to get home, to tell her everything?

'Is someone going to tell the police what he did?' She heard her words come out sharper than she'd meant them to. This too had been preying on her mind.

Her mother didn't reply.

'Don't you think they should know?'

'I don't know, Laura.' Her mother's voice became a small tremble. 'Maybe Jane will tell them.'

'I hope so. How long will you be at Katherine's? Are you going to go back to Dad?'

'I don't know, I can't decide anything just yet.' Her mother's tone changed. 'Do you think Marmaduke will be alright on his own with your dad? He's only got four tins of Whiskas left. Your father might forget to feed him.'

'I'm sure he'll be OK, Mum.' She couldn't help a trace of annoyance entering her voice. Her mother seemed more concerned with the cat's well-being than trying to deal with this situation.

After their conversation, Laura carried on washing up. Her mother's voice lingered in her head. Mum hadn't sounded herself at all, more like someone having a breakdown. If she had the strength, she might leave Dad. But most likely she wouldn't. After a few weeks she would convince herself that he was going to change, and he'd never do any of those things again, and she'd give him one more chance. And if he had one more chance, what would happen? If no one reported him to the police, he would be free to go after other girls. Once again, she found herself imagining her father with Emma. Fucking a girl of twelve – how had he managed it? Had Emma struggled, or had she been too shocked and too scared to resist? Had he sweet-talked her into giving way, sapping her resistance bit by bit?

It was too horrible to think about. The poor girl, she would have to carry this around with her for the rest of her life. Of course, Emma would probably try to forget it had ever happened. It wouldn't work; the knowledge would make itself felt. Perhaps she would find it harder to trust people, and easier to think bad things about herself. The bad things men did wouldn't surprise her. In one way or another, Emma's life would be changed because of what Dad had done.

Laura picked up the scouring pad to attack the grimy layer at the bottom of a saucepan. That awful feeling was back. Guilt struck at her core. There was no doubt; she should have stopped her father from going after Emma. He had lied to her about his intentions – all that guff about how he would never think of harming Emma. Why, oh why had she believed him? It was obvious, looking back, that her father would have tried to find a way to see Emma again. If only she hadn't been so concerned about protecting her mother. Mum had found out the truth anyway, in the end.

It was done now; there was nothing she could do to change the past. But she did have the power to change the future. Whatever else happened, her father couldn't be allowed to get away with what he'd done to Emma.

Only it looked like he *was* going to get away with it.

She kept scrubbing, not noticing what she was doing she was so deep in thought.

If Emma hadn't told anyone at the time, and if she didn't want to talk to the police, there would be no evidence against him. Her father wouldn't be charged or prosecuted and he'd be free to carry on as before, wouldn't he? How soon would it be before he found his next victim?

Laura put down the saucepan and slowly dried her hands on a towel.

What if she told the police what he'd done to her when she was a child?

Her mind raced. The things he'd done to her in secret were crimes – indecently touching an underage girl, forcing her into a sexual act – they were serious crimes, surely, especially if that girl was his daughter.

But, if she reported it now, ten years on, would the police take any notice? There was no evidence, no witness. She hadn't kept a diary and she hadn't told anyone about those things, not until years later. Her father would simply deny it all.

Her heart began to speed up. A strange surge of excitement, almost exhilaration, went through her, along with an undercurrent of trepidation.

Perhaps if she went to the police about what her father had done to her, it might convince Emma to go to the police too. Then they'd have to listen. Jane might change her mind about Emma giving evidence if it was by video link. If her father was found guilty of having sex with a child he'd be put away, surely. He'd be unable to harm any more girls for a good while. He'd be monitored afterwards, put on the sex offenders register. Even if he got off, or it didn't get to court, at least the police would be alerted to her father and his predilections. Most of all, he would be forced to face himself and the things he'd done.

It was scary, the thought of giving up her own father to the police, but she had to stop him from hurting anyone else. He couldn't be allowed to get away with what he'd done.

23

Suzanne

29 April 2011

She stared at the blurred lime-green shape that had appeared in front of her, and realised it was a mug.

'Here you are, m'dear. This'll pep you up.' Katherine smiled at her with coral lips, pleased about something. 'That was David on the phone.'

'David?'

'He said he might drop by later. He's staying in Chelsea for a conference. He's got some cuttings for us.'

She nodded, not getting what her friend meant. It was as if she'd been marooned for months on a remote island. Katherine was miles away. Her words floated by, one by one, out of reach.

Katherine sat in the armchair opposite. Two converging creases appeared above her eyebrows.

'You're in a bad way, aren't you, love? You've hardly said a word since you got here.'

Suzanne took a sip of tea. It tasted quite unlike tea. She put down the mug.

'I don't know what to do,' she said.

'Give yourself time for things to settle. You can stay here for as long as you want to, you know that.'

'Aren't you supposed to be at work today? It's Friday, isn't it?'

'I'm working Monday and Tuesday next week to make up. It's alright, Suzy, I don't mind. I can't leave you alone while you're like this.'

She looked down at her hands lying limply in her lap. The thought that had filled her head for the past few days was back.

'How could he have done those things? Every time I think of him … I can't bear to think about it.'

'It's hard. You've just got to hang on in there, love.'

Katherine disappeared. Her attention was drawn back to the sculpture that was staring at her from the mantelpiece: a warrior with a spear in his outstretched arm, and a frightful expression on his face. Suzanne looked away. Wherever her gaze landed, exotic objects plucked from Katherine and Jeremy's travels popped disconcertingly into view. It hadn't bothered her before, but today … The room's maroon walls were oppressive, more suited to an opium den than a living room. She tried to concentrate on a beam of pure white light, imagine it washing over her, lifting the dreadful images from her mind.

But it was no use. Paul's mouth was on Emma's belly button. His hand lay on her thigh, next to her pubic hair. Soon, he would put his fingers inside her most private, most sacred place. The same fingers he used to caress her own body.

She bit down hard on her lip, tasted blood.

'I've made some soup for lunch.' Katherine's head appeared at the door. 'Will you have some?'

'No thanks, I'm not hungry. But you go ahead.'

'Are you sure? What about a sandwich?'

The door closed. Suzanne listened to the muffled clatter of plates and saucepans coming from the kitchen.

It was a relief to be left alone; she didn't have to pretend she was coping when she wasn't, or that everything would be alright when she knew it wouldn't. She dug her nails into the top of her hand, imprinting a series of dark curves on her skin.

Her husband had betrayed her as surely as if he'd had an affair. Only this was a thousand times worse.

Well, he could sod off out of her life. She never wanted to see him again.

No. How could she live without Paul? He was her blood, her backbone.

She closed her eyes, felt herself drift away. She was brought back suddenly when Katherine burst into the room, holding a handset.

'It's Jane, for you.'

She took the phone.

'Jane?' Her heart beat faster. Why did Jane want to speak to her? Had she told the police about Paul?

'Hello, Suzanne.' Curt, emotionless.

'Jane, I'm so sorry I didn't believe you—'

'I didn't call to make up with you.' Her voice had the tone you'd use for someone you didn't like. No, someone you hated.

'I just wanted to ask you about something,' Jane continued. 'Has Paul abused anyone else besides Emma?'

For a moment, she was tempted to lie.

'Laura told me some things on the weekend that I didn't know before. I would have told you if I'd known.'

'So, tell me, what did he do to Laura?'

'I'm not going to go into the details, Jane. It was when she was about Emma's age. He touched her. He did things that were ... indecent.'

'But you didn't find out until a few days ago. You didn't have any knowledge of it before, any suspicions? There was nothing you could have done to prevent Paul raping my daughter?'

She felt herself shrivel. 'No, there was nothing definite. Except ...'

'Except what?' The question was barked at her, as if she were under interrogation.

It would make things worse, she knew that before she opened her mouth.

'They were just little things. The way he looked at young girls sometimes seemed ... a bit odd. There was one time ...' She remembered the girl in the hotel restaurant and shivered. 'But, Jane, I never imagined what he would do to Emma, not in a million years.'

Jane laughed, a short, humourless croak. 'Just like you never imagined him doing anything to *your* daughter?'

The words struck her deep in the belly, pulling the air from her.

'I'm not saying that what happened is your fault, Suzanne.' Jane's words sounded distorted, as if they were being strangled. 'I was the one who trusted him with my daughter. I should have realised from the start how vulnerable she was, how—' Jane stopped abruptly. When she spoke again, her voice was composed, hard-edged. 'Anyhow, I'm sure you understand what I'm saying.'

For a few moments, neither of them spoke.

'Emma told me today that Laura came by to see me, the evening before Paul ...' Jane cut herself off. '... the evening before that day. She said Laura was worried that he might be up to something. She warned her not to be alone with him.' Her tone sharpened. 'Did you know that Laura came to see me?'

'She mentioned it at the weekend – when she told me about Paul. I had no idea before that she suspected him. I would have said something if I'd known.'

'I'll have to take your word for that.' A brief pause. 'Well, I won't disturb you any longer.'

Suzanne hesitated. She tried to keep the anger and frustration out of her voice.

'So, Emma didn't tell you that Laura came over?'

'She told me. I didn't listen.' A deep sigh at the other end of the line. 'You may as well know the whole of it. I was delayed getting home from work that Friday. Emma tried to tell me that Laura had been over when I finally got home, but I didn't take it in. Toby ran at me as soon as she started talking. He was in tears, saying that she'd hurt his arm – they'd been fighting again. I lost my rag with Emma, told her she was old enough to know better and sent her up to her room. Then a friend phoned and asked if I knew that Mandy had been suspended from school for spray painting the gym – the girl Emma was going to go shopping with on the Saturday. It was the last straw. I phoned Paul afterwards and told him to come over on Saturday after all, I needed him to keep an eye on Emma – I wasn't having my daughter turn into a delinquent too. He texted Emma right away with his modelling bullshit, so I've found out, and she swallowed it.'

She could almost hear Jane spit the final words into the phone. Before she could say anything, Jane carried on.

'The silly girl didn't try to tell me again about Laura coming over, and kept quiet about her warning not to be alone with your husband. She went off with him the next day because she was pissed off with me for getting mad at her – and she thought he could help turn her into Rosie fucking Huntingley-White.'

She waited for Jane to catch her breath.

'She didn't dare tell me any of this until this morning, she was so scared I'd think badly of her. She thought that because Laura had warned her away from him, I would blame her for what happened.'

'If only she'd …' She didn't dare to say the rest.

'What?'

If only Emma had listened to Laura, they wouldn't be having this sodding conversation.

'Oh, never mind.' Emma had suffered enough already, and so had Jane, and what was done was done. 'Jane, before you go.' She braced herself for Jane's reaction. 'Have you talked to the police? Has Emma?'

'Oh, so that's what you're worried about.' A fake laugh. 'You needn't worry. I'm not going to make Emma go through any more than she has already. Endless questions from the police and lawyers … she doesn't want to talk about it to them. She doesn't want to give a load of total strangers a blow-by-blow account of how he humiliated her, and I don't blame her. Frankly, she's in no state to go through all that.'

'How … how is she?' As soon as she formed the words, she wished she could take them back.

'Oh, please.' Contempt. The voice had become a stranger's. 'I'm sorry, I have to go. I won't be phoning again. Goodbye, Suzanne.'

The phone clicked loudly in her ear.

'Are you alright, love?' Katherine put her head round the door. 'What did Jane want? Suzy? What's the matter?'
Suzanne tried to meet her friend's eyes, which were too kind. She'd felt she'd been knocked flat, a mouse mowed down by a lorry.

'She's not going to the police. And she blames me for what happened to Emma. Herself as well, but mainly me.'

'Suzanne, listen to me. You're not to blame and neither is Jane. Paul is. He's the one who needs to get whatever's coming to him.' Katherine's hand throttled a cushion as she spoke. She put it down and frisked dog hairs from her corduroy skirt. 'How about a drink? You look like you need one.'

'I'd murder a gin and tonic, Kat, if you've got any of that bottle of Gordon's left.'

'I'll join you. Come and help me in the kitchen. It's Jeremy's bridge night so we'll be alone for dinner, unless David wants to join us.'

David? Oh, yes, the man from the party.

'I don't mind if you ask him,' she said. She didn't care one way or another.

Suzanne pulled a layer of tough outer skin from the onion that was set out on the worktop. Taking a knife from the rack, she began to slice it.

Katherine put her drink down beside the chopping board and stood there, rubbing her cheek thoughtfully.

'Did Jane say why she's not going to the police?'

This couldn't be happening. If she closed her eyes, and concentrated really hard, maybe it would all go away.

'For Emma's sake,' she replied. 'Jane doesn't want her to have to go through a trial, all those questions. It would be too much of an ordeal.'

'I don't like to say this when you're so upset,' Katherine said, without hesitation, 'but what about the next time he molests someone? They say that men who do these things often can't stop. It's like an addiction.'

Suzanne drew a sharp breath. She concentrated on chopping the onion as finely as possible. Next time, Katherine had said, as if it were a foregone conclusion that there would be a next time. Paul wouldn't do anything like this again, would he? Surely, now his depravity had been discovered, he'd have to stop.

Then she was afraid. What if the police investigated and Paul were put on trial? What if he were sent to prison? He would never survive that.

'Sorry, Suzy, but I have strong feelings about what Paul's done. I think he's dead lucky Jane hasn't gone over there and walloped him. If it were my daughter, I'd be over there with a fucking carving knife, anything I could find. He deserves everything that's coming to him, in my opinion.'

A shrill ring interrupted them from the other side of the kitchen. Katherine picked up the phone on its third ring. 'It's your husband,' she said curtly, scowling. 'Will you take it?'

'No, tell him I can't talk to him.' It was the third time he'd rung that day.

Katherine frowned. 'He says he has to talk to you.'

'I don't want to talk to him.'

Katherine turned away from her for a few moments, then put the phone back into its base. 'He says he hopes you're OK and he wants you to come home,' she said, in a matter-of-fact voice. 'And to call him as soon as you can.'

Suzanne sliced a courgette in half and scored deep crevices into its moist flesh. It was Paul's flesh, or her own, she didn't know which. She picked up the salt shaker and ground in the white crystals with the flat of the blade.

The front doorbell rang. Katherine wiped her hands on her apron and left the kitchen, pulling the door behind her. Suzanne strained to hear the voices from the hall; she could make out David's bass voice below Katherine's. Then the door opened and David stepped hesitantly into the kitchen, each hand grasping a plastic bag bulging with green shoots.

'Hello, Suzanne. It's good to see you again.'

In a suit, David looked quite different from the man she'd met at the party, but his eyes were the same gentle blue. He bent down and put the bags on the mat against the back door.

'If this is a bad time … I don't want to intrude. I only came to drop these off.'

'It's alright. You're not intruding.'

He looked at her for a few moments. 'Kate's told me you're going through a rough time at the moment.'

She nodded, unable to think of anything to say.

Katherine came in, holding a bottle of wine. 'Have a drink, won't you, David? And won't you stay for dinner? It'll be just the three of us, Jeremy won't be back till late.'

'I was going to have dinner at the hotel, but you could twist my arm. I'd much rather have dinner with you two ladies.'

'My mushroom risotto isn't bad,' Katherine said, giving the frying pan on the hob a quick stir. 'If I do say so myself.'

'Yes,' Suzanne added. 'You'll stay for dinner, won't you? I'm not up to much conversation, I'm afraid, but Kat needs a respite from all my doom and gloom.'

David took off his jacket. He would have to leave shortly after dinner, he said.

Suzanne went upstairs. She was sleeping in Debbie's old bedroom, which was decorated in a sugary pink. A glass tray on the dressing table contained a hotchpotch of girlie things: hair accessories, body paint, and oddly coloured lipsticks. The noticeboard on the wall was covered in photographs. Debbie as a little girl holding a kitten, grinning toothily. Debbie in her black graduation gown, shaking hands as she collected her certificate. Debbie in a long dress, grinning from ear to ear, a young man at her side.

A lump came to her throat. If only Laura's life was as happy as Debbie's.

She took off her cardigan, put on a blouse, and retouched her lipstick.

Downstairs, the table was set for dinner. A vase of vivid red and yellow tulips stood in the centre. At each end, white dinner candles flickered. Suzanne sat at the place that had been laid for her, opposite David.

Katherine poured the wine. 'Tuck in, guys. No need to be polite.'

David enthused about his latest project: converting his shed into an art studio. Suzanne pecked at her food. She wasn't in the mood for talking.

'What are the women like, at your firm?' Katherine asked David, during a lull in the conversation, with a teasing smile. 'Any talent there?'

'I told you, Kate, I'm steering clear of women at the moment.'

'I thought you said your divorce didn't leave you bitter and twisted,' Katherine continued playfully.

Suzanne put down her fork. Divorce. The word was so bleak, so final. If she left Paul, what would happen to her? Would she end up skittering between dating websites and meet-up groups like some of her divorced friends? How would she cope with the loneliness? How would she begin to rebuild her life?

She stared at the tulips. They were glorious. Yet within a week they'd be wilting, ready to be thrown away.

'I don't know how I'll live without Paul,' she said.

Katherine blinked at her, mouth open.

David spoke softly, as if to himself.

'You think it's the end of the world, when your marriage ends, but it's not. It's a new start, another chance to be happy.'

He didn't know how she felt. He couldn't possibly.

David's eyes met hers. They seemed to contain the strength that she lacked, the assurance that she didn't have. 'You're going to leave him, aren't you?'

'Yes,' she replied, without hesitation. 'I'm going to leave him.'

No one spoke; it shocked her too, but she would manage. Somehow.

'Good on you, love,' Katherine said.

Suzanne searched her pockets for a tissue. 'I'm sorry about this.'

Katherine dabbed at her own eyes with a finger. 'I'll get the Kleenex.'

David stood, his arms open. 'How about a hug?'

Although she hardly knew him, she didn't hesitate. This was right. His arms enclosed her with a light pressure. She felt his heart beating and his warmth, and wished this simple touch could go on forever.

24

Laura

30 April 2011

A sluggish light slipped through the curtains. Laura raised her head from the pillow. A bee in her ear? No, someone was at the door. She turned over, hoping whoever it was would go away. Her dream caught mid-frame, trapped in her head.

A younger version of herself, holding Emma's hand, walking towards the front door of her childhood home. The front door is on the latch. No one seems to be in, it is so quiet. They go upstairs. *We can play in my room*, she's thinking, *out of everyone's way*. She pushes open her bedroom door.

He is there. Lying on her bed.

'Come in, girls,' says her dream father, pulling back the covers, 'climb in beside me.'

Laura shuddered. The front door buzzed again then her mobile rang. She sat up and gulped some water, tested the firmness of the floor.

'Hi, I'm outside, can you let me in?' It was her brother's voice.

She buzzed him in and went to put on her dressing gown and her slippers.

'Hiya, sis. Sorry to wake you up. I didn't mean to get you out of bed.'

Her brother put down his bag and bent to hug her. He was wearing a sweater over jeans. She noticed how broad he was across the chest, how big and capable he seemed.

'It's alright, it's time I was up. I'll make some coffee.'

'I phoned an hour ago but there was no answer. I'm in London to see some friends, thought I'd drop by.'

Daniel sat on the only stool in the kitchen while she dried some mugs.

'Still working at the nightclub?'

'No, I don't work there anymore.'

'What happened?' He raised his eyebrows. 'Did they sack you?'

'No, I left. It wasn't the right place for me.'

'That's probably a good idea, you know.' There was a serious note in his voice. He seemed to be turning something over in his mind. No words came out though. 'So, what are you going to do now?'

'I might have found something. I had an interview yesterday.' A job agency had rung her earlier in the week, out of the blue, and said they'd got an unusual role and it looked like the perfect opportunity for her. 'This woman is writing a book about archaeology – the latest Roman finds in Britain – she's getting on a bit and can't see too well, and then she was hurt in an accident. She wants someone to help with the research – read to her, help her with interviews, go to places with her.' It was the first job she'd gone for where the interviewer had shown the slightest interest in the modules she'd taken on ancient civilisations, not to mention the first job where her knowledge had been relevant; the first job for which she'd had any enthusiasm, full stop.

'Hmm, that doesn't sound like you, sis. Helping an old biddy.' A mischievous smile.

'I went to see her at her flat in Earls Court. I couldn't get her to stop talking. We spent an hour chatting about my history course at Durham, then another hour on the ancient Minoans. She loves all that stuff too.'

'Fingers crossed you get it then.'

She put a cup of coffee in front of her brother and sipped hers, standing with her back against the sink. Daniel tapped his foot against the metal legs of the stool. He seemed distracted.

'The reason I came by ... I was wondering if you might know what's going on with Mum and Dad? I called the house last night and Dad answered the phone. He sounded really down. He's been on his own at home since last Tuesday. Mum's gone to stay with her friend and he doesn't know when she's coming back—'

'Yes, I know.'

He looked at her sharply. 'What's going on, Laura? I asked Dad why she'd gone and he said to ask Mum. But Mum wouldn't say. She just said she needed to be away from him, she'd explain it all later. Have they had a fight or something?'

This was the moment she'd been dreading. What was she going to say? She turned away so he couldn't see her face.

'You know what's going on,' he said, 'don't you?'

'Yes, I do. Some of it is to do with me.'

'To do with you?'

'Dan, I don't know what to say. Maybe it's better you don't know.'

She wanted so much to tell him. But how could she shatter his existence in one moment? Daniel was getting on much better with Dad these days. The two seemed to have a lot more to talk about, he'd told her. He'd taken up sailing too, like their father. Last summer, the two of them had spent hours together – tinkering about on boats, drinking beer, talking man to man. What right did she have to spoil all that for him?

'What you tell me is up to you, I guess.' Daniel waited, holding her gaze. 'But I'm part of this family too, aren't I? Don't I have a right to know what's going on?'

'OK,' she replied, putting down her cup. 'I'll tell you what he did to me.'

On cue, the fridge stopped its thunderous drone. She began her story, trying to keep her voice calm. How her father had started touching her in the garden, and downstairs in the house, and then how he'd started coming into her room. How he'd warned her not to tell anyone. Daniel sat rigid, staring at her, not saying a word and ignoring his coffee.

'I kept it to myself for a long time. I didn't even tell Mum until last Sunday.' She swallowed the stickiness in her throat. It had clogged up, wouldn't let any more words out. 'I wasn't going to say anything to her. But I had to.'

'Why?'

'Because …' Her heart thudded.

'Because, what?'

'A twelve-year-old girl has accused Dad of having sex with her.'

'Shit, Laura. You're kidding me, aren't you?'

Daniel's face was pale, his mouth hanging open. She felt sorry for him; he wanted her to say it was all a joke.

'What girl? Who are you talking about?'

'Remember Jane, Mum's friend? It was Emma, Jane's daughter. She told Jane what he did to her and Jane told Mum. Mum didn't believe it at first, but later he admitted it to her.'

'I can't believe it.'

'Daniel, I'm sorry. You said you wanted to know.'

The fridge sputtered back into life. Daniel looked at the floor for a long time before speaking.

'Jesus. I know Dad acted a bit unhinged at times when we were growing up, hey, most of the time, but what you're telling me … you're saying he screwed this girl? That's totally unbelievable.'

His head drooped over his shoulders. Finally, he looked at her.

'Look, Laura, I'll have to go or I'll be late for my meeting.' He scraped back his stool and got to his feet. His untouched cup of coffee where she'd placed it. 'I'll call you soon.'

Laura followed her brother to the front door. He didn't kiss her goodbye, and just let himself out without looking back. She went back to the kitchen and dumped the two cups in the sink with a clatter.

Oh, fuck. What have you done?

Dismay grew inside her. What had been the point of that? She kicked the fridge to make it shut up. The whine of a vacuum cleaner started next door, too loud. She pressed her nose against the kitchen window. A thin drizzle had begun.

Her thoughts began to pile up, each one darker than the one before.

Everything had been tainted by what her father had done. He had betrayed Emma, despite his claim that he would never think of harming her. In doing so, he'd betrayed every one of his family. Her mother. Her brother. Herself.

Her mouth was dry, her heart was beating too fast. A pool of anger welled inside her. She knew it then, as much as she'd ever known anything: her father wasn't going to get the better of her. He wasn't going to win this game.

25

Suzanne

Morning, 4 May 2011

As Katherine's car turned into Elgin Drive, Suzanne noticed that the rambling, pale pink house on the corner had a For Sale sign outside. It wasn't there when she'd left home last week. The lower room's curtains were shut too, hiding the usual sight of a grand piano and shelves stacked with books. She wondered what had happened to Della, the woman in her mid-sixties who'd been living there alone in the months since her divorce. Had she finally moved in with her son, as she'd said she might have to? Or found a retirement flat?

Her own future was as bleak, perhaps.

Suzanne lowered her head. With each second, her resolve was eroding. In its place, trepidation, and something else – beyond fear. It was like that cold panic she'd felt years ago on her only attempt at abseiling. The ground had been a mere fifty feet below, yet it could have been thirty miles.

She clenched the hand on her lap into a fist. Time to face him. It was going to happen; it was too late to call a halt to it. Soon, she would have to take that first step backwards off the cliff and pray that the rope would hold her.

Katherine pulled up outside number 31. The house peered back, its face unwelcoming. The hedge was badly in need of a trim – its straggly top almost obscured the lower windows. This meant, she realised, that Katherine wouldn't be able to see into the living room. But her friend would be close enough, should anything happen. And they had both made sure to bring their mobiles.

'Here you are, madam. That'll be twenty pounds, please.'

'Thanks, Kat.' Suzanne unbuckled her seat belt, unable to raise a smile. 'See you soon.'

'Good luck, kiddo.' Katherine's hand warmed her own. 'Remember to come out straight away if you feel unsafe.'

Suzanne glanced at her face in the rear-view mirror. She looked haggard, the skin around her eyes purple and puffy from lack of sleep. She reached for her handbag and stepped out of the car. As she did so, her last strands of courage strained to hold. What if Paul got angry with her? What if he tried to stop her from leaving?

His Porsche was parked across the driveway, as shiny as ever. She opened the front gate and walked down the path. A clutch of orange poppies in the flowerbed caught her eye, incongruously bright. She pressed the doorbell.

Paul opened the door. In just three days his face was thinner, his hair greyer, and the lines across his brow deeper. A thick layer of stubble sprouted from his jaw – he hadn't been going to work, presumably. Nothing had ever got in the way of work before.

'Hello, Paul.'

He was wearing the sweater she'd given him for Christmas – was he trying to win her sympathy? It wouldn't work, if he was. This time, she wasn't going to let him crawl back into her heart.

'Suzanne, I'm so glad you've come.' He sounded hopeful, even a little excited. Surely, he wasn't expecting a loving reunion?

She gave him a warning look. 'I'm not staying long. Katherine's waiting outside, she's giving me a lift back.' She stepped into the hall and he closed the door. The house was silent.

'I was having a beer. Can I get you anything?'

She'd become a visitor in her own home. 'No thanks.' She scanned the kitchen. 'Where's Marmaduke?'

He shrugged. 'He was here earlier.'

'Have you been feeding him?'

'I put food out for him and he turns his nose up at it. I threw away the last lot after the flies got to it.'

Marmaduke would be missing her, she thought with a pang of guilt.

He opened the living room door. 'Come and sit down. I need to tell you something.'

She sat stiffly on an armchair.

Paul, standing against the sideboard, cleared his throat.

'You have to forgive me, darling,' he said. 'I'm so sorry for what I've done.'

She stared at him. His voice sounded small.

'I know what I did was wrong. I'll regret it for the rest of my life, every single day. If only you knew—'

'How can you say that?' It wasn't enough, this hollow apology. He thought he could make everything right by saying the right words. 'I'll never understand how you could have done what you did. You really pulled the wool over my eyes, didn't you? You fooled me into believing I could trust you. You fooled me about everything. I thought you loved me. When we made love, I thought it was for real. I thought—' The words caught in her throat. 'I thought it meant the same to you.'

'Suze, I love you. I've always loved you. You must believe me. What happened with Laura and Emma. It was like something took me over. It was so strong, I couldn't—'

'You couldn't keep your hands off them, could you?' She spat out the words. 'You don't need to explain.'

He seemed to shrink before her. 'I know, I disgust you. I have no right to ask your forgiveness.'

'I can't forgive you, Paul.'

He seemed not to have heard. 'I'm asking for one last chance. I swear I'll never do anything like that again.'

She had a vision of herself, in twenty years' time, with sagging skin and aching joints, living alone in some cramped flat, waiting for the phone to ring and her children to visit. But it wasn't enough.

'I'm sorry, it's too late. Our marriage is over. I want a divorce.'

He turned his head away to look out of the window; she couldn't see his face. All she could hear was the solitary tweet, tweet, tweet of a baby bird in the front garden. When he turned back to her, his eyes glistened.

'I love you, Suzanne.'

It took a few seconds before she was able to speak.

'You love me? You have a funny way of showing it. You do those disgusting things to our daughter, and my friend's daughter.' Her voice faltered. She couldn't draw in enough air. 'Then you expect me to put it aside like everything else, and carry on as if nothing's happened? Well, I can't. I won't.'

'Please, Suzanne.' Paul clutched his hands together as if he were praying.

'I've made up my mind, Paul.'

His hands unclasped and his eyes fell away from hers. A muscle above his mouth moved. He seemed defeated. Finally, he spoke.

'What are you going to do?'

'I'm going to stay with Katherine for a few weeks. I'll go to a solicitor. We'll have to sell the house, I suppose.' Suzanne stood and walked towards the door. Her composure wouldn't hold out. 'We can discuss the details later. I'm going upstairs to pack some things.'

Their bed was unmade. Towards the middle, a single crumpled pillow. She slid open the wardrobe door and stared at the array of clothes inside, resisting the urge to flop on the bed and howl. Leaving Paul was like chopping off her own hand: there was no painless way to extract him.

When she came downstairs with a suitcase, he was waiting in the hall, and as she put it down he came towards her. She prepared herself for a last show of defiance.

'I'm sorry,' was all he said.

Katherine opened the car door for her. 'How did it go, love?'

Suzanne stumbled inside and sat staring through the windscreen. She couldn't look at her friend. So many emotions jostled inside her – relief, exhaustion and, most of all, disappointment. An acrid disappointment that made her throat ache. It couldn't end like this. Paul had been everything to her. After twenty-five years together, it couldn't end like this.

'He wasn't angry.' She fastened her seat belt. 'He said he loved me. I thought he was going to cry. He's never cried, not in all the years we've been together.'

Shortly after they got back to Katherine and Jeremy's house, she rang Laura to say that she had left Paul. But Laura's home number was set to the answering machine and her mobile rang out.

26

Laura

Afternoon, 4 May 2011

Laura got off the Tube at Wimbledon station and walked towards the house. An uncomfortable sensation had taken over her chest, eroding the calmness she'd felt earlier. But that didn't matter. At last she was ready to do it.

The streets of Wimbledon were busy with mothers and children on their way home from school. Trees and hedgerows spread their new green against a clear, pale blue sky. The sunshine was warm. It seemed like summer already – she wore a T-shirt and jeans, with her leather jacket over her shoulder. But she walked on steadily, looking neither left nor right, hardly noticing what was around her, aware only of what lay ahead.

She rang the doorbell.

After nearly a minute the door opened. Her father was shabby. A beard clung to his jaw and an old business shirt, frayed at the collar, hung over his jeans. He looked at her blankly for a moment or two, as if not recognising she was his daughter.

'Hello, Laura. It's good to see you.' An unpleasant odour leaked from his mouth – tooth decay merging with whisky. 'Come in.' He sounded subdued, yet also pleased.

She followed him into the kitchen. It smelled of disinfectant. The table was bare. All the surfaces shone, their usual clutter gone. A lone side plate bore a green scroll of apple peel and a paring knife.

'Do you want something to drink?'

'No thanks.' She stood near the door leading to the hall. He didn't ask her to sit down and she didn't want to, in any case. 'You're not going to work this week?'

'I'm taking some time off.' He moved to stand across from her, by a row of spotless cupboards. 'They owe me a week's holiday. I thought I could get some work done on the house.' He picked up a pencil from the worktop and placed it inside a metal container that was filled with similar items.

She looked around the kitchen. None of the windows were open. The disinfectant smell was starting to react with the eggs she'd eaten earlier.

'Your mother was over earlier,' he began. 'She said she was leaving me.'

He was looking in her direction, but not at her. The quietness of the room intensified. From outside she heard the distant hum of heavy machinery and a periodic rattle that she couldn't identify. Then those noises stopped and she could make out a faint trill of birds.

'I can understand that,' she replied. 'I don't know why she didn't leave you years ago.'

'I know it was wrong,' he said, quietly, as if he hadn't heard her, 'what I did to Emma. I wish I hadn't ever gone near her.'

'Why did you lie to me? You said you wouldn't do anything to harm her.'

A look of ... what was it? Irritation? Self-reproach? It was gone before she could decipher it.

'I thought I could resist her. I tried to. But I couldn't stop.'

Like the trip of a switch, anger overtook her.

'I hate you, for what you did to her, and for all those horrible things you did to me when you were supposed to be my father.'

He stared at her. Drops of sweat began to form on his brow, blue veins clinging to his temples like a peculiar creeper. But she had no sympathy towards him. He was beyond sympathy.

'Who are you going to go after next, Dad?' She stepped towards him. 'Do you have your next victim lined up?'

'Laura, please. Don't talk like this. Can't you try to forgive me?'

'I'll never forgive you. You're not my father anymore, as far as I'm concerned. I never want to see or hear from you again.'

He didn't speak. He just moved his head slightly as if he hadn't heard properly.

'There's one more thing,' she said. 'I want you to go to the police and tell them what you did to Emma.'

'I couldn't do that—'

'If you don't go, I will.'

She walked through the doorway into the hall, then stopped and looked back. His hands hung at his sides, fingers fluttering like trapped moths.

'You can't do that,' he said. 'They'd send me to prison. You know what they'd do to me there, don't you? You know what they do to men who …' He moved his head slowly from side to side. His face had drained of colour. 'I'd be done for in prison.'

She didn't reply. A twinge of pity threatened to overtake her anger.

No. His pleading couldn't reach her. He had to be punished for what he'd done, and he had to be put out of reach of other girls – whatever might happen to him in prison.

'You haven't told Daniel about any of this, have you?' His eyes scoured her face. 'He doesn't have to know, does he?'

'I told him this morning. About what sort of a father you were to me, and what you did to Emma.'

'What did he say?' His voice just above a whisper.

'I'm not sure he believed it. He didn't think you could do anything like that.'

'Now he's going to hate me as well.' It was more to himself than to her.

'You deserve it, don't you?'

She left him then, pulling the front door firmly behind her and breathing in the fresh, sweet smell of a spring afternoon.

27

Paul

Afternoon, 4 May 2011

Paul went to the drinks cabinet in the dining room. He poured himself a tumbler of Scotch and drank it quickly, not bothering to sit down. Then he poured another.

His daughter had abandoned him as his wife had – as his son would too, sooner or later. Worse than that, she had disowned him. She had judged him and found him guilty. In her eyes, as well as Suzanne's, he was incapable of redemption.

The thought burrowed into him.

He could change – no, he *would* change. He would no longer think about girls, or look at pictures of them. He would never again do what he'd done. He would do good deeds instead, to atone for his mistakes.

But what if Laura really meant what she had said? What if she went to the police about Emma? They'd speak to Jane … He could be charged with having sex with an underage girl; a girl, not even a teenager. A child in the eyes of the law. Sex with a girl under sixteen was automatically rape, wasn't it? They would investigate him and everything would be public knowledge. There'd be a trial. His photograph would be in all the papers. He'd be crucified.

Even if he denied it all, even if he got the best defence lawyer in London, and Laura and Emma's evidence was called into doubt, how would he cope with the humiliation of exposure? They'd question him about the most private, intimate things. His life would be on display for the world to see. Even if the jury found him not guilty, people would always look at him askew. He'd be labelled as a suspected paedophile, a dirty old man. The streets for miles around would be full of it – the respectable Wimbledon businessman who secretly abused his own daughter then fucked a twelve-year-old girl, the daughter of his wife's best friend. He would lose his job. He'd become an isolated old man, unvisited and rebuffed by everyone. His friends would wash their hands of him, so would his family. Whatever he said, or did, he would never be able to make amends for what he'd done.

And what if he was found guilty? What if they sent him to prison?

He shivered.

Sex offender. He would become one of *those*, the most hated breed of prisoner, the lowest of the low. There would be nowhere safe for him to go. He would be set upon by his fellow inmates at any time, day or night.

His heart began to race. He heard the clang of the cell door, the scrape of metal in the lock. The voices gathering around him, the coarse jibes, the spits. The fists raised, the contempt in their eyes. What would they do to him?

Anything … Everything. They'd make him pay for his crimes in ways he could not bear to think about. They'd take away every ounce of his dignity, every iota of what made him a man. And then they'd do it again.

He poured more whisky then set the empty tumbler down on the cabinet with a clunk.

No. It couldn't happen. He wouldn't let Laura do this.

28

Laura

Afternoon, 4 May 2011

She walked on without seeing what was in front of her, her thoughts twisting and tumbling, one upon the next without respite. What was she going to do? Could she really turn him in to the police, her own father? The relief she felt earlier, walking away from the house, had been replaced by a creeping sense of foreboding. At last she stopped, and wiped the perspiration off her face with a disintegrating tissue from her jeans pocket. She must have walked several miles since leaving the house.

Looking around, she saw squat, grimy-fronted terraces punctuated by corner shops. The area wasn't familiar. The moon, a sickly yellow clown's smile, low in the sky. It was nowhere near sunset, but the light was being sucked away by dark towers of cloud. The weather had turned – it was way too hot for May. Moisture-laden air clung to her skin like a damp blanket. A storm would come, sooner or later.

The evening commuter rush had started already. Streams of Lycra-clad cyclists dodged packed buses. The grocery on the corner was doing a brisk trade. She went inside, and bought an apple and a bottle of water. She was more thirsty than hungry, though she'd eaten nothing since breakfast.

Outside, she leaned on a garden wall. Her legs were starting to ache and her left toe was sore where it had rubbed against her trainer. She munched into the apple and juice dribbled down her chin. It was wonderfully sweet and refreshing.

Well, are you going to do it? Are you really going to do something, or was all that talk earlier just bravado?

She tossed the core into a dustbin on the other side of the wall. She didn't have a smartphone, reluctant to pay extra just to be able to use the internet when not at home, but it would have been handy to find out where the nearest police station was. She went through what she would say.

Hello, my name's Laura Cunningham. I've come to report a crime. Two, actually.

They would ask lots of questions, ask her to make a statement. They would thank her for taking the trouble to come in, and assure her they would do all they could to investigate everything fully. Maybe they would do, maybe they wouldn't, but what other choice did she have?

Her mobile rang, making her start. Daniel's name flashed up on the screen.

'Hi, Daniel.'

'Where are you? I've been trying to get hold of you.'

'I'm out, walking.' She raised her voice as another bus trundled past. 'Sorry, I didn't hear the phone. There's a lot of traffic.'

'I talked to Dad earlier. He says you're going to report him to the police.'

Around her, rain began to thwack on the pavement. She looked up, her cheeks catching fat wet drops.

'Is that true, Laura?' His voice louder. Loud enough to overcome the traffic noise.

'It's true. I'm going to tell them what he did to me. And, while I'm there, I'll tell them what I've heard he did to Emma. They'll find that interesting, I think.'

'Are you having me on? You're going to turn Dad in to the cops?' Her brother's voice bellowed into her ear. 'You can't do this, whatever you think he may have done. He's our father, not some fucking criminal!'

She pulled the phone away from her ear, nearly dropping it. Daniel's reaction sent a bolt of shock through her body. She'd never known him to be this furious. But it awoke the anger inside her too.

'Indecent assault, sex with a minor, rape. Whatever you call it, Daniel, it's a crime.'

'If you believe that.' He didn't try to keep the scepticism from his voice.

'Did he tell you what he actually did?' Her voice came out too loud, distorted.

'He said she was egging him on and he lost control.' Her brother sounded embarrassed, took a long time to finish his sentence. 'She was touching him and he couldn't stop himself, he started touching her back.'

'What?' The heat left her body. She couldn't find any words.

'I know, it's totally gross. But he swears that's all he did—'

'He's lying, can't you tell? He's trying to shift all the blame onto Emma—'

'OK, OK. I get you, Laura, I do. But do you really want Dad to end up in court? Think for a moment.'

'I think he should have to go to court, yes. Absolutely he should.'

Her brother carried on. If their father was prosecuted, their lives would change. Even if he wasn't found guilty, people would assume he was. His name would be in the papers and on social media, and so would theirs. Even if they could keep their names out of the media, people would find out somehow. This would follow them around for the rest of their lives. He'd be ashamed to use his real name. He'd have to admit to his fiancée that his father was a child abuser. If he had kids, what the hell would he tell them about their granddad? Did she want to bring all that down on him? On herself too? And what about Mum?

Daniel's voice faded into the sound of rain and tyres on wet tarmac. A tear slipped down Laura's cheek.

'Hello, are you there?'

She couldn't speak. She switched off the phone and fumbled for a tissue to wipe her face. It was useless. More tears came, mingling with the rainwater sliding down her face. Without thinking, she started to walk. She stepped off the kerb to cross the side street, straight into the path of a cyclist turning right. Just in time she stepped backwards, feeling the whoosh of air as they brushed past. Another cyclist flashed by, close behind, draped in fluorescent yellow.

Back on the pavement, her legs gave way. She sank onto a damp paving stone beside the kerb, hugging her knees, hiding her face in her arms. The rain came more steadily, heavier now.

'Oh, God.'

She said it aloud. A prayer, of sorts. She was utterly drained; she couldn't think, couldn't move. She would just have to sit until the rain floated her away.

For several minutes, footsteps came and went around her, as if it were quite normal for a young woman to be sitting by the kerb in the pouring rain. Her hair was sticking to her brow and her T-shirt's cool dampness hugged her skin. She closed her eyes.

Someone was tapping on her shoulder.

'Excuse me.' A face came into view. A guy in a raincoat, carrying an umbrella. 'Sorry to disturb you, but hadn't you better get out of the rain? If you stay there you might get pneumonia or something.'

The guy hurried off before she could speak.

At home, Laura made a cup of tea and peeled off her damp clothes, put on her dressing gown and turned on the hot water for a shower. The light on the phone handset was flashing. She played the message. It was from her mother:

'Hello, darling, I'm in Woking. I saw the solicitor this afternoon about getting a divorce. I'm having dinner with a friend now. I'll be back at Katherine's later tonight.' The line crackled, making her mother's voice hard to hear. 'Daniel phoned earlier, he's very upset. He says you're going to the police about your father. Please, Laura, don't do anything yet. I need to talk to you—'

A static-filled announcement interrupted.

'I know he's done some terrible things, but he's still my husband. What if he ended up in prison? I don't know if I could cope with that on top of everything else. And your father … it would finish him off—'

A long beep cut her off mid-sentence.

Laura drank more tea. Her hands were trembling. She was being squeezed, bit by bit, into a small box. Both her mother and Daniel wanted to shut her up – what chance did she have now?

She undressed and stepped into the shower, staying in until the water ran cold, ruminating on her mother's voice in the message. Composed, just about. Yet there was something jagged and frayed below its surface, like the howl of an animal in pain.

She dried herself slowly, thinking she ought to eat something. There'd be leftovers in the fridge, enough to make a meal. Against the bathroom window, the steady swish of rain. It was properly dark now.

The ring of her mobile phone cut across her thoughts. She wrapped the towel around her and hurried to the bedroom where she'd left her bag. It would be her mother, most likely.

But 'Dad' flashed up on the screen.

'Hello?'

'It's me. Your father.'

She flopped onto the bed. After their last conversation, she hadn't expected to hear from him.

'What do you want?'

'I want to know what your intentions are. You're not going to tell anyone about this ... situation, are you? You wouldn't do that to me, would you?'

His voice was badly slurred. She'd not heard it like this for a very long time. It contained an echo of something from years ago, which she couldn't quite bring into memory. He'd drunk Scotch in the evenings sometimes when she was growing up, not usually enough to affect his speech, just enough to make him darkly morose and even more unpredictable. But it wasn't that. It was something else, something icky.

'I haven't gone to the police yet, if that's what you—'

'Laura, listen to me. You can't tell them about me and Emma. I'm fifty-three years old, I'm hanging on to my job by a thread. If this comes out, I'll never work again. Your mother has left me, and now you've gone too. I've got no one left except Daniel, but if you keep down this path he'll be gone too. Is that what you want?'

Pity and revulsion washed over her.

'I don't know what I'm going to do.' It was the truth.

'You can't go to the police, Laura.' His voice altered. Anger obliterated all traces of the wheedling, self-pitying tones. 'Are you listening to me? I won't let you do that. You can't go to the police.'

'Yes, I understand. Sorry, I have to go now.'

She ended the call and put her phone on the bedside table. It was almost out of battery, she should put it on charge. But she stayed sitting on her bed, her heart drumming against her chest. Her father's anger was seeping into her, removing what was left of her resolve. She began to shiver. It was happening again, this attempt to control her, to shut her up, to stop her telling the truth.

Would there never be an end to it? What was she going to do? Could she let him do this to her again?

She put her head on the pillow and pulled the duvet over her head. Her mouth was dry and her heart thumped hard, too hard. Another pulse of fear. It had lodged deep down and was steadily gnawing into the sane, healthy part of her.

Oh God. Please, help me.

Her eyelids became heavy. She lay in the near darkness listening to the sighs of wind, the uneven tap of raindrops on the pane, the gush of water down the drainpipe.

It came when she was almost asleep. A memory, swift and ruthless.

His whisky breath as he kisses her. The smoky sweetness, the almost liquorish taste of his mouth. The retch that begins in her gut as he pushes his tongue into her mouth. Then something else. His iron grip on her wrist as her head is pushed down, towards that place ...

She can't do it, she just can't. But there's no choice.

What's next is beyond words. Trapped. The gag at the back of her throat. Hope withering, darkness surrounding her. Only the long, private agony of death awaiting her, or whatever would take the place of death.

317

Laura sat up in bed, her eyes wide open, her heart beating erratically. It wasn't her fault, what she'd done to him. She knew that now, with all of her being. She'd had no choice.

And then she knew for sure. Even if her mother and brother never spoke to her again, even if her father's life was ruined as a result, she had to do this. Yes, it would be difficult for Daniel, even more so for her mother, but she had to do something.

She pulled a thick jumper and a pair of jeans from the chest of drawers and hauled them on, her mind in tumult. Then she hurried to the kitchen and opened the drawer next to the cooker. She rifled through a mess of electricity bills, bank statements and takeaway leaflets before finding what she was looking for: a leaflet from West Kensington police station; the phone number, and beside it 10am to 6pm. She checked her mobile for the time: 8.32pm. The station would be shut now. What fucking use was that?

She started up her laptop, typed in Metropolitan Police on Google, and clicked Report a crime.

Is it an emergency?

No.

Was anyone threatened, verbally abused or assaulted?

She clicked Yes. A message came up:

Report threats, verbal abuse or assault

Thank you. You can report this crime online. Click 'Start' below to complete our quick and simple online form. Please give as much information as you can so we have everything we need to start an investigation. Our team will review your report and get back to you within 48 hours. You'll also be able to download a copy of your report for your own records.

She read on. Oh, Christ. It would take an age to complete this form. They wanted the date and time of the crime, the contact details of anyone who witnessed the crime, and information about any evidence that could help their investigation. How the hell was she going to give them all that?

She thought back to the time her father had done those things. The dates were hazy – no, totally absent. She was thirteen years old the last time her father had come into her room, wasn't she, while she'd been alone in the house with him for a week? It was 2011 now and she was 22, so that would make it nine years ago ... 2002. Daniel had been away camping with his school, so it would probably have been June 2002, or July. She jotted it down on a piece of paper.

And the first time, in the garden? It was so hot that day. Definitely summertime, early in the school holidays; July. But was it the summer of 2000 or 2001? Suddenly, she wasn't sure. And what about all the other times in between? She had no idea about those dates – the memories had merged together without any helpful date stamps. It was no use. She'd have to talk to a police officer.

On the website she found another page with a phone number to report crimes. She dialled the number. A recorded message told her they were experiencing a high volume of calls at the moment and she was ninth in the queue. She hung up, swearing.

A tight ball of frustration was building up, reducing her thoughts to an incoherent mush. But she wouldn't be defeated. She'd go to a police station and tell them everything she knew. There had to be one open somewhere.

She went back to the website and entered her postcode. Hammersmith police station showed first on the list. Thank God, it was open twenty-four hours. She wrote down the number and the address. Shepherd's Bush Road wasn't that far. She could get there by Tube.

The decision brought a sense of relief, along with a pang of hunger. She hadn't eaten for hours. Before leaving she'd have a quick bite.

Laura lay on the sofa with another cup of tea, and a slice of toast spread with banana and peanut butter. She thought about turning on the TV – something light-hearted to take her mind off what she was going to do, just for a few minutes. But then she wouldn't hear if …

If what?

She took a few more mouthfuls and sipped at her tea, warming her hands on the mug. She was on edge now, over alert. Outside, the rain and wind were getting stronger, removing the normal sounds of traffic and planes, even the fridge's noisy chatter.

The window frame jolted, making her start.

What was it her father had said to her earlier, on the phone? Something she should have remembered. A threat, or a warning.

I won't let you do that.

The words struck her as menacing now. What if he came here? What if he tried to stop her from going to the police?

She got up from the sofa, spooked. She had to leave, right now. Without another thought she stuffed her mobile phone, house keys and some coins into her jeans pocket, pulled on her raincoat and grabbed her umbrella.

29

Laura

Late evening, 4 May 2011

Outside, rain lashed the pavement. There was no one about – no one with any sense would be out in this. She tried to steer the umbrella into the direction of the rain, as she pushed the contraption open, but it jammed halfway. She'd be soaked again before she reached West Kensington Tube station, a five-minute walk. Sometimes one could hail a taxi on North End Road, but that wasn't likely in heavy rain.

Laura started to run. Before she'd gone fifty yards, a black cat streaked in front of her from under a parked car.

'Shit!'

She stumbled and nearly fell. The cat sprang over a wall into a garden. She slowed to a fast walk. The pavement was scarcely visible between gauzy nets of artificial light. In the distance she could make out the streetlights of the main road. Shoving her free hand into a raincoat pocket, she brought out half a Mars Bar and a theatre ticket. *Les Mis.* She'd gone with Rachel an aeon ago to celebrate Rachel's success at the end of her first year at work. That peal of flirtatious laughter sounded in her memory, as if Rachel were still beside her.

A loud smack of glass against plastic. Her heart took off, scudding against her chest. She glimpsed a lit hallway behind a closing front door. Only someone chucking stuff into a dustbin. She let out a long breath. Once again, a gust of wind tugged at her umbrella, allowing more rain to land on her. She tossed the useless thing away.

It was a while before she realised there was a car behind her, moving slowly so it kept a short distance away from her. Its engine was almost inaudible over the noise of the wind and rain, but she could just make out a deep thrum, like the purr of a giant cat. She couldn't bring herself to look around, because she knew what she would see.

She gripped her phone in her hand, walking as fast as she could without running. Should she call 999? No, it was hardly an emergency. She scrolled down to her mother's number.

'Hello, Mum? Are you there?'

She heard her mother's voice briefly before it was gobbled up by a warbling noise. She couldn't tell if it was her mother's voicemail or her mother actually speaking at the other end.

'Mum, can you hear me? Dad is over here. I've just left the flat. He's following me in the car.'

A garbled voice in her ear, indecipherable. Laura shoved the phone into a pocket.

The car moved slightly ahead and her heart jumped. She could see it clearly now, without turning her head – a silver-grey Porsche. *His* car.

It stopped ten yards ahead of her. The passenger window opened. Her father's head leaned out. She couldn't see much of him in the half dark. His hair, uncombed. A dull gleam in his eyes. She wanted to run away as fast as she could.

'Laura, stop! I need to talk to you.' The voice marred by wind and rain.

She hurried ahead, speeding up to a fast jog.

The car moved forward. Half a minute later it stopped again, right beside her. Her father's head appeared through the open window.

'Please, Laura! I want to talk to you, that's all.' There was a note of desperation in his voice.

'I don't want to talk to you,' she replied.

'I just need to say a few things I never had the chance to. It won't take long.'

She hesitated. He wasn't going to go away. Even if she ran it would take her two or three minutes to reach the main road.

The passenger door opened. 'Please,' he said. 'Get in.'

'No, I'd rather not.'

'You'll get soaked,' he insisted. 'We can go somewhere to talk, if you want. A pub?'

'I don't want to go anywhere with you.'

'Well for Christ's sake just get in the car then, you'll catch your death out there.'

What to do? Water began to drip from her sodden hair down her brow. Her jumper was already damp against her skin. It would be ridiculous to stay out here.

'OK, just five minutes.'

Laura sat down on the sculpted, pale leather seat beside her father, and pulled the door shut against the slanting rain. The dashboard's green glow suffused the car's interior with a faint light, and the fan heater spewed a noisy stream of air. Raindrops smacked the roof. She listened to the rhythmic flick of the windscreen wipers, a coil of tension tightening in the pit of her stomach.

'So, what do you want to tell me?'

She was aware of him beside her, though she couldn't bring herself to look properly. There was a fug of whisky coming off him. That same smoky-sweet smell of years ago ...

A tremor caught her stomach. She clenched her bladder muscles tight against the sudden panic and tried to still the violent flutter of her heart.

He reached forward and switched off the engine then turned to her.

'If you go to the police, Laura, my life will be over.'

How could such a simple statement have so much force? It expanded to fill the space in the car, snuffing out her rational thoughts.

'I understand how you must feel,' she replied. 'How frightening it must be.' She met his eyes. Before she could look away her eyes were drawn to his, down and down into a well of pain and darkness.

'I want you to know that I did try. I tried so hard to let it go, to do what a good father would have done.'

His voice reminded her of a hypnotist's. Despite her instinct to recoil, she couldn't help but listen.

'The first time it happened, that afternoon in the back garden. I hated myself afterwards. My little girl, my one source of joy ... I'd ruined everything. I'd taken what I loved most away from her.'

His tears glinted as he raised his left hand and held it, palm up, above her lap. In the centre, a taut white thickening of the flesh in uneven ridges. The scar was roughly circular, the size of a pound coin.

She stared at it, trying to remember. She'd noticed it before, as a child, and remembered how he'd tried to hide the palm of his left hand.

'I burned it that evening. With a cigarette lighter. I told your mother the pan caught fire while I was deep frying chips, my hand got caught in the flame. I did it again, the next time, to try to stop things getting out of hand. But it wasn't enough.'

A flicker of anger warmed her cheeks.

'Why did you do those things? Tell me.'

He didn't answer.

'You nearly ruined my life. I can't begin to tell you how desperate I've been.'

'I know what I did was wrong.' He was addressing the dashboard.

'Do you really?'

'I fucked up, Laura, I fucked up big time.' A crack opened in his voice. 'You didn't deserve a father like me.'

'A father who, for years, made me too scared to sleep at night? Who treated me like—'

'I know. I'm ashamed of what I did. Of who I am.' He leant his head back against the headrest, his eyes shut. 'I'm not a monster, Laura. I'm just an ordinary man who's made some terrible mistakes.' He looked straight at her. 'Please, you must forgive me.'

She turned her head away from him. Dark forms merged beyond the window – bushes, houses, parked cars. Someone hurried across the road, head down, oblivious to them.

'If you go to the police,' he went on, 'they'll put me in the dock. What if they send me to prison? Do you know what they'd do to me in there?' His voice increased in pitch. 'Do you?'

She felt pity for him, and something stronger than pity. Contempt.

'Do you really think,' he went on, 'I deserve to suffer like that? I'd sooner kill myself.'

He was trying to squeeze the resolve out of her. He was still trying to win this game that wasn't a game.

'If I don't go to the police,' she replied, 'nothing will change. You won't stop what you're doing, will you? You'll find someone else, another Emma.'

His eyes opened wide, as if she'd slapped his face. Then he laughed.

'You'd like me to end it all, wouldn't you?' His mouth twisted, distorting his face. 'Then you wouldn't have your old man around to bother you anymore.'

Something jolted inside her like an electric shock. She stared at him, open-mouthed. Her father leaned towards her. A flicker of metal in his eyes. His voice low, accusing.

'You're going to the police, aren't you? I know that's where you're off to. Why else would you be out on a night like this?'

She shuddered, had a desperate urge to pee. She had to get away from him. Now.

Slowly, carefully, she moved her hand towards the passenger door and felt for the latch.

'Yes, I am. I'm going to the police and you can't stop me.'

It was instinct talking, nothing more. She pulled the handle and pushed open the door, planted one foot on the pavement and prepared to launch herself from the car. But he was ready. He pulled on her free arm, twisting as he did so. Pain stabbed her shoulder. She gasped, a rush of nausea in her gut. Next thing she knew he was out of the car and on the pavement beside her, shoving her back into the seat. His hands, big and strong, pinned her in place. Panic flashed through her. Before she could think of a response, her hand was already hurtling towards his face, fingers outstretched.

In the semi-darkness, she could not see the strike but she felt it. The contact with something gelatinous, like the over-firm jelly that her mother sometimes made in the trifle for Sunday lunch. At that moment her father screeched, a shrill, girlish sound that she remembered from distant playgrounds, as piercing as a teacher's whistle. He stumbled back, slamming a hand over his eye.

'Fuck, fuck! What have you fucking done? You've fucking blinded me!'

Then she was running, faster than she'd ever run in her life. Towards the distant strip of lights on the main road, where there would be other people, where she could find help; rain piercing her clothes, her mouth filling with spittle, a hoarse warmth in her windpipe, the ache of her calf muscles. Only one thought. *Get away.*

No following footsteps, no shouts. Laura ran on. Suddenly, the road ahead lit up, the colours of parked cars leaping out of the monochrome. Behind her, the deep-throated roar of a powerful engine. She glanced behind. Her father's form was just visible behind the wheel. He would reach her in no time.

Ahead, a turning to the left. A side street. She darted into the secluded darkness. She had not been down it before. Where it went – if anywhere – she had no idea. The lamp posts were further apart here, gathering shadowy islands between them. The pavement was empty but the road was crammed with cars in shades of grey. Tall brick houses loomed on either side of the road, three storeys high, guarded by rows of black dustbins. Bedsit land. Rented-out flats. Homes where you have to buzz to get in. Most people wouldn't answer, probably.

The possibilities zipped through her head. Run up to one and press all the buzzers in turn until someone let her in? If they didn't, start to scream? There wouldn't be enough time. She ran on, scanning each side of the road in turn. Gasping for breath, a jag of pain in her side. Not daring to slow even a fraction. Hunting for some dark recess where she could hide.

Nothing. Only a sprinkling of shrubs and low walls.

Then she heard them. Footsteps, slapping the pavement in a rapid, even rhythm; their echo cut off abruptly by the landscape of the street. He was coming for her.

Her heart beat with renewed force. She veered and ran towards a three-storey house. Up some steps. She hesitated. She could ring the doorbell and hope for the best. But what if no one answered?

She looked around. Clumps of shrubs in a flowerbed, not quite high enough – there was only one place to hide: a small, covered area set against the dividing wall between two properties, a holding place for dustbins. She crouched among a clutter of plastic bins, between a low wall in front of her and the high wall behind. They were child height, and just wide enough to conceal her.

She waited, straining for the sound of him. But there was nothing except the splash-patter of rain on roofs and the gurgling suck of water into a drain. Laura pressed on her jeans pocket for her phone. A wave of relief at the answering bulge. She pulled out the device. It was still working but the battery indicator showed a long strip of red. It was almost dead.

She pressed 9 three times. A man's voice, infused with a calm firmness.

'Police.' She heard her voice waver. 'There's a man coming after me. I think he might hurt me …'

Footsteps again, from the street. Slower now. Close, getting closer.

The phone went black. With shaking hands she stuffed it back in her pocket. Her body was cold, as cold as the inside of a freezer. Her breath came in hoarse rasps, too loud. She clamped a hand over her mouth and waited for her father to find her.

30

Suzanne

Early hours, 5 May 2011

Suzanne lay in bed listening to the wind. The breeze had become a restless, shifting, snarling creature. A branch creaked loudly as if in pain. Her back twinged in sympathy. She would have turned over only the mattress in Debbie's room had moulded itself to her body, making movement difficult.

It must be gone midnight; she couldn't see the clock but its unrelenting tick bore into her. Though bone tired, dozing off on the train back to London, and going straight to bed at 10pm on arriving at Katherine's, she'd been unable to get to sleep for thinking about Laura. Since Daniel's frantic phone call, just as she'd stepped out of the solicitor's office, a thought had gnawed at her. How would Paul survive if Laura went to the police? He'd be questioned, arrested perhaps, and put in a cell. He would never cope with the suspicion, the humiliation.

A ripple of fear began, as it did when she let herself think about it. What if Laura was right?

Suddenly she was uncertain. What if Paul did look for another girl to groom, who would eventually succumb to his base urges? Could they let that happen? And didn't he deserve to be punished?

Her thoughts turned to the solicitor's assessment. The divorce could become a real thing now, not just a threat or a distant possibility. The process would be painful and difficult; there'd be financial matters to sort out, property and investment splits, and pension arrangements. But the children weren't children anymore, which would make everything much easier.

She sipped from the glass of water by her bed, trying to forget an urge to use the loo. It was at the far end of the landing and had a noisy flush that could wake up Katherine and Jeremy. But, if she didn't flush it, it might get blocked with toilet paper. She berated herself for having such trivial thoughts when her life was crashing down around her. What did it matter if she woke them?

Yawning and groggy, she sat up and switched on the light. 12.13am. Katherine's hairdryer lay on the dressing table with all the other things she'd had to ask for or borrow. She felt like one of those seashore creatures on nature programmes – a particularly inept one, waking up to find she'd made a home under the wrong shell.

Although she'd been there for a week now, every time she woke during the night she wondered what she was doing in this room, in this narrow bed, all alone. And every time, despite knowing what her husband did, a grief came over her for the loss of him, and all the intimate things she had got used to over the years: his warm body beside her as they lay down for the night, his jaw-clenching in his sleep, the tigerish yawns in the mornings that never failed to startle her. Even those things that had become rare over the years: his jokes and anecdotes, the pats and squeezes …

She put on the long brown cardigan – her makeshift dressing gown – stepped into her slippers and padded to the bathroom. Katherine's stuff was piled on top of the large mirrored cabinet. On the shelf beside it, a mess of ointments, lotions, tablets, tonics, hair products, skin products and depilatory creams. She wondered if Jeremy minded.

Leaving the toilet unflushed, she went downstairs to get a banana. On her return she picked up one of Katherine's books that she'd started reading a few days ago. A romance about a divorced woman who meets the man of her dreams in an online chatroom. Kat had planted it, no doubt.

Struggling to reach the end of the chapter, she put it down again. She couldn't concentrate on anything with this storm raging outside. Why hadn't Laura phoned her back after getting her message? Or had she been out somewhere for the evening and not had a chance to play it? She hadn't answered her mobile either, though that was hardly unusual. If she'd gone to the police station she'd be back by now, wouldn't she?

Another gust of wind creaked the branches, jolting the window. Suzanne checked the clock again: 1.05am. Finally, she fell back into a fitful sleep, broken from time to time by the sound of the wind and rain.

31

Laura

Early hours, 5 May 2011

The shiver flitted across her shoulders, along with an insane leaping of her heart, the urge to empty her bladder. The footsteps were back.

They had come and gone several times during the seemingly endless time she'd been sitting here. Was her father waiting for her, just out of sight, ready to ... what? Could he really be angry and scared enough to hurt her? He must know he couldn't stop her from going to the police indefinitely, unless he killed her – which was crazy, wasn't it?

Get a grip, girl. Come on, get your act together.

Again, a doglike pant mingled with the slap of feet on wet paving stones. Was the sound even real? Or was it a tape replaying in her head, her mind playing tricks on her?

The footsteps changed in texture, as if meeting another surface, then stopped. She closed her eyes. A squirt of hot urine soaked into her underwear. She held her breath, squeezing in her fear, biting hard on her lip to stop herself from screaming.

Don't let him find me. Please, don't let him find me.

Minutes passed. No more footsteps. Nothing now but the whoosh of rain, slowly rising in intensity, and the deafening pump of her heart. Was he still there, waiting for her to come out of her hiding place?

Her body was going numb with cold and her shoulder ached badly where it had been wrenched. There was an odd tapping noise too. Where was it coming from? She realised it was her teeth tapping together. A surge of relief, followed by anger at herself – what was she going to do, sit here in the dark all night?

But what if her father was sitting in his car on the street just a few yards away, waiting for her to emerge? He would be livid after what she'd done to him. His eye would be hurting like hell, if not permanently damaged.

No. This is ridiculous.

Careful not to wince, or nudge the row of bins in front of her, she forced herself up into a crouching position and peeked around the edge of the outermost bin. A section of the street was visible.

The rain was less heavy now. She took a step towards the pavement, part of her still unwilling to leave the refuge of the bins, then another.

He's not there.

She walked slowly along the edge of the wall until she had a clear view of the road. The pavement was empty. No car with its engine idling. None of the parked cars were lit inside, nor, as far as she could see, did they have anyone inside. She walked along the pavement in the same direction as before, scanning the cars, glancing over her shoulder a couple of times.

He's not here, she told herself, picking up speed. *He's gone home.*

But whose home? Her heart fluttered in panic. He might be waiting for her now, outside her flat. That would be the obvious thing to do. She couldn't go home.

She checked her wrist and remembered she wasn't wearing a watch. Had the last Tube gone?

A tear rolled down her face, then another. She wiped her eyes with her hand so she could see the pavement. Houses gazed down, pitiless.

She stopped. The sound of voices, laughter. Ahead, two women carrying umbrellas, trying their best to hold them in the windy squall. They were on their way home from the pub, she guessed. Their voices unguarded, over-loud.

'Please, could you help me?'

They appraised her suspiciously, not stopping. She tagged along beside them.

'There was a man following me. He's gone now but I'm scared he might come back.' She could hear the madness in her voice. Rain-soaked and straggly-haired, she must look a bit mad. 'Would you let me use your phone please, so I can call the police? There's no battery left on mine.'

She looked at each woman in turn. Both had the same anxious-hostile expression, as if at any second she might lean over and bite one of them.

'Sorry, it's late,' one said. 'I've got to get home, I've a childminder waiting.'

'It doesn't look like there's anyone following you now, love,' the other added. 'Why don't you get on home?'

Laura ran down the street in the other direction, towards the main road and buses. There was only one place she needed to get to, and she'd walk there, if necessary.

After she'd been walking for about ten minutes, a night bus loomed in the distance. She ran to the next stop, turning to put out her arm. The bus pulled up just beyond the stop. Grateful, she climbed in.

'I only have one pound twenty on me,' she told the driver. 'Is that enough?'

He gestured for her to get on board. The lower deck was empty except for two youths on the back seat. She sat next to the exit doors and tried to make herself presentable by combing through her hair with her fingers. The recorded announcement informed them of the next stop and where the bus was headed. Soon, the bus slowed. Three teenage boys got on. She sighed, her impatience rising, and hoped the bus would not stop again.

At the police station, the male officer behind the counter looked surprised to see her.

'I want to report a crime,' she began. 'My father abused me when I was a child. Also, I understand that a month ago, he had sex with a girl I know. A twelve-year-old girl.'

The officer's eyebrows raised and he jotted something down. He said he would set up an interview as soon as possible.

'I need to use the toilet, if you don't mind, and you wouldn't have a jumper lying around, would you? I'm really, really cold.'

She was shown to the toilet then taken to a well-lit, sparsely furnished room, where she was given two blankets and a mug of scalding tea. She had no anxiety anymore, just a wonderful sense of relief. She'd made it.

After a while another officer appeared, not in uniform. He took her to a smaller room with a table, a tape-recorder and two chairs, and asked her to tell him what had happened.

'It started about ten years ago,' she began, and she didn't stop until she'd told him everything.

32

Paul

Early hours, 5 May 2011

Paul went to the kitchen and poured a tumbler of whisky. Some spilled over the edge of the glass. The pain was more bearable now, less like a spike was being driven through his eye. But his vision on that side was still blurred and patchy, darker than it should be, as if he were trying to see underwater. Christ, he was in a state. How the fuck had he made it home without having an accident?

After downing the contents of the glass, he went to the downstairs bathroom and looked at his face in the mirror. He breathed in sharply. His left eye was a mess, spotted and streaked with red where the white should be. In the corner, a clump of congealed blood. He looked pitiful.

He lurched into the hall, considering whether to drag himself upstairs. He could lie on the bed and fall into a stupor. But the large, empty bed would be yet another source of pain, another reminder that he had lost Suzanne. Instead, he went into the office, the room that had once been his sanctuary.

The room was dark, the curtains drawn. He didn't bother to turn on the light. He sat at his desk, leaned his head into his hands, and closed his eyes. The fury in Laura's face, that moment before she dug into his eye, came back to him. He recalled his surprise at the excruciating pain, and at the fact she had the stomach for such a thing. How it had left him gasping, unhinged, and made him want to hurt her in return – hurt her very badly. How, as she was running away, he'd started the engine, intending to smash into her at high speed, to crush her with his metal machine. How, when he lost sight of her, he'd searched for her on foot, winded and stumbling, his one thought: to stop her for good. And how, much later, anger spent, he'd gone back to the car, put his head on the steering wheel, and sobbed for the man he'd become.

He listened to the soft chug chug of a distant train. His thoughts came and went; the happy times, early on. Fishing with Grandpa by the river on drowsy golden afternoons, sharing tangy homemade lemonade and cookies. Holding the net for him, asking why the fish let themselves get caught. Later, the long summer days left alone to do whatever he pleased: building cities out of handfuls of Lego, climbing into next door's garden and stealing their best apples. And when he was older, after things had got worse at home, the sweet relief of escaping for a while to train at the local pool. Jacko, the swimming coach, who'd told him he had the potential to be a champion. Holding a trophy for the first time …

Then he saw Emma's look, just before she'd climbed out of his car for the last time, as if he were the scum that floated on a pond. He felt himself falling into a deep, impenetrable darkness.

He opened his eyes. His heart was pounding, like a volley of hammer blows nailing down his own coffin. A chill went through him. He thought of the knife rack in the kitchen. It was filled with high-quality knifes, kept sharp.

He hated cutting anything with a blunt knife. The largest had a blade that was seven inches long and capable of doing serious damage. He imagined the blade breaking the surface of his skin, the ease with which the steel would rip his flesh.

He didn't want to die. The thought of perpetual nothingness scared him. But how could he go on living?

Heart racing, he turned on the desk lamp, opened the top drawer and removed last year's leather-bound desk diary from the back-left corner. There, still tucked between the pages, was the photograph of Emma. It was the only one he'd printed. Not the one on his camera, which he'd left there as a decoy, just in case anyone questioned him about the photo shoot, but the image that had mattered the most. Several times he'd gone to the drawer to get rid of it, scared that Suzanne might find it as she'd found the other one, but he'd been unable to destroy it.

Emma looked back at him from the photograph. Her smile tugged on his heart again. That alluring, mischievous, all-too-familiar smile; her breasts cupped in the pale blue bra, her slim hips gently stretching the skimpy briefs. Desire rose like sap through his body, becoming an ache in his groin. He still wanted her, despite everything that had happened, despite the wrongness of it. If, by some magic, Emma could be here with him now, standing in this room, he would not be able to resist her.

He pushed away the photograph in horror. What was he truly, if not a monster? His daughter had only done what he deserved. She should have stabbed both eyes and blinded him.

The pain wasn't only physical now, it was a mental anguish. It cut into the part of him that contained the residue of a decent man – the part that had once held fantasises of future happiness and was now no more than a husk of shrivelled dreams. The pain plunged and twisted, intolerable.

He found the cigarette lighter in the kitchen, the one used for lighting dinner candles. Sitting back at the desk, he guided the flame to Emma's paper face. It distorted and blackened, then began to disintegrate. He watched the photograph become a pile of ash then pressed the lighter button again. Carefully, he guided the flame to the centre of his palm. The pain was pure, focussed, distracting him from the other, deeper pain. Ignoring the smell of charring flesh, he kept his hand open to receive the flame until he could take no more. Dropping the lighter, he slumped over the desk.

There was nothing left for him, he knew that now. Whatever he did, wherever he went, there would be no escape from his own mind.

He opened the front door.

The rain had stopped. A gust of wind scattered white blossom across the path.

His Porsche waited for him on the driveway. He unlocked it, lowered himself into the driver's seat, and turned the key in the ignition.

33

Suzanne

Early hours, 5 May 2011

S uddenly she was wide awake. Someone was at the window. The brisk rap of knuckles against glass. Suzanne pulled back the curtains. All she could see were streaks of rain on the windowpane and the swaying branches of the monkey puzzle tree, one of which came close to the window.

It's only a branch.

Getting back into bed, she caught sight of a wispy light in the wardrobe mirror. Heart thudding, she went closer. But now there was only the vague reflected features of her own face. Outside, the wind flurried and sighed.

She switched on the bedside light. Her small collection of possessions lay on the dressing table, exactly as they were when she'd gone to bed. She glanced at the alarm clock: 2.17am.

At first she thought it was a church bell – in her dream she was walking out of a church, beside Paul, confetti drifting down.

The shawl of sleep began to dissolve but the ringing wouldn't go away. What could it be? A burglar alarm? Or was the house on fire?

Reluctantly, she opened her eyes. No, it was the doorbell. Someone was walking across the landing. Suzanne sat up.

A rap on her door. Katherine's voice.

'Suzanne? Are you awake?'

'Yes, what is it?'

'The police are here. They want to speak to you.'

She glanced at the clock. Nearly 3am. What on earth could they want with her in the middle of the night?

Laura. Something's happened to her.

Suzanne put on her long cardigan, went into the bathroom and splashed her face with cold water. She'd hollowed out with dread.

In the hall stood two uniformed officers. A stocky, plain woman looked at her with dull eyes. Towering beside her, a youth with stuck-out ears like small Yorkshire puddings. The sleeves of his uniform were a fraction too short for his arms.

'Are you Mrs Suzanne Cunningham?'

She stared at each of them in turn. 'Yes. What do you want?'

'Hello, Mrs Cunningham. I'm Sergeant Richards from Wimbledon Police.' The woman's voice grasped at warmth. 'And this is Constable Trimble.' The youth gave Suzanne a silent nod. 'I'm sorry to disturb you so early in the morning. Would you mind if we came in and sat down?'

Katherine gave her a reassuring smile and headed upstairs. The police officers followed Suzanne into the living room.

The woman officer made a small head movement. 'This isn't your home, Mrs Cunningham?'

'No, I'm staying here with my friends, Katherine and Jeremy. What are you here for?'

'There's been an incident.'

The back of her scalp tingled.

'Can I just check your home address, Mrs Cunningham?'
The PC, this time.

'31 Elgin Drive.' She gave the postcode. 'How did you know where to find me?'

'There was an address written down on a piece of paper in the glovebox of your husband's car,' the sergeant said. The constable showed it to her. She recognised her own writing: Gone to stay with Katherine. The phone number was given and Katherine's address.

She looked at them, a horrible suspicion growing in her. What were they doing, looking in the glovebox of Paul's car?

'Is your husband the registered keeper of a silver Porsche, registration GX04 VYA?'

'Yes, he is. Why, what's happened?' Suzanne looked from one officer to the other. She wiped her clammy palms on the cardigan. 'Please, tell me what it is.'

'Mrs Cunningham, I'm afraid I have some bad news.' The sergeant blinked, and shifted a fraction in her seat. 'There's been an incident involving your husband. Emergency services were called to the scene just after two am. A vehicle was found crashed into a tree at the end of Elgin Drive – a silver Porsche. It had been driven at a high speed, judging from the amount of damage—' The sergeant stopped, her eyes becoming duller. 'We believe it was your husband at the wheel, Mrs Cunningham. He was dead when we arrived at the scene.'

Tree. Husband. Dead.

The words refused to make sense. She looked into the officers' faces. Both wore such serious expressions.

'I don't understand. He crashed into a tree?'

'Yes, that's right,' the sergeant resumed. 'I'm very sorry, Mrs Cunningham. A nearby resident heard the crash take place and came out to see what had happened.'

'What time did you say this was?'

The sergeant brought out a notebook and glanced at it. 'It was fifteen minutes past two.'

Her scalp prickled. It had been him, earlier.

'Your husband wasn't wearing a seat belt,' the constable said. 'Did he normally wear one?'

'Yes, always.'

She realised she was staring at his ears and wrenched her gaze away. Her mind was off on a tangent. Why didn't he have an operation to fix his ears?

'Mrs Cunningham?'

She forced her mind back to the PC's question; no seat belt. What did that mean? Either Paul had been in a great hurry to go somewhere, or he was in such a state he hadn't cared about belting up.

An icy clamminess settled over her. She was certain of it now: Paul had killed himself on purpose.

'I'm sorry, Mrs Cunningham, I know this must be hard for you. But I have to ask you a few more questions.' The sergeant turned the page of her notebook. 'When did you last see your husband?'

She answered the questions, despite not feeling fully present in the room. Her mind drifted. She was alone, far out at sea, and there was no one to rescue her.

'Mrs Cunningham?'

'I'm sorry, what did you say?'

The constable repeated his question. Would she be able to visit the mortuary later to identify her husband's body? A family liaison officer would be available to offer support and would explain all about the post-mortem procedure and the inquest.

When they'd gone, Suzanne went upstairs. The door to Katherine and Jeremy's bedroom was ajar and she could hear them talking. Jeremy's voice followed by Katherine's fainter reply. Something about someone snoring. The exchange sounded ridiculously ordinary.

She went into her bedroom and shut the door. She would tell them in the morning that Paul was dead. How could she tell them now, when she didn't believe it herself?

She lay down in bed and closed her eyes. A murky light seeped into the room and she found herself thinking about ordinary things: her back pain was getting worse, with this mattress, perhaps she should go to the osteopath again; what was Marmaduke doing now? He was all alone with Paul.

No, that wasn't right. Paul was gone now. He would never be coming back.

She sat up, imagining the thud of the impact, the buckling of metal, the lifeless body slumped against the steering wheel.

Suzanne found her mobile on the dressing table and switched it on. She ought to tell Daniel and Laura. She was about to call Laura when she saw there were two voicemail messages. She played the most recent, sent at 1.32am:

'Mum, I'm OK. I'm in the police station at Shepherd's Bush. They're taking my statement now.'

Then an earlier message, inaudible except for the words 'Dad' and 'following me'. The fear in her daughter's voice made the hairs on the back of her neck rise.

Suzanne pressed the call button. Laura picked up immediately.

'Hello, Mum. I'm so glad to hear from you. Did you get my messages?'

'I did, just now. What are you doing at the police station?'

'I'm waiting here with a cup of tea. I don't want to go home yet and the police might want to talk to me again.

I told them about Dad, I told them everything.' Laura sounded drained of energy. 'He was waiting for me in his car, outside my flat. He tried to stop me going to the police. I thought he was going to hurt me.'

Suzanne felt a numbness settle over her. She couldn't process her daughter's words. Paul had been trying to hurt Laura? How could that be?

'They were trying to get hold of him,' Laura went on. 'Then they told me he's been in some sort of incident. Do you know where he is? They won't tell me.'

'He's dead, Laura.'

'What?'

'He drove into a tree. The police told me twenty minutes ago. It was just up the road from the house.'

A small gasp, then silence.

'I've got to go and identify the body,' Suzanne continued. 'Will you come over later?'

'Of course. I'll get a cab.' Laura lowered her voice. 'Was it on purpose, Mum?'

'Yes. Yes, it was.'

Suzanne drove into the vacant driveway of number 31. The storm had bashed the poppies in the flowerbed; bruised heads sagged from bent stalks. She turned her key in the lock, pushed on the front door. The smell of glass cleaning spray struck her first. The light had been left on in the hall. She put down her things and opened the living room door.

The room had changed since the last time she was there: the wood of the sideboard and the coffee table shone; the cushions were neatly arranged and the carpet had been vacuumed, as if he'd wanted to leave the place looking nice for her to come back to.

No note. The police had said to look out for a suicide note.

She went into the kitchen. No empty beer cans lying around, no sign that any food had been prepared. Everything had been put away and the surfaces were spotless. No note in the kitchen either. She checked the dining room and the conservatory, then opened the office door. The desk had been cleared of his papers – of everything, except for the computer screen, a cigarette lighter and a scattering of ash. Something papery.

She went closer, wondered briefly what it had been and if this little heap was something the police or the coroner might be interested in. Then she brushed the debris into her hand and dropped it into the kitchen bin. Whatever it was, she'd rather it was gone.

There was no note anywhere. She allowed a vague disappointment to drift away. Perhaps it was better that way. Yes, it was definitely better that way. She didn't want to read some concocted explanation of his actions, or a pathetic goodbye. She didn't want to know that he couldn't live without her, or Laura, or Emma, or whatever else had gone through his head, or any more of his words that meant nothing.

Her thoughts shifted – Marmaduke. Where was he? She'd forgotten all about him. Why hadn't he come to greet her? She peeped under the kitchen chair, alarmed now. Marmaduke's bowl contained a few pieces of dried-up food. Quickly, she unlocked the back door.

'Marmaduke! Here, kitty-kitty!'

She tapped her fingers against the glass and called him several more times, but he didn't appear. Leaving the back door ajar, she went inside, sat down, and tilted her head back against the wall. Despair rolled through her. The emotion was bigger than she'd expected, bigger than she knew how to deal with.

This was it then, the moment of reckoning. She was alone. Her husband was dead and now her cat had disappeared. What the hell was she going to do?

She'd never been good at facing reality, it was so much easier to run away and hide. But she couldn't hide from this pain. Once again, she saw Paul's face as it was revealed on the mortuary slab: the long red gash across his brow, the eye misshapen and dark with blood. Had he really loved her, despite everything?

She closed her eyes. Why couldn't he have been an ordinary man? An ordinary husband, an ordinary father to her children? That was all she'd ever wanted.

Her shoulders heaved. She began to cry, the sobs crashing out of her, seemingly unstoppable. Then something rubbed against her legs, purring noisily.

'Marmaduke! Where have you been?'

She picked him up, stroked his back, and tickled under his chin. He was thinner, but otherwise seemed fine. Suzanne put half a tin of cat food into his bowl and watched him eat.

Laura arrived first, then Daniel. The three of them sat at the kitchen table, one or other occasionally getting up to bring cups of tea or coffee. No one said much at first. They all sounded unlike their usual selves, tentatively treading around what they really wanted to talk about.

'So, it was suicide?' Daniel asked at last, rubbing his chin.

'That's what the police think,' Suzanne replied. 'All the signs were there. The whisky, no seat belt, no other vehicles involved.'

'Why? Why did he do it?'

'I don't know, Daniel.' But she could guess. What did he have left to live for? He'd lost everything.

'He must have felt terribly alone,' Daniel went on. 'Like we'd all abandoned him.'

'It was shame too, I think,' she said. 'He always hated people judging him.'

Laura lowered her face onto her folded arms. She looked terrible: her eyelids puffy, her face greyish in tone.

'He didn't want to go to prison, that's what he was afraid of. He knew I was going to the police. When we were talking in the car, he begged me not to go. He tried to stop me.'

Daniel gave his sister a hard look. 'He hurt my arm.' Laura glared back at her brother. 'I thought he was going to … I don't know what he might have done. I pushed my fingers into his face, to stop him hurting me. That's why his eye was damaged.'

Suzanne stirred her tea. It was extra strong and made with sugar, which she never normally took. Today though, she needed all the help she could get. She tried not to think about the torn and bloody eye that had stared up at her from the mortuary slab. Why hadn't they closed it? Perhaps it was because they were going to examine the body.

'You did what you had to do,' she said.

'But did she have to tell the coppers?'

Laura's face flushed. 'What do you think we should have done, just sat around patiently and waited for him to find his next victim?'

'Stop it, you two!'

Her voice was louder than she'd intended. Both Laura and Daniel stared at her.

'Your father chose to do what he did,' she said. 'He chose to act like a total prick and then he chose to throw his life away. This is no one's fault but his.' She got to her feet, surprised by the certainty she felt.

Neither Laura nor Daniel spoke. They both looked shamefaced. Laura heated some chicken soup and Daniel busied himself with his phone.

'I'm sorry, Laura,' Daniel said.

'It's OK.'

The hostility between them disappeared, replaced by an attempt at banter. They did their best to help with the practical things and clearly wanted to be on hand should their mother fall into a pit of despair. In the late afternoon she tried to shoo them away, reassuring them that she'd be OK, she needed to rest now, but they refused to leave.

Suzanne opened the door to the bedroom she'd shared with Paul.

It was too early to go to bed, but she desperately needed to sleep. She lay on the bed, fully dressed, glancing around the room. The chair was no longer piled with his clothes and Laura had changed the sheets. Paul's comb, watches and bottles of scent still rested on the chest of drawers.

It was difficult to believe that her husband had actually gone, that he wouldn't put his head around the door any moment and ask what was for dinner, or did she want a glass of water. But he wasn't coming back. She was a widow now.

The thought was too strange, it didn't slot in anywhere. A wobble, deep in her psyche.

Katherine's recent advice came to her. Try to think of something funny when you can't deal with things anymore. She tried, but nothing came to mind. She noticed the tapping of her heart, louder now and a little too fast. She took a deep breath and exhaled slowly to the count of five.

Five, four, three, two, one.

She repeated this several times. After a while, she was calmer.

It's going to take a while, but you'll get there.

A wry smile came to her lips. Yes, she'd get there. The old geezer up above had surprised her, yet again, but she wasn't going to fall apart this time. Somehow, she would get through this latest crisis. Deep down she was a tough old bird.

34

Laura

12 May 2011

The remains of the buffet lay on the dining table: dented balls of deep-fried mozzarella, nibbled sandwiches, and the crumbling remains of quiches and cake. At last, apart from her mother and Daniel, everyone had gone.

Laura went to the French windows. Outside, yellows and blues studded the flowerbeds. The sun came out from behind a cloud and went in again.

Everyone had spoken well of her father this morning, and no one had mentioned the likelihood that her father had killed himself. None of his relatives had made it to the funeral, except for a great aunt and a cousin from Canada, and they'd said little about him. But many of his friends and work colleagues had turned up. To them, her father had been a different man, it seemed. A likeable, charming man who had done many kind and helpful things, who'd laughed with them and had made them laugh. It was as if the man they were talking about wasn't her father at all, but a good-natured imposter. Perhaps each had decided not mention the less pleasant side of him. Or perhaps, to them, he really had been a different man.

She thought back to when she was growing up, how he'd never stayed the same person for long. Every so often, the brooding silences would build into rage, for no discernible reason. Then, hey presto, the anger was put aside and a jovial, contented man would appear. In a similar way, when he touched her, he went into a sort of altered state. Once he'd finished, he'd snap out of it. As if he were a magician performing a conjuring trick, the man with glazed eyes would instantly transform, from the ogre she feared into a father like anyone else's.

'Hi, sis. How's it going?'

She turned to Daniel, now standing behind her. He was wearing a black shirt and his grey suit, the jacket now removed. He hadn't had time to buy a black suit for the funeral, he'd told her earlier. Hadn't wanted to, perhaps.

'It was an effort,' she replied. 'I wasn't in the mood to talk to anyone. I hardly knew most of them. And they all seemed so positive about him.'

Daniel shrugged, gave a small sigh. 'Yeah, I know what you mean. You'd never think he'd topped himself.' He looked into the garden. 'Or he'd done all that other stuff.'

She noticed again the absence of his girlfriend. 'Where's Karen? I thought she would be here.'

'She's OK. She had something on today.' His voice was guarded.

'Have you told her what really happened with Dad?'

'No, definitely not.' He glanced behind as if Karen might suddenly appear. 'She wouldn't understand.'

'Why don't you try talking to her?'

'What do you think I should say? "Hey, my dad was a child molester on the side, how about that? He abused my sister and then he went for the daughter of my mum's friend, and, when he got found out, he decided to top himself"?' He glared at her then closed his eyes for a moment.

352

'I'm sorry, Laura, all this has shaken me up. Everything I thought I knew about him ... I know he could be a real bastard at times. The way he ranted at Mum when she was just trying to make him happy, the way he used to come down on us like a ton of bricks for the slightest thing. He wasn't that hot as a father, I always knew. But he was my dad. And now ...'

He looked away from her, his eyes wet.

'I loved him once too.' She swallowed to remove the sudden tightness in her throat. 'A long time ago. But the last time I saw him, I hated him more than I've ever hated anyone. Now, I feel nothing.'

Neither spoke. Her brother stared at the un-cleared table.

'I'm thinking of breaking off the engagement,' Daniel said, rubbing the back of his neck.

'Because of Dad?'

His eyes flicked to her face. 'If we get married, I'll have to tell Karen the truth about him, won't I? I don't think I'm up to that.'

'You don't have to tell her, if you don't want to. You should go ahead and get married. Don't let him change anything.'

Daniel didn't reply.

'Have you said anything yet to Karen? About calling it off?'

'Not yet. I haven't told Mum, either.'

'Wait a bit and think it over, won't you?'

He shrugged and looked at his watch. 'I'm heading off now, sis. I've got stuff to do.'

'Daniel, before you go. Can I ask you something?'

He waited for her to speak.

'Do you still blame me for Dad killing himself?'

'No, I don't blame you. I'm sorry I said that.'

'I'm not sure he'd have done it,' she explained, 'if I hadn't said what I did. If I hadn't wanted to tell the police.'

'It was his choice, Laura. After all that he did to you, he must have known he'd have to pay the price one day.' He checked his watch again. 'It's getting late, I have to get back.' He put his hand lightly on her arm. 'See ya, sis. Take care of yourself.'

35

Laura

Four months later

I t was a warm afternoon, one of the last days of summer. The garden's greenness was tinged with dusty yellows and golds. Marmaduke, lazing on the patio, rolled onto his back. Laura yawned and stretched. She was sleepy from the sun and the bottle of wine that she and her mother had shared at lunch.

Her mother, laid out on a reclining chair, raised her head. It was hidden by a large-brimmed straw hat. 'How was Mrs Harris this week?'

'Oh, she's alright. She said I've been a massive help and she's sorry for being so tetchy.'

It was the end of another week of helping Mrs Harris research her book. They'd travelled to Doncaster to talk to a farmer who'd discovered valuable Roman relics in the corner of his field. At last, she'd found a job she enjoyed. It was demanding, working for an irascible seventy-something woman who was greatly frustrated at her reduced sight and mobility, but never boring. The research was likely to go on for another six months, at least, and after that … She could help Mrs Harris write her book. Or she could apply to do a postgraduate degree in archaeology. After a few years she

Jennie Ensor

might end up on a dig in Crete or Italy. Perhaps she would discover something important herself.

'The garden's so lovely now,' her mother said, under her breath. 'I'm going to miss it.'

'I can hardly believe you've sold the house, Mum.'

'Nor me. It seems odd to think that I won't be coming here when I get back.'

It was hard to imagine anyone else living in this house, but in just under four weeks it would be occupied by two doctors, and her mother would be off to Texas for a month, to stay with a friend she hadn't seen for years, followed by two weeks in Spain with another friend, then an 'old girls' get-together' in the Lake District. After all that, her mother was thinking of renting a house near the sea for a few months before buying somewhere else.

'What sort of place are you going to look for?'

'Somewhere bright, modern. Somewhere without memories.'

She knew what her mother meant. Dad had been dead for nearly half a year, yet the house still held many reminders of him. Several times, alone in the kitchen or the living room, she'd felt signs of him. A small disturbance in the air like someone walking close by. An odd quiver in the light, the faint spill of his voice into the room. It could well have been her imagination – she didn't believe in ghosts – but she wouldn't be sad to say goodbye to this place.

'It's time you got away from here,' she said. 'And away from the past.'

'Yes, there's been a bit too much of the past, lately.'

The inquest into her father's death had been held three weeks ago. Both she and her mother had been summoned as witnesses. Not as many people as Mum had feared turned up. Daniel hadn't gone, said he wasn't interested in 'a rehash of the past'.

'You loved him, didn't you, Mum?'

'I loved the man I thought he was. Or the man he wanted me to see, perhaps. It's as though he put me under a spell when I met him, and I never realised. Katherine always thought I was mad to put up with him, so did Irene. But I didn't see it – just as I didn't see what he did to you.' Her mother rubbed the bridge of her nose. 'It's a strange thing, Laura. Lately, it's like a weight's been lifted from me. I was dreading the inquest and what might happen.'

Her mother had handled it quite well in the end, staying composed and clear and succinct in response to the coroner's questions about what had led to Paul's distressed state of mind. Jane had given a guarded account of Emma's accusations, staring icily at Suzanne the whole time. She herself had decided to be as open as possible. She mentioned everything relevant – his abuse of her when she was a child, her reaction after learning of Jane's accusation, her final confrontation with her father before her visit to the police. Oddly enough, talking about it had been OK. It was another chance to be heard, perhaps. Five hours later the verdict was death by misadventure, as they'd expected.

'It's not just that the inquest's over.' A sad smile fluttered onto her mother's face. 'Now Paul is gone, I can breathe again. It's terrible that he felt he had no choice but to kill himself, and I'd never have wished him dead, but now it's happened … Part of me wonders if this could all be for the best, in some strange way.'

She looked at her mother in surprise as she carried on.

'You were right about him going after other girls. Even if he'd gone to prison, I don't see how that would have stopped him. They'd have let him out sooner or later. We'd have always been wondering what he might do next.'

From high above, the cawing of a wood pigeon. Laura ran her fingers through the stems of grass.

'I'm glad too,' she said softly. 'That he's not around anymore.' Maybe, she thought, in years to come she would be able to forgive him. Was it easier to forgive a dead person? She wondered if Emma would ever be able to forgive him, or if Jane would.

'What your father did to you, when you were a child.' Her mother spoke carefully. 'It's affected you a lot, hasn't it?'

Laura looked away from her mother. A sadness washed over her, chafing the same raw places. She tried to put her feelings into words.

'For years I felt like I was always alone, no matter what. Even though I knew you were around, and Daniel.'

Her mother's head dipped.

'It's like I'm coming out of his shadow,' Laura continued. 'He's not there, following me wherever I go.'

'We're both coming out of his shadow.' Her mother reached across and squeezed her hand. 'I know we haven't been close, darling, as far as mothers and daughters go, not for a long time. But I'd like to change that.'

'Me too.'

Their eyes met. Above the nearby borders, bees hummed and climbed in and out of flowers.

Laura picked a head of clover. 'Any news of David?'

'Last week he asked if I'd go walking with him one weekend in Dorset.'

'Did you say yes?'

'I said I'd go – once I'm back from Texas.'

'Playing hard to get?'

'Maybe.' Mum smiled. 'It's been a while, I'm a bit rusty when it comes to romance. He'll jolly well have to be patient!'

They laughed in unison. Since her father's death, she'd felt closer to her mother than she could remember. If only the same were true with Daniel. She'd not seen him since the funeral. They had tentative plans to meet soon, for his birthday, unless he took off for a contract overseas instead.

Her thoughts drifted, punctuated by the rumble of wood pigeons. In a short time, so much had changed. Her father was gone and was no longer able to harm anyone, and her mother would get along fine without him – that was clear. Hopefully, her brother would learn how to get along without the father he'd always imagined. As for herself ... the bad dreams hardly came at all now. She was finally getting on with her life. That desperate, hopeless girl of a few months ago would soon be a memory.

Laura looked up at the trees along the edge of the garden. How wonderful they were in their haloes of green. Her fingers played among heads of clover.

I'm alive, right here, right now.

With that thought came a stirring of excitement, a childish wonder at the possibilities of the world. It lay open to her like a meadow waiting to be explored, full of secret places where rare birds and butterflies lived, and plants that had no names. Perhaps it had been waiting for her all along, only she'd never noticed.

She lay there for a while, looking up at the sky, watching clouds slowly form, break apart and reform.

THE END

Acknowledgements

Thank you to the first editor of my manuscript, Philippa Brewster, the team at Bloodhound and all the writers who have who have helped me with nearly endless revisions of this novel. To name a few: Joanna Stephen-Ward, Richard Rickford and Alan Franks from the old days of the Richmond Writers Circle; Hillary Bailey, Gail Robinson, Iris Ansell and Margaret d'Armenia from the former novelists' group, and Gail Cleare, Kate Murdoch, Kali Napier and Ann Warner from the many authors I've got to know online. Your help has been invaluable.